DANCE WITH THE DEVIL

THE DEVIL'S OWN, BOOK ONE

DANCE WITH THE DEVIL

JD MARCH

FIVE STAR

A part of Gale, Cengage Learning

GALE
CENGAGE Learning·

Farmington Hills, Mich • San Francisco • New York • Waterville, Maine
Meriden, Conn • Mason, Ohio • Chicago

GALE
CENGAGE Learning®

LIBRARY OF CONGRESS CATALOGING-IN-PUBLICATION DATA

March, J. D., author.
    Dance with the devil : the devil's own, book one / by JD March. — First edition.
        pages cm. — (Devil's own Book one)
        ISBN 978-1-4328-2931-5 (hardcover) — ISBN 1-4328-2931-9 (hardcover)
        ISBN 978-1-4328-2933-9 (ebook) — ISBN 1-4328-2933-5 (ebook)
        1. Gunfights—Fiction. 2. Revenge—Fiction. 3. Families—Fiction. 4. Mexican-American Border Region—History—19th century—Fiction. 5. Western stories. I. Title.
PS3613.A7325D36 2014
813'.6—dc23   2014025061

First Edition. First Printing: November 2014
Find us on Facebook– https://www.facebook.com/FiveStarCengage
Visit our website– http://www.gale.cengage.com/fivestar/
Contact Five Star™ Publishing at FiveStar@cengage.com

Printed in the United States of America
1 2 3 4 5 6 7 18 17 16 15 14

ACKNOWLEDGEMENTS

I am indebted to CC, who found me, and taught me how to tell a story; to Whistle, who spent countless, painstaking hours poring over all of those drafts; to Shelley, for her unswerving encouragement and advice; and to Anna, who persuaded me to take a risk and sent me to Albuquerque. I couldn't have done this without your generosity and support—thank you!

PROLOGUE

Mexico—April 1870

The sound of hammering jarred his nerves.

It had been going on all morning. Whatever he did he couldn't block the sound out.

Each thud of the hammer was like a bullet hitting home. This was the last day he'd live. Tomorrow they'd walk him across the courtyard and hang him.

Reaching above his head, he grasped the iron bars of the cell window and hauled himself up to peer out, blinking as the brilliant sunlight stung his eyes. As if on cue, the carpenter hammered another nail into the gallows, securing the cross beam. On the far side of the courtyard was a scarred wall, pockmarked with the bullets of the firing squad.

He eased back down, sinking onto the pile of torn blankets that served as a mattress. It was kind of funny. He'd always thought a bullet would kill him, but here he was facing a hangman's noose. A firing squad would be better. There was no loss of pride with that. A man could face the guns with dignity and go out unbowed and unbeaten—if he had the guts. He wasn't afraid of bullets. Getting shot was a quick death. But hanging was another matter. It was possibly the only thing that frightened him. He certainly wasn't scared of dying. Hell, death was an old friend; he'd looked it in the face often enough. And that gave him his edge. Men looked into the eyes of Johnny Fierro and felt fear; they saw he didn't care if he lived or died.

He leaned his head back against the stone wall. Maybe men were frightened of death when they had something to live for, but he wasn't sure he'd ever had that. But hanging . . . That was something else. He swallowed hard, thinking of crowds of people watching a man jerk on the end of a rope, like it was some kind of a show. And then the way they'd poke the body with sticks and jeer . . .

He shut his eyes briefly, trying to block out the memories of seeing three men hang. He could only have been about seven at the time, pushing through the jostling people gathered in the plaza for the big show, hoping to maybe snag some food. The crowd had cheered as each man made that long drop. One of them took a long time to die . . . Someone at the front of the crowd had suddenly lifted him and swung him in the air toward the gallows, and he'd seen the piss trickle down the trouser leg of the hanging man. He remembered screaming and the crowd laughing.

And here he was facing the same death because he'd been dumb enough to get involved in that peasants' uprising. But work had been thin on the ground and the idea of making life more difficult for the Rurales had appealed to him. Arrogant bastards! They swaggered around the countryside like they owned it. And made life hell for the poor peasants trying to scratch a living from the dirt.

He'd known the villagers wouldn't be able to pay him when he delivered the guns, but it had amused him to take the job. He'd figured that maybe it would give the poor devils something to fight back with. They'd maybe grow cojones enough to stand up for themselves.

What he hadn't figured on was el capitán from the Federal Army being there to take him prisoner for gunrunning and treason.

Treason! Madre de Dios!

Right now the capitán, Morales, was having the last laugh. The man strutted around like a farmyard rooster because he'd captured Johnny Fierro.

He hated losing to a bastard like Morales. No, not only to Morales. He just hated losing. He'd spent his whole life fighting to survive, not because he enjoyed living, but because he was too damn stubborn, and too damn proud, to let anyone beat him.

Narrowing his eyes, and with perfect timing, he aimed a kick at a rat that emerged from a hole at the bottom of the wall of his cell, its nose twitching as it sniffed the air. It scuttled off with a squeak, disappearing back under the stones. Mierda! The rat had more freedom than he did.

Freedom. The word had a nice sound to it. He'd been here a month hoping that an opportunity for escape would open up. And now he had just a few hours left.

He huffed out a breath. He was done waiting. He'd be damned if he'd give Morales the chance to crow that he was the man who'd hanged Johnny Fierro. And if he was going to deprive el capitán of his entertainment, he'd best quit waiting and get to planning.

CHAPTER ONE

New Mexico—September 1868

The rhythmic beat of hooves could lull a man the way a mother singing could soothe a crying child. Maybe that was why he always enjoyed returning from a cattle drive. The journey to the stockyards stretched nerves to the breaking point: the choking dust and the noise of bawling cattle, the shouts of the vaqueros, and the never-ending whooping and whistling.

On reaching the stockyards he'd given the men his usual orders to look out for each other, bought the first round, and then left them to drink, brawl, and, all too often, end up in jail. Now, tired and dusty and smelling of sweat, they were almost back. The hazy mountain ranges in the distance were familiar friends beckoning them home.

The journey home had been more restful, a time for reflection on the success of the trip. The stock had fetched top dollar. The ranch was having a good year and had a healthy balance sheet. He should be happy.

He shook his head. Here he was, Guthrie Sinclair, owner of 150,000 acres of prime cattle land in the Cimarron, a success in business, respected by his fellow ranchers—and yet his life was empty. One wife dead, one missing. Written on the balance sheet of life, it didn't look good. One son a virtual stranger, the other lost. That didn't look good on life's balance sheet either.

He'd sent the child of his first marriage to be raised by his

11

wife's family in Boston. It had seemed the right thing to do at a time when the ranch was repeatedly under attack by raiding Indians. And, yes, it had been a good decision; Guy had thrived in Boston. He'd been happy there, surrounded by his mother's family. He'd been well educated, even going to Harvard. But as soon as he turned eighteen he'd seized the opportunity to join a cavalry unit, and serve in the war. He'd gone back to Harvard once the fighting was over and graduated top of his class. The one thing Guthrie hadn't figured on was the boy becoming so immersed in Boston society that he now had no interest in traveling west to reclaim his heritage.

And then there was John.

Even thinking of him brought a sharp, stabbing pain deep inside.

Guthrie snorted to himself, startling his horse, which skittered sideways and sent a jackrabbit running for cover. Was the boy still alive? He had to believe that he was. But ever since Gabriela had stolen away in the night, taking their two-year-old son, there had never been a word. The boy had vanished. Not that he was much of a boy now. He would be almost twenty. Almost a man, if he were still alive.

And that was the worst part—that gnawing doubt. If only he knew, one way or the other.

The men were hollering now. They'd be returning to wives and sweethearts, to their families. He pushed away the pang of envy.

He reined in on the ridge overlooking the ranch. The sprawling adobe hacienda seemed to grow out of the meadows around it, as if planted there. It was as fitting a part of the landscape as the mountains that rose behind it in the west, their slopes splashed with gold where the aspens were already wearing their fall colors.

As if by some unspoken agreement, his vaqueros took off

down the hill, galloping flat out, anxious to be home. He hesitated for a moment before turning his horse toward town. He could do without witnessing the family reunions. Better to go and put the money in the bank.

The town was busy as he rode in. Cowhands and drummers jostled for space on the narrow boardwalks. Plump Mexican mothers bustled along with baskets bursting with tomatillos and glossy green chilies, sloe-eyed children clinging to their hands.

He hurried to the bank and deposited the draft from the stockyard. Stepping back into the street he cannoned into a fellow hurrying along. An apology died on his lips as he looked into the face of the town doctor. "Ben! Good to see you."

His old friend pumped his hand. "Guthrie, you've been gone a long while. Good trip?"

He nodded, smiling. "Aye, it was. And prices are holding up."

Ben clapped him on the back. "Come and join Steen and me for a drink. He's in the saloon."

He followed Ben, pushing through the doors into the dim light of the smoky saloon. His old friend and neighbor, Steen Andersson, nursed a bottle of rye whiskey and a couple of glasses at a battered corner table. Steen jumped to his feet to bang Guthrie on the back and call for another glass. He grinned broadly. "This is a surprise. I wondered when you'd be back. Welcome home!" He raised his glass in a toast.

Guthrie smiled. "It's good to be home. I'm getting too old for long cattle drives." He swigged down a mouthful of whiskey. "So tell me, what's been going on in my absence?"

Ben shrugged. "We've had a busy time while you were away. I've delivered three babies, treated old Otto Lutz, who managed to fall off his own roof, and coped with all the other ailments that people seem to save up so they can all get sick together. And then we had two gunmen here earlier this week, trying to kill each other. That livened up the town, I can tell you."

Guthrie raised an eyebrow. "We're seeing too many damn gunfights in these parts. What happened?"

"Oh, they were neither of them good shots. So I patched them up and sent them on their way. I doubt that either of them learned a lesson from it. I've seen hens with bigger brains than those two. But, as you can imagine, it has people all stirred up, and now all they can talk about is gunfights."

Guthrie snorted. "Shootists are scum. They live without principles and die without principles."

The men at the next table were raucous, their banter heard by everyone as they swapped stories about gunfights they had seen and commented on the speed of the participants. "Tell you who I seen, I seen Bill Hickok over in Missouri. He was fast—I saw him and another fellow shoot it out. And I saw Carlos Panchez down in Texas, too."

A hush fell, and then they broke into an excited clamor. "Is he really as fast as everyone says?"

The man ran a hand over his rough beard. "Yeah, he was like lightning—he gunned down a fellow who never even cleared leather. Reckon he was faster than even Dan Beard—and we all know how fast he is."

His drinking partner shook his head. "Beard's fast, but he ain't near as quick as Fierro. I saw him down in Nogales one time."

Another man slammed his glass down on the battered table. "Hell, I've heard tales of Johnny Fierro from here to the other side of the border. I've heard he's real mean. You see him draw?"

The man was silent for a minute as he considered his answer. "I'll tell you something; he scared the shit out of me. He faced down two men but he looked real relaxed, sorta smiling like he was playing with 'em. It was like watchin' a cat with a mouse. He told the one man to get the hell out 'cause it wasn't his fight, but the man stayed; that was a big mistake. Fierro killed

14

him outright with a clean shot but the other man . . . Fierro gutshot him, like on purpose, and then stood smiling, watchin' him die. And the fellow was trying to get his hand to his gun, but instead of finishing him off, Fierro just shot him in the hand. I tell you, it was something awful to see. And when the poor devil was dead, Fierro tossed a coin down for buryin' the first man but said the second wasn't worth a dime.

"I tell you, I never seen anyone draw so fast. I bumped into him on the sidewalk later, comin' round the corner. His hand went straight to his gun and the way he looked at me . . . Hell, I found myself apologizing! Even called him sir . . . Almost shit myself, his eyes was so cold."

Ben shook his head at the story and turned back to Steen and Guthrie. "What is it that turns men into evil killers? I mean, what possesses a man that he should end up like that?"

The whiskey was sour in Guthrie's mouth. Gabriela had come from those border towns. He'd always believed she'd taken John there when she left. But if he'd grown up there . . . God forbid he should have seen men like these killers in action. Men who could stand unmoved, watching someone die. He hated to think his son might have witnessed such sights.

Steen shrugged. "Who knows? Maybe some men are just born bad?"

Guthrie found his memory drifting to a small blue-eyed boy with a winning smile who tottered around on chubby legs causing mayhem. And he knew with a sudden sense of urgency that he had to find John if he were still alive and get him away from places where gunmen held sway. He thought of the very large sum of money he had just deposited in the bank. What good was it doing there?

He downed his drink and stood up. "Will you both excuse me? I've just remembered an important message I have to send at the telegraph office. I'll catch up with you both this weekend."

Five minutes later he was riding back out of town, thinking of the message he had sent to the Pinkerton Agency. "Find my son, no expense spared."

There was still no news.

It was months since he had sent his message to the Pinkertons. They were quick enough to send him bills. There'd been plenty of those since Gabriela had run off. He'd used the agency on and off over the years, whenever he'd been able to spare the money, hoping they'd be able to trace John.

There were times when he wanted to kill Gabriela for stealing the boy. He could imagine his fingers around her throat, throttling the life from her.

She'd been the first woman he'd really desired after Marianne died, leaving him alone with Guy. Gabriela was beautiful, with dark flashing eyes. He'd been obsessed with the thought of possessing her. The idea of marriage hadn't entered into it, not at first. He just wanted to bed her, again and again.

But when he discovered she was carrying his child, he'd done the decent thing and married her. And it seemed then he had it all, an impressive hacienda, land, cattle, a beautiful wife that other men desired, and a baby on the way.

He'd been delighted to have a second son. The boy was quick at everything; he walked sooner than his elder brother had . . . Walked! Hell, John had run. The boy never stood still. He'd attacked life with glee, taking knocks and tumbles with few tears, and was mulishly obstinate, always determined to succeed.

He'd set the younger boy on his horse in front of him, while Guy rode a small pony at his side, and shown them the land they'd one day inherit. Guy had been a serious, dutiful little boy. He was the total opposite of his younger brother—fair-haired and angelic, while John had a mop of silky hair as dark as a raven's wing. And while Guy was courteous and smiled politely at visitors, John was willful and mutinous. Even so . . . John had a smile that could melt the sternest heart.

When Gabriela left, he'd known that some of the smaller ranchers had crowed to see him brought down. But he wasn't going to be beaten by her. He'd been determined to find his wife and claim what was his.

He'd tried to track her through the stinking hellholes that were the border towns, becoming more embittered each day. How dare she steal his son!

But his desperate hunt along the border had been useless. The towns were full of tight-lipped people with closed faces; no one was going to help the gringo. In the end he'd returned home. He instructed the Pinkerton Agency to look for his family. And they had, on and off for years, always drawing a blank. The trail had gone cold.

The sound of hoofbeats stirred him from his reverie. He glanced out of the window by his desk to see Ben and Steen riding in together. He hauled himself out of his chair and headed out to welcome them.

Steen smiled broadly. "Ben was coming out to look at one of your ranch hands, so I thought I'd ride over with him and bring your mail." He held out some envelopes.

Guthrie grimaced at the familiar Pinkerton Agency return address. "It'll be another account for their outrageous fees! That's all I ever get."

Steen shrugged. "One of these days maybe you'll hear something."

Guthrie knew that Steen privately felt he should give up and accept the inevitable, that the boy was dead and probably had been for a long time. There would have been some sign otherwise; no one could just disappear the way Gabriela and the boy had done. They were probably both dead. He was also all too well aware that Steen thought he was better off without

Gabriela. She'd been trouble from the first. Flirting outrageously with his friends. She didn't care if they were married or not.

She would run her hands over them in a provocative fashion, even when their wives were there. He had felt mortified at times; he'd wanted to strike her. Hell, she'd even come on to Steen. They'd never discussed it but he'd seen Gabriela flouncing out of the sitting room one night, and Steen flushed and disheveled. Steen would have been embarrassed: Guthrie was a good friend. But God, he'd be prepared to bet Steen had been tempted. What man wouldn't be? He'd seen desire flare in many men's eyes when they'd looked at Gabriela. God, she'd been beautiful, a fiery, voluptuous, sultry temptress. And however angry he'd been with her, she only had to run her hands over him and he'd succumb again.

Steen and Ben followed him into the hacienda. Guthrie poured them a drink before slitting the envelope open. He cautiously took out the contents to read.

The words merged in front of his eyes, and he felt sick and dizzy as he read. He heard a strangled gasp and realized the noise had come from himself. Ben rushed to support him as he staggered to a chair. God no, please, no! It couldn't be. It wasn't possible. He clutched the letter in his hand.

Raising his eyes to look at them he could almost see the thought flash across his friends' faces. Steen looked sadly at him. "The boy's dead, isn't he?"

An icy shroud wrapped itself around him as he stared at the letter again. And when he spoke his voice was barely a whisper. "Fierro."

Steen stared back, puzzled. "Fierro? You mean Fierro the gunfighter? What's he got to do with this? You're not telling me he killed the boy?"

Guthrie just shook his head in despair and repeated the name Fierro, more to himself than Steen and Ben.

"Guthrie, what the hell happened?"

He swallowed hard, choking back the bitter taste of bile, as he tried to put the news into words. He didn't know if he could even own to it. He felt ashamed, so ashamed. How could he even say it? But, no. It couldn't possibly be true.

He turned dazed eyes toward them, feeling the heat flushing his face. "No. You don't understand. They say they've found him, but . . . but, my boy, my John. They say he is Fierro. They say there's no doubt." His voice cracked and he swallowed hard again. No! The Pinkerton Agency had to be wrong. Not his son. Fierro couldn't possibly be his son.

God only knew what they were both thinking, as neither man spoke for a few beats. Then Steen shook his head decisively. "No, Guthrie, it makes no sense. We've been hearing stories about Fierro for years. He has to be a much older man. Your boy, well, he'd be way too young. Just doesn't add up. It's crazy; he'd have to have been a gunfighter by the time he was about fourteen."

Wordlessly, he handed Steen the letter to read.

He couldn't get that damning final paragraph out of his mind. The one warning him that Fierro was "a very dangerous man" and should be viewed with "extreme caution." The Pinkerton Agency strongly advised against any form of contact.

Steen hunched over, reading the letter, before looking back up. "No! They've got it wrong. It can't be your John. Surely not. I'll bet my life that Fierro is older. Besides, I've never heard of him being mixed."

At least he didn't say that awful word, *breed*. Steen would know how much he'd hate it.

Ben reached out and took the letter. "I agree with Steen. Fierro has been around for years. Your John isn't old enough."

Guthrie felt a surge of relief. Ben and Steen agreed with him. Fierro couldn't be his son. The Pinkerton Agency was wrong.

Fierro . . . He frowned as he tried to remember that evening in the saloon after the cattle drive. Damn it, who the hell was it who said he'd seen Fierro? Then he remembered. "Buck Lee. Remember that afternoon in the saloon? He's the one who was bragging about seeing Fierro in action. Go ask him, Steen. He's down in the barn—I hired him last month when one of the hands left. Ask him what Fierro looked like. That would settle it." Yes, that would be the best thing. If Lee could describe Fierro it would remove all doubt.

Steen nodded, his face grave. "I'll go now."

Ben rubbed his chin as he read the letter, slowly shaking his head. "It makes no sense, Guthrie. Like Steen said, surely we'd have read of Fierro being mixed. I've only ever heard reports of how fast he is." Ben hauled himself up to lean across for the whiskey bottle. He poured them each another measure. "Even so . . ." Ben paused. "The Agency seems very positive that Fierro is your boy."

Guthrie reached out for the glass, his hand shaking. He hated gunfighters. Damn it, he hated anyone who broke the law or didn't conform. His upbringing had been strict. His parents had been religious and demanded high standards. No. Fierro couldn't possibly be his son. No Sinclair could turn out that way.

It seemed like hours before Steen returned, and when he did he poured himself a drink before turning to face them. He hesitated, as if uncertain how to start. "OK, these are his words, not mine. He told me what really struck him about Fierro was how young he was. Maybe around eighteen or so. A half-breed with crazy blue eyes." Steen trailed off, unable to look his friend in the eye.

Guthrie felt his gut clench again and heard himself give an almost primeval roar as the hope died inside him. He hurled his glass at the fireplace. "Damn her! Damn her to hell! This is all her doing, the bitch! How could my boy end up like that? It's bad blood, Ben. It's bad blood from her. To think I've wasted all these years looking for him. A gunfighter! My God! We've heard what Fierro is like. A killer, nothing more!"

Ben shook his head sadly. "Who knows, Guthrie? The Pinkerton people could still be wrong."

"And if they're right? And Fierro is my John?"

"Then I suggest you have nothing to do with him. He'll just bring trouble."

Steen interrupted. "Ben, that's pretty damn harsh. We don't really know anything about him. It's all just saloon gossip. Hell, you know what fellows are like when they have a drink inside them! Things get exaggerated."

"We know enough, Steen, to know we wouldn't want a man like that anywhere near this ranch or yours. Think of your daughter. Would you want Fierro near her?" Guthrie spoke softly.

Steen stood silently, reflecting on that. But then he said, "Guthrie, he's your son. He's just a boy. We all remember him. He wasn't born bad. He was a good kid. Yeah, he was always into everything, but it wasn't 'cause he was bad, just adventurous. Cute little bugger, too, couldn't stay mad at him the way he was always laughing."

"Maybe he was still too young to show his true nature. Even if the tales are exaggerated, it doesn't alter the fact that he may be a boy in years but he's a hardened gunman. Damn it, he's one of the most infamous shootists of all!" Guthrie sighed, staring into the fire before continuing. "I know one thing for certain. I don't want him anywhere near Sinclair Ranch."

CHAPTER TWO

April 1870

Guy Sinclair was jarred awake as the stage jolted over a particularly rough bit of track. He made a frantic grab for Gibbon's *Decline and Fall,* which lived up to its name by almost falling from his lap. The sour-faced lady sitting opposite him sniffed loudly, and snatched her feet out of the way. She frowned and Guy murmured a word of apology as he sat back wearily. He was relieved that this nightmare journey was almost over.

The farther southwest he traveled, the more uncivilized it became. The frontier was populated by people who didn't seem to be on nodding acquaintance with any form of manners or etiquette. And why did they all carry guns? Overnight stops in dead-end towns had become something to dread. He all too frequently had cause to wonder when the bedding in the rough little hotels had last seen soap and water. And as for the food . . .

He wondered, yet again, why he had let his uncle talk him into this visit. Talk! That was a joke; his uncle had practically ordered him out of Boston. It seemed that the latest in a long line of invitations from his father couldn't have arrived at a more auspicious time.

He wasn't sure which annoyed his uncle more, his failure to show any interest in the business or his innumerable dalliances.

He gritted his teeth as he recalled their recent conversation.

His uncle had looked at him disparagingly. "Guy, if you're out of town it will allow the gossip to die down. This latest escapade with Cecily was the last straw. However, if you're out of sight for a while, people will soon tire of discussing your indiscretions and find something else to occupy their attention. And a trip to such an uncivilized part of the country will make you appreciate Boston more when you return. Perhaps then, you'll be less inclined to womanize and fritter away your time in such an idle fashion and more inclined to settle down to business and marriage. It's one thing going after the serving girls; I can tolerate that. They are of little consequence and are easily paid off if there are any complications. But the daughters of my business colleagues are a different matter. They are young ladies and should be treated as such."

But there was the rub: it was the daughters of his uncle's business colleagues who provided the biggest thrill. Because they were out of bounds, it made the chase so much more exciting. Anyone could have a whore; he wanted the forbidden fruit. And if one or two, or three or four, mistook his intentions for something more serious, that hadn't mattered to him. He felt a sudden surge of guilt. His uncle was right—his behavior had been reprehensible.

He swallowed hard. If he were honest he'd almost taken pleasure in shocking his family. He'd been so damned restless since the war. He couldn't settle to anything. Life seemed meaningless and his dalliances served as diversions in an effort to block out the memories of brutal warfare. He needed something more in his life than figures, stocks, shares, and hours looking at balance sheets. He was searching for something, but for the life of him he couldn't figure out what.

And then Cecily's father had raised such a furor when he'd caught Guy and the girl together. Guy grimaced. The latest in a long line of irate fathers . . . But, as fate would have it, it coincided with the latest invitation from his father to return to New Mexico.

This was a trip he'd been reluctant to make for years. He barely remembered New Mexico. He'd left when he'd been how old? Eight? He'd been sent away to his mother's family in Boston. To be educated, they said. But it had always felt like a rejection. Oh, there'd been numerous letters from his father and gifts on his birthday. But the man had only made two brief visits in all of those years.

Logic told him it was a very arduous journey from New Mexico to Boston. Logic told him his father was a busy man with a large ranch to run. But it had still hurt. When he was young he wondered if it was his fault that his mother had died when he was born. And was it his fault that Gabriela had left them? Was that why his father had sent him away? Of course, now, with the benefit of maturity, he could see that his father's decision to send him to stay with his aunt and uncle had been a wise one. But there was no denying the consequence: Boston was home now, not the West.

He reached inside his traveling coat for the letter and smoothed it out to read his father's words. The letters were usually full of names that meant nothing to him. He shook his head. Surely it should have occurred to his father that Guy wouldn't have any idea who those people were.

This latest letter related how Steen Andersson had been killed in an ambush on a journey in Arizona. Guy furrowed his brow. He had vague memories of "Uncle" Steen: a big Swede with a mop of white blond hair and a very loud laugh. He remembered the laugh—it used to make the plates shake on the table. It seemed that his father was now guardian to Steen's daughter. A daughter? He didn't remember a daughter.

He remembered his little brother, John, though. Guy could only have been five or six when Gabriela had disappeared one night, taking John with her. And he still remembered vividly how distraught his father had been. The man had taken off after them, leaving Guy in the care of the housekeeper, but he'd returned alone after several weeks.

Guy laid the letter on his lap, thinking back to the small brother he'd known for two short years. After John disappeared, Guy had told everyone that he would find him one day. He'd told his aunt and uncle in Boston the same thing. And then, just before his father's first visit, his uncle had taken him to one side and explained that John was dead, and that he shouldn't mention him to his father; it would cause him too much distress. After that day, John was never mentioned again.

He'd had little time to grieve. Life on Beacon Hill had been a hectic social whirl, even as a child. There had been a constant round of parties and picnics and summer visits to the family's other home in Duxbury. It had come as a shock after the narrow society of New Mexico. But he'd quickly settled into his new life and built up a wide circle of friends. He smiled, remembering warm summer days sailing off Duxbury, and the new sailing club that his friends had formed in Marblehead since the war. Heavens, he'd miss sailing. It was one of his chief pleasures in life. He'd have to ensure that he was back in Boston by the fall. It was bad enough having to miss this summer's sailing; he certainly didn't want to miss the hunting parties at the estates of his wealthier friends.

He sighed. Even so, it was time that he visited the place where he'd been born. It must be almost seventeen years since he left. But one thing was certain: it wouldn't feel like home.

He glanced down at the letter again. His father hinted at a "range war" brewing over Steen's land. What the hell was a range war? Surely the daughter would inherit the land and that was the end of it. Guy shook his head. His uncle was right—the West was an uncivilized place.

A clatter of hooves, and the raucous cries of the driver and the shotgun rider, roused Guy from his reflections. The stage had arrived at its destination; his journey was almost over. He'd wired his father to announce his arrival. Presumably someone would be there to meet him. Maybe even his father would have exerted himself? He tried to push away the barbed thought. Someone would doubtless be there, and that was all that mattered.

Moving stiffly, he eased himself out of the stage and then held his hand out to help his fellow passenger down.

He winced as the shotgun rider tossed his bags to the ground. They landed with a dull thud at his feet, sending up a shower of dust over his legs.

"Guy."

He left the bags where they were, turning to face his father. With a sudden pang, he saw how the man had aged. He still had the thick hair Guy remembered, but now it was completely gray, and so was his beard. His face was deeply lined, too, revealing a life spent outdoors under a scorching sun. The only thing unchanged was the faint Scottish burr. Guy held out his hand, suddenly unsure of how to address him. Father didn't seem appropriate for this burly stranger. "Sir, thank you for meeting me."

His father had a firm grip. "I won't ask if it was a good journey. I can imagine it was purgatory. But Peggy is over there with the buggy. That at least will be more comfortable."

"Peggy?" Guy stared at his father blankly.

Guthrie Sinclair nodded. "Steen's daughter. Her real name is Margarethe." The man smiled. "Peggy is less of a mouthful."

Guy followed his father to a neat buggy where a young, flaxen-haired girl stood waiting. She had a wide, engaging smile and she leaned forward to kiss Guy on the cheek. "I have been so looking forward to your arrival. I have always wanted a brother and Uncle Guthrie says that you'll be a brother to me." She slipped her arm through his. "And now I'll want to hear everything about Boston."

Guy inclined his head. "That's a tall order, but I'll do my best."

The journey back to the ranch was full of inconsequential chatter. Guy had the distinct impression that both his father and Peggy were struggling to keep the conversation on the most superficial level. It suited him; he was too tired for anything much. But he couldn't help but feel the two of them were wound as tight as springs about something. Doubtless he would learn more about that later.

Guy hardly recognized the hacienda. His father appeared to have added at least two new wings to it, doubling the size of the central courtyard. Why he'd felt the need to enlarge it was something of a mystery. Guy eyed him curiously. Maybe he was the type of man who liked the world to know of his success. The sprawling adobe house certainly boasted wealth, but Guy felt it was a little vulgar for his taste.

The one thing that hadn't changed was his old room. He looked around with a slight smile. The paintings of Scottish cattle on the wall were unchanged, and there were even some of his old books on the oak desk. French doors opened out onto a balcony with a view of the main corral, where Mexican workers were watching someone break a young horse. As he stood admiring the mountainous landscape fading into a heathery haze, and breathing in the soft, warm air, he felt an unexpected surge of excitement. Maybe this wasn't such a big mistake after all.

Dinner was excellent. At least his father didn't stint on the table he kept. Or his wine cellar, if the excellent Burgundy was anything to go by. Peggy chattered throughout, full of eager questions about the latest fashions in Boston. He tried to answer as best he could, but had to confess that he really hadn't noticed whether hats were smaller this year.

It wasn't until Peggy had cleared away the dishes and retired to her room that he was finally alone with his father. They sat facing each other in awkward silence, sipping a good malt whiskey, which his father imported from "the old country."

The man sighed heavily. "I have to tell you, Guy, we're going through a rough time."

Guy raised an eyebrow. "You mean finances are . . ."

"No!" His father set his glass down firmly, the contents splashing over the mahogany side table. "No, this is nothing to do with money. I think I hinted of a possible range war in my last letter. Well, that's what we have starting. One of my neighbors—Ramon Chavez—is keen to get hold of Steen's land. His spread is east of Steen's old ranch and he's looking to expand. It would make his access to water more secure for a start. But I'm holding that land in trust for Peggy. If she marries a boy who wants to ranch, she will have her land. If she marries someone who doesn't wish to use it, then I will purchase it, at a price agreed upon a couple of years ago with Steen after he bought it from Maxwell. He wanted to make provision for the girl in the event of his death. And Chavez isn't the only one interested. I had an inquiry from one of the mine owners from Elizabethtown, a man I know called Wallace."

Guy leaned forward, puzzled. "Why would he want it? If his business is mining, what possible attraction could ranch land have for him?"

His father shrugged. "Steen's land has a lot of timber, and the mines need it to shore up the diggings. I suppose he was hedging his bets there and thinking about ensuring a supply. But Wallace isn't my problem. Chavez is. He's rustled some of my cattle. His men have cut our fences, and the latest news I have is that he's talking of hiring guns."

Guy cocked his head. "Can't you just take out an injunction against him? Surely there is some law around here?"

Guthrie shook his head. "There's precious little law in these parts. Lucien Maxwell ran the area like his personal fiefdom and there was some law under him, but now that he's left, things are deteriorating fast. Men who already own their land have to protect what's theirs, while the tenant ranchers resent the landowners and are battling for control of their own spreads. And I know this is just the start. If Chavez gets control of Steen's land, it will only be a matter of time before he comes after mine. Even so, I find his move surprising. He dislikes all the Anglo settlers, but I had never taken him for the type of man to stir up a range war and hire guns. I suppose it's a symptom of the unrest since Maxwell left."

Guy frowned. "When you say hiring guns, what exactly do you mean? And should we be doing it too?"

Guthrie grunted dismissively. "I won't stoop to hiring gunmen. They're paid killers, nothing more. We've got good ranch hands here, and I pay them well. We'll fight for our own land, die fighting if necessary, but I'll be damned if I'll take on professional shootists." He leaned across to top up Guy's glass before pouring himself another tot. "I think we'll have a good while to prepare ourselves. It will take Chavez time to gather enough men together to launch an attack. But we'll need to get down to some serious planning. Hopefully your army experience will help there."

Guy inclined his head. So was this why his father had been so insistent he should return? Had the last letter been fueled more by the need to make use of Guy's cavalry experience rather than any deep desire to be reunited with him? Certainly the most recent letter had a sense of urgency that earlier letters lacked. It grated a bit, this assumption that he would be prepared to risk his life fighting for a piece of land with which he felt little connection. Oddly, the thought that his father simply saw him as cannon fodder hurt. Although they were essentially strangers, part of him had hoped that the man wanted to get to know him and re-establish a relationship. Now, it looked as though that had been a vain hope. Guthrie Sinclair wasn't interested in his son, only in the experience Guy could bring to the battle ahead.

Eventually, he headed upstairs to bed, his arms full of maps of the ranch and of Steen Andersson's spread, so that he could plan an effective defense. But it could wait until the next day. He was far too weary to even consider the problem on his first night home. Home. It had a strange sound to it. Maybe, given time, it would be home. Provided they managed to hold onto it.

He slept the sleep of the gods in crisp sheets scented with lavender, lulled to sleep by a gentle lowing of cattle carried on the light breeze that stirred the muslin drapes.

A pounding on the door jarred him out of peaceful dreams.

"Guy! Guy!"

Grabbing a robe, he moved swiftly to open the door to face Peggy, tears streaming down her face.

"It's your father." She stumbled forward, leaning into him for support.

"What about my father? What's happened?" He was vaguely aware that he must have overslept. The sun was well above the horizon.

"He's been shot. He was heading to one of the line shacks with a work crew. Someone shot him . . . One of Chavez's men, we think." She gave a short gulping wail before rushing on, words tumbling from her mouth. "He's not dead. The men got him back here, and the doctor is on his way. But what if he dies? I can't lose him too . . ."

It was as though someone had swept the ground from under

him. His father had been shot? It was crazy. They'd been drinking together only hours previously. Fumbling and dazed, he pulled the girl into a comforting embrace, patting her gently on the back as he tried to collect his thoughts. He forced himself to sound calm. "Hush, Peggy. My father's a tough old devil. Let me go and see him. Who's with him now?"

Peggy sniffed, rubbing her sleeve across her face. "Carlita, the housekeeper."

"Right. I'll go and see him, and you make us coffee. I'm sure the doctor will need coffee when he arrives." He turned her around and pointed her toward the stairs, before hurrying to his father's room.

He paused in the doorway, shocked by the sight of his father, deathly pale and so still. He swallowed hard. So much for Chavez biding his time. This was a declaration of war.

Footfalls on the stairs dragged his attention back to the present. A short, curly-haired man carrying a black bag hurried toward him, thrusting out a hand. "Guy? It is Guy, isn't it?" Guy nodded as the man carried on talking. "I'm Ben Greenlaw, the doctor and old friend of your father's. Luckily I was on my way out here to welcome you home. Is Guthrie in here?"

Guy nodded again, standing to one side as the doctor sped past him.

Greenlaw wasted no time in getting everyone organized to bring hot water and towels. He removed the bullet swiftly and proceeded to stanch the blood, clean the wound, and stitch it in a very efficient manner. Having seen many army surgeons during the war, Guy was impressed by the man's competence.

Finally, satisfied with his work, Greenlaw stepped back and accepted a cup of steaming coffee. "All we can do now is hope the wound doesn't become infected. If he starts a fever, Peggy, you know what to do. Guthrie's as strong as an ox. That's his best hope." He shook his head sadly. "He, Steen, and I, we've

31

been close friends for many years. Losing Steen was bad enough. I don't want to lose Guthrie too. Not much of a homecoming for you, Guy. But I'm glad you're here. You have tough times ahead. You're going to need your wits about you."

Guy sucked in a deep breath. "So it seems. And to think I thought I was going to be bored here . . ." His voice trailed off before he pulled his shoulders back and stood a little straighter. "You'll visit again tomorrow, Dr. Greenlaw?"

The man nodded, clapping Guy gently on the arm. "Sure, I'll be back tomorrow, and it's Ben, please, not Dr. Greenlaw. I'm sure that we'll be good friends. And hopefully this business will be over before too long."

The day passed in a blur while Peggy tended to Guthrie, cooling his face with damp cloths, and Guy tried to organize some sort of work schedule with a man who said he was the "segundo"—a type of foreman apparently. Guy regretted he'd forgotten almost all the Spanish he'd known as a child. All the Greek, Latin, and French he'd learned at Harvard was useless now. He'd have to learn Spanish again.

He was poring over the maps when Peggy came in to press yet another cup of coffee on him. She was coping manfully with their situation, only occasionally succumbing to a brief lip wobble. Now she perched on the desk, toying with the corner of one of the more ornate maps. "It would have been so much more sensible if he'd done as my father wanted, and sent for John."

Guy glanced up. "John? John who?"

Her brow furrowed. "John! Your brother."

Guy set down the cup with a clatter, spilling coffee over the desk. "My brother is dead, Peggy. He died when I was a child."

Peggy stared wide-eyed at him. "Who told you that? It's not true. All through my childhood I remember your father trying to trace him. And then a while ago he had news. He had paid the Pinkerton Agency to trace him. And my father thought Uncle Guthrie should contact him. I overheard them talking about it." She flushed slightly as she said the last words.

Guy sank down into the chair by the desk. "He's alive? You're sure?"

She nodded vigorously. "I do know that much, but I don't know why Uncle Guthrie didn't send for him."

Guy didn't speak. Even now he could hear his uncle's words as he'd told him of John's death. Why had he said that if it wasn't the truth? Why would they let him believe his brother was dead?

He shook his head as another odd thought struck him. "But if John's alive, why hasn't he come home?"

Peggy seemed to have no answer for that. Guy chewed on his lip, trying to figure out what might have happened. "I suppose," he said slowly. "I suppose he might not even know about us. John was very young when he left here. Maybe his mother never told him . . ." It seemed the only logical explanation.

He stood up, suddenly determined on the right action. "Do we know which branch of the agency my father used for his search?"

Frowning, Peggy nodded. "Yes, I know how to contact them."

"Then, Peggy, you and I shall send them a wire, this very afternoon. There's no time to lose and in the battle ahead we need all the help we can get."

Later they stood in the telegraph office in town as Guy carefully wrote out the message. "Urgent: Contact my son John. Stop. Will pay expenses plus $500 for him to hear something to his advantage. Stop. Sinclair."

CHAPTER THREE

Six by four paces. Four paces by six. Nothing he did would make the damn cell any bigger. He was tired of counting the stones in the walls. And tired of counting the cockroaches.

Or maybe he was just tired of fighting. For a long time now the only reason he'd fought so hard was because of his pride. He reckoned if someone wanted his reputation they could damn well earn it like he'd had to. And there was no shortage of young guns wanting his reputation. Young! Hell, some of them looked like they hadn't started shaving. Sometimes he'd try and talk them out of facing him, offer them a drink instead. But they mistook his reluctance to face them as weakness. Trouble was they were too easy for him. He could take no pride in gunning down a kid. He enjoyed a more worthy opponent.

If it wasn't for fear of the hangman's noose, he could maybe welcome death. But he was damned if he'd give Morales the satisfaction. He paused in his pacing to scratch the fleabites that covered his belly. He wasn't sure which was the worst part of being held prisoner: the boredom, the fleas, the cockroaches, or the rats.

He leaned back against the wall, listening to the sounds from the town. The guard who'd brought him what passed for breakfast had been talkative, boasting that the men would be having a good time this evening because today was a holiday. There was to be a fiesta. They'd be drinking and whoring. The guard had laughed. "And all you can do, amigo, is look forward to the gallows!"

He'd smiled and let the guard talk and brag. And all the while an idea was forming in his mind. The men would want to be out celebrating. Maybe that meant they'd only leave one man on duty tonight. And if there was only one man, it could open up all sorts of possibilities.

He thought of the knife hidden in his boot. They'd found the other knife—it had never occurred to them that he would carry two. And what did that say about him? One knife was enough for any normal man. But maybe he wasn't normal? He laughed out loud at that. No, he wasn't normal. But he survived.

He always survived.

He scratched at the lice in his hair. First thing he'd do when he reached the border was get a bath, a decent meal, and a woman.

A smile pulled at his mouth. He really liked whores; he respected them. Hell, it wasn't like they'd dreamed of being whores when they were little kids. Circumstances usually left them with no choice. They might sell their bodies but they hadn't sold their souls. Not like him. He'd made his deal with the devil a long time ago. And now a night in a whore's bed was as close to comfort as he was ever going to get. After a killing, he'd take two or three of them to bed, it was easier. It was the only way he could block out the memory of a gunfight . . . And then, if he tired of the whole game, well, they could entertain each other.

His instincts had been right; all the guards wanted to be out eating and dancing with their wives, or sweethearts. So they'd left the youngest guard on duty, a real greenhorn, assuring the kid they'd be back to relieve him before the party was over.

That should have pleased him, for it would make the job easier. But he felt a twinge of regret that it wasn't one of the more brutal guards they were leaving. He would have had no hesitation in killing one of them.

The fiesta was getting under way. He could hear music and laughter, people singing. They were sure making a hell of a lot of noise. He grinned. Things were looking good. All he had to do was sit and wait for the guard to bring him a drink of water, the way they did every night. He always had the same joke with them that it was actually the best sipping tequila.

He fingered the knife, checking for the hundredth time that it was really sharp, before sliding it up inside his sleeve. He could hear the kid moving around in el capitán's office, and he could smell the rich, smoky aroma of coffee brewing. He licked his dry lips. What he wouldn't give for a decent cup of coffee. And a decent meal, not the slop they served in the jail.

He dragged his mind back to the job in hand. The kid would be coming in at any minute. He fingered the knife again. Was it really sharp enough for the job? Was it long enough?

The heavy door from the guardroom creaked open. "Hey, hijo de puta, I have your sipping tequila." The kid was carrying a grubby jug. "But we used the jug to piss in before we added the tequila."

Johnny's eyes narrowed. He wouldn't have put that past the bastards. And he didn't feel so bad about what he was getting ready to do. He stood with his left hand resting on the bars as the young guard swaggered toward him, slopping half the water over the floor. He knew it was deliberate. It was like a fucking oven in the cells and they knew he was always parched.

The keys of freedom jangled from the belt at the kid's waist. He smirked at Johnny and then spat a stream of saliva into the jug of water. "Here's your water, Fierro." Laughing, he passed the jug through the bars toward Johnny. It was the last thing the boy ever did.

The jug fell to the ground as Johnny grabbed the boy around

the back of the neck with his left arm, forcing him against the bars even as Johnny's right hand swung up with the knife, plunging it straight into his heart. Johnny kept a firm grip on him as the kid's legs buckled, didn't want him falling out of reach. The guard's eyes widened with surprise before the life went out of them and Johnny eased him down to the ground. Reaching through the bars, he unclipped the keys and unlocked his cell door.

Moving silently he stepped over the kid's body and paused, listening hard, by the door to the guardroom. Satisfied that there was nobody in there, he gently pushed the door open and stepped into the room. It was deserted; everyone was at the fiesta. He grinned. Morales would be furious to discover Fierro had slipped through his fingers.

He quickly rifled through the drawers of Morales's desk, pocketing some American dollars, and sighing with relief when he found his holster and fighting gun in the bottom drawers, along with his other knife and spare gun. He took some bullets from the gun belt and loaded his gun, before buckling the holster around his hips. He grabbed a dark, broad-brimmed Stetson from a stand in the corner of the room. He smiled at the sight of his saddle sitting in pride of place on a saddletree, together with his saddlebags. It had been made for him by the finest saddler in Santa Fe. The leather was beautifully and elaborately tooled, and adorned with real silver conchos. Morales had obviously decided to keep the saddle for himself. It made seizing it back doubly satisfying.

Hefting the saddle over his shoulder, he peered cautiously through the window onto the side street. It was deserted; everyone must be out on the main street. Pulling the hat down low to cast his face in shadow, he slipped out the door and walked quickly toward the back of the livery stables. He passed a group of laughing children tussling over a ball, but they paid him no heed. They were too busy wrestling and falling around in the dust to bother with him.

The stables were hot, and his nostrils filled with the sweet smell of hay and straw. The scent was almost overpowering, as if it were a solid living thing forcing its way into his lungs. He wondered briefly which was Morales's horse, toying with the idea of stealing it. Something else to goad the man . . . But he saw his own buckskin pulling at a hay net. Doubtless Morales intended to sell the animal and pocket the money. The buckskin nickered at the sight of him and he ran his hand down its neck. They'd been through a lot together, and the horse would run its heart out for him.

Moving swiftly he heaved his saddle onto the animal and fastened the cinch. He snagged a bridle from the rack and slipped it on before leading the horse out of the side door of the livery. Stepping up into the saddle, he walked the horse to the edge of town and turned north. He felt a surge of triumph— he'd done it. By the time they discovered his empty cell he'd be miles away. With a whoop, he kicked the horse into a gallop and headed toward the border.

He needed a job.

He'd washed the worst of the dirt off himself in a lake on the way north. The water was cool and inviting, dappled by sunlight that filtered through a canopy of overhanging trees. After crossing the shimmering ribbon that was the Rio Grande, he'd hesitated, thinking of heading for one of the scruffy border towns. But he knew he'd feel safer away from the border, so he'd carried on north until he reached Santa Fe, where he paid for a steaming hot bath, reveling in the luxury after the discomfort of his cell.

But the bath, a good meal, and a cheap room had made a dent in his money. He needed a woman, but was reluctant to settle for one of the cheapest whores. He'd got his eye on a dark-haired girl who curved in all the right places, but her price was too high for him. So he spurned her come-on, feigning indifference although his dick pushing against the confines of his leather pants told him a different story.

He'd been in town for a couple of days and spent most of his time at a corner table in the saloon, a bottle of tequila near his left hand. Not that he drank much. He rarely drank much. Drink made a man slow and that was one thing he couldn't ever afford. And although he looked at ease, his hand never strayed far from his hip.

Everyone knew exactly who he was and gave him a wide berth, and that suited him just fine. It amused him to see how nervous he made the regulars at the saloon. He even succeeded in putting the poker players off their game when he fixed them with a cool, unblinking gaze. They sat stiffly in their seats, making foolish errors. He'd have taken advantage of their discomfort and joined the game but he didn't have enough money for a stake.

He glanced up as the gray-haired barkeep brought him a plate of tamales and beans, licking his lips and shuffling awkwardly like he'd got something on his mind.

Johnny waited. The man would spit it out eventually.

"Someone was asking about you earlier." The man blurted the words out.

Johnny raised an eyebrow. "A gunman?"

The man shook his head. "No. Looked more like a drummer or a businessman. Said he'd heard you were in town."

Johnny beat a tattoo on the table, his fingers restless. "What did you tell him?"

"That you'd be in this evening. Figured that way I could tip you off and if you didn't want to see him you could avoid him."

Johnny nodded. "Good thinking. I appreciate it."

Relief, like a big tide, flooded the barkeep's face. Johnny bit back a grin. His name sure had a way of scaring folk. He liked that. Helped keep his edge.

"I'll be here. When he comes in, give me a nod. OK?"

The barkeep nodded eagerly. "I'll do that, Mr. Fierro. Be a real pleasure, Mr. Fierro."

Johnny waved him away, forking in the food. He was still damn hungry. He'd gotten thin in the jail and it felt like his clothes were made for someone else. Who was the fellow asking for him? Maybe he had some work for him. But a drummer? Probably not. Drummers couldn't afford his price—he was an expensive gun to hire. Maybe a businessman? Successful businessmen usually sent their lackeys to hire him. But they sure didn't mind using him when it suited them.

He scraped up the last of the beans, wishing he could afford another helping. Maybe this man would have work for him. Then he could get himself a woman and another decent meal.

He had a mouthful of tequila and sat back to wait, avoiding the eye of the girl he wanted. The last thing he needed was to start talking with her. No way could he admit that he couldn't afford her. Dios! Morales had a lot to answer for, leaving Johnny Fierro scratching around for enough money for a whore.

He didn't have to wait long. The barkeep tipped him a nod when a skinny fellow walked in. Johnny sneaked a look at him over the top of his glass. He wasn't a cowpoke, that was for sure. He wore a badly fitting, dusty suit, and the sleeves looked slightly frayed at the ends. Yeah, the man looked like a drummer. This sort of man didn't look like he could afford to hire Fierro. And he was damned if he was taking another job for no money. He grunted—he'd told himself that more than once in the past but it hadn't stopped him from taking the gunrunning work. He was getting too damn soft.

He sat back in his seat as if watching the card players, but

never let the fellow out of his sight. He was talking to the
barkeep, who nodded his head in Johnny's direction. The man
glanced across at him and then walked purposefully toward
him. "You're Johnny Fierro?" It was a question, not a statement.

Johnny didn't move. "Who wants to know?"

"My name's Stanton. I'm a Pinkerton agent." The man
moved to pull out a chair.

"Did I ask you to sit down?" Johnny kept his voice very soft.

Stanton hesitated, swallowing hard. A bead of sweat trickled
down into his large moustache. "I've a business proposition for
you. A very lucrative business proposition."

What the hell did lucrative mean? He kept his face expressionless. "Since when do Pinks hire gunmen?"

Stanton's eyes widened a touch. "We don't . . . Oh, I see
what you mean. I'm sorry, I didn't make myself clear. The
proposition is from a client of ours. He's very keen to get in
touch with Mr. Fierro. And he's prepared to pay a great deal of
money."

Johnny eyed him silently, and then nodded briefly toward the
seat. "You got two minutes, Pink. And then I get bored."

Stanton pulled out the chair. "You are Mr. Fierro?"

Johnny sighed softly. "The clock's ticking. Get on with it."

Stanton sat down heavily, causing dust to waft out of his suit.
"Five hundred dollars, Mr. Fierro. Does that interest you?"

Johnny stayed motionless, not allowing any reaction to show.
Five hundred dollars? Who the hell wanted to pay him five
hundred dollars? And more to the point, what would he have to
do to earn it?

Johnny reached for the bottle of tequila and poured himself
another small measure. He let Stanton sweat for a few seconds
before speaking. "And what do I have to do for this money?"

"Hear a man out, that's all. I'm also instructed to give you traveling expenses."

"You telling me that someone is prepared to pay me five hundred dollars just for going to listen to what they have to say?" Whoever it was must be loco. Either that or it was some sort of trap.

The Pink nodded. "That is the proposition. And you will receive the money when you reach the destination."

"And exactly where is this destination?"

Stanton smiled. "The Sinclair Ranch up on the New Mexico border with Colorado. It's close to Cimarron."

He just managed to stop himself jolting forward. Wha—Sinclair? Hell! Sinclair. He swallowed hard. Had Stanton noticed his reaction? Had he given himself away? His mouth was dry. He forced himself to say the name although it almost stuck in his throat. "Sinclair?"

Stanton nodded. "Man called Guthrie Sinclair. He's a rancher; he owns a big spread. And he wants to talk to you."

But probably not as much as Johnny Fierro wanted to talk to Sinclair. The question was: did Sinclair know who he was? Or was he looking for a gun? "Why does he want to see me?" He studied Stanton, trying to gauge if the man was hiding something.

"A private matter. I'm not at liberty to divulge that." Stanton said the words like he'd practiced them.

"And my expenses?"

Stanton smiled smugly, like he knew he'd got Fierro on the hook. "Thirty dollars, Mr. Fierro. Very generous, I'm sure you'd agree."

Johnny ignored the comment. Guthrie Sinclair. Hell, it was like everything he'd ever wanted was being handed to him on a plate. Because what he wanted more than anything was to kill Sinclair. He'd wanted to do that for a very long time. And here he was being paid handsomely for the opportunity.

He shrugged, kept his voice disinterested. "I guess I could make the time to travel up there." He grasped the notes that Stanton offered. "But you tell him to make sure he has my money ready and waiting. I don't take kindly to being played for a fool. And if someone tries to cross me . . ." He paused and smiled coldly. "I kill them."

Stanton's Adam's apple bobbed. "He's a straight kind of man, from what I hear. He'll pay you, Fierro."

Johnny shrugged. "He better."

Stanton looked at him uneasily. "So, I can say that you'll go?"

Johnny nodded. "Yeah, I'll go." He turned away, hoping Stanton would take the hint and leave.

Stanton coughed. "Can I say when you'll be there?"

Johnny sipped his tequila. He didn't glance at Stanton. "No, you can't. I don't dance to no man's fiddle. I'll go when I'm ready."

Stanton shuffled to his feet. "Right. Well, I'll tell him that you'll go." He stood waiting, kind of like he expected a farewell.

Johnny sipped his tequila and ignored him. Stanton sighed heavily before turning and walking out of the door.

He stared down at the notes in his hand. Thirty dollars. His own thirty pieces of silver. Did Sinclair know who he was? No . . . How could he know? Had Sinclair ever given him a thought since he'd thrown them out? Probably not.

He could hear the echo of his mother's voice, the bitterness as she told him for the hundredth time how they weren't good enough for the great Guthrie Sinclair. He'd heard that story so often through the years. And he'd watched his mother sink lower, drinking away the pain, and opening her legs for any man who passed by. That was what Sinclair had driven her to. And that was what he was going to pay for. And five hundred dollars wasn't going to save him.

Another voice echoed in his head. A voice telling him that there were two sides to every story. A voice telling him to hear the man out if he ever met Sinclair. Johnny sat back in his chair, chewing on his lip. He'd promised that he'd hear Sinclair out, so he'd keep his promise. But he didn't believe that Sinclair would have anything to say that would make him change his mind. It would just buy the man a few more minutes of life before Johnny Fierro sent him to hell.

Guthrie Sinclair had one hell of a shock coming. A smile pulled at his mouth. Revenge could be real sweet. And the joke would be that Sinclair probably thought he was hiring a gun to take care of business, when in fact he was paying for his own death.

Glancing around the saloon he caught the eye of the dark-haired whore. Hell, he had thirty dollars now; he might as well have some fun. A night in a whore's bed—it would be a little comfort before he headed north to kill his father.

Yeah, life was suddenly looking a whole lot more promising. Pushing his chair back, he rose and beckoned to the girl to follow him, before heading up the creaking stairs.

CHAPTER FOUR

Guthrie had lost all track of time. Days and nights blurred together in a haze of pain. He couldn't make sense of anything; sometimes he was convinced it was daytime but then there would be lamps lit, glowing softly in the corner of the room. And yet surely he had just seen the sunlight casting shadows across the wall?

Peggy always seemed to be sitting there. And sometimes Guy too. He could hear Peggy's voice—snatches of words of everyday, mundane things as he fell back into a sleep.

But sleep brought no peace. His dreams were confused, and sometimes everything was colored blood-red. Sometimes he saw Marianne, calm and serene, and that made him feel safe. But then he'd see Gabriela taunting him, beckoning him to follow her as she retreated out of sight. Always out of reach. He called to her, begging her to stay, to tell him where his son was. And he would hear her laughter. Then he'd catch a glimpse of a small, dark-haired boy, laughing and running away from him. But when he went to follow the child, the boy turned with cold, hard eyes and fired a gun straight into him. He could feel the bullet's heat as it seared his flesh and he would awaken, crying out and soaked in sweat.

Peggy held his head as she helped him to drink. She was tender and gentle. She smelled of lavender and rosemary, her soft fragrance wafting on the air. Her presence calmed him and he prayed to stay awake. Or die. Anything was better than the dreams.

But gradually he found he could stay awake for longer periods. He was starting to focus and follow conversations. He could respond to some of Peggy's questions. He could hear himself reply. He'd found his voice again.

Each day he felt a little stronger. He was starting to fret about the ranch and grouch at Peggy. He was on the mend, despite the pain in his back.

Although Guy had made a habit of checking on him each day and giving brief reports on the ranch, today was different. Guy came to sit with him, apparently confident that his father was up to a more serious discussion. He looked different from when he'd arrived. He was tanned and he'd lost his Eastern city pallor. It seemed the ranch was good for him.

"We believe that it was one of Chavez's men who shot you." Guy paused. "Not that we can prove it. And the word is that he's gathering guns. We've moved the cattle in so that they'll be easier to guard and I've been working on ways to defend the hacienda if they launch a full-blown attack. I've been giving the hands some basic military drills to make them a more effective fighting force. It's asking a lot to expect vaqueros to take up arms and risk their lives to defend this ranch. I want them to be as well prepared as possible."

Guthrie nodded. "That's a good, sound move." He flinched as a wave of pain swept over him. He swallowed hard before speaking again. "Was anyone else shot? We didn't lose any men, did we?"

Guy shook his head. "No, it seems that you were the sole target. I found that surprising, because it enabled the hands to get you back here safely without coming under attack. So whoever it was who shot you, it wasn't a professional gunman. I've been told that no professional would have let them off that easily; a professional would have wanted to take out as many men as possible. An army or any effective fighting force would certainly have seized the advantage in that situation. So, we can only assume his hired guns aren't in place yet.

"Luckily Ben was on his way here to welcome me when you were brought in, so there was barely a delay. He's been coming in every day since to check on you. He says you're going to be fine." Guy flushed, and smiled a little sheepishly. "Which is a huge relief! I don't think I'm quite ready to run this place without you."

Guthrie forced a smile. "Aye, you've been away a long time. You've got a lot to learn about ranching. But that'll have to wait—the first thing is to ensure we have a ranch to work and that we hang on to what's ours. We're certainly not going to roll over for the likes of Chavez. He resents any landowner who isn't Spanish. He hates me because I got most of my land before the big land grant came into effect. And he hated Peggy's father for persuading Maxwell to sell him the land he'd rented. I guess he saw Steen's death as an opportunity to wage war on us. But I bought my land, fair and square, and I'll fight for it, and for Peggy's land too while she's under my care." He hissed in a breath as another stab of pain lanced his body. When the pain eased off he glanced again at Guy. The young man seemed ill at ease; he was fidgeting and chewing on his lip.

Guthrie felt a cold clutch of fear; maybe Guy didn't want to stay here and risk his life for the ranch? After all, he'd been in Boston for a long time . . . Did he want to return to that life of comfort and ease instead of fighting for what was his? But what should he say to him? Guy was a virtual stranger. He sighed heavily. He should have brought his son home to New Mexico when he was younger, at a more biddable age. Guy had no experience whatsoever in running the ranch while Guthrie was out of action. He didn't even know if Guy had the guts or the brains to run it. The young man sitting in front of him was an unknown quantity—but a man, not a boy. He favored his mother; he'd inherited her fine features and fair skin. But had he inherited his father's determination? Damn it, he should ask Guy what his intentions were instead of lying here fretting.

"I need to know, Guy, are you planning on staying? Or do you wish to return to Boston? You seem . . ." He hesitated. "Somewhat distracted, ill at ease."

Guy shrugged, not meeting Guthrie's eyes. "There's a lot to think about. I'm trying to plan the defense of the hacienda, learn about ranching, and cope with everything else as best I can while you're laid up."

He knew the young man was avoiding his question; his response hadn't even been subtle. "I asked if you were planning on staying."

Guy jerked his head up, his eyes narrowed. "Of course I'm staying. Do you think I'm the sort of man who'd leave you and Peggy to face this alone?"

"But there's something you're not telling me?" Guthrie couldn't stop himself pushing.

Guy sighed. "I don't think you're well enough to discuss it yet."

Guthrie glared. "Just damn well tell me what's on your mind. I've spent my life building up this ranch, and if there's a problem I need to know about it. Someone has to make decisions, and right now, that's me. This isn't the time to be concerned about my health."

Guy's mouth tightened. And a nerve was pulsing at his temple. "In that case, as you insist. But it's nothing specifically to do with the ranch. What's really on my mind is my brother. Why was I told that John was dead?"

"John?" Guthrie frowned.

"Yes!" Guy snapped the word out. "John. My brother."

Guthrie shook his head slowly. What on earth had Guy heard? Why was he asking about John? Play for time—that was the best option. Try and find out what Guy had heard. "I didn't know that you were told he was dead."

Guy narrowed his eyes. "My uncle told me years ago that John was dead. Now I hear from Peggy that it isn't true."

"Peggy?" How the hell had Peggy known that John was alive?

Guy nodded. "You look somewhat surprised that she should know that, but it seems she overheard you and her father discussing John." He stared intently at Guthrie.

Guthrie swallowed hard. What had Peggy heard? Surely not that John was Fierro? Please, God, not that. "As I just said, I didn't know you'd been told that John was dead." Maybe a bland statement would make Guy open up, make him reveal whatever he had heard about his long-lost brother.

"My uncle told me just before you visited when I was ten or eleven. You really didn't know?" Guy cocked an eyebrow.

"No, I didn't. And I have no idea why your uncle told you that; I was still hunting for John, as your uncle knew full well."

Guy fiddled with the cuff of his shirt. "Maybe they thought it would distress you if I kept asking questions."

Guthrie nodded slowly. It was a distinct possibility. Doubtless it had been kindly meant. Perhaps Guy had worried about his younger brother? If he was honest, he'd hoped that Guy might have forgotten he ever had a brother. He was only five or so when Gabriela left. "I'm sure they meant well. To be honest, I assumed you'd put it behind you as you never mentioned him in letters or when I visited."

"Put it behind me?" Guy's voice sounded bitter. "The disappearance of a brother is not something that I was inclined to forget."

Guthrie bit his lip. "I didn't phrase that well. I just meant that you had moved on, that part of your life was past."

49

Guy's face hardened, but then the look was gone and he looked once more his impassive self. "The fact remains that you have apparently traced John. I am at a loss to understand why you didn't send for him too."

He almost welcomed the wave of pain from his wound; it gave him a few seconds of thinking time. How should he explain his decision? One thing was certain; he wouldn't be telling Guy what John did for a living. Nothing would induce him to reveal that. "I feel John should be left to get on with his own life now. He is obviously unaware of our existence and I see no point in upsetting whatever he has grown up believing." It sounded weak, but it was the best he could come up with.

Guy didn't look impressed. "This ranch is as much his birthright as mine. He's entitled to know he has a family. He should be free to make an informed choice. He's a man, not a child."

Guthrie waved a dismissive hand. "Well, we have no time to worry about that at present. We have to concentrate on the ranch. We have a fight ahead of us . . ."

"A fight in which another man would be useful." Guy looked smug.

Guthrie snorted. "We don't have time for that now . . ."

"Which is why," Guy carried on inexorably as if Guthrie hadn't spoken. "I instructed the Pinkerton Agency to contact John and offer him five hundred dollars to come here to hear something to his advantage."

Guthrie fell back against his pillow, the color draining from his face, and he felt icy cold. "You did what?" His voice was just a whisper.

Guy raised an eyebrow. "I instructed the Pinkerton Agency to contact John. I felt it was time to act. He should be here, where he belongs. This was his home too. I also assumed he doesn't remember and Gabriela never told him about us, since I can't think of any other explanation for why he hasn't returned. I felt it prudent to offer some money to bring him here, so that we could explain things in person. It's not the sort of information he should receive from a Pinkerton Agent."

His gut was churning, and he shivered, unable to suppress the chill sweeping through him. What the hell could he say? He'd be damned if he'd tell Guy what John had become. He couldn't; he didn't want to admit that John was scum and not a man to even allow over the threshold. He flinched, remembering what a joyful child John had been. There'd been no clue in those first years that he'd turn into a killer.

Guy was watching him intently, apparently expecting some sort of response. And he still couldn't think what to say. He cleared his throat, playing for time. But what the hell had Guy unleashed? Fierro coming here . . . God almighty.

"I'm sorry." Guy sounded contrite, but there was no mistaking the curiosity in his eyes. "You aren't well enough yet to receive this piece of news. I should have left telling you to later."

"Aye, I don't feel too good." He deliberately made his voice sound feeble. He needed time alone to figure out what the hell to do. Fierro. God in heaven!

"I'll leave you to rest. Ben will be here shortly. I'll send him up when he arrives."

Guthrie nodded weakly, relieved to see Guy leave and to be left alone with his thoughts.

He was jarred from his worrying by the arrival of Ben, who blew into the room like a small whirlwind. A surge of relief swept over him—Ben would know what to do. He'd have sound advice for his old friend.

His attempts to describe what Guy had done were thwarted by Ben's insistence that he give Guthrie a thorough examination. "Damn it, Ben! Never mind examining me. I need to talk to you."

"After my examination." Ben's tone brooked no arguments.

Guthrie gritted his teeth while Ben prodded and poked at him and checked that his wound was healing. "That's coming on well, Guthrie, it's looking good. Now, what is this momentous news that you have to tell me?" Ben perched on the edge of the bed and folded his arms.

Guthrie rapidly outlined what Guy had done, still hardly able to believe it himself. But if he'd hoped for a considered response from Ben he was disappointed. Ben looked as shocked as he had been.

"He's sent for Fierro?" Ben's voice was barely a whisper. "My God. The last thing we need is a man like that."

A man like that? Guthrie frowned. Maybe Ben was forgetting that he had delivered John—one of the first babies the man had delivered as a fresh-faced young doctor. But no, Ben was right, of course he was right. A man like Fierro could only mean trouble.

"Guy doesn't know who John is. He thinks of him as his young brother." Guthrie felt compelled to explain Guy's action.

"You haven't told him?" Ben stared at him through wide eyes. "Have you taken leave of your senses?"

Guthrie shuffled uncomfortably. "How can I tell him what John is? And anyway," he was defensive now. "John might never arrive here." Even though he suspected it would be a cold day in hell before a gunman turned down the chance of such easy money.

Ben raised a disbelieving eyebrow, obviously thinking exactly the same thing. "Leaving that very unlikely scenario to one side, the fact remains that Fierro is a dangerous man. You don't even know if he knows that you're his family. Although, I would have thought that if he did know he'd have turned up here looking for money a long time ago. It's the sort of thing a man like that would do."

There it was again: a man like that. That was what his son had become, a man nobody trusted or wanted around. A paid killer. But Ben had a point. Surely if Fierro knew his father was a wealthy man, he'd have shown up before this. Perhaps he'd arrive when Guy wasn't around . . . Then he could be paid off. It would be a small price to pay to get rid of him. And then nobody need ever know that Fierro was his son.

"I know one thing," Ben looked at him hard, through narrowed eyes. "I'd have that money ready and waiting if I were you. There's no telling what Fierro might do if he thinks you're trying to swindle him."

"Yes, I thought the same thing myself." Guthrie hesitated, the ghost of an idea forming in his mind. "If he does know I'm his father, I thought a partnership offer might scare him off. I could offer him a share if he stays and works on the ranch. I'll bet that he's never done a real day's work in his life. And then, when he refuses, I can give him some extra money to get rid of him. Do you think that would work?"

Ben furrowed his brow and then shrugged. "It might. It would be easy money for him. But on the other hand . . ."

Guthrie's head jerked up. "But?"

"Maybe he'll threaten you. Demand more. What if he does that? Damn it, Guthrie!" Ben stood up and stalked to the window. "He's a dangerous man. And Guy has no idea what he is bringing down on you all. You should warn Guy."

Guthrie shook his head. "No. It may be possible that Guy will never find out. Let him keep his dream of his little brother. I don't want to destroy that if I can help it. And there is a chance that he won't show. He may be killed in a gunfight before he even gets here." But even as he said the words he felt a chill deep inside of him. His little blue-eyed boy, killed in a gunfight.

What the hell had happened to his child to turn him into a cold-hearted killer?

"Frankly, that might be the best thing. For all of you." Ben sighed. "I know that sounds harsh, Guthrie. But you've heard the stories. You'd be a fool to underestimate him, or not to view his presence as a threat. And with Chavez hiring guns, what's to say that Fierro won't throw his lot in with them? Chavez would welcome him with open arms."

"Except he doesn't like mestizos," Guthrie muttered to himself. There was no getting away from the fact that John would be viewed as that by many people here. With a mixture of Mexican, Apache, and Scottish blood, John would have doubtless encountered prejudice from people in all walks of life. And Chavez hated anyone who wasn't of pure Spanish descent.

Ben nodded slowly. "That might work to your advantage. Although, if Chavez is set on getting that land at any cost, he might set aside his prejudices. I'm sorry, Guthrie, but I find this development very worrying. I know Guy had no idea what he was unleashing, but heavens, this could bring no end of trouble and I do feel that you should warn him of the danger. If Fierro does turn up here, Guy needs to know the risks so that he can be alert. It's only right to prepare him for what could happen."

Guthrie shook his head decisively. "No. I'm not going to tell him."

"Because you're ashamed." Ben threw up his hands. "That's what this is really about. You're ashamed to admit that your son is a gunfighter."

Guthrie swallowed hard. Trust Ben to see beneath the bluster, and the excuses that he didn't want to destroy Guy's illusions. Ben knew him too well. He huffed in a breath. "Yes. I'm ashamed. Are you happy now? I am ashamed to admit what John has become. I don't know if he was born bad, or if this is

Gabriela's fault. All I know is that I want nothing to do with him."

Ben turned back to the window and stood staring out, apparently lost in thought. Guthrie could hear the sounds of the vaqueros in the corral; judging from the shouts of approval someone was breaking a horse. Ben sighed heavily. "I suppose there's a chance we're wrong. What if there's more to Fierro than just a gun for hire? What if half of what we've heard is just barroom gossip?"

Guthrie hesitated. Could that be the case? "No. Buck Lee saw him in action. He's an honest man, and I don't believe he invented that tale of Fierro gutshooting someone."

Ben shrugged. "Lots of people like to embellish a story."

Guthrie furrowed his brow. "I don't understand you, Ben, a few minutes ago you were warning me against Fierro and now you're arguing the other way?"

Ben flinched, looked embarrassed, and gestured toward the corral. "Seeing the men out there breaking that horse . . . It made me think of that time when John crawled in among that small herd someone rounded up for breaking. How he didn't get hurt was a miracle, but he wanted to be in there with all the action. We found him sitting among those wild horses as happy as a pig in mud. Do you recall what Steen said to us about young John and how he was always laughing and into everything? Steen was right about that. And I remembered John's smile . . . It made me wonder if perhaps the stories are exaggerated. It just seems unlikely, when I think of that child, that he could turn out all bad."

Guthrie nodded slowly. "But whether the tales have been exaggerated or not, the fact remains that he's a hired gun. A man who'll kill if the price is right. What sort of man does that? You know me, Ben, I despise gunfighters. Even thinking of John as that type of man makes me feel sick to my stomach." He set his jaw. "I believe in the law. I want to see this wild land of ours become a civilized place that's safe for people to live and grow. And hired guns like John are standing in the way of that. While men like him have free rein, this land is safe for no one. As a God-fearing man, I hate his kind, and everything they represent."

CHAPTER FIVE

It was an easy journey from Santa Fe to Cimarron. He toyed with the idea of following the Rio Grande through the gorge and then looping around through the mountains to Cimarron, but in the end decided it would be far quicker to follow the Santa Fe Trail. He wanted to find out what Sinclair wanted with him. So, just this once speed won.

He avoided most of the popular places to stop, preferring to make his own camp and keep clear of trouble. Because trouble always found him—it seemed to be the one certainty in life. But as he drew closer to Cimarron he spent a night at a crowded way station; he figured it was one way to pick up any gossip about what might be happening in the area. Surely Sinclair must have had a particular reason for sending for him?

After listening to the talk at the table where the travelers gathered to swap tall stories over a meal, he figured he knew. It sounded like there was a full-blown range war brewing, with Sinclair's ranch right in the middle of it. Doubtless Sinclair wanted to hire guns, and Fierro was one of the best. But the question still remained whether Sinclair knew that Fierro was his own son. And not knowing the answer to that was eating away at him. He'd be going in blind, and he hated that. He hated not having control of the situation. The only thing he had on his side was that Sinclair wouldn't know when to expect him—maybe he could use that element of surprise to his advantage. And Johnny Fierro always had to have the advantage.

He made an early start the next day. He wanted to reach Cimarron to gather as much information as he could about the range war, and then ride out to Sinclair Ranch and face his father. It was odd though. He'd waited so long for this and he thought he'd feel good about it. Excited, maybe? But there was an icy knot in his stomach, which he could almost have taken for fear if it wasn't that Johnny Fierro wasn't afraid of anything. Except hanging.

It was kind of funny really. He'd spent years avoiding Cimarron, always telling himself he'd go there to face his father when he could spare the time. But if he was honest, there had been lots of times when work was thin on the ground, lots of times when he'd passed near the town . . . So what the hell did that say about him? He pushed the thought away. He needed to concentrate on the now of it, not brood on the past. The time had come—that was all that mattered.

The buckskin made short work of the last few miles to Cimarron. The town nestled in the shelter of the mountains rising behind it to the north, while wide windswept plains lay to the east. It sure was pretty scenery but probably damn cold in the winter. Too cold for his blood.

The town was a sprawl of rough wooden buildings mixed in with a few more solidly built structures. Mexicans and gringos hurried about their business while groups of cowpokes and miners sidled in and out of saloons, anxious to blow the wages burning holes in their pockets.

He was glad of the bustle; it was easier to go unnoticed. Pulling his hat low to cast a shadow over his face, he headed for the busiest saloon, ordered a beer, and sat in a corner where he could see and hear most everything. And there was plenty to hear with a group of hard-eyed men discussing some rancher called Chavez who seemed to be the one stirring up trouble. Chavez was hiring guns—lots of guns—and if some of the names being discussed were, in fact, signing on with the man, it looked like Sinclair had trouble coming. Big trouble.

When he'd heard enough he slipped out of the bar and returned to where he'd left his buckskin. Stepping into the saddle he headed west toward the Sinclair spread. What he wanted was to get a look at the place and then slip in unnoticed. The element of surprise would give him the edge he craved. He chewed on his lip—trouble was if Sinclair had any sense he'd have posted lookouts all over the place, preparing for the trouble to come.

He rode west for several miles through the hill country and rangeland, before reining in sharply as he rounded a bend on a narrow ridge. The breath caught in his throat as he stared across to the sprawling white hacienda of the Sinclair Ranch, which seemed to grow out of its surroundings. It was huge. His mother had never told him that Sinclair was this rich, or that the house was this big or this beautiful.

Flat-roofed in parts, it was built around a large courtyard with high metal gates opening out on to its range, which spread toward the mountains. A long sweeping driveway approached the other side of the house, so long it must run right back toward the Santa Fe Trail.

He sat for several minutes drinking in the beauty, scarcely able to believe that this was where he'd been born. This was where he should have been raised. He closed his eyes tight, trying to block out the memories of the series of shacks he'd lived in with his mother, and everything his mother's men had done . . . He shook himself; this was no time to start thinking about what might have been. A man had to play the cards that life dealt him, and that was the end of it.

He reached inside his jacket for a small spyglass and studied the hacienda. Peering through it, he could see a couple of guards pacing the flat roof, but the raised roof to one side meant the men had blind spots, and there weren't enough guards. Either Sinclair was dumb or he didn't have the men to spare, and that was dumb in itself because if an attack came, he wouldn't have a ranch left at the end of it.

A group of vaqueros were riding out with some young, fair-haired gringo with a big mustache. Johnny shook his head wondering if that was the segundo. If it was, then Sinclair really was a fool—the young man rode like he was in the army, not like a seasoned ranch hand. But hell, Sinclair had thrown him and his mother out because he didn't want a half-breed for a son; maybe he didn't want a Mex segundo.

He huffed out a breath. Leastways it seemed that Sinclair didn't have any proper defenses—he was certain that he could get into the house without being spotted. He laughed softly. That would give Sinclair one hell of a shock.

Keeping in the long shadow of a steep bluff, he skirted around to the west before tying the buckskin in a small clump of trees some distance from the main courtyard. Keeping a close eye on the guards he crept toward the house, using the scrub sagebrush for cover. Once when a vaquero swung suddenly to peer in his direction, he flattened himself to the ground, glad of his faded leather charro jacket, which blended in against the muted colors of the landscape.

The vaquero turned away once more and returned to his pacing on the roof as Johnny edged, Apache-like, across the ground until he reached the cover of a big water trough. He breathed in deeply a couple of times, trying to calm his thumping heart. The next problem was to make it from here to the house without being spotted. Leastways the courtyard had some sort of raised flowerbeds built from stone, which would provide some cover. Even better there was a pond in the center with a small fountain. Johnny shook his head—damn but this was an impressive place. Sinclair obviously liked people to know he was a rich man. But not a man who wanted a half-breed kid . . .

He grunted, irritated with himself. He couldn't let Sinclair get to him. He needed to concentrate on the thought of five hundred dollars, and then he could worry about exacting revenge for what the man had inflicted on him and his mother.

He forced his attention back to the guards, counting their paces until he was certain there was a brief moment when none of the guards would be watching the courtyard. That would be his cue to speed to the house and slip inside.

He timed his move perfectly, racing to the house before quietly pushing the door open and stepping into a dim, cool corridor. Lots of doors led off it. All was quiet, although some distance away at the other end of the house he could hear the sounds of pans rattling—doubtless the cook preparing dinner.

Leaning down he unfastened his spurs and slipped them into his pocket, before silently padding along the tiled corridor to the middle of the house where another wing led off on the far side of the courtyard. A staircase with an ornately carved banister rose from the central hall where a log smoldered in a stone hearth. A heavy cedar door stood ajar; through the gap he could glimpse a gray-haired man working at a desk—presumably this was Sinclair.

Moving cautiously he pushed the door open. It creaked on its heavy hinges causing Sinclair to glance up. He paled and stumbled to his feet, rubbing at his side as if it pained him to move quickly. "Who the hell are you, and how did you get into my home?"

Johnny raised an eyebrow, and then ghosted a smile. "Now that ain't much of a greeting, Old Man."

"I asked how you got in and who you are . . ." Sinclair's voice trailed off and he sat down abruptly.

"Getting in wasn't hard. Those guards of yours are shit. If you think they're going to protect you from an attack by Chavez you're a fool. And as to who I am . . ." He laughed. "You know who I am."

Sinclair swallowed hard. "Fierro?"

Johnny nodded.

"How do you know about Chavez?" Sinclair's voice had an edge.

"Oh, I know all sorts of things about you, Sinclair. You'd be real surprised at just how much I know . . ." Johnny left the words hanging. That would get the bastard wondering. The question was did Sinclair know Fierro was his son? It was hard to gauge from the man's reaction—he was too shocked that someone had walked into his house without being seen. Now that was bound to make a man feel vulnerable. Johnny bit back a grin; he'd gotten the upper hand here, and Sinclair was way out of his depth.

Johnny glanced around the room. The walls were lined with books, hundreds of damn books, and a fire burned in a big hearth that took up half of one wall. The worn leather chairs and couch were draped with colorful blankets like the Pueblo made. So Sinclair didn't mind Indian blankets—just part Indian sons.

"There's the matter of my fee, Sinclair. Five hundred dollars, the Pink said. I expect people to keep their word. I get real pissed if they don't."

The man glowered at him. "You'll get your money. It's in my desk." He bent to open a drawer, jerking back as Johnny drew his gun.

"Just reach for it nice and slow. I get jumpy when men reach into open drawers."

Sinclair snorted. "Then you're mixing in the wrong company. I'm a man of my word. Here it is." He half threw the envelope across the desk. "Perhaps you'd better count it."

Johnny thumbed through the notes. It was all there. Five

hundred dollars! He kept his face expressionless—didn't want the old man to guess that Fierro wasn't used to having that much money.

Sinclair was looking at him intently, studying him hard, like he was looking for something . . . or trying to recognize him? Maybe Sinclair did know who he was? He met the man's scrutiny with his own hard-eyed stare and he could swear he saw a flicker of recognition in Sinclair's eyes, but maybe not. There was only one way to find out.

"So, you hiring guns? Is that why I'm here? You're going to need them to deal with Chavez."

"I'm damned if I'll stoop to hiring a bunch of shootists." Sinclair snapped the words out.

Johnny laughed softly. "But you sent for me, and I can't help but wonder why." He paused. "Seeing as how I'm a shootist, Sinclair." He smiled wolfishly. "Sinclair. Now there's a name to think about. Is that what I call you? Sinclair? Maybe you prefer 'Old Man'? Or is there some other name I should call you?"

The man narrowed his eyes. "Don't play games with me. What exactly do you know about me?"

Johnny shrugged. "Like I said, I know all sorts of things about you."

Sinclair sighed heavily, and looked oddly defeated. "So you do know. You know I'm your father."

Johnny nodded. "Oh yeah, like I said, I know all about you. So, if you ain't hiring guns, why am I here? I can't believe you suddenly got some urge for a cozy family reunion."

Sinclair limped across to a side table where there was a cut glass bottle filled with amber liquid. He looked questioningly at Johnny. "Scotch?"

Johnny shook his head. "No. Just tell me why I'm here, Old Man."

Sinclair scowled. "I'll come to that. But if you know that I'm your father, why've you never come here before? I'd have thought a man like you would be only too keen to see if there was money to be got from a wealthy man like me."

"A man like me?" Johnny echoed the words. "Let me tell you, Sinclair, you don't know nothing about a man like me."

"I know you're a hired gun. What else is there to know?" Sinclair tossed back his drink.

The words stung, hitting their mark as sure as a bullet. Johnny turned away, determined not to let him see any reaction. "Just get to the point, Old Man."

"Fine. Your birthright." Sinclair gestured out through the window. "One third of everything I own. But you'll damn well work for it. Ranching is hard work, and I don't believe in carrying anyone. If you want what I'm offering, you'll have to earn it, and we'll have to drive off Chavez and his gunmen first. If you're afraid of the thought of hard work, then I'll pay you now to go away. But you'll never get anything else from me."

Johnny sucked in a breath. Whatever he'd expected it sure wasn't this. Why the hell would Sinclair want to give his half-breed son a share of his ranch? There had to be a catch; there was always a catch. He shrugged, like the offer didn't mean much. "Only a third, Sinclair? Hell, why not make it half?"

Whatever Sinclair was about to say was cut off as the door swung open and the gringo he'd seen with the vaqueros burst into the room. "I think we may have an intruder. One of the men found a horse tethered just out of sight of the . . ." The man paused, and stared hard at Johnny, before looking at Sinclair. "I'm sorry to interrupt; I didn't realize you had a visitor."

"That's my horse, gringo. I guess we could say I'm your intruder. So why don't you butt out? Sinclair and me have business to discuss." Johnny glared as the man continued to stare at him with a frown creasing his brow. Johnny turned to Sinclair. "You want to tell him to go?" Johnny's lip curled as he looked the gringo up and down. "Who is he anyway? He don't look much of a hand."

Sinclair shook his head. "He's not a ranch hand—he's your brother."

Johnny turned his head sharply, even as the gringo strode toward him with an outstretched hand.

"John! As soon as I saw you, I knew you looked familiar!" The gringo tried to grab his hand but Johnny jerked it back.

Brother? He had a brother? But this fellow looked older than him, and that made no sense. If he had an older brother his mother would have told him.

"This is Guy, your older brother." Sinclair's voice was kind of even but he was looking hard at Johnny, as if trying to gauge his reaction. "Now you know why the offer is only one third."

The fellow, Guy, was looking like he'd won a big pot in a poker game, grinning from ear to ear like he was pleased to claim Johnny Fierro as a brother, and that really was crazy. Nobody would want Fierro as a brother . . . Johnny glanced at Sinclair. The man was refilling his glass and there was the slightest tremor in his hand as he poured the whiskey. Yeah, Sinclair was nervous, so maybe the gringo didn't know exactly who his brother was. And that could make life real interesting.

"Guy, perhaps you could give John and me a few minutes alone, please." Sinclair's voice sounded strong, but the tremor was still there in the hand.

The gringo nodded. "Of course, sir, I'll get back to work. I'll make sure that one of the men feeds John's horse and puts it in the corral." He opened the door before he paused and turned to face Johnny. "I just want to say how pleased I am that you came. Welcome home."

As the door closed behind him, Johnny stared hard at Sinclair. "He doesn't know who I am, does he?"

Sinclair shook his head. "He's been out east for many years.

He's probably never even heard of Johnny Fierro."

"And you didn't think to tell him?" Johnny raised an eyebrow and walked across to one of the bookcases. "Hell, anyone would think you're ashamed of me." He laughed softly as Sinclair drew in a sharp breath.

"And do you really think any father would be pleased to have a gunman in the family?" Sinclair snapped out the words.

Johnny ran his finger along the spines of books. "But a gunman in the family comes in real handy at times like this. And so I can't help but wonder what happens after I deal with Chavez and you get your ranch back safe and sound. Will you still want your gunman then?"

"You seem very confident that you can deal with Chavez."

Johnny nodded. "I can deal with pretty much anything. But you didn't answer the question."

Sinclair narrowed his eyes. "I am a man of my word. Maybe you've never met one before. But if you want a piece of this ranch you'll damn well have to work for it. Have you ever done a day's real work in your life?"

Johnny ducked his head before meeting Sinclair's eyes. "My life ain't none of your business. But I'm not afraid of work if that's what you're thinking. And, I'm a man of my word. If I take your deal I'll work for it." He paused and chewed on his thumb. "Are there any more brothers or sisters I should know about? And where'd you get this gringo, anyway?"

"Your mother never mentioned Guy?" Sinclair sounded puzzled. "He's the son of my first wife, who died. I married your mother later so Guy remembers you, although you would have been too young to remember him when you left."

Johnny's hands balled into fists. When he left? The old man was referring to throwing them out like they'd just upped and left? He sucked in a breath and tried to calm himself. There was plenty of time for a showdown with Sinclair—this wasn't the time. "Like I said, are there any other brothers or sisters I should know about?"

"No." Sinclair sounded riled now. "I've never remarried. The only other person you need to know about is Peggy, the daughter of an old friend of mine. He was a rancher. After he was killed I became her guardian. It's her land that has brought this business with Chavez to a head. I'm holding the land in trust for her."

"And how old is this Peggy?"

"She's almost sixteen. Why?"

Johnny smiled thinly. "Oh, I just wondered exactly what your relationship with her is. If maybe there'll be some more brothers and sisters coming along."

Sinclair flushed. "Good God, she's the daughter of an old friend. She's only fifteen, I said!"

Johnny shrugged, but he couldn't resist the urge to goad his father. "Probably about the age my mother was when you fucked her." His words hit home and he stood his ground as Sinclair took two strides toward him. A pulse was beating in the man's temple and his face was scarlet.

Sinclair sucked in a long breath, like he was trying to calm himself. "I loved your mother. I married her. And, I won't tolerate that sort of language in my home. Now, do we have a deal, or am I paying you off?"

Johnny smiled coldly. "We got a deal, Old Man." He hesitated, his mind racing. "But maybe it would be best not to let folk know I'm Fierro—we might be able to play that to our advantage. Let's just keep it between ourselves for the time being." He saw the relief in Sinclair's eyes. Yeah, it would suit the man very well if he didn't have to admit to being the father of Johnny Fierro. "Of course, there's always the chance someone will recognize me, but for now we'll keep it quiet—until the time comes to take down Chavez."

Sinclair nodded. "I'll show you your room."

Johnny followed him as the man slowly climbed the staircase, half surprised that he wasn't being shown to the bunkhouse. His father opened a door into a big airy room with a view of the mountains to the west. "This is your old room. Dinner is prompt at six. A gong will sound five minutes beforehand. Don't be late." With a gruff nod the man limped out of the room and closed the door behind him.

Johnny sank down onto the bed. Mierda! Things hadn't gone the way he'd planned them. And whatever he'd expected it sure wasn't to be offered part of a ranch. Not that he believed the offer—why would Sinclair want to give him a chunk of something like this? No, Sinclair doubtless wanted to use him, and then, when it was over, he'd be thrown out. People never wanted him around once the dust had settled on whatever troubles they'd brought him in to deal with. It was always the same—use Fierro and then send him on his way.

He hauled himself back to his feet and paced over to the window. A group of vaqueros were gathered around a corral where one of them was breaking a horse, cheered on by his compadres. And beyond the corral the mountains stretched away into the distance, a purple haze in the late afternoon light. But one peak in particular caught his eye. It was different from the others. Instead of being roughly hewn out of the landscape, it had straight sides and a bald tip. He grinned; it was the kind of shape that a child would draw for a mountain. But it sure was pretty here. What would it be like to belong here? Hell, to belong anywhere?

Irritated, he turned away. Why the hell hadn't he handled things differently? He should have just shot the man and be done with it. Or at least demanded to hear Sinclair's side of the story. But he'd felt overwhelmed at finally meeting the man who'd sired him. And then when the man had made this amazing offer, part of him wanted to believe the offer was genuine. That Sinclair was as good as his word . . .

And a brother? Shit, that had thrown him too. Why hadn't his mother told him he had a brother? If Sinclair was to be believed his mother had known. But in all those years she'd never mentioned a brother. Guy. What kind of a name was that? It sure wasn't one he'd ever heard before.

He stared around the room. His room? That's what Sinclair had said. He screwed his eyes shut, desperately trying to remember anything of the time he'd lived here. But those years had disappeared, lost in the depths of his memory. Nothing remained. Nothing to link him with a time when he'd been safe.

Sinclair had to have thrown them out. No sane person would have walked away from all this to live like he and his mother had lived. Hell, this room alone was bigger than some of the shacks they'd lived in. And his mother wouldn't have lied to him about the past. She just . . . she just wouldn't.

He huffed out a sigh, and threw himself down on the bed. He had to stop brooding. Take things as they came and try to figure out what game Sinclair was playing, and not let any of this get to him. Dinner would be a good time to test Sinclair. See how far he could push the man. But one thing was certain; he'd be damned if he'd go down on time for dinner. He wasn't dancing to no man's tune.

Chapter Six

Guy fidgeted with his napkin. His father's constant finger drumming was enough to drive a man mad. It was ten minutes since dinner had been served but his newfound brother hadn't appeared.

"What's keeping that boy?" Guthrie glared at Peggy. "You did sound the gong?"

She rolled her eyes. "You know I did. But maybe, as he's had a long journey, he was tired and has fallen asleep."

Guthrie snorted derisively. "He's not asleep. He's just being difficult . . ."

"Evening." John's soft drawl broke across his father's words. Guthrie jerked forward, his wine spreading a red stain across the cloth.

"You're late. I said dinner was prompt." Guthrie narrowed his eyes. "And do you always creep around like that?"

John ignored the question, nodding toward Peggy. "We haven't been introduced."

Guthrie inclined his head. "Peggy, this is John."

"Johnny. Nobody calls me John." Taking her hand, he bowed and kissed her fingertips. She pulled her hand away, blushing while he slid into the seat next to her.

John hadn't bothered changing. He was still in the same dusty clothes he'd arrived in, and it didn't look as though he'd even bothered washing the dirt from his hands. He was still wearing his gun, too. Guy wondered how long it would take before

Guthrie commented on that. Well, maybe it had all proved overwhelming for him and he had indeed been asleep. Guy grinned encouragingly as he helped himself to a large helping of stew. "So, we finally get a chance to talk. We have more than twenty years to catch up on."

John glanced at him, his eyes cool and distinctly unfriendly. "I don't reckon we'll have much to talk about. My life ain't none of your business."

Guy tried another smile. "Well, tell me where you've been living all these years. Where did you grow up? Where did you go to school? Like I said, we've a lot to catch up on."

"Guy went to Harvard. That's a very well-known school in Boston." Peggy beamed.

John hunched over his plate, forking in the food, before looking at Guy with a sardonic smile. "Harvard, huh? Well, that's real nice for him, ain't it?"

Guy forced another smile; it seemed that this was going to be a more difficult evening than he'd expected. "So, where did you go to school? Somewhere down in Mexico?"

Johnny put his fork down and stared at him silently. Just when Guy thought he wasn't going to bother answering, he said, "Well, I s'pose you'd say I got my learning in the school of life. The border towns where I grew up, they're sort of here today, gone tomorrow, kind of places. You'd fit in real well down there." He paused and looked Guy up and down. "Especially in them fancy clothes." John gestured vaguely toward Guy's cravat and laughed but there didn't seem to be any mirth in it.

Guy bit his lip, determined not to rise to the taunt. "And what sort of work do you do in these . . . here today, gone tomorrow sort of towns?"

John looked at him steadily through narrowed eyes. "I don't reckon that's any of your business, either."

Guy frowned. Why did John have to be so surly? He gritted

his teeth. Still, they couldn't eat dinner in total silence; someone was going to have to make an effort at conversation, and judging from the sour look on his . . . their . . . father's face, that dubious privilege was obviously down to Guy.

John had returned to shoveling food in. Guy winced. His brother's manners were appalling. He tried desperately to think of something to say. "How's Gabriela?" Out of the corner of his eye he saw his father flinch.

John laid down his fork and stared at him through narrowed eyes. "Gabriela?"

Guy nodded reluctantly. "Your mother."

John looked even colder, if that was possible. "I know who she is. As to how she is, last time I saw her she was dead."

Guy flushed. "I'm sorry; I didn't know that she had died. My condolences."

John shook his head, as if unable to believe what he was hearing. "Your condolences?" He stumbled slightly over the word.

Guy inclined his head. "It means my sympathies . . ."

"I know what it means," John snapped. "But your . . . condolences . . . are a bit late. She's been dead more than ten years."

"More than ten years?" Their father sounded shocked. "But you were a child. Who looked after you?"

John laughed softly. "I don't see as how that's any of your business, Old Man. Let's just say I got by."

"Someone must have taken care of you. Her family or friends maybe?" Guthrie leaned forward, his eyes fixed on John.

John forked in another mouthful of stew before glancing across at his father and then smiling sardonically. "Like I said, I got by. Tell me about Chavez."

Guthrie opened his mouth to say something, but John cut across him. "Chavez."

Guthrie swallowed hard and started telling John about

Chavez, describing the man and where his ranch lay. When Guthrie explained that he'd been shot by one of Chavez's men, Johnny's mouth quirked into a sardonic smile, but their father didn't react. He just set his jaw and carried on talking. Guy was puzzled by his father's behavior. He seemed almost nervous of John. It was as if he didn't want to risk annoying his brother and yet that was, he frowned, bizarre. That was it; his father's behavior was bizarre. And even allowing for the fact that he barely knew his own father, he'd observed enough of the man to know that he wasn't someone who backed down or was easily intimidated. But he was intimidated by John; Guy felt certain of that.

There was no point in dwelling on it. He turned his attention back to his food. Doubtless in time things would settle down, always assuming that John intended staying. Even so, if there were a battle ahead, he'd have felt easier if John was a more . . . amenable . . . yes, amenable sort of person. Had his brother ever had any military experience? Somehow he doubted it. John didn't look like he'd be good at taking orders. But at least he wore a gun, so hopefully he knew how to use it. From what he'd seen of the West, all young men seemed to wear guns. He felt a pang of regret for Boston. Life had been so much more civilized there.

He breathed a sigh of relief when Peggy cleared the dishes from the table. But it was short-lived as he noticed John eyeing Peggy's figure up and down like a man might leer at a saloon girl, a smile playing at his mouth. Peggy, leaving the room with the dishes balanced precariously on a tray, didn't notice. But Guthrie did.

As soon as Peggy closed the door behind her, Guthrie snapped. "You'll treat Peggy with respect. She's my ward, like a daughter to me. While you're under this roof you treat her accordingly."

John just laughed softly and drawled, "You sure you just see her as a daughter, Old Man? She's way too young for you, however much you might want her."

Guthrie's fists balled, and for a fleeting moment Guy thought his father might hit John, who slouched against the table with an insolent smile. But oddly, Guthrie backed down, sucking in a breath as if struggling to gain control of himself. "I suggest we go and sit down with a drink and plan our next move." He stood and beckoned them into the living room.

"I'll pour us all a drink." Guy picked up the heavy decanter and poured his father a hefty measure; from the look on his face he needed one. He proffered another measure to John, who shook his head. "No."

Not no, thank you. Just a plain no. God, but his brother was rude. But he'd be damned if he'd let John see that his rudeness was getting to him. Instead he inclined his head and kept the Scotch for himself before sinking on to the couch. Leaning back, he watched as John prowled around the room, stopping at the bookcase to run a finger along the spines of the books. Then John picked up each ornament from the side tables, tossing them casually from one hand to the other, until Guthrie, who was turning an interesting shade of purple, snapped. "Stop that. Those are fragile. They belonged to your grandmother."

John fumbled with a fine porcelain figurine, pretending to drop it and catching it at the last moment with a smirk.

"Can we get down to business?" Guthrie sounded as though he was talking through clenched teeth. Actually, he *was* talking through clenched teeth. Guy bit back a reluctant smile; he had to admit that John was certainly very good at annoying their father. The only puzzle was why John seemed so intent on annoying him.

John went and perched on the arm of the couch. "I'll tell you something, Old Man," he drawled. "You got trouble coming. Your man Chavez is putting out to hire a lot of guns. A lot of big names being talked about in town. He's looking at serious fire power. And you need to stop him dead before they arrive. No way could you fight a range war, not with the dumb ranch hands you got." John smiled wolfishly. "Unless you want to hire some guns yourself."

His brother's words certainly annoyed Guthrie, who was turning a deeper shade of purple. Guy jumped in quickly, before an argument could develop. "What makes you think our ranch hands aren't capable? I've been giving them drill, and some of them are good shots."

"Drill?" John laughed.

"Like in the army," Guy snapped.

John sighed, as if irritated. "I know they have drill in the army. But these ain't soldiers; they're Mex ranch hands. They round up cattle. They mend fences. They ain't gun hawks. And it's one thing doing some target practice, but it's a whole different game when the target is a man. And yeah, they are dumb. I got in here without anyone noticing. And you got a blind spot where you got them guards on the roof. That's how I got in without being seen. And if I could figure out how to get in here, I reckon any professional gunmen that Chavez takes on will figure it out too."

Guy frowned. "You talk as if you have military experience. I was in the cavalry . . ."

John laughed sourly. "Now why don't that surprise me? But you don't need to have been in the army to figure that this place is easy to take. This ain't an army fight, Soldier Boy. Ain't no generals sitting all cozy and safe giving orders and looking at their maps. No, this will be a quick and bloody attack. And believe me; the fellows that Chavez is looking to hire don't take no prisoners."

Guy cocked an eyebrow. "You've heard of these gunmen?"

His brother shrugged, glancing at Guthrie, who sat stiffly clutching his glass. "Yeah. Their names. Of course," he paused and looked across at Guthrie with a strange smile, "there are better known gunmen. Better shootists. But these men, they ain't bad."

"How well known they are is irrelevant." Guthrie glared at them. "What we need to do is decide how to deal with the threat."

"Kill Chavez." John smiled coldly. "That'll put an end to it."

Guthrie slammed his glass down and rose to his feet. "I'm a law-abiding man. My God, but you've got a nerve. How dare you suggest such a thing? I will not stoop to murder. It's not the way I deal with trouble."

"He'll murder you to get what he wants. Hell, you said one of his men already took a shot at you. So, now, you got to do it to him before he kills you." John stood and stretched. "You got to get tough, Old Man. There's ways of doing it so it don't look like murder. And trust me, you need to stamp on this before his guns start arriving, because they'll slaughter you. And that pretty little ward of yours. So you got two choices. Kill Chavez and do it soon. Or hire your own guns."

Guthrie paced around the room, a nerve pulsing at his temple. "We will do neither. Guy, do you have any suggestions?"

John snorted dismissively. "Yeah, Soldier Boy, let's hear what the cavalry would do."

Guy gritted his teeth. He wasn't going to rise to this. "I think we should conduct a survey of the land tomorrow, become familiar with it so that we can anticipate any move that Chavez may make. Look to see where the weak spots are in our defenses."

"I could tell you that without going for a fucking ride," muttered John.

Guthrie swung around. "I won't have that language in my house." He sucked in a breath. "But I think that's an excellent suggestion, Guy. You haven't visited Steen's ranch yet. It will be helpful for both of you to see what has triggered this fight."

John shrugged. "Yeah, well, we're bound to do what Harvard wants, seeing as how he's all gringo with fancy manners and fancy schooling. The fact that he don't know squat about life out here doesn't matter. But I tell you, Old Man, he's wrong. You're wrong. There's only one way to deal with this sort of fight—and that's to cut off the head."

Whatever Guthrie was going to say was interrupted by Peggy bustling into the room. "I'm off to bed in a few moments. Does anyone need more coffee or anything before I turn in?"

Guthrie shook his head. "No, thank you, Peg, we're fine. And we won't be up much longer." He hesitated. "Don't forget what I said earlier, dear."

Peggy frowned. "What did you say earlier?"

Guthrie flushed. "Oh, forget it, it doesn't matter."

John laughed softly. "I bet he told you to make sure you locked your door."

Peggy's eyes widened in surprise. "Yes! He did. How did you know that, John . . . Johnny?"

Guthrie opened his mouth but John cut across him. "Because you got a real bad hombre in the house."

"That's enough." Guthrie moved quickly to hold the door for Peggy, who had paled and stared nervously now at John. "Goodnight, dear. Sleep well." Guthrie patted her shoulder as she left the room before turning to glare at John. "If you're staying, you will learn some manners. This is my house, and it's my rules."

John ducked his head briefly before looking up, his eyes cold and hard. "I don't take orders from no man, Sinclair, including you."

Guy ran his fingers through his hair; he didn't think he could take much more this evening. If he stayed any longer he might knock their heads together. "I think I'll turn in too. I'll see you in the morning." With a curt nod he strode out of the room, offering up a silent prayer for patience. He was going to need it if life was going to be like this.

He was tugging his boots off when he heard footsteps hurrying along the passageway outside his room. He smiled. Peggy. She was always hurrying; running a house this big was a lot of responsibility for such a young girl. Then he heard her exclaim as she bumped into someone.

"Oh, you made me jump, Johnny, I didn't hear you." The girl sounded very nervous. Guy ground his teeth. His brother's offensive remark had obviously bothered the girl.

He heard John's voice. "Sorry. I didn't mean to make you jump. I was just turning in." There was a pause, and although he knew good manners dictated he shouldn't, he listened intently. Then he heard his brother speak again, but gently, kindly, not at all how he'd been during the evening. "There's no need to be afraid of me, Peggy. I shouldn't have said what I did. I ain't gonna hurt you. You can sleep sound and you really don't need to worry about locking your door. You're safe, I promise. G'night."

He heard his brother's door close, and Peggy's footsteps, slowly now, tapping down the passage. Frowning, he stood by the open window, looking out into the night. John was certainly an enigma. Aggressive and sarcastic, rude and ill-mannered, but just then, he had sounded so different. He had sounded kind and gentle with Peggy. He had sounded—genuine. It seemed there was a lot more to this strange new brother than met the eye. Guy shook his head. It was late and he was too tired to ponder it any more. Perhaps tomorrow, things would be clearer. Now, all he wanted was to sleep.

He smiled wryly. It would certainly surprise his uncle that he wasn't hightailing it back to Boston. Ranching and range wars certainly presented a more interesting prospect than balance sheets. And, he had to admit, this intriguing brother he had suddenly acquired, well, that was going to be interesting too.

CHAPTER SEVEN

Closing the door softly, Johnny looked around his room. His room? Still couldn't figure that. But the bed looked real inviting, and God, he was tired. He hadn't slept in a bed since he'd last had a woman and that was too long ago. But right now, he was too tired for that as well.

He placed his gun under the pillow and put another one next to the bed before shrugging himself out of his clothes. The sheets, smelling faintly of lavender, felt crisp and cool against his skin. He tensed at the sound of footsteps outside on the terrace, but relaxed as he recognized them as the old man's. Cattle lowed gently in the distance and he felt more comfortable than he'd felt in a long time.

He felt a pang of regret for scaring the girl with his comment about locking her door. The trouble was the old man brought out the worst in him. He'd only said it to rile him, and hadn't stopped to think it could upset her. Harvard hadn't thought much of it either judging from the look on his face. In fact, he reckoned Harvard hadn't been impressed by much of anything that evening. Give the man his due though: he'd been polite and hadn't reacted to any of the jibes Fierro threw at him. Even so, the man was obviously way out of his depth in the West. What with his strange clothes, and his strange way of talking. Hell, he'd even smelled strange, kind of like women were meant to smell.

How the hell could Harvard be his brother? He'd never

figured on a brother. And why hadn't his mother ever mentioned him? He pushed the thought away. He needed to start planning because it was obvious that Sinclair hadn't a clue how to deal with the threat to his land. And old Harvard was looking at it like he might look at a military problem. But the men Chavez would be hiring weren't a military problem. They were far more dangerous: men who'd hit rock bottom and who didn't care who they hurt. There was no telling what men like that would do.

If only he could catch some sleep tonight, maybe he could figure out a plan in the morning. And he was so damn tired. Perhaps, just for once, the demons that haunted his dreams would leave him to sleep undisturbed.

But the demons didn't leave him alone. There was never any escape. However tired he was, they still came visiting in the night. Faces of men he'd killed. Faces of his mother's men. And then there were the other memories of childhood—things he never wanted to think of; they were the worst of all.

He woke, sweating and striking out at his ghosts, as the golden dawn spread across the distant mountains. He left the warmth of the bed and knelt naked at the window. The funny shaped peak he'd noticed the previous day was flushed with pink. The breath caught in his throat then as the sun came full up, triumphant and brilliant, welcoming the start of a new day. Touched with dew, everything looked clean and fresh. Everything except him. He just felt old and tired. He'd come here for revenge but now he couldn't help but wonder if it was worth the effort. And as for the money Sinclair had given him . . . What the hell would he do with five hundred dollars anyway?

He could maybe buy a piece of land, set up on his own. Raise horses? But the men who wanted his reputation would find him. They'd still come looking, whatever he did they were going to keep coming. And it was only a question of time before one of them was fast enough. No, there was no point in trying to start over. He'd just fritter the money away, same as always. Maybe get yet another gun, but he'd spend the rest on women, getting himself fucked as often as possible. It was his only comfort. It was only during that brief spasm of pleasure that he could forget the demons.

He couldn't believe that the old man thought he'd fall for that promise of a piece of this ranch. He'd seen the look in his father's eyes. The look that said he just wanted Fierro to get the hell out. He'd seen the contempt. But he'd also seen the fear. A smile pulled at his mouth. Yeah, the old man had been real nervous. Fierro had him on the run. Now he could look forward to scaring the shit out of him. And then, when he had Sinclair just where he wanted him, well then Fierro would kill him. He was looking forward to pulling the trigger. He certainly hadn't heard anything to make him change his mind. But he'd like to see the old man beg. That would make everything worthwhile. He would achieve what he had set out to do all those years ago. And his chance had finally come. Leastways then, Fierro could die happy when his time came because he would have nothing left to live for once the old man was dead.

He shivered at the open window. The cold air had cooled his body, and its early morning needs, he noticed with a grin. It would keep till he got a chance to visit town. He padded softly back to bed and eased himself down under the covers. He could still see his mountain from the bed. His mountain? Where the hell did that come from? And what a damn stupid thought. His mountain! Funny though, the peak drew his eye, almost like it was an old friend.

He wondered again about what the hell Harvard was doing out West. It sounded like he'd been settled in Boston. Had the old man summoned him back? It seemed the most likely answer. But he couldn't believe that his brother would stay out West for long. He still found it hard to believe they could be related. They sure didn't look alike. Still, at least the man had been thoughtful when the girl had been embarrassed the previous night. Johnny bit his lip—he felt kind of bad about that. None of this was her fault. Wasn't old Harvard's fault either, but hell, anyone who dressed like that, well they were asking to be laughed at. He hadn't been able to stop himself poking fun at Harvard. The man probably had fancy clothes to sleep in. Why anyone needed clothes for sleeping was a mystery to him. They'd just get in the way of whatever else a man might feel like doing.

But what the hell should he do about the threat to the ranch? The names he'd heard mentioned in town were all fast guns, but he reckoned he was faster. He could take any of them individually, no problem, but even if he got the chance, did he want to? He knew what they'd do to the old man if they took him alive. Sinclair would suffer a very slow and painful death. And that would serve him right. It would be justice for the life his mother had been forced to lead, and for him too. But old Harvard, he might smell like a woman and dress odd, but that was no reason to kill a man. Those gunmen would really enjoy themselves with Harvard.

And then there was the girl, and the cook. Those men would take turns at 'em, over and over and then over again. All watching and laughing. And if the mood took 'em they might cut the women too. And finally, when the women were almost dead, they'd finish them off. Shit, shit, shit!

The old man was one thing, but the others didn't deserve that. No woman deserved that and not many men deserved it either, certainly not Harvard. Oh fuck it. He'd have to do something. But he'd be damned if he'd leave the old man to enjoy his ranch. Sinclair would have to die, when the time was right, but he'd keep for now. In the meantime, he could have fun riling him. Get him on the run, get him scared.

He could hear the hands moving about in the barns and corrals now, clattering buckets as they called out to each other. He supposed he ought to get up but it was good to lie in a decent bed for once, even if he was alone. Reluctantly he swung his legs over the side and bent and picked up his things from where he'd dumped them the night before. Pulling on his trousers he found he still needed to do his belt up a couple of extra notches. God, he really had gotten thin in that damn prison. What little food there was had been barely edible, made him gag trying to get it down. But the rats and lice had been the worst. Lice, rats, fleas, and cockroaches. To go from that to all this comfort amused him. Just for once he'd allow himself to enjoy the little bit of luxury. He pulled on his boots and then fastened his rig around his hips, tightening it and then pulling it up one more notch. Methodically he checked his gun before sliding it into the holster. Slipping a spare gun inside his jacket, he headed downstairs in search of breakfast.

He could smell bacon and followed his nose to the kitchen, where his father stood swallowing what looked like very strong black coffee. Harvard arrived just seconds later.

"Morning, everyone. I smell coffee." His brother sniffed the air like a dog after the scent of a bitch in heat.

His father gestured toward the pot. "Help yourself." His gaze rested on Johnny. "Did you sleep well, John? Have you got everything you need?"

"It's Johnny. Not John, Old Man." Johnny reached for the coffee pot and poured himself a cup. "And, yeah, I got everything I need."

His father sighed. "If you insist, Johnny it is. And while we're on the subject of names, mine isn't Old Man." He hesitated. "If you won't call me father, my name's Guthrie. That'll do."

Johnny shrugged; he'd call his father what he damn well pleased and the old man had better get used to it. "Whatever."

He swallowed a gulp of coffee. "What's the plan today? Are we going to look at this other piece of land? I guess you'd best show me around so I know what we're dealing with here."

Sinclair set his cup down with a clatter. "Aye. As soon as you've finished breakfast, we'll head out to Steen's old place. I'll see you outside. I'll give my segundo today's work schedule." He pulled on a jacket and strode outside.

Harvard nodded toward the tray of bacon. "Help yourself. It's every man for himself at breakfast." He frowned, gesturing toward a plate piled with tortillas. "I assume these are for your benefit. We don't normally have those for breakfast." He peered at the eggs. "I think these must be in your honor too. They look as though they have peppers in them."

"Makes them taste of something. Better than your boring gringo food." Johnny heaped his plate with bacon, eggs, and tortillas. Hell, it was worth sticking around for a while just for the food. He could maybe regain some of the weight he'd lost in the Mexican jail.

Harvard cautiously tasted a small portion of eggs and flinched, screwing his face up like he'd been poisoned. "Hmmm. I think I'll pass."

Johnny smiled coldly. "This ain't Boston. You need to get used to how things are done down here if you're reckoning on staying. This was part of Mexico. Some would say it still is, or should be. But this is how we like our food in these parts."

His brother grinned, seemingly unbothered by Johnny's coldness. "I guess I will, given time. But for now, we'd best not keep our esteemed father waiting. He's not the most patient of men."

Esteemed? What the hell did that mean? But no way would he let this fancy brother see that he didn't understand, so he nodded and forked in the rest of his breakfast. Then, grabbing his hat, he followed Harvard outside and across to the corral where his horse was already saddled, and dozing in the sun. His

85

father stood talking to some fellow who Johnny assumed was the segundo. The man had the look of someone who lived his life outdoors, his face heavily lined by the sun and wind, and his shirt barely hiding his muscular frame.

Johnny nodded an acknowledgment at his father's brief introduction of Alonso, and swung himself up into his saddle. He watched Sinclair move stiffly to mount. Judging from the way he flinched as he threw his leg across the saddle, he was nowhere near recovered from the gunshot wound he'd received from one of Chavez's men. Still, the man had grit. Lots of men of his age would still be resting up after that sort of attack. It seemed that Guthrie Sinclair was no pushover.

They rode southeast for a few miles at an easy lope, away from the mountains toward flatter grazing. It was good land, lush and green and watered by streams still swollen with the snow melting in the mountains. Johnny reined in, pausing to look back over his shoulder to the towering mountains behind. Early morning mist still shrouded the higher slopes, but in places the tips peaked through, their outlines sharp against the sky. He sighed softly—it sure was pretty here. The sort of place a man could settle, and never want to leave. And it was where he should have belonged . . . He pushed the thought away. No point in brooding on what might have been; it was the here and now that mattered. Spurring his horse, he sped on to catch up with his brother and father. He muttered an oath—brother and father? An Eastern dandy, and a bastard he'd sworn to kill, that was more like it. And he was damned if he'd let any of this get to him.

The Andersson ranch was neat and tidy but nothing as grand as his father's place. Even so, he was impressed that his father was obviously ensuring it was kept in good order. He could understand the old man caring for the land, but maintaining the house took money. Most men would have left it to run down. Yeah, the old man was a puzzle, a man who'd throw out his wife and kid, but take care of a place like this because of a promise to a friend.

He dragged his attention back to his father, who was droning on about where the boundaries were, and where the water supply came from. Johnny chewed on his stampede string, listening with half an ear, while he tried to figure out if this place would be useful when Chavez attacked. But no, it was too far away from the hacienda. There was no point in even thinking on it. They'd need all the hands at Sinclair if they were to mount a successful defense, because that's where Chavez would attack. The man wouldn't take this until he'd done away with Sinclair. He huffed out a grunt. Damn but Sinclair was a stubborn man. They needed to hire guns. Any normal man would hire extra guns.

A cloud of dust in the south caught his attention. Squinting into the sun, he could make out horsemen approaching, maybe four or five of them. Pointing to the figures, he cut across his father's lecture. "We got company. And there're more of them than us."

Shielding his eyes from the sun, his father stared at the group. "Too far away for me to see who they are. Probably just ranch hands passing through."

Johnny shook his head. "Nope. They're coming here. And since they ain't coming from your place, they can't have no good reason for being here."

Harvard glanced at him. "Are you always this suspicious of everyone?"

Johnny narrowed his eyes. "When there's a range war brewing, yeah. You got a lot to learn about the West, Harvard. A man needs to watch his back out here, and take nothing on trust. Unless he wants to wind up dead."

Harvard's mouth twitched, like he was trying not to laugh.

"I'll bear that in mind, Johnny."

"You'd be well advised to." The old man swung around to look at them, a nerve pulsing in his temple. "Johnny's right, those men are heading this way. And they're trouble. That's Chavez riding in. I'd know that big grulla of his anywhere. Looks like he's got some hands with him." He paused, still peering hard at the men closing in on them. "But that man riding out front . . . He's no ranch hand."

Chapter Eight

"How can you tell?" Harvard leaned forward, shading his eyes to stare at the fellow riding in.

"The three at the back are hands, but not the fellow out front. Look at the way he wears his gun, and sits a horse. He's no ranch hand." Sinclair shot Johnny a sharp look. "Would you agree?"

Johnny nodded. He knew exactly what the fellow was, but he didn't recognize him.

"So what is he, if not a ranch hand?" Harvard was curious, but Johnny could see the sudden tension in the man's shoulders.

"A shootist." Johnny spoke softly, easing down from his horse, and flicking the loop that secured his gun in the holster when he rode. "Seems that Chavez's guns are starting to gather. But it seems crazy for him to ride in here with a small group. I wonder what he's up to."

His father shrugged. "Maybe just showing the shootist the lay of the land."

Johnny ducked his head, rubbing his chin. Somehow he couldn't believe that. "Or he knew we were coming." Johnny moved away from his horse and leaned against the corral fence like he hadn't a care in the world. But every muscle was tense and he could feel the familiar surge of excitement racing through him. He loved this feeling before a gunfight, when his blood was pounding and every nerve in his body seemed on fire. And he'd lay money that this meeting was going to end in a gunfight.

Hell, he'd make sure it did.

"There's no spy on my ranch," Sinclair snapped. "It's a co-incidence that they're here at the same time as us."

"I hope you're right." Harvard slid from his horse and tied it to the rail of the corral. "What should we do?"

Johnny raised an eyebrow but kept his mouth shut. He didn't believe in coincidences.

"See what they want, and keep a lid on things," muttered the old man.

"Cut off the head." Johnny smiled icily at his father. "We could end it here and now."

His father scowled. "I told you, that's not the way I operate."

The riders skidded to a halt in front of Sinclair, kicking up a cloud of dust and sand. The man riding the grulla motioned three of the men to hold back, and edged his horse forward, with the shootist keeping pace with him. Johnny narrowed his eyes, studying the gunman: a Mexican with a hard face and a thin moustache. Nope, he was certain he hadn't seen him before.

The man on the grulla tipped his hat. "Sinclair. Having a last look at the Andersson spread? Maybe you have reconsidered my offer? It was a fair price."

Sinclair snorted. "Fair price! I wouldn't take an offer like that even if the land were mine to sell. But it's not—I'm holding it in trust for Steen's daughter. I promised him that and I'm a man of my word. So, it's not for sale and if you've any sense, you'll take your hands and leave. Now."

Chavez shook his head as if sad. "I heard you'd been shot. My condolences." He turned toward the gunman. "Poor Mr. Sinclair was shot not long ago. It has obviously made him short-tempered and unreasonable. It was shocking—he was riding his own range." Chavez tutted. "It's a terrible thing when a man cannot ride on his own land in safety. When he never knows if a bullet will catch him in the back." He gestured toward Harvard.

"And I am guessing this is your son, returned home from the East, I heard. It would be a tragedy if some accident were to befall him too."

"I think we know who shot me, Chavez. And don't threaten my family." Sinclair's fists clenched tightly.

Chavez leaned back, as if shocked by the accusation. "Yo! Yo nunca haría amenazas." He gave an oily smile and made a slight bow toward Harvard. "My apologies, for speaking in Spanish, doubtless, being from the East, you do not understand our language."

Harvard stood a little straighter. "Don't be bothered on my account. I'm a fast learner, and I assure you I'm picking up all sorts of things. And I recognize a threat when I hear one."

Johnny bit back a smile. Harvard was no pushover for all his fancy manners. "You know, Chavez," he drawled, "I reckon you're so oily that if I heated you up I could cook my frijoles in what oozes out of you."

Chavez glanced at him, his fake smile fading as fast as frost in the sun. "So you're taking on extra hands, Sinclair. He doesn't seem your usual type. Worried you don't have enough hired men for what lies ahead? I can't imagine that many of them will want to spill their blood over water rights and mineral deposits. You'd be better off hiring guns, but instead you hire insolent boys who need a good whipping." He turned to the gunman. "You'd give him a good whipping, would you not, Mendoza?"

Johnny laughed at that, but his mind was whirling. Mendoza? Yeah, the name was familiar, but he wasn't a top gun.

"I'd give him more than a whipping." Mendoza spat on the ground and narrowed his eyes.

"He's not a hired hand." Sinclair snapped the words out. "This is my younger son, John."

Chavez's brow furrowed, then he threw back his head with a

laugh. "Oh, but I'd forgotten about that most unfortunate second marriage of yours." He turned to Mendoza. "Mr. Sinclair married a half-breed. Can you imagine? And an Apache half-breed at that. She was a beauty but we know what that race is like, do we not?"

Mendoza spat on the ground again. "Apache, huh? Well, they're the worst kind of Indians. They're only good for target practice. We should kill them all." He stared at Johnny. "You're not dressed right, boy. You should have a bow and arrows, not that gun on your hip. And shouldn't you be wearing war paint and feathers, like the rest of your breed?"

Johnny shrugged. "Oh, I keep those for special occasions. Ain't worth getting prettied up to take out scum like you, Mendoza."

The man hissed in a breath. "You need to be taught a lesson, breed. You need to learn some respect for your betters. And I tell you, a man who wears a gun on his hip must be prepared to use it." He paused, looking at Johnny hard. "Do I know you from somewhere?"

Johnny smiled coldly. "I don't think so. I'm pretty sure I'd remember meeting a talkin' jackass."

Mendoza stepped out of the saddle. "I'm going to make you wish you'd never been born, mestizo."

"What sort of man picks a fight because he doesn't like the color of another man's skin?" Harvard stepped forward, his fists clenched.

"Stay out of this, Harvard," Johnny hissed. "This ain't your fight. And it sure as hell ain't going to be a fistfight."

"Guy . . ." Sinclair had paled. "Johnny's right. Stay out of it. Chavez, call your man off. This isn't the time to start this."

Chavez shrugged. "You are free to leave with your other son, Sinclair. But this one," he looked at Johnny and curled his lip. "This one has annoyed Mendoza. Mendoza can have him—he's of no consequence. But if you stay, Sinclair, Mendoza can have you too, and that Eastern dandy son of yours. Ride out now while you can. But the half-breed stays."

"That's fine by me." Johnny smiled thinly.

Chavez raised a brow. "I hope you know how to use that gun, mestizo."

"I hope you do too, Chavez. When I finish with Mendoza I'll take you next. I'm in the mood for a killing." Johnny tipped his hat.

The Mexican laughed. "Well, you have nerve, I grant you that, lots of nerve. But you're a fool. You obviously have no idea who Mendoza is."

"I ain't never heard of him, so I'm guessing he's a nobody." Johnny lied, knowing it would rile Mendoza. He looked like the sort of man who would want people to know his name. Johnny bit back a smile. That was the difference between them—not many people would have heard of Mendoza, but everyone knew Fierro's name. And Mendoza had no idea who he was facing down.

"John!" His father sounded real tense. "Leave it alone. We don't need a gunfight . . ."

"Too late for that, Sinclair." Chavez smiled. "There's no backing down now. Your breed has asked for this. But as I said, you and your other son may still ride out. You should take the chance while you can."

"Chavez, you don't know who Johnny . . ."

"Shut up, Old Man! And stay out of this." Johnny rounded on his father. Shit. The last thing he needed was the old man announcing that he was Fierro. "I mean it. Stay out of it. This is my fight, not yours." He looked at Mendoza and curled his lip. "I'm ready any time, Mendoza. You started this. Let's finish it."

Mendoza adopted the usual shootist pose, standing tensely with his hand close to his gun. Johnny tilted his head to one side and ghosted a smile. "Is that meant to scare me?"

The gunman narrowed his eyes. "You think this amusing, mestizo? Believe me, I will have the last laugh."

"Oh, I doubt that," Johnny drawled. He stood casually, and then sighed softly like he was bored by the whole thing. But hell, he felt good—every nerve was tingling and his blood was pulsing faster. "So, you going to do something, Mendoza? Like go for that gun? Or we going to stand here passing the time of day?" That should trigger it.

And it did.

As Mendoza's hand moved, Johnny drew. Mendoza staggered as the bullet hit him dead center, and disbelief showed in his eyes before he dropped like a stone. Even as he fell, Johnny turned on Chavez. He glimpsed the man's shocked face, Chavez's mouth gaping open. Then the man made a move for his gun but Johnny was ready for that. He fired two rounds into the man before turning to face the three white-faced ranch hands who rushed to throw their hands up.

He was vaguely aware of the old man and Harvard staring at him wide-eyed, silent, and motionless. Ignoring them, he moved toward the trembling, sweating ranch hands.

"I ain't got no fight with you." He spoke softly. "You can ride on out of here, put the word out that there ain't anybody going to be paying those gunmen now, and then you get the hell out of the Cimarron. Or . . ." He paused, to make them sweat a little more. "Or you can make a stand of it here with me. Your choice."

They licked their lips, glancing at each other. One of them pushed his hat back and then shrugged. "We leave, Señor. We don't want trouble." He pointed to Chavez, who lay in a pool of blood. "He was our boss, not an amigo. We are hired hands, not gunmen."

Johnny nodded. "Go on then. Get out of here." He could

almost feel their relief as they fumbled with their reins, before spurring their horses and galloping away.

He could feel his father's eyes boring into him. Turning, Johnny smiled coldly. "Like I said before, cut off the head. That ends it." But even as he said the words he had the uneasy feeling that he'd missed something. Something Chavez had said . . . something that wasn't quite right . . . He pushed the thought away. This wasn't the time to think on that.

Harvard seemed to have forgotten how to speak and was looking at Johnny like he'd grown two heads. But the old man was building up to say plenty; that was pretty damn obvious. His face was vivid red, and that nerve was pulsing in his temple. Johnny folded his arms and glared. The thought flashed in his mind that maybe he could get the man so angry that he'd try and draw. "Yeah? You got something to say, Old Man, spit it out."

"What the hell did you think you were doing? I told you, this isn't the way I operate." His father spat the words out. "I was trying to avoid anyone being killed."

"Well, I got news for you," Johnny cut across him. "People were going to get killed and my way stopped it getting out of hand. Are you so dumb that you think Chavez was bringing in guns just for a show of strength? He was going to use them— against you. Against your men. Against your precious ward. And against old Harvard there." Johnny flung his hand out to point at his brother. "And I'll tell you something else. You didn't stand a chance in hell of beating them."

"I'm not so naïve that I didn't know he meant business," Sinclair snapped. "I wanted to play for time. I wanted to be better prepared . . ."

"We couldn't afford to wait. The longer you delayed, while you were busy preparing, the more guns he'd have had to turn on us." Damn, but his father was mule-headed.

"You manipulated this gunfight. Every word you said to them was calculated to bring it about. You were playing them like fiddles and you forced this situation."

Johnny laughed sourly. "Of course I forced it. That's what I do, didn't you know?" He saw Harvard's head jerk up as if puzzled by Johnny's words, but if he was going to say something he didn't get the chance because the old man wasn't done yelling.

"You must be crazy. It was insane." The old man shook his head, his brow furrowed. "Have you no regard for your own safety? Don't you care if you live or die? You were totally reckless. You were outnumbered . . ."

"I'm still here, still breathing, ain't I?" He pointed to the bodies. "And they're not. So now you can go back to your precious ranch and get on with your life. This way you didn't have to get blood on your hands. And neither did Harvard there. You can both sleep safe in your beds with easy minds. You ain't done any sinning—it's all on me."

"You could have been killed." His father sounded bewildered now.

Johnny grunted in irritation. "Of course I could have been fucking killed. It goes with the territory. Live by the gun, die by the gun, sooner or later. It wasn't my time today."

Harvard opened his mouth again, but the old man cut across him. "How can you be so . . . so blasé . . . so unbothered?"

Johnny shut his eyes briefly. The rush he always got from a gunfight had gone, leaving him empty and sick inside. Same as always. All that was left was two more dead men to come visiting at night. But he'd never admit that the killing got to him. Never. "It was a gunfight. That's all. It's just another couple of dead men. And it don't mean nothing. Nothing at all." He trudged to his horse and stepped into the saddle. "I'm going to town. I'll see you later." With a brief nod he turned his horse and took off at a gallop.

CHAPTER NINE

"Are you going to tell me what just happened here?" Guy had his hands on his hips and sounded furious. Looked furious too. His mouth was a tight hard line and his jaw jutted out.

Guthrie sighed heavily, turning away from watching John's fast retreating figure. "I'll explain everything later. First we need to get back to the ranch. We'll take their horses back with us and send a wagon for these two." He gestured toward the bodies with a grimace. Two men dead by his son's hand. It wouldn't be quite so bad if John had shown some emotion, but there had been nothing, not even a flicker. It was as if killing two men had no effect whatsoever on him. "Then, I'll send word to the governor. I'll explain what happened here."

Guy shot him a sour look. "All right, and then you can explain to me too. We have some serious talking to do, sir."

"Later," snapped Guthrie. "We deal with Chavez and Mendoza first."

Guy inclined his head before turning away to his horse and swinging up into the saddle.

They returned to the ranch in silence. Guy's head was down as if deep in thought and Guthrie's gut clenched at the thought of the conversation that lay ahead. He'd been a fool to hope that Fierro would just leave and that he wouldn't have to tell Guy what his younger brother had become. He should have known it would blow up.

As soon as they arrived at the ranch he gave Alonso orders to retrieve the bodies, and wrote a brief letter outlining the morning's events to send to the governor. Guy paced around the living room, his hands clasped behind his back, intermittently stopping to stare out of the window into the distance as if searching for something. His brother, maybe?

Finishing his letter, Guthrie laid down his pen and studied Guy, who swung now to face him. "Well?" His son's tone was insistent. There would be no more delaying this conversation.

Guthrie rose slowly and went to the liquor cabinet. "Drink?" He proffered the bottle. "You might need it."

Guy nodded slowly, his eyes curious. "I think so. It's been a long day already, and it's barely noon."

Guthrie poured them each a stiff measure before sinking back into the chair by his desk. "I don't know where to start. This isn't easy."

"He could have been killed, but you made no real effort to stop that fight. Why?" Guy's brow furrowed in bewilderment. "Thank God he was so fast. Fast! I couldn't believe anyone could draw a gun that fast. It was a blur. But you couldn't know that he'd be that fast . . ." Guy paused, staring hard at him, shaking his head slowly. "And yet you didn't look surprised . . ."

Guthrie swallowed a gulp of his whiskey. "When I was laid up, sick, you asked me why I didn't send for John when the Pinkerton Agency first traced him. The reason I didn't send for him . . ." He hesitated, chewing on his lip and feeling the color flushing his face. "The reason was because I discovered that he'd become a shootist."

"A shootist? Like Mendoza?" Guy sounded shocked. "Are you seriously telling me my brother is a paid killer? Shootists are paid killers, are they not?"

Guthrie nodded, unable to think of a damn thing to say.

"A killer? And you didn't think it would be prudent to tell

me of this before he turned up here?" Guy's voice was icy cold. "To warn me? So that I could be alert to the danger of inviting a killer into our home?"

"I didn't think he'd show," snapped Guthrie. "And I hoped maybe he didn't know who we were. I thought maybe he'd think I was just looking to hire extra guns because of the threat of a range war and then I could have paid him off if he did turn up, saying I'd changed my mind."

"Well, that plan backfired, didn't it?" Guy snapped back. "And for that much money it was fairly certain he'd show. Presumably a man like that will do anything for money. And how could you be sure if you turned him away that he wouldn't have gone and offered his services to Chavez?"

Guthrie shrugged, the color burning his face again. "Chavez, as you learned this morning, didn't like the Apache, much less anyone who is part Apache. I didn't think he'd hire your brother."

"And did you then have second thoughts when he showed up? Did you think he'd be of use to us? Is that why you didn't send him packing as soon as he arrived? You thought that maybe having a shootist for a son could be useful in the short term?" Guy spat the words out.

"A shootist!" Peggy stood in the doorway clutching a tray— their lunch, Guthrie supposed.

"Are you saying John is a gunfighter?" She set the tray down as Guthrie nodded. Turning to them, she frowned. "I've never heard of a gunfighter called Johnny Sinclair."

Guthrie sucked in a deep breath, and then licked his dry lips. "He doesn't use that name." His voice was barely a whisper.

Guy and Peggy exchanged puzzled glances. "So what name does he use?" Guy leaned forward, staring into Guthrie's face.

Guthrie shut his eyes briefly. "Fierro. Johnny Fierro." He knew the name would mean nothing to Guy, but Peggy gave a little cry and clapped her hand to her mouth, paling as she sank into a chair.

Guy narrowed his eyes. "I take it from Peggy's reaction that my brother's name is not unknown to her." His voice was heavy with sarcasm.

"He's famous," Peggy squeaked. "Everyone's heard of Johnny Fierro. He . . . I mean, really famous . . . The papers say he's fast and really dangerous . . ."

Guy shook his head. "This goes from bad to worse. So, my brother isn't just an ordinary gunfighter, he's a famous one! Oh, wonderful! That's just wonderful." If he'd sounded sarcastic before, it was ten times worse now. "No wonder you weren't worried about him in that gunfight this morning."

Peggy shot him a puzzled look. "A gunfight? What gunfight?"

Guthrie grunted with irritation and quickly outlined the events of the morning.

Guy sank down onto the couch. "Well, I suppose we should be celebrating. Our homegrown gunfighter has put an end to things before they developed into a range war. The question is, what does he want? Is he staying? Does he want money . . . or what?"

Guthrie shook his head. "I don't know what he wants. I offered him a share in the ranch . . ."

"I can't believe you did that in the light of what you knew about him." Guy ran his fingers through his hair. "I mean, it was crazy." He gave Guthrie a sharp look. "Why did you?"

Guthrie spun his chair and looked out of the window to the corral and the mountains beyond. He huffed in a breath and then sighed heavily. "I thought the prospect of hard work would frighten him off. Maybe it still will. I don't suppose he's ever done a day's work in his life. Although, if I'm honest, part of me longed to be wrong about him. But having seen him in action this morning . . ." he swallowed hard. He certainly wouldn't tell

Guy that he had a Pinkerton report on John sitting in his desk. Or that he'd taken it out to read three times, but had been unable to get beyond the first page because it sickened him.

"Having seen him in action this morning?" Guy prompted him.

"You saw him. I hoped he was different, that there was more to him. I hoped the newspaper reports and the gossip were wrong, but he was so cold and hard. Emotionless—it was as if killing those men meant nothing at all. What happened this morning, well, it was just two more dead men to mark down to Fierro's gun." Guthrie turned back to face Guy. "And look at his behavior last night. He was rude, ill-mannered, offensive. I saw nothing to make me feel that the talk about him is wrong."

Guy sat silent, apparently lost in thought, swirling his drink around in the glass. His brow furrowed and he looked across at Guthrie. "And yet, something else happened yesterday evening. Something you didn't know about. I mean, I agree his behavior really was appalling. And yet, later, I heard him speak to Peggy, promising her that she was safe, and he sounded totally different. Gentle almost . . . I mean, was that an act, or was that real?" Guy tailed off, glancing at Peggy, who nodded.

"It's true, Uncle Guthrie, he was totally different when you weren't around. He seemed kinder. His eyes were kind. I didn't like him at dinner. He scared me. But later . . ." She shrugged apologetically, "Later, he was nice, just like Guy says."

Guthrie eyed them doubtfully. He suspected that this was a case of them not wanting to believe the worst of Johnny Fierro. He wondered what they'd say if they knew the story of Fierro gutshooting a man in the street and standing smiling over the dying man. He took another swig of whiskey; that was an image he wanted to shut out, but it kept coming to mind. It invaded his dreams too—confused dreams of a small, dark-haired, happy child who would suddenly turn to face him holding a blood-red smoking gun.

He turned away from Guy to stare once more out of the window. The question was, what should he do now? Would John stay or leave? Could he withdraw the offer of a part of the ranch? Guy was right—he'd been crazy to offer that. Could he offer to pay him off? Hell, would John even come back? Had they maybe seen the last of him?

Had they seen the last of him?

He felt a pang of something deep inside. Regret maybe? Damn it, he should feel relieved if John didn't return. He was a very dangerous man.

But he was still his son.

But he was also a killer. That's what all the papers said. That's what the Pinkerton Agency said.

"Sir." Guy's voice broke into his thoughts. "Perhaps the best thing is to wait and see if he even returns before we start worrying about the future. It may be wishful thinking, but I have a feeling that maybe there's more to Johnny than meets the eye. I would like the opportunity to get to know him." Guy laughed ruefully. "Or I think I would."

Guthrie nodded reluctantly. There was nothing they could do at present, and there was work to be done. "Aye, we'll wait and see. But for now there are jobs to do. We've let everything slide because of the threat from Chavez. We need to move some of the cattle to better range, there's fences needing mending, the roof of the feed barn is leaking." He got slowly to his feet, hissing as the pain from his recent injury stabbed at him. "But, Guy, I think for now it's for the best that the fewer people who know that John is Fierro, the better. As you gathered, the name Fierro is notorious. And it'll certainly distract the men from their work, so let's keep it to ourselves for the time being. The men will find out soon enough if he sticks around."

Guy nodded and followed him outside to start getting the work parties organized.

Peggy was serving dinner when the chink of spurs announced Johnny's arrival. He stood in the doorway with that strange sardonic smile pulling at his mouth. Guthrie swallowed hard; the boy seemed to wear an air of menace like other men wore a jacket or hat. But he was damned if he'd allow the boy to intimidate him. "You're late," he snapped, hoping that maybe the tone would throw Johnny off balance.

It didn't. Johnny shrugged. "I don't dance to no man's tune. Never said I'd be back for dinner."

"No, you didn't." Guthrie glared at him. "It would have been courteous to tell us what your intentions were. I didn't know if you were even coming back."

Johnny smiled wolfishly. "And I'll just bet you were hoping I wouldn't. So, I'm real sorry to disappoint you, but all of this is way too good to pass up on." He gestured around the room. "And as for my long-lost family . . ."

"Come and sit down, Johnny." Peggy's voice was overly bright as she cut in with a forced smile.

Johnny inclined his head and slid into the seat next to her.

"And I don't like to see guns worn in the house." Guthrie glared at him. It was his house, his rules, and he was damned if he'd let Johnny run the show.

Johnny laid down his fork and narrowed his eyes. "Nobody tells me what to do, Old Man, and they sure as hell don't tell me where or when to wear my gun."

"You don't need to wear it inside. It's just family here, there is no threat."

Johnny snorted. "You don't know that. This was all too easy. I don't think this fight is over."

Guy set his cutlery down with a clatter, and Peggy jerked

around to look at Johnny. Guthrie opened his mouth to speak, but for a few seconds he couldn't think of a thing to say. He took a deep breath and tried again. "Chavez is dead. You killed him, if you recall?" He couldn't keep the sarcasm from his tone. "That's the end of it."

Johnny spooned in a mouthful of chili verde before looking around at them, his eyes remote. "Like I said, it was too easy. There was something wrong with what Chavez said, I just can't figure out what. I got a feeling in my gut that this ain't done yet."

Guy grinned. "I think you're overdramatizing things. Are you always this suspicious and cynical?"

Johnny sighed softly. "Yeah, I am. That's how I lived this long. This is tough country, Harvard. I learned my lessons the hard way, and when things are easy I reckon they're too good to be true—and they usually are. There's trouble coming. I can smell it."

Guthrie snorted. "Well, your gut and your nose are wrong on this occasion. And instead of dwelling on this, I think we need to turn our attention to the work that needs doing." He looked hard at Johnny. "Always assuming that you're staying."

Johnny smiled thinly. "For now, yeah. I ain't done here yet."

Guthrie shivered at the words, feeling an icy tingle down his spine. He cleared his throat. "Anyway, back to the matter of work. I thought it would be a good idea if you two boys go with Alonso and some of the hands this week and move the cattle from the pasture on the south boundary before it's overgrazed. There are about a thousand head down there and it'll give you both a chance to get the lay of the land."

Guy looked up from his meal. "You won't be coming?"

"No." He tried to ignore the look of relief that he saw flash briefly in Johnny's eyes. "Once you get to my age, sleeping out on the trail loses its appeal. I do it on the cattle drives and that's quite often enough, thank you. I enjoy the comfort of my own bed these days. This is just moving one of our herds to new pasture so you don't need me, anyway."

"You want us to check the lines at the same time?"

He tried not to register his surprise that Johnny had actually asked that question. "Yes, that might be a good idea. I mean, we've got men out riding the lines but with a spread this size it takes a while for them to cover the distance. It'll mean you staying away longer." That, he suspected, was probably why Johnny had suggested it.

"When do you want us to go?" asked Guy.

"I suggest you head off later tomorrow or early the next day, once you get everything organized. Alonso will show you both the ropes."

"Yeah, well, moving a herd and checking fence lines is real difficult." Johnny's voice was heavy with sarcasm.

Guthrie counted to ten and bit his tongue. When he spoke he made a supreme effort to sound friendly. "I meant he'll show you what's what."

"And where's where."

"Something like that, yes, Johnny." He concentrated on eating. He was not going to rise to the bait.

"We should have a party when you get back," said Peggy suddenly. "So you can both meet all our neighbors."

Guthrie shuddered inwardly and couldn't help but notice that Guy looked slightly alarmed too. Somehow he couldn't see Johnny making any effort to be polite to the neighboring ranchers. And God only knew what their neighbors would think when they discovered that Johnny Fierro was living at Sinclair. An image came to mind of Johnny gunning down Chavez . . .

"I don't like parties." Johnny's tone was sullen.

"Oh, you'll like ours, Johnny. We have nice neighbors and they'll all want to meet you and Guy," Peggy said happily.

"They might want to meet old Harvard, but I can promise you they won't want to meet me. And I sure as hell don't want to meet them." Johnny put down his spoon, looking mutinous.

"I think, Peggy, there is far too much work to do to be worrying about parties at present." He tried to sound relaxed. "Perhaps later in the year, when the boys have had a chance to settle in." He avoided meeting Johnny's eyes. "Anyway, as I said, the two of you can move the herd tomorrow. It'll be good experience for you both."

Johnny rolled his eyes and then turned his attention back to his meal, hunched over and shoveling in the food.

Guthrie pushed his plate away, his appetite gone. He wondered if he'd ever be able to enjoy a meal again. Was this what life would be like from now on? Worrying about what to say, avoiding certain subjects, having an image of his son killing someone hovering in his mind? No. The boy would never stay—hard work would drive him away. Wouldn't it?

With a grunt of irritation he rose to his feet. "I'll go and sort out the arrangements with Alonso for the drive. I'll see you later." With a curt nod he headed outside.

CHAPTER TEN

Guy watched his father leave the room and glanced at Johnny heaping more food onto his plate. His brother's face was impassive, as if the events of the day had made no impression on him. How could he be like that? Guy thought back to the war—even now, after all these years, he still relived that horror. Surely Johnny should feel something?

"You done staring at me, Harvard?" Johnny didn't look up from his food as he spoke. "You been staring ever since I came in this evening. Anyone would think I'd grown another head. Or done something to shock you."

Peggy rose and hurriedly picked up the empty dishes before speeding from the room. Johnny stared after her, smiling sardonically. "Seems like I'm driving everyone out, Harvard. Why do you think that is? Hell, a man could get to think that folk don't enjoy his company. It's almost like you're all scared of me." He laughed softly. "So I'll bet you had a nice cozy chat with our old man this afternoon and he told you all about me. Except, of course, he knows fuck all about me. Still, I'll bet he dressed it up real good for you."

Guy shrugged. "He said you're a gunfighter. Is that not true?"

Johnny leaned back in his chair and nodded slowly. "Yeah, Harvard, it's true. It's . . ." He paused briefly. "What was it you asked me last night? Something about how I make a living? Well, now you know. That's what I do."

"Killing people for money?" Guy couldn't disguise his

108

contempt, but he felt a pang of disappointment. He'd hoped to see some contrition, or even for Johnny to say that Guthrie had got it wrong. But Johnny just looked amused by Guy's discomfort.

"Yeah, for money. Sometimes I even do it for free." Johnny put his hands behind his head and leaned back into them, a picture of relaxation. "It ain't illegal if that's what you're thinking. Not if I play by the right rules."

"There are rules for gunfighters?" Guy was stunned.

Johnny nodded. "Yeah, there are rules. I even stick to them." Johnny paused, smiling coldly. "Most of the time."

"How very reassuring. I'll sleep better knowing that." Guy wondered briefly if the sarcasm was lost on his brother, but he suspected that Johnny was very astute. He sighed, but had to ask. "How many times have you, um, failed to stick to them?"

Johnny's face was impassive. "I don't think that's your business, Harvard. And believe me you don't want to piss me off by pushing it. But leastways you'll be able to go on this cattle drive knowing you got a real live gunfighter at your side. A real bad hombre. Now I bet that'll make you sleep well."

"Like a baby," Guy said softly, determined not to rise to the bait. He felt a change of subject might be prudent. "So what did you do in town today? You disappeared very quickly this morning."

"I went to the saloon—whoring. A man needs a little relaxation now and then." Johnny shrugged.

"Whoring?" Guy raised his eyebrows.

"Yeah, Harvard, whoring. You do know what whores are?"

Guy glared. "Yes, Johnny, I know what whores are. And this is your usual form of relaxation? This is when you let your guard down?"

Johnny shook his head, his eyes suddenly bleak. "I don't ever let my guard down, Harvard. I can't afford to. How do you think I've stayed alive this long? I don't trust nobody. Ever."

Guy shifted uncomfortably. It seemed that this hadn't been a good line of questioning. He changed tack again. "Have you ever been on a cattle drive?" He could have bitten his tongue off—why on earth would a gunfighter have been on a cattle drive? It was odd, though, because Johnny nodded.

"Yeah, I done some droving." Johnny raised an eyebrow. "And you didn't expect that, did you? A real bad hombre like me knowing about driving cattle, kind of surprising, ain't it?"

Guy inclined his head. "So you haven't always been a gunfighter then." It was a statement more than a question. He hoped his brother would confirm it.

Johnny laughed softly. "Oh I've always been a gunfighter, Harvard, but sometimes a man needs a . . ." Johnny scratched his chin thoughtfully. "A disguise? A cover? Some word like that anyway. Or sometimes, if work's thin on the ground, droving brings in a few dollars. But deep down? I'm a gunfighter, so you'd best get used to it. Like I said, it'll be a real comfort to a city boy like you knowing I'm right by you on this trip."

Guy pushed his chair back and got to his feet. "If you're trying to intimidate me, it won't work. I don't scare easily."

Johnny shrugged. "Now why would you think I'm trying to scare you, Harvard? Don't you trust me?"

"Trust you?" Guy raised an eyebrow. "Not one iota. But you don't intimidate me either, so you might as well get used to it, brother. I'm turning in. I'll see you in the morning." He trudged out of the room, ignoring his brother's soft laugh even as he wondered how they'd survive a cattle drive without one murdering the other.

Perhaps it was a reaction to the day's events, but Guy slept surprisingly well, waking refreshed to prepare for the drive. The main corral was a hive of activity with hands loading packhorses with supplies. Alonso was at pains to explain to him that this wasn't a proper cattle drive, which involved huge amounts of logistical planning including a chuckwagon and numerous spare horses for each hand, but merely several days' work moving a large herd to the ranch's farthest pastures. He was curious to note that the hands gave Johnny a wide berth, and Alonso made no effort to volunteer any information to him. Had Guthrie told them who Johnny was? He suspected not. If he was certain of one thing it was that his father was deeply ashamed of having a gunfighter for a son, and wouldn't be advertising the fact to anyone.

Guthrie appeared in his element giving orders and directing the preparations for the drive. He was certainly more relaxed now that the threat of the range war had gone. Presumably he didn't give any credence to Johnny's assertion that the trouble wasn't over. The worry lines that had filled his face over the past few days didn't look as deep, although Guy noticed that every time his father's gaze rested on Johnny, his face hardened again. Maybe that was understandable; what man would welcome a gunfighter as a son?

The men were mounting up when Guthrie called Guy and Johnny over for a private word. "I think you're all set. This drive will be a good introduction for you to the business of ranching. Just let the men do their work and try not to get in their way. Watch and learn." He gave Johnny a long hard look. "And if you could stay out of trouble, I'd appreciate it. Do as Alonso tells you and don't get into any fights."

"Fistfights?" Johnny raised a questioning eyebrow. "Or were you thinking more of gunfights, Old Man?"

Guthrie glared. "Any fights. Just do as you're told, right."

Johnny looked at him impassively. "I ain't too good at taking orders, Old Man." He tipped his hat and spurred his horse to follow the crew.

Guy forced a reassuring smile at his father. "Don't worry. I'll keep him in line."

Guthrie snorted derisively. "I doubt there's a man alive who could keep him in line. You watch out for yourself and I'll see you in a few days." He raised his hand in farewell and turned back to the hacienda.

The men were already some distance ahead with the herd by the time Guy caught up. Johnny was riding slightly apart from the rest of them or they were avoiding Johnny. Guy wasn't sure which. But he cantered over and settled his horse alongside Johnny's buckskin.

Johnny, however, ignored him, seemingly intent on scanning the territory ahead. Guy thought briefly about what Johnny had said about never letting his guard down. He certainly seemed on his guard now, and silent. Was he brooding about the gunfight? Would Johnny talk about it? Or would they ride for hours in silence if he didn't initiate a conversation himself? Figuring the latter, he gave in. "Is there something on your mind? You're very quiet."

Johnny ignored the question and continued to stare ahead.

Guy pushed his hat back in exasperation. "I asked if there was something on your mind."

"I heard you the first time." Johnny still didn't as much as glance at him.

"Do you have a problem with me?" Guy snapped the words out. God, Johnny was irritating. Even more irritating than when he was a toddler. That had been bad enough and it seemed he'd gotten worse with age. If they'd grown up together he was prepared to bet he'd have throttled him at some stage.

Johnny shook his head. "Nope. If I had a problem with you, Harvard, you wouldn't still be breathing."

Guy hissed in a breath. "I told you that you don't intimidate me. You're forgetting, I remember you in diapers and that memory doesn't engender a fearsome image. So, you might as well stop trying."

Johnny shrugged. "I don't need to try. Trust me, if I wanted to intimidate you, I could. And I bet you're dying to ask about the gunfight. It's written all over your face. Must have been a shock seeing men killed like that."

Guy clenched his jaw. "Oddly enough, Johnny, having been in a war, I've seen killing before."

"But you ain't seen a gunfight. A gunfight's personal; war is more . . ." He pushed his hat back and swatted a fly away. "More impersonal!" There was a note of triumph in his voice, as if pleased to have come up with the right word. "Hell, you got the law on your side in a war. But a gunfight, well, that's different. It's close and it's bloody. Real bloody. And law don't have much to do with it."

"War's bloody too," snapped Guy, irritated that Johnny still hadn't so much as glanced at him.

"Ain't saying war's not bloody. Just saying gunfighting's different and now you've seen me in action."

Guy pushed his hat forward now, sighing with exasperation. "Yes, I saw the great Johnny Fierro in action. Peggy tells me that everyone knows your name. But at the time of the fight, when I didn't know about your, um, what shall we call it, your unusual choice of profession? At the time my overriding feeling was fear. I couldn't imagine how you could take on two men." Guy shook his head in wonder. "I thought I was going to see you gunned down. And yet you didn't look concerned. Are you not scared of being shot?"

Johnny gave a humorless laugh. "No, I ain't scared. It's what gives me my edge. And taking on those two? Take more than those pieces of shit to outdraw me. I knew I could take Mendoza." Johnny shrugged.

"How could you know that?" Guy was curious.

113

"Like I said, he's a piece of shit. That's how."

Guy didn't feel that Johnny's laconic reply clarified the situation. Still, at least Johnny had actually spoken. It was better than silence. But how could he not fear death? All men feared death . . .

"Anyway," Johnny shot him a chilling smile, "what you saw, well, that was nothing. That was me on my best behavior, being as how I knew you were watching." And with that, Johnny spurred the horse into a lope, leaving Guy covered in dust.

Guy ground his teeth in frustration. Why the hell was Johnny so difficult? He'd hoped that a few days like this, away from the ranch, and more importantly away from Guthrie, would make Johnny a little more forthcoming. When they were young, Johnny had followed him everywhere, always tagging along and trying to keep up despite Guy's best efforts at times to leave him behind. Now all he wanted was to get to know this enigmatic man, but it didn't feel like they were getting off to the best of starts.

The men made camp under the shelter of a ridge near a meandering river. Alonso got them building a fire and soon the smell of cooking mingled with the scent of wood smoke. Guy was fascinated to see how wary the men were of Johnny. No one sought out his company or ventured any remarks toward him. Had one of the men recognized him? He thought back to Peggy's reaction to the name Fierro. He found it bizarre that a gunfighter's reputation could engender so much awe in people. Or fear. And he noticed that the men's attitude certainly suggested they were afraid of Johnny and reluctant to relax in his presence.

But Johnny appeared oblivious to the atmosphere. Or just so used to receiving that sort of reception that he accepted it as natural. He ate apart from them all. While Guy sat and chatted with Alonso about the plan for the following day, Johnny ignored everyone, remote and unapproachable.

It was only later, when they were settling down for the night that Guy realized that Johnny had disappeared along with his horse.

"Alonso, have you seen Johnny?"

The segundo pointed to the west, where the last glow of day could still be seen on the horizon. "He rode in that direction."

What the hell was Johnny up to now? Cursing Johnny, Guy wearily saddled his horse again, and headed off after his brother.

He could smell the fire before he saw the faint flicker of flames, about a mile from the main camp. Johnny sat huddled by the small fire, while his horse grazed nearby.

"What do you want now, Harvard?" Johnny sounded more irritated than angry.

Guy glared. "I wondered where the hell you'd gone."

"Just prefer my own company. And I can hear things better away from that crowd."

"What things?" Guy furrowed his brow, puzzled.

Johnny lifted a small mug from the heat of the fire with a gloved hand and sipped at what Guy presumed was coffee. "Like someone creeping up on a camp, Harvard! You born yesterday or something?"

"You really don't ever let your guard down, do you?" Guy smiled, amused by his brother's caution.

Johnny looked at him impassively. "You get all sorts of outlaws in this territory, and I don't want my throat slit in the night. How do you think I lived this long? I've spent more nights sleeping under the stars than I ever have in a nice safe bed."

Was there a reproach in his words? Resentment? Oddly, he thought not, more that Johnny was just stating a fact. "You must have slept in a bed as a child; you can't have been sleeping under the stars then." Guy slid off his horse and squatted by the fire. "Mind if I join you?"

Johnny looked at him without expression. "Seems like I don't have much choice. Unless, of course, I shoot you."

Guy grinned. "Somehow I don't see you doing that. Didn't you say there were rules?"

"You shouldn't underestimate me, Harvard."

"Oh, I don't, Johnny. But I don't think you'd shoot me either. Or at least, not just for coming to your camp."

"Don't bet on it," muttered Johnny, taking another sip of his coffee. His face was lit by the flickering flames of the fire, and he studied Guy silently for a few seconds, holding his gaze before sighing as if exasperated. "Make yourself some coffee, Harvard. You look fucking frozen. But you'll have to make it in the mug; I don't run to coffee pots."

Guy grinned. "It is rather chilly this evening. Thanks." He snagged his cup from his saddlebags and proceeded to make himself some coffee while Johnny watched impassively. He raised his mug to Johnny. "Cheers."

Johnny didn't respond, he just sipped his coffee and carried on staring at Guy. His silence was unnerving. Guy sighed heavily. "So, what do you make of the ranch? Are you staying?"

Johnny looked away, into the fire, and didn't respond for a few seconds. Finally glancing at Guy, he shrugged again. "It's big."

"It's big? That's all you can say?" Guy settled himself closer to the fire, glad of the warmth. "Why've you never visited before? You apparently knew you were a Sinclair."

"Do you think that's any of your business?" Johnny's tone was icy.

Guy shrugged. "We're brothers, so yes, I think it's my business."

"Just because we got the same father, that don't mean a thing, Harvard. You ain't nothing to me. And since he threw me and my mother out, why would I think I'd be welcome?"

Guy jerked forward, spilling his coffee and scalding his hand. "What the hell do you mean, threw you out? You weren't thrown out." He sucked his hand trying to take the heat out of it.

Johnny laughed but there was no mirth in his laughter. "Yeah, we were. The old man didn't want no breed. He only married my mother because he got her in the family way. And I guess once I came along, he realized that having a half-breed wife and brat didn't sit too well with his fancy friends. So he threw us out."

Guy shook his head. "You've got it all wrong. Who on earth told you that nonsense? Surely not your mother?"

Johnny's eyes narrowed. "My mother wouldn't lie to me, Harvard. And seeing as you were how old at the time? What five, maybe six years old? I don't suppose our old man told you much about it. He wasn't going to tell you that he kicked us out. But that's what happened."

"But he spent years searching for you . . . I remember how upset he was. How upset I was."

Johnny grunted dismissively. "Searching? He was probably off whoring. He threw us out. My mother said so." There was an air of finality in Johnny's words. "Anyways," Johnny's tone was aggressive. "He didn't keep you around either. He sent you off to Boston. Why'd he do that?"

Guy flushed and paused. "Indian attacks." Johnny was part Indian; would he resent the comment? There was no knowing.

"Yeah, well, them Indians are real savage. Can't trust any of them." Johnny's tone was heavy with irony. "And so he didn't want his precious gringo kid hurt so he sent you to Boston." Johnny paused. "Why Boston?"

"My mother's family lived there. I was sent to live with my aunt and her husband. They had no children and raised me as if I was their own child. But I missed you." Guy spoke softly and Johnny jerked his head up at the words. "I promised myself I'd find you one day, but when I was about ten, my uncle told me you were dead. I have no idea why. I suspect they assumed you were dead and possibly found my constant assertions that I would find you very wearing." Guy bowed his head. "It was quite a shock to discover you were alive after all."

"And I guess I ain't exactly what you were hoping for." Johnny sounded amused.

Guy smiled ruefully. "Well, I never imagined a gunfighter for a brother, that's true."

Johnny nodded. "So tell me about Boston. What sort of house did you live in?"

Guy grinned. "You mean while you were living under the stars? Just a house, a big red brick house on Louisburg Square with a grand staircase, me, my aunt and uncle, and the servants."

"Servants? So they were rich then?"

Guy inclined his head. "Oh yes, they were rich. We had a housekeeper, butler, parlor maids, cook, groom . . ."

"Shit! Where did they all live? In the stables?"

Guy was about to laugh at the preposterous notion that the servants lived outside, when he realized that the question was serious. "No, Johnny. They had their own rooms in the house."

"Rooms? You mean more than one?" Johnny leaned forward.

"Well, the housekeeper had her own parlor and bedroom. So did the butler. The cook certainly had her own bedroom, but I think perhaps the parlor maids shared a room."

"Your servants had their own rooms?" Johnny sounded amazed. "Dios! I never had a room of my own. We had just one room when I was growing up."

Guy looked at him. "You mean you shared a bedroom with your mother?"

"No. I mean we had one room. Cooked in it, slept in it." Johnny grinned. "When I wasn't sleeping under the stars." His smile faded. "Or under the porch." He shook himself, as if to bring himself back to the present, and stirred the fire with his booted foot.

The glow in the west had disappeared and the sky turned deep violet as the first stars appeared. "So what did you do for fun, Harvard, growing up out East?"

Guy smiled. "I liked the winters. I loved skating on the lakes, sledding, tramping across Boston Common. And waking in the morning to seeing the patterns Jack Frost made on the windows."

"Who's Jack Frost?"

Guy laughed. "He's not a person. But frost makes wonderful pictures and people tell children that Jack Frost visited in the night."

Johnny pulled his jacket tighter around him. "Sounds cold. I hate the cold. What's sledding?"

"A sled is a sort of seat on runners that carries you really fast down snowy hills. It's great fun, even when you fall off. And in the summers we'd go to our home at Duxbury on the coast. I learned to sail . . ."

"Two houses? Shit! What for?" Johnny shook his head.

Guy paused, embarrassed now. "Sorry, I wasn't boasting . . ."

"I didn't think you were." Johnny shrugged. "I just can't think why anyone needs two houses."

Guy nodded. "They don't, but the families we mixed with, well, everyone had a summer house. What did you do for fun, when you were growing up in Mexico?"

"Fun?" Johnny sounded puzzled. "I dunno that there was much fun. More worried about getting enough to eat."

Guy eased himself round, so he could see Johnny's face better by the light of the fire. "There must have been some fun? What about birthdays? How did you celebrate those?"

But his brother's face was blank. "Dunno when my birthday is. Don't remember ever celebrating it."

It felt like a punch in the gut. He remembered celebrating Johnny's first two birthdays. They'd had a special cake and games and Johnny had eaten too much cake and been violently sick . . . It hit him how totally alien Johnny's life was to his own experiences. He swallowed hard. "There must be something good. Come on, what was the best day, ever?"

Johnny furrowed his brow, as if desperately trying to recall something. Then he grinned. "I remember that. I guess I was maybe nine or ten. Some of the village kids had cornered me, got me on the ground. Normally I could outrun them, but this one time my back had been whipped up real bad . . ."

Guy interrupted. "Johnny, this is meant to be a happy story?" And what on earth did he mean about a whipped back? He must have meant kicked by the other children; that was it.

Johnny frowned. "It is. I'm getting there. Anyway, I'm on the ground and I hear some fellow riding in and asking about a bordello. But then he called to these kids and got off his horse and came over. He pushed 'em away and looked at my back. The next thing I know he picked me up, sat me on his horse, and asked where there was a doctor. We rode down the street and I could see by the way he wore his gun he was some kind of gunfighter. Up there on his horse, I felt like I was king of the world.

"He told the doc to see to my back. But the doc said I was only the half-breed whore's bastard so wasn't worth the trouble." Guy hissed in a breath but bit back the question on his lips. He didn't want to interrupt Johnny. He'd never known him to talk so much. "And shit . . ." Johnny paused, shaking his head, "This gunfighter, he drew his gun and ordered him to take care of me. The doc put stuff on it. Felt really good." Johnny smiled to himself at the memory. Guy wondered if Johnny had even forgotten his presence. He seemed to be talking to himself now. "Then the gunman asked the doc how much he owed. But I reckon the doc was shit scared by this time because he said the man didn't owe him nothing, but the gunman said he always paid his debts. And when he paid the doc he took a big stack of notes out and said he was going to pay him to treat my back again if I needed it. Even told the doc he'd be back to check up on him. And if he found the doc hadn't looked after me, he'd kill the doc's family. Hell, but that made me feel important.

"He took me for a meal, asked what I wanted to do with my life. I told him I was going to be the greatest pistolero anyone had ever seen—it's what I'd always dreamed of. And how when I was famous I'd hunt down my gringo father . . ." Johnny kicked the fire again with his boot and stared into the glowing embers.

He had to ask, couldn't stop himself. "The whore? Not your mother . . ." Guy paused, uncertain of how to continue. It didn't fit with his memory of Gabriela. Even as a young child he'd thought she must be the most beautiful woman in the world even if she was given to stormy outbursts. She'd been very fond of throwing things, he recalled. But a whore?

Johnny eyes hardened. "Yeah, Harvard, she was a whore. But if you ever tell the old man, I'll kill you."

Guy felt a sudden chill, realizing Johnny meant what he said. "I wouldn't tell him, but . . ."

"No point in telling a man his wife was a whore. I mean, I don't mind whores, but somehow, I don't think the old man would see it in the same way and I ain't having him thinking bad of her."

Johnny clutched his coffee cup tight as if to get every last scrap of warmth from it. "I said I'd heard the pistolero asking for the bordello. Told him my mother was a whore and all the men liked her. Seeing as how he'd seen to my back, she'd probably do him for free. Told him she was a real good fuck." Johnny

121

shook his head slowly, lost it seemed, in his memories. "But he looked kinda sad, said he'd got to be moving on. He sat me on his horse again and rode with me to near where I lived. Gave me a silver dollar. Hell, I'd never even seen one before. He said to hide it from my mother. Then he rode off."

Guy smiled at the thought of a skinny little boy gazing wide-eyed at his first ever silver dollar. "What did you spend it on?"

Johnny laughed. "Oh, my mother found it. Hit me round the head, wanted to know what I'd had to do to earn it and kicked me down the steps. I expect it went for tequila."

Guy shivered. The night air was chill but it was more than that. This was Johnny's happy story? The best day of his child-hood? How the hell had he ever survived? He looked across at his brother. "But this was a good day, right?"

Johnny looked back, bewildered. "Shit, Harvard, don't you get it? That day, I was somebody." Johnny stood up and picked up his bedroll. "I'm turning in now, I'm beat."

"May I share your camp?"

Johnny looked at him levelly. "S'pose you'll have to now. You'll only get lost in the dark or something going back to the other one. Then I'd have to go and fucking look for you. So, sack in and just shut up, OK?"

Chapter Eleven

As always, the dreams woke him. There never was any sleeping through them. Instead, he woke sweating and fearful, thrashing out at the ghosts with their lifeless eyes. Why couldn't they leave him in peace? Just for one night. All he wanted really was one night when they didn't all come visiting. The moon cast a silvery light across the camp and he could make out the shape of Harvard sitting and watching him. Shit! He knew he shouldn't have let his brother stay in his camp. Should have sent him back to join the men. What the hell should he say? He wasn't going to tell anyone about the dreams. Wasn't no one's business.

"Are you all right? You were calling out in your sleep."

Johnny shrugged. "Bad dream, that's all." He laughed, tried to sound casual. "Ain't like me, normally I sleep real well. Go back to sleep, Harvard." For a second he thought his brother was going to say something but then seemed to think better of it and lay back down. Johnny huddled closer to the embers of the fire, but there was little warmth there. It would be good to be in a whore's bed. To feel the heat of her body and her legs wrapped around him. A woman could always provide some fleeting comfort. Blot things out for a while.

Didn't even know why he'd thought about that gunman the night before. Hadn't thought of him in a long while. And Mama sure hadn't believed that the man gave him the silver dollar for nothing . . . That had hurt. He'd been honest but she still gave him a beating. He'd told her that the man was just being kind.

Kind! That was something she couldn't understand. Why would anyone be kind to a breed, she'd demanded. People weren't kind, she'd said. Well, wasn't that the truth? There were few enough kind people around where he grew up.

But he couldn't figure why the hell he'd told Harvard that story. He never told anyone anything and yet he'd ended up spilling that story. It was crazy. It wasn't like having a brother meant anything. And yet . . . And yet there was something about the man. He shook his head, irritated with himself. So what if they were brothers? Didn't mean a thing. Did it? Hell, he should have just shot his old man like he'd intended to and ridden out. But a brother . . . He hadn't expected that. It had thrown him off his game. So he'd stayed and helped them. And now here he was, on a fucking cattle drive, sharing a camp with a so-called brother. And the old man was still breathing instead of cold in his grave.

He shivered. Damn but it was cold as the grave here. If only there was still some warmth in the fire. He lay back down, pulling his blanket tight round him. If only he could get some sleep without the dreams. And the latest gunfight made it worse. Two more men. Would it never end? And he felt so damn tired. Trouble was, he was afraid to sleep now, with Harvard there. Afraid Harvard would hear more of his nightmares. This was the last time he'd let anyone share his camp. He pulled his gun closer, hugging it to him. Felt better like that. He rested his face against the barrel. So tired. Just wanted to sleep. A deep sleep with no fucking ghosts.

He woke again at first light, striking out at one of Mama's men who was . . . Shit. Sitting up, sweating and shaking, he clutched his gun. Breathing deeply, he tried to slow his heart, which felt like it was jumping out of his chest. He hated that dream, it was worse than all the ghosts together. Why did he have to remember these things? If only he could forget it all.

Looking up he saw his brother, leaning up on one elbow, a look of concern on his face. Johnny shut his eyes briefly before glaring at the other man. "Don't say it, Harvard. Just mind your own fucking business."

He felt a pang of guilt as Harvard flinched slightly like he'd been hit.

Johnny was turning away as the other man spoke. "I have really bad dreams, too."

Johnny gave a short laugh. "What do you have bad dreams about, Harvard? Getting lost in that big house? Or not knowing what to choose for dinner off some fucking menu?" Even as he said it, he regretted it. He knew it was a cheap jibe, but he needed to push him away. He sure as hell wasn't going to talk about his dream.

His brother looked at him steadily. "About the war."

Johnny sighed. Yeah, it had been a cheap shot. Why did he do these things? And why did Harvard keep coming back for more? "Sorry," he muttered, unable to look his brother in the eyes.

It's OK." Guy gave a short laugh. "I sort of expect it from you, now."

Johnny shut his eyes briefly, the sharp blades of shame stabbing at him. Tried to think of some way to explain. Trouble was he didn't know why he was like this, so how could he explain? Flushing, he looked his brother in the eyes, but he couldn't read the expression there. And he couldn't think of a single damn thing to say. Hell, whatever he said would only make it worse. Maybe, if he'd been to some fancy school, he'd be better with words. "I . . . I just don't want to talk about some stuff, OK?"

Guy nodded his head slowly. "OK. But I just wanted you to know that there's no need to feel embarrassed about your bad dreams. I have awful dreams about things we did in the war. Things I'd rather forget." He gave a humorless laugh. "And then there are the dreams about the battles. The cries of men in pain, they seem to stalk my dreams."

Johnny chewed on his lip, trying to think of the right thing to say. To get it right, just once. Then he grinned. "Seems we got something in common then, even if it's just bad dreams."

And to his relief Harvard grinned back. "It would seem so." He shivered. "Shall we light a fire, make some coffee?"

"No. Be easier to join the others. They'll have kept the fire going all night." Johnny hefted his saddle across the buckskin as he watched Guy get ready to mount up. They couldn't be more different and it was real strange to think they were brothers. Well, half-brothers. He knew the old man was impressed by Guy; he could see the pride in the way the man looked at his older son. His father sure as hell wouldn't ever look at Fierro like that. "I'm sorry. Just always seem to bite your head off." He shrugged. "Dunno why I do it, can't seem to help myself. Ain't used to talking much." He tightened the cinch and secured his bedroll behind the saddle.

Harvard grinned. "I give you due warning—you'll have my company again tonight. I think you need practice at talking so I want another story."

Johnny bit back a sharp retort. He should tell him straight out he didn't want him in his camp, but he couldn't bring himself to say it. Hell, the fellow seemed to mean well enough. He couldn't help being an Eastern dandy. And Harvard kept right on grinning at him. In spite of himself, Johnny found himself grinning back as he sprang into the saddle. "Another one? You must sleep real bad if you need my bedtime stories. Now, you ready to get moving?" And Johnny spurred his horse into a gallop, kicking dust all over Guy as he raced past him.

It was odd, he thought later, but he didn't really mind the thought of Guy sharing his camp. He'd never have expected it from his first impressions of the man. Then he'd thought he was merely a stuck-up fancy dandy. Now he suspected there was more to the man than that, and he wanted to get to know him better. But God only knew what his brother would think if he knew that Fierro had only come to the ranch to kill their father. That plan had gone to hell. But it was odd Guy being so convinced that their father had been searching for him. So sure they hadn't been thrown out . . . But hell, why would Harvard know about it? He'd only been a kid himself when it happened. And Mama wouldn't have lied. Would she?

He reined in and sat watching the men driving the cattle on to the next good graze, keeping them from spreading out. He had a pricking sensation at the back of his neck, as if from some unseen danger. Screwing his eyes up against the dazzling light he peered at the hills behind them but could see nothing out of the ordinary. He shook his head. Maybe he was imagining things.

Harvard was trying to persuade a cow and her calf to join the main herd. Cows might be dumb but it seemed this one was a hell of a lot smarter than Harvard as it kicked up her heels and trotted off in the other direction. Johnny grinned. This Eastern dandy still needed to learn which side of the cow to ride on to push it the way he wanted it to go. So much for fancy school-ing. With one last glance at the hills, he took off at a gallop and delighted in pushing the cow and calf back into the herd while his brother watched. Johnny turned his horse and loped across to join him. "You gotta lot to learn, Harvard. You're riding too close to them when you're driving them on. Give them some space; you don't want to spook them."

Harvard inclined his head. "Thanks. The men are all very respectful but they aren't giving me any advice at all."

Johnny shrugged. "You're the patron's son. They probably don't like to."

"You're the patron's son too, but they all seem to be avoiding you. Why? Do you think they know who you are?"

Johnny pushed his hat back and tried to ease the crick in his neck while he thought about that. He shook his head slowly. "I don't think so. I mean one of them might have recognized me, or think I look familiar, but I reckon it's the way I wear my gun. They all know what that means, even if they don't know my face."

"I noticed that you wear it very low. Is that significant?"

Johnny grinned. "You really are a greenhorn. Yeah, it sends a message. You only wear a gun like this if you know what you're doing and you're ready to use it."

"Which you are?" Harvard's tone was cool.

Johnny tensed and narrowed his eyes, speaking softly. "Yeah, Harvard, I am. I told you before, don't underestimate me. I'm dangerous, and you'd do well to remember that."

Mierda, it was dusty. The dust in his throat felt like it was choking him, and the dust in his eyes stung like hell. And he couldn't remember having worked so hard in his life. What a way to earn a living. So what was Harvard doing out here when he could be living it up in Boston? It wasn't like he'd lived life on the edge of the law and was trying to escape. Or salvage what was left of his soul. So why was he here? Maybe the man would open up a bit, in return for another bedtime story. Johnny grinned. He'd already chosen the story for that evening, one he thought Harvard might actually like—and there were few enough of those. And because he felt guilty about his cheap jibe, he'd tried to think of a story the man would enjoy. He sighed. He really was getting soft.

By the time the hands made camp for the evening he felt like he was going to snap in two. There had to be easier ways of making a living than gunfighting. But punching cattle sure wasn't one of them.

He sat apart from the men when they ate. He knew he made them uncomfortable but that was their problem. He certainly had no intention of buddying up. The only thing a man could rely on was his gun. And while he figured his brother was probably an honest man, he sure as hell wouldn't be relying on any blond gringo either. Because his instincts told him there was trouble ahead on this trip, although for the life of him he didn't know why he felt that.

He stretched his aching back and went and saddled up again, to go and make his own camp. Amused, he saw that Harvard was quick off the mark this time and riding not far behind. Johnny rode for about a mile before choosing a quiet spot. They set about making a fire and then just as Guy settled down next to it stretching his legs out, Johnny took more branches and scattered them around their camp.

"What on earth are you doing now?" Guy leaned forward watching.

"You really are an innocent, ain't you, Harvard? This way, anyone approaches the camp at night, they tread on a twig, you hear them coming."

A smile spread across Guy's face. "I have to say, that's very clever. Unnecessary, but clever."

"Unnecessary? Better than getting your throat slit or a bullet in the head." Johnny shrugged. "A man can't be too careful. Now, what about that coffee?"

His brother handed him a mug of steaming and somewhat foul-smelling coffee. "What about my story? And make it a good one."

"You better make the most of it; it's the last one you're getting. And in return you'll have to give me a straight answer to a question, agreed?"

Harvard nodded. "Anything you say, partner. But it's got to be a good story. About something that mattered to you."

129

Johnny hesitated, before nodding his head slowly. "Yeah, you'll like this one. I guess it happened about two, maybe three years ago. I was sitting in a saloon in Nogales."

"That's down on the border, right?"

"Yeah, down around the border. Like I said, I was in the saloon. I'd had two gunfights in two days. I was . . ." He paused, trying to think of a way to describe how drained he'd felt, without giving too much away. "Fucking exhausted. I figured I'd get me something to eat and then go find me a couple of women, same as always. Anyway, I was in the corner . . ."

"On your own? Or with friends?"

Johnny stared at Guy. Was the man really dumb? "Friends? Harvard, ain't hardly any people I'd call a friend. Gunfighters like me don't trust too many people, y'know. Now, are you going to let me tell this story or not?"

Guy grinned. "Sorry. Pray, continue."

Johnny closed his eyes briefly. Pray continue? What a damn stupid expression that was. Could they really be related? He glared at him. "Like I said, I was in the corner, watching the room when this man walks in. I didn't know him, but I could see he was a gunhawk. He spotted me straight off but he walked to the bar and stood there, both hands on it. So he's sending me a message right, that he ain't looking for no trouble."

"But if you'd never seen him before, how did he know who you were?"

Johnny smiled slightly, kicking at a spark that flew from the fire too close to his leg. "Harvard, believe me, everyone knows who I am. He'd have heard that there'd been two gunfights. Hell, it was the talk of the town, and he'd have recognized me for what I was and who I was straight off. Any rate, he's at the bar and I dunno, I just got to thinking I knew him from some place, but I couldn't figure where. So I just sat watching him."

Johnny grinned. "Made him feel real uncomfortable, too. He

could feel me watching him. He glanced over, nodded at me, and then turned his back again, making sure he kept both hands on the bar."

Guy leaned forward, warming his hands by the fire. "What was he doing?"

"Sending me a message again. He didn't want trouble. Hell, he knew he was way out of his league and me watching him was scaring the shit outta him. He ordered a meal and sat there trying to eat. Then it came to me. I knew where I'd seen him before.

"So I walked over and stood right next to him." Johnny laughed softly, remembering the fear he'd seen in the man's eyes.

"I told the fellow behind the bar to put the man's meal on my bill. That surprised the barkeep. I wasn't known for being too friendly. And this gunhawk looked even more nervous. I think he was wondering if I paid for people's meals before I shot 'em. He looked at me an' said 'That's real generous of you, Fierro, but I'm wondering why you want to pay for my dinner.' So I told him I owed him, an' I always pay my debts.

"He looked puzzled and said maybe I was confusing him with someone else. And he looked at me, and just for a second hesitated, like he was wondering if there was something about me he remembered. But he shook his head and said how he was sorry, but he thought I was mistaken. Then he said 'Hell, Fierro, I sure wouldn't want you to find you'd paid for my dinner thinking I was someone else and then get mad and shoot me.' I told him I wasn't mistaken, and I picked up his meal and said I'd be real honored if he'd come and share my table, and I turned my back and walked back to my table with his plate in my hands."

Guy furrowed his brow again, looking real confused. "What's the significance of that?"

Johnny sighed in exasperation. "Well, if I turn my back on him an' I got something in my hands, I'm telling him I ain't gonna shoot him. Hell, I'm giving him a chance to shoot me in the back. Times you seem real dumb, Harvard. Any rate, he comes over and sits down. Still staring at me, trying to place me. But he shook his head and said, he was sorry but he was sure we'd never met before. Then he said, 'Hell, I sure wouldn't forget meeting Johnny Fierro.' I told him I didn't expect him to remember me. I said, last time he saw me I was being kicked around like a ball on the ground in a dusty street."

A smile spread across Guy's face. "You mean it was . . ."

Johnny cut across him. "Anyway, he stared at me real hard, trying to remember. So I reminded him he'd bought me dinner too. And then he said 'My God, the greatest pistolero anyone's ever seen! I've never forgotten the fire that burned in your eyes when you told me that.' Then he said how I'd achieved my ambition." Johnny grinned, remembering the stunned look on the man's face.

"I told him I owed him for taking care of me. And he wanted to know if the doctor had kept his promise to take care of me."

"And had he?" asked Guy.

Johnny nodded. "Yeah, he did. Mind you, if the doc was away for a day or two, I made sure to tell him when he came back that the man had ridden in to check on him, so it kind of encouraged him to keep doing the right thing by me."

Guy grinned. "Johnny, you are positively Machiavellian!"

Johnny frowned. "Maccky what?"

"Devious, scheming."

"Oh, yeah, I'm all of that. The gunhawk thought it was kinda funny, too. Wanted to know if I'd spent the silver dollar on something good. I told him my mother had taken it. He said he'd kind of expected that. But it was strange, he said he'd always remembered me but figured I'd be long dead." Johnny smiled, remembering the evening. "It was real good to find someone to talk to. We spent a couple of days in the town together. He thought it was great when everyone started stepping outta his way and being all respectful because he was with me."

Johnny bowed his head, wondering what his brother would say if he knew about the promise the gunhawk had extracted from him. Because when Johnny had said how he was going to hunt down his old man and kill him, the gunhawk had made him promise to hear the man out first. The same promise Johnny had already made to someone else—to the only man he'd ever really trusted. Two sides to every story, he'd said. Well, Johnny hadn't killed the old man yet, but he couldn't imagine what the old man's version would be of what happened all those years ago. It didn't make sense for his mother to have left a life of luxury for no reason. Sinclair had to have thrown them out. Didn't he?

Guy's voice brought him back to the present with a start. "This man sounds like a decent, good type. Why did he become a gunfighter?"

Johnny flicked a spark from his jacket. "Kinda sad, really. He was a family man, but some comancheros came, tied him up and raped his wife, and then killed her and the kids. Left him next to their bodies. Took him over a day to get free. He was hunting for them comancheros, that's why he became a gunhawk." Johnny sighed softly. "And I tell you something else, Harvard, if he came now and asked for my help, I'd kill them for him."

Johnny threw another branch on the fire and the flames licked up, making shadows dance against the slender trunks of the aspens. "Shit, Harvard, I killed a lot of men, but some of them fucking deserved it. So, I guess I'm damned, 'cause I sure as hell ain't repentant over all of them." He stared at the flickering flames; that's what hell would be like. One day, Johnny Fierro would pay the price. He shook himself back to the present. "I'm beat, Harvard. I'm turning in. My question will keep."

"Johnny, what happened to the man? Did you ever see him again?"

Johnny looked across at his brother's face, lit on one side by the glow of the fire. "No. But I wish I had. Hell, he's probably dead by now. But I'd like to have seen him." He shrugged and then shook out his bedroll and huddled down inside it. He needed some sleep. Maybe tonight.

"Goodnight, Johnny." Harvard's voice was soft. "And thanks. I did like the story. I'm glad you had the chance to thank the man at least. He sounds like a good man."

"G'night, Harvard, and try not to snore."

CHAPTER TWELVE

Guy felt like he'd been through a mangle. Every muscle of his body was crying out for a long soak in a hot tub, and Johnny had woken him frequently in the night, muttering incoherently or calling out. And while he felt rough, Johnny looked a hell of a lot worse. Guy was sure it wasn't just the disturbed nights taking their toll. But when he'd asked Johnny what was bothering him, he'd shrugged and said he wasn't sure; he just knew there was trouble ahead.

Reluctantly, Guy hauled himself back into the saddle for another hard day's work. No wonder Guthrie hadn't wanted to come. Sleeping on the trail was rough even for young men, although Johnny seemed less bothered by the hardness of the ground than most. Presumably he was more used to it. From what he'd said, he'd spent a lot of time "sleeping under the stars."

Although Guy felt inclined to be dismissive of Johnny's unease about trouble ahead, a part of him had to admit that presumably it was his brother's sixth sense that had kept him alive. He was surprised that Johnny had opened up as much as he had. But he also realized that if Guthrie had been there, Johnny's lips would have been sealed tight. Perhaps if Guthrie knew more about the circumstances of Johnny's childhood, he would be more sympathetic. Not that he would be betraying Johnny's trust and telling their father—his brother would probably shoot him for that. He smiled ruefully. He suspected Johnny was more than capable of shooting both of them.

"Stop sleeping on the job and get after that damn cow." The yell broke into his thoughts and brought him back to the present. Guiltily he took off after the recalcitrant cow. He was starting to agree with Johnny's view that they were really dumb animals. Why did one always go off on its own instead of sticking with the herd? Or else they'd get stuck in thick undergrowth or just do anything that would make life more awkward for everyone. Dumb animals—'nough said. Dear Lord, he was even starting to sound like his brother.

He looked across at Johnny riding the far side of the herd. But it was odd, because instead of doing his usual job of keeping right on top of any stragglers, Johnny was staring off at the distant plain. Guy took advantage of a break in the herd to cross over. "Falling asleep on the job?"

Johnny gave him an icy look. "No, Harvard, watching our tails."

"Sorry, what are you talking about?"

"Just wondering who finds our drive so interesting that they've been following us for miles. And they were watching us yesterday too, I reckon."

Guy peered into the distance, but damn it, he couldn't see anything suspicious. "Where?"

"They give off a trail of dust, and it's following us."

"Who do you think they could be? Indians?"

Johnny shook his head. "No. They aren't hereabouts, wouldn't kick up no dust cloud, and wouldn't bother trailin' after us anyhow."

"Comancheros?" He felt pleased that he could roll the name out. He suspected that Johnny wouldn't have expected him to remember the term, which he'd used in his story of the previous night. But Johnny looked singularly unimpressed by the suggestion.

"No, too far north for them."

"So, who, Johnny?"

"Well, Harvard, if I knew that, I wouldn't be sitting here trying to figure it out." Johnny sounded very irritated.

"Maybe it's rustlers."

Johnny looked at him as if he was stupid. "Harvard, rustlers tend not to hit moving herds surrounded by ranch hands. No." He chewed the end of his stampede string. "No, this is trouble, take it from me."

Guy looked once more at the horizon. He thought Johnny was fussing unnecessarily. Chances were it was just people headed the same direction. He was faintly amused by his brother's reactions. Come to that, everyone in the West seemed to overreact wildly to everything. Life was far more civilized in the East. Still, if Johnny wanted to fuss and worry, it was up to him. He would enjoy ribbing him when the drive passed off without incident. Turning his horse he moved on again with the herd, leaving Johnny chewing his stampede string, still staring intently at the horizon.

It was later in the day when Johnny started arguing with Alonso about the best place to make camp. The segundo had chosen a sheltered site with a wooded hillside behind it. And Johnny was far from happy. He was rattling away in Spanish at the man, while the hands stood around fidgeting, obviously uncomfortable at the tirade.

"Johnny, what the hell is the matter with you?" Guy felt embarrassed and annoyed by Johnny's truculent attitude.

"This ain't a good spot for us, Harvard. If someone's going to attack this camp, we can't see 'em coming with all these trees."

Guy sighed in exasperation. "You're being ridiculous. You've no reason to believe that the camp is going to be attacked because you saw a trail of dust in the distance, and your supposed instincts. Father said we were to follow Alonso's instructions, so I suggest we do that."

"Alonso ain't a fucking owner of this ranch, Harvard, but according to the old man we can be. Leastways on paper. And you might sneer, but there's trouble coming, and I for one don't want my throat slit or a bullet in my gut."

"I suggest, Johnny, that you and I discuss this quietly and in private," Guy hissed. Arguing in front of the hands was inexcusable. Why did Johnny have to be so damned awkward?

Johnny looked even angrier now. "You backing Alonso, Harvard? Against me?"

Guy walked out of hearing of the men and stood waiting for Johnny, who stormed over with a face like thunder. "OK, Harvard, happy now? So, you backing Alonso? Just give me a straight, fucking answer."

"Yes, Johnny, I am. This seems a good, sheltered spot for the camp. There's water for the herd and protection from the weather. Set up a guard if you're that worried, but I am backing Alonso. It's what Father would expect."

Johnny's eyes were icy now. "Oh, well, we must do what the old man would want. Can't possibly be allowed to make a decision of our own." He paused. "In case you ain't noticed, Harvard, the old man ain't here. And this is a fucking stupid place to make camp, given what we know."

"We don't know anything, Johnny. All we have is your hunch and that's not enough to convince me." He turned on his heel to tell Alonso to start making camp.

Johnny stalked over to his horse and swung himself into the saddle. Guy stood and waited until his brother was turning the horse away toward the trees. "Where are you going?"

Johnny gave him another icy stare. "I'm going to see if I can spot anything and decide where to set up guards." And with that he rode off into the trees. Guy pushed his hat back. God,

Johnny could be stubborn and pigheaded. Always had to have the last word and always thought he was right. And if the men repeated these events to Guthrie when they got back, there'd be hell to pay. And that would only crank up the antagonism between Guthrie and Johnny. Boston suddenly seemed a very long way away. At least there life was calm and orderly. And very dull. He sighed, pushing his hat forward to keep the low sun out of his eyes. Hopefully the men would have forgotten about this by the time they got back. But he had a nasty feeling that Alonso would say something. Johnny had openly challenged the segundo in front of the hands, putting the man in a difficult position. It would only be natural for the man to go to Guthrie to seek clarification of his position. Damn. And damn Johnny. He was too suspicious for his own good. If only he'd relax a little, life could be so much simpler for everyone.

Taking his gloves off he walked over to join the men where the cook was heating up a pan of beans—again. He longed for a proper meal. One without beans, served on a proper plate and coffee out of a proper cup. He'd known enough hardship in the army but here he was, actively seeking out a tougher life. What did that say about him?

He felt Alonso's gaze upon him and wondered what to say that didn't put Johnny in a bad light.

"Señor, this is a good place to camp. I don't expect to be insulted for doing my job."

Guy forced what he hoped was an apologetic smile. "I'm sorry, Alonso. Johnny wasn't insulting your ability to do your job; he was just concerned because he thinks there is some sort of threat to us."

Alonso stared at him impassively. "You do not speak Spanish, Señor, you do not realize what your brother said. And if there is some danger, which, Señor, I doubt, I would say it has more to do with your brother than this herd."

139

Guy felt a flash of irritation. No, he didn't speak Spanish and didn't understand what exactly had been said during the short exchange between the two men. But neither did he like the inference that Johnny was trouble. Did Alonso know who Johnny was? Had he recognized him as Fierro? "Alonso, I am sorry you were offended. I am sure that wasn't Johnny's intention, but he is concerned, so we will post guards if that's what he wishes."

Alonso looked as though he was about to say something else, but then nodded curtly before turning away.

Guy sighed and hoped that Johnny would be back soon so that they could sort out sentries before dusk. The smell of the beans was making him feel queasy. Or maybe it was just the upset, but right now he felt like strangling his brother.

The sun had sunk very low by the time Johnny returned. Guy watched as Johnny, without any reference to him, set about posting guards and organizing shift changes. Guy gritted his teeth. He was the one with military experience, which made his brother's behavior doubly irritating, and when Johnny was standing alone a little later, he went over to tell him so.

Johnny stared at him coolly. "I might not have been in the cavalry, Soldier Boy, but I've run enough range wars to know how to organize men. Trouble is I ain't convinced this bunch of innocents is up to the job. Maybe, if my brother had backed me up, they might take the threat a little more seriously."

"For heaven's sake," Guy rolled his eyes. "I'm not going to back you without any proof that there's trouble brewing. All we know is that you saw some dust in the distance. What on earth are you trying to prove? You made Alonso look small in front of the men and you tried to do the same to me. I would remind you that I'm the one with military experience . . ."

Johnny snorted derisively. "And don't you want everyone to know it."

Guy's fists clenched. "And," he carried on as if Johnny hadn't spoken. "Your experience as a gunfighter, killing for hire, hardly qualifies you to talk down to me in front of the hands, organize the shifts, or act as if you're in charge."

There was a flicker of something in Johnny's eyes, but it was gone before Guy could read it. Johnny turned and stalked away even as Guy felt a stab of guilt. Following him, he called out, "Johnny, I'm sorry . . ."

"Fuck off, Soldier Boy."

"I'm sorry. I shouldn't have said what I did. It was uncalled for and patronizing. Please, Johnny." He held his hand out, hoping his brother would take it and shake.

Instead, Johnny just stared at it, bewildered almost, as if not knowing what Guy expected. "I said fuck off."

Guy shook his head. "I spoke rashly and I'm sorry. Haven't you ever said the wrong thing?" He smiled wryly. "I guess the last few days have shaken me up. We were getting along better too, I don't want to put us back to the beginning again."

Johnny's face was impassive. "You just did, Harvard. I should've known better than to give an Eastern dandy any credit. I don't usually give anyone any credit—I find it saves a lot of disappointment. Now, like I said. Fuck off."

He was turning away when there was the click of guns being cocked.

"Easy now, boys, and no one need get hurt."

He and Johnny stared at the two men who had stepped from the shadow of the trees. Johnny made the slightest move of his hand and one of the men said, "I wouldn't do that, boy. Not if you want to see another sunrise. And don't go thinking your guards are going to help. They won't be helping anyone again."

Flinching, Guy glanced at Johnny, but his brother showed no emotion. It was as if he was carved from stone. Guy swallowed hard. "What do you want from us?"

One of the men, with wiry hair and a rough beard, spoke.

"We're going to take the money, stampede your herd, and then we'll be gone."

Guy shook his head, bewildered. "We're moving a herd. We're not carrying money."

The bearded man jerked his gun at them, motioning them to move over where two more men had guns trained on the ranch hands. "Yeah, you do. You got a nice tidy sum of money here. And we're going to relieve you of the bother of having to deliver it."

"Seems like you men are in for a disappointment," drawled Johnny. "We sure as hell ain't got no money with us."

One of the men suddenly stepped across and struck Johnny hard in the belly with his rifle. Johnny doubled over, hissing in pain. "Shut your mouth. Now you stand good and still while we relieve you all of those guns you're carrying. Then we'll take the money."

He took the gun from Johnny's holster while another of his group moved swiftly among the ranch hands, removing their guns and throwing them into the edge of the woods. "Now, give us the money and we'll be gone."

"And we told you, we ain't got no fucking money," Johnny said hoarsely.

The bearded man went and put his gun against Johnny's head, cocking the hammer. "I count to three and then I pull the trigger—unless someone produces the money. One, two . . ."

Guy's gut clenched. "We aren't carrying money. For God's sake, let him go." One of the men grabbed Guy, holding his arms tight. "I swear we haven't any money other than the cash in our pockets. You have . . ."

"It is here." Alonso's voice broke the tension.

Guy tried to pull away from his captor to look at Alonso. "What money, Alonso? No one mentioned money."

Alonso didn't reply. He passed his saddlebags to one of the

men, who snatched out a thick pile of notes with a yell of glee.

The leader stared at Guy through narrowed eyes. "You're lucky I ain't gonna shoot you, Blondie, for lying to me." He nodded toward Johnny. "But maybe that kid will shoot you for messing with his life." He jerked a thumb at two of his men. "Go stampede their cattle, and then we get the hell out of here."

The men rode off toward the herd at a gallop, firing their guns even as the bearded man turned back to face Guy. "We'll be taking one of your men with us as a hostage. Follow us, and I'll kill him. That's a promise."

One of his men grabbed a young ranch hand, and Guy realized he didn't even know the kid's name. "You'll let him go later?"

"Yeah, so long as you don't follow. We'll let him go later." They bundled the kid onto a horse and rode out.

Guy sucked in a deep breath. His heart felt as though it was going to explode in his chest. He stared wide-eyed at Johnny, who'd moved swiftly to retrieve his gun from the edge of the trees. "Are you OK, Johnny? God, I thought he was going to shoot you." He barely recognized his own voice.

Johnny ignored the question. Cocking his gun, he walked over to Alonso. Pushing the barrel under the segundo's chin, he hissed, "You got some talking to do. And you'd better have the right answers, because otherwise I'm going to take great pleasure in blowing your brains out of the back of your head."

Chapter Thirteen

The man had guts, Johnny had to give him that. The thought slid into his head as he stared into Alonso's eyes; the segundo looked uneasy but not terrified. Well, that was about to change—he was in no mood to go easy, because he wanted answers, and he wanted them now. He grabbed the back of Alonso's head by the hair, jerking it back as he rammed the gun in hard under the man's chin until Alonso gasped in pain. He heard Harvard exclaim in protest but Johnny paid him no heed.

"Now, Alonso, s'pose you start telling us what the hell is going on. I want to know what the money was for. And who it was for. And more to the point," and he jammed the gun harder against the man's throat, "just how those men knew we was carrying this fucking money."

Alonso grunted at the pressure, struggling to breathe. Johnny smiled. "And don't think I won't use this. Because, believe me, right this moment, I've got a real ache to shoot someone. And you'll do just fine." Now he could see fear in the man's eyes. Yeah, this was what he was good at. Not punching cattle.

"I cannot speak," Alonso whispered hoarsely, "with that gun in my throat."

Johnny stared into the man's face, keeping his expression ice cold, but easing the pressure just slightly. But not too much. "Talk."

Alonso swallowed hard again. "It is the patron's money. He ask me to deliver it to a rancher friend of his, later on our drive."

Johnny narrowed his eyes, pushing the gun again, enjoying the feeling of power. God, he'd missed this. "He ask you to do this a lot? Have you done this sort of job for him before?"

Beads of sweat tracked down Alonso's face. He licked his lips and tried to shrug. "It is not first time. His friend doesn't trust bankers' drafts. If he and the patron do business, it is always cash."

"So, tell me, Alonso," Johnny kept his voice silky soft. "Exactly how do you think those men knew we had the money? You see, I'm wondering if you didn't have something to do with that . . ." Johnny's smile didn't reach his eyes. He'd got Alonso where he wanted him—the man was shaking slightly and his eyes were wide with fear. And, he noted, Harvard wasn't interfering either, simply standing and watching. That surprised him. He thought Harvard would have tried to stop him. Maybe Harvard had a little more respect now for Johnny's instincts, and maybe even a few suspicions of his own.

"I do not know, Señor. I have often carried money for the patron. I have been with him for many years. He knows I am loyal. And honest. He would not be pleased at your treatment of me."

Johnny gave a mirthless laugh. "Well, Alonso, I guess the patron wouldn't be too pleased by anything I do. But I do think he'll be kinda worried about that money. So tell me, who were those men? Friends of yours?" He watched Alonso's face closely, looking for some flicker to indicate guilt. But all he saw was wounded pride.

"I tell you, Señor, I do not know these men or how they knew about the money." His voice had the ring of truth to it.

"Who else knew you had the money?"

Alonso stared back, grimacing as Johnny suddenly jerked his head back by the hair again, even as the gun dug deeper into his neck. Alonso tried to pull away. "The men, they know that sometimes we take money if we are riding in this direction. It is not the first time. But these are good men, Señor. These men are not outlaws or shootists."

Johnny glared at him, the meaning of Alonso's words not lost on him. Even if the segundo hadn't recognized Fierro, he knew what Johnny was. Still, he was inclined to believe Alonso's account. Whoever had been in on this robbery, it wasn't Alonso. But in that case who the hell was it? Someone had to have tipped those men off. There had to be a spy in the Sinclair crew. But who? He chewed on his lip and then huffed out a grunt of irritation. Shit! He could have kicked himself. It was obvious who the guilty man was. "Alonso, that kid, the one they took as hostage, how long's he been working for the ranch?"

Alonso furrowed his brow, puzzled, but relief flickered in his eyes as Johnny let go of his head. "Not long, a few weeks."

Johnny turned away, thoughtful. He holstered his gun. Things were starting to make sense. The kid had to be a plant. There to tip the others off. Because someone, maybe a former hand, knew that sometimes money was carried on drives like this one.

"Johnny." Harvard's voice broke into his thoughts.

He looked at him coldly. "Yeah? Come to preach at me? Still think you know best?"

His brother looked at him steadily. "You were right, I'm sorry I doubted you. Question is, what do we do now?"

"Well, Harvard, I suggest you go on with the remainder of the crew and round up all them damn cows—if you're sure you can manage that. But I'm going to find those murderers and get our money back. Because let's not forget, it's our fucking money too if we're going to own a share of the spread, even if the old man didn't see fit to mention it to us. Hell, a man could get to thinking that our father don't trust us." Johnny laughed humorlessly. "Or that he don't trust me."

"We'll send Alonso on with the hands and the herd then."

"We? I don't recall asking you along on this jaunt."

"You're not going on your own, Johnny." Harvard's voice was hard, like he wasn't going to back down.

"Why? Afraid I might take off with the money, are you?" The dry heat of anger was building and Johnny shoved his brother back a couple of paces.

Instead of reacting Guy sighed and shook his head slightly. "No, I'm not afraid that you'll take off with the money. But I am coming with you, as your backup."

"Backup? You? Don't make me laugh." Johnny stared, looking for some sign of his brother giving up the damn stupid idea. Like old Harvard could be any help for what he was planning. Just get them both shot, more like.

But Guy just stared right back at him, holding his gaze. "I can watch your back, Johnny, if nothing else."

Watch his back? That was a joke. "Don't think you'll like what I got in mind. Those men are killers, not just thieves, and they're going to pay." Johnny's voice was hard. "Ain't going to be pretty. An' seeing as how you don't trust my instincts, it might make you real uncomfortable."

"I dare say I'll survive. But I am coming with you. You're not going to do this alone, not this time. We're a team." His mouth lifted in a smile. "But you can run it; you call the tune."

Johnny grunted in exasperation. "Hell! You could get us both killed. Have you thought of that? I don't like amateurs. They get in the way. Why don't you stay with the hands and do what the old man wants? Leastways then you can be sure you're still the apple of his fucking eye. Because believe me, he ain't gonna like my plan. And he sure as hell ain't gonna like what I got to say to him later."

But Guy smiled again. "I'll take the risk, Johnny. I'm backing you on this one."

Damn but the man was stubborn. Very stubborn. But his

brother was backing him . . . Shit. Why did he let Harvard get to him? How did the man do that? He should never have let his guard down with the man. Shouldn't trust nobody, Fierro. That was always his first rule. Never give anyone credit, and never let anyone get close. Fuck. He ran his hand through his hair in exasperation. And Harvard stood there, giving him that sort of level look he used. All calm. But like he wasn't going to budge, no matter what. Shit.

Johnny sighed, defeated. "Fine. You can come, but you do as I fucking well say, otherwise I will shoot you. That's a promise. You want to get killed that's your business, but you ain't playing around with my life."

Guy smiled. "I thought you weren't afraid of dying. That's what you said if I recall correctly."

Johnny shut his eyes briefly. "I ain't afraid of dying. That don't mean I'm gonna let some tin soldier mess things up and get me killed. So, if you come, I run the show. You're only coming along for the ride."

"Fine—it's your show. So, when do we leave?"

"Firstly we sort out the men. And bury the dead guards—poor devils. We give Alonso his orders. I don't care if he likes it or not. He can damn well do as he's told. And then we'll leave before dawn." Johnny smiled as he made another decision. "Tell you what, Harvard, you can give Alonso his orders. He might take it from you. I reckon he ain't too keen on me right now. See how generous I am, already giving you a job to do."

Guy raised an eyebrow. "You're too kind." Then, with a brief nod, he walked toward Alonso, who was huddled in a group with the rest of the hands.

"Oh, and Harvard."

Guy half turned, a questioning look on his face.

"Find out where all the nearby towns are. Alonso should know that."

His brother nodded and scooted over to talk to the men.

Johnny hurried over to where he'd dumped his gear and grabbed his saddlebags. He wanted to check how much ammunition he had with him. Not that he needed to check, he always carried far more than he could ever need. But he could never stop checking and double-checking everything. He wondered sometimes why he did that. He worried constantly about ammunition. He always bought bullets when he went to a town. Sometimes he wasn't even aware of having done so. Even now he had shells and bullets in his pockets, and he'd already put some in a drawer in his room at the ranch. Hell, he usually had enough bullets to start his own private war. But he kept buying more. And even now, he couldn't relax till he'd checked the bags. Checked his gun. Checked his rifle. And he knew he'd do it all over again later. Maybe he was plain loco. Would Guy have plenty of ammunition too? Better check. And better check his guns for him. Harvard might not do it right.

He fetched Guy's saddlebags, grunting with irritation when they turned out to be full of all sorts of junk. A razor and shaving soap? This was a cattle drive, not a town social. Extra shirts? Why couldn't the man just wear the same shirt each day, like everyone else did? A book? No, two damn books. Madre de Dios! Spare socks? He felt tempted to set fire to the whole lot. There didn't seem to be any extra ammunition other than half a dozen shells for the rifle.

"Looking for something in particular?" His brother's voice jolted him out of his search. The tone of voice was mild, but Johnny couldn't suppress a flash of pleasure that Harvard looked pissed.

Johnny threw the bags down. "I was checking your stuff for this trip, Harvard. And all you've got is a load of junk." He kicked at the contents. "I mean you brought a razor but no ammunition? We're moving cattle; we ain't going to no churches.

We won't be meeting fancy women. If you're real lucky, best you can hope for at the end of a drive is fucking some saloon girl and they won't turn you down because your shirt ain't clean. But, oh no, old Harvard, with his fancy fucking education takes books and spare socks on a cattle drive."

"What do you suggest I take next time, Johnny? Pray, do enlighten me."

Johnny shut his eyes briefly, shaking his head. Why the hell couldn't his brother talk normal like other people? "Bullets, Harvard, bullets. They tend to come in handy because of situations like this. You're out West now. This ain't Boston—and a man needs to be ready for anything. It's a wild land. And there's a lot of folk out here who don't have Sunday manners. Men who'd shoot you just because you look at them for a second longer than they like." Johnny paused to draw breath, forcing himself to calm down before he started yelling at his brother. "Anyway, did you sort out Alonso or have you screwed that up too?"

Harvard bent down and started cramming his belongings back in the saddlebags. "No, I have not screwed that up. I pulled rank on him. He's not too happy with you at present, but he'll take the men and move the herd on—once they've gathered them back together. I also asked him to check the farthest fence lines when they finish moving the herd. I hoped it might delay them sufficiently for us to get back and see Father before he does."

Johnny shook his head, giving Harvard his coolest look. "Won't matter who gets back first. It won't change anything. The old man is going to be mad as hell with me. I know exactly what he'll think and he'll say all of this is my fault."

"That's just stupid, Johnny. It's not your fault we were held up. In fact, you were the only one with enough sense to see the risk. He won't think this is your fault."

"Wanna bet? Because one way or the other, he'll turn it so that I'm to blame." Johnny kicked at the ground thinking of the argument ahead when they got back. Assuming they got back. He knew the old man would turn this around on him one way or another. He knew exactly what his father thought of him—he'd seen it in his eyes. And now things had gone belly up so it was bound to be Fierro's fault. Yeah, his old man would love being able to blame Fierro. It would give Sinclair the chance to welsh on the offer of a share in his ranch. Well, he'd never believed in that offer so it wouldn't be no surprise. But he was damned if he'd let the old man have things all his own way—he'd got quite a lot to say to Sinclair, too. About not trusting them to know they were carrying money. And how much money had they been carrying? Shit, they didn't even know. Yep, they'd be bound to fight and he'd probably end up shooting his father if only to shut him up.

Johnny sighed. "You better see if one of the hands can give you some extra ammunition. I sure as hell can't spare any. Then try and get some sleep. We got a long ride ahead tomorrow."

He watched Guy scrounging ammunition from the men. Why the hell had he agreed to let his brother come along with him? He really was losing his grip. He was getting soft—way too soft. Well, that was all about to change. No one was taking his money and getting away with it. He felt a surge of excitement. He was going to enjoy payback time.

Chapter Fourteen

He tried to sleep but his damn ghosts came calling. Lying with his gun cradled against his face, he listened to the snoring men around him. What would it be like to sleep like that? The only time he got any real sleep was when he was with a whore, and then the sleep was all too brief. Harvard was curled up and sleeping soundly in a cozy spot near the dying embers of the fire. His face, lit by the moon, looked peaceful. Like he didn't have a care in the world. A real innocent. And it was probably best he stayed that way. He had no place in what was ahead. Because it was going to be bloody, Fierro would see to that.

Looking at the position of the moon, he figured it must be about an hour before dawn, so he got quietly to his feet and moved swiftly and silently to the horses. His buckskin, Pistol, nickered softly at him as he hefted the saddle onto the animal's back. "Hush, amigo," he whispered, as he secured his saddlebags and rifle.

He was about to swing himself into the saddle when the crack of a twig made him whirl round, gun in hand.

"You're going to make me feel left out if you're not careful." Harvard stood, hands on hips, a faint smile on his face. "Surely you weren't thinking of going without me?"

Johnny holstered the gun. "Shit, Harvard! You could get yourself killed creeping up on a man like that. Why don't you go back and stay with the men? Ain't no place for you on this trip. What I'm planning is going to be ugly."

Guy stared back at him, all calm and easy. "As we agreed, I'm coming along for the ride. Don't worry, it's your show." He smiled slightly. "But I am coming. Partner." And this time, there was a real hard tone to his voice, like it was made of steel or something.

Dios! He was one stubborn son of a bitch—who wasn't about to change his mind in a hurry. Johnny threw his hands in the air. "Fine, I give in. But hurry up, we need to get moving."

At least the man moved quickly. He was mounted and ready in a minute. Didn't make no noise either. Maybe he'd learned one or two tricks in the cavalry.

"Come on then, let's move out." Johnny turned Pistol and headed out of camp.

They rode in silence toward the farthest ridge where they'd seen the robbers disappear. In the east the first glow of dawn was edging across the sky. It was going to be a good day, make it easier to follow the trail. But would the men lay a false trail? Well, they could try, but not many men could fool Johnny like that. He was a mean tracker and he didn't think the men were that smart. He was looking forward to getting even. Payback was going to be fun. He'd missed this feeling. He'd sure been tempted by the old man's offer, but hell, this was what he was. And if he was honest with himself, he knew that it was what he always would be.

But there was the other part of him too. The part that realized that there was no glory in this life he'd made for himself. The part that knew he'd sold his soul to the devil. The killing had gotten to him, and the buzz he got from the gunfights faded quicker than it used to. All too often now he felt sick and empty inside. And that part of him wanted nothing more than to leave this sham of a life behind. But his ghosts were never going to let him forget so maybe he should just settle for doing what he did best.

He'd worked hard enough to get to this place over the years. He'd grown up hating. Hearing his mother's stories had made sure of that. All he'd ever wanted was to be the fastest pistolero. And now here he was—fast with a gun, but damn it was a lonely life. He'd never expected it to be quite so lonely. As a child he'd thought gunfighters were admired and respected. People stepped out of their way in the street. They didn't kick them, or whip them, or . . . But now, he knew it hadn't been respect he'd seen—just fear. He was all too familiar with fear now. He saw it in the eyes of most everyone he met. Still, nobody had forced a gun into his hand. There was no one to blame but himself. And so, he guessed he'd carry on because there was no escape. At least he could get a little justice for those dead ranch hands. Those killers would regret the day they messed with Fierro. He'd make them pay. He felt the familiar surge of excitement and grinned. He was going to have himself some fun.

"What are you smiling about?" Harvard's voice broke the silence.

"Just planning on payback, that's all. But it's going to be real sweet."

"And legal, I trust."

Johnny laughed. "Legal, Harvard? Let's just say the law won't be able to touch me. Like I said though, you're only along for the ride. This is my show, you remember that. And I warn you, don't get in my way, because that'll make me real mad."

"Well, that would never do." His brother sounded real cool. "Never do at all."

Johnny reined in Pistol and slid down to search for tracks. The ground was giving way to rough rocks and stony outcrops and the tracks had almost petered out.

"We can't track them over rocks, Johnny."

"They won't have gone far over them. That money will be burning a hole in their pockets. This is just a false trail; they'll double back off these rocks and head for a town."

Johnny threw Pistol's reins to Guy and clambered up across the rocks, looking for signs of the odd broken bit of weed sprouting haphazardly in the cracks. He was right—the men were stupid, hadn't stayed on the rocks for much more than quarter of a mile before they'd taken a path heading off to the northeast. Dumb sons of bitches. The feeling of power made him feel almost light-headed, gave him a real rush. Yeah, he was looking forward to what lay ahead and the looks on their faces when he got even.

It was a fairly easy trail to follow. The men must have figured they'd lose any trackers on the rocks and not made much effort after that. It was open country so there was nowhere they could set up an ambush ahead and Johnny relaxed slightly. Even better, Harvard was quiet, intent on studying the route ahead. Johnny shifted in his saddle, casting an eye at the sky. The sun was climbing higher; the only clouds were way up high. It was going to be hot later.

He'd been really mad at Harvard the previous day. If he was honest he'd been hurt too when the man didn't back him. Trouble was old Harvard really was an innocent. He might have been in a war, but he knew nothing about life out West, so he probably really hadn't understood Johnny's concerns.

Johnny sighed; he wasn't usually the forgiving type. But he kinda liked Harvard, even if he was odd. And despite everything, he felt he could trust him. That was strange in itself. He could count on one hand the number of men he'd trusted in his life, and still have a spare finger or two.

He studied his brother thoughtfully. Why was the man out here? He sure as hell wasn't like most men who traveled West. And it wasn't like he was trying to make his fortune. It sounded like he'd enjoyed a life of luxury back in Boston. What would make a man turn his back on that? His brother didn't give the

155

impression of being a devoted son, so why? Well, he'd warned Harvard that he'd want an answer in return for the stories, so maybe now was the time.

"So, Harvard, it's time for that question. What I want to know is why you came out here. It's a lot different from Boston, and I can't help thinking that you're running from something. Can't be the law, so what?"

Harvard choked back a snort of laughter. "The law? Well, you're right there, I'm certainly not running from the law." His shoulders shook as he gave way to the laughter.

Johnny raised an eyebrow. "So, what? And don't say it was because you wanted to see the old man. I figure there's more to it than that."

Guy nodded slowly, almost to himself it seemed. "You're very astute, Johnny. You certainly don't miss much. In the future I will always listen to your instincts."

He fell silent again, but Johnny just waited. Still, it felt good to hear Harvard's words. To know that the man didn't think he was dumb. Yeah, real good.

"You're right, of course." Harvard spoke soft. "If you must know, my uncle ordered me out of Boston to allow for a bit of a scandal to die down. But, of course, he didn't expect me to stay. He thought sending me out to the uncivilized West would make me appreciate the delights of Boston. Make me want to return and settle down to a more serious life." He smiled. "No, the last thing he expected was for me to want to stay here and yet I find myself very tempted to do so."

"Scandal, what scandal?" Johnny was looking forward to this. It sounded real interesting and he noticed that his brother was flushing a deep red.

"It involved a young lady." Guy pushed his hat forward, and pulled off his gloves.

Johnny grinned. "Now, I think I'm gonna need a bit more

information than that. Hell, you've had two stories from me." He could hardly keep from grinning at his brother's discomfort. And boy, was he coloring up real good.

"The young lady and I . . . Well . . ."

"What was her name? Come on, you ain't being let off the hook. We had a deal."

"She was called Cecily. I was in her room."

"I take it you mean her bedroom, Harvard?"

Guy glared. "I was in her boudoir. I mean, there was a sofa and table and my intentions were misunderstood."

Johnny's grin broadened. "Misunderstood? In her boo dwah? And just who misunderstood your intentions?"

"Her father." Guy pushed his hat back.

"And what were your intentions, Harvard, in her boo dwah?" He'd heard bits of ladies called all sorts of things before but he never knew that they had parts called a boo dwah.

His brother grinned now. "Well, maybe my intentions weren't too honorable, but I assure you she wasn't objecting. She never had before."

"So this wasn't the first time you'd been in her boo dwah? Just her pa never caught you before?"

Guy nodded. "It was somewhat unfortunate. I was forced to make my getaway out of the window over the balcony. I had to climb down using the plants on the wall for handholds. It was a close shave, that's for sure."

Johnny started laughing. He could hardly keep from falling out of the saddle. The thought of his brother climbing through windows and shinnying down walls was too good to be true. Guy looked offended by his laughter, which set him off even more. Grinning broadly, he said, "So, her old man kicked up a stink, did he?"

"Somewhat. The trouble was there had been other fathers . . ."

This new bit of information caused Johnny to laugh even more. He couldn't imagine this man as a womanizer—he looked so formal and serious. "So, Harvard, you'd been spreading it around in Boston, had you?" Johnny snorted as he said this, tears rolling down his face.

"I'm really glad that my misfortunes amuse you so much. To answer your somewhat crude inquiry, I had enjoyed one or two dalliances."

"Dally ounces?" That was another word for it that he hadn't heard before. He snorted again and grabbed hold of the saddle horn as he almost slid from the saddle. He could see Harvard was struggling now to keep a straight face, and trying hard to look offended. And that made Johnny laugh all the more.

"Yes, brother, dalliances. Unfortunately, the ladies concerned misunderstood my intentions for something more serious. Marriage was mentioned." Harvard shuddered as he said the word. "Cecily, however, never misunderstood, it was her father who proved to be the problem."

Johnny let out a snort and a splutter together. He was glad now that he'd let Harvard come with him. This was too good to have missed. "So I take it your uncle ain't too impressed by all this."

"That, Johnny, is something of an understatement. If I kept a mistress he wouldn't have minded, and he didn't mind me enjoying the odd servant. But these were the daughters of his business acquaintances . . ."

Johnny stopped laughing now. "So it's OK for you to fuck a serving girl and maybe put her in the family way, because they don't matter. But it's not OK to fuck 'ladies' because they do matter?"

Harvard flushed. "I suppose that is how he saw it."

"And you, Harvard, how did you see it?" Johnny looked at him coolly. "Did you think the servant girls mattered?"

Guy sighed. "I admit that some of my behavior doesn't bear close examination, and I'm certainly not proud of myself or my indiscretions."

Hell, why couldn't the man use normal words like other people?

"And, of course, the serving girls mattered. But I just seemed to go crazy when I came back from the war; it was as if I wanted to risk losing everything. My behavior was appalling but I couldn't bear the thought of fitting into some role carved out by my uncle. I went back to Harvard to finish my education, but then was expected to join my uncle's business. It was what had always been expected of me, and I'd never questioned it before the war. But afterwards . . ." He paused, shaking his head. "I found it all so dull, not just the work, but my life too. I did everything possible to relieve the boredom. I was involved in setting up the Boston Sailing Club—I love sailing and out on the sea I could feel free for a while. And I had countless affairs. I was looking for something but I didn't know what. And you can't begin to imagine how rigid and claustrophobic that level of Boston society is. I felt . . ." He paused, seeming to struggle to find the right words. "I felt as though I was drowning under all these layers of pompous people. They were set on squeezing the life out of me, pigeonholing me and I wasn't ready for that."

Johnny was silent. Funny, he knew in a way what Harvard meant. He sometimes felt like he was drowning under the weight of the bodies of the men he'd killed. "I guess then, you were pleased to be ordered out of Boston?"

Guy shook his head slightly. "No, not at first. I was dismissive of the idea. Our father had been asking me to visit for some time, but the West held no appeal. I'd been away for too long. But all the fathers, particularly Cecily's, raised such a furor that my uncle thought it was a good way to get me out of Boston until the gossip died down."

Johnny tilted his hat farther forward to shield his eyes from the sun. "Well, seems like we got a lot more in common than we ever thought. Except you've fucked a lot more ladies while I've probably fucked a lot more whores."

"You really do have a delightfully colorful vocabulary, Johnny. Limited, but colorful. And please, do tell me, just how many ladies have you had?"

Johnny grinned. "I've had just one lady, Harvard. And trust me, you'd have liked her. She was a real lady, and you and she would get along real well."

Harvard shot him a disbelieving sort of look.

"So, yeah, just one lady but a helluva lot of whores. I like whores. They're honest." And there'd been a lot of them over the years. Yeah, a helluva lot.

"You'll have to raise your expectations if you become a partner in one of the biggest ranches in New Mexico."

Johnny stared at him. What the hell was Harvard talking about now?

"I mean you'll have to put your promiscuous life behind you and start courting young ladies, instead of spending your time in bordellos. At some point you'll have to make a suitable marriage."

"A suitable marriage? What the hell is that?"

Guy laughed. "Well, to a nice young lady, preferably from a family with a little money, possibly the daughter of a rancher. Someone suitable to bear you future heirs for Sinclair."

"Shit, I hope you ain't serious. And nice girls ain't any fun, not for the sort of things I got in mind. No nice young lady is going to get her claws into me. Mind you, can't imagine any respectable ranchers letting their daughters near me anyhow." He found this thought soothed him. Yeah, no one would want him near their daughters. He should be pretty safe.

Harvard grinned. "Oh, give them time, Johnny, give them

time. We're both probably fated to turn into copies of our father over time and be considered very respectable. Even you."

"That ain't even funny. And if I got to become respectable it seems like that's a damn good reason for telling the old man to shove his ranch." He sighed. "Anyway, he won't want me around once he hears about all of this. And, I think it's time we stopped pissing around because I can smell a town."

His brother raised his eyebrows questioningly. "What do you mean, you can smell a town? I know that sailors can smell land before they see it, but I've never heard of someone being able to smell a town." He scanned the horizon as if looking for some sign of life.

"We ain't far. I can smell it. The stench of folk gets carried on the air. So, time to start concentrating." And with the lightest touch of his spurs Johnny pushed Pistol on, while he did what he did best and slid back into Johnny Fierro.

CHAPTER FIFTEEN

Guy looked at Johnny's profile as they rode on. It was impossible to read any expression there now. The difference in him from just a few minutes before was remarkable. Almost as soon as Johnny had made the comment about being able to smell a town, he'd seemed different. Watchful and . . . dangerous. How could anyone change so quickly? And it was odd because he had the strangest feeling he was riding with a different man now. Johnny Fierro, perhaps?

Yes, that was it—he seemed dangerous again. Just like he'd been in the run up to the showdown with Chavez. Then danger had emanated from him, it had been palpable.

He couldn't help but wonder what Johnny would have done if Alonso hadn't come up with some answers. Although he hated to admit it, even to himself, he suspected Johnny was more than capable of shooting the man. But would he have shot him? With all the hands watching? No. Johnny was too smart for that.

He was certainly an enigma. Given the tiny glimpse he'd been permitted of Johnny's past, the only surprising thing was that he had any decency. The way he'd spoken to Peggy that first night—he'd sounded kind, and it had been a thoughtful thing to do to allay her fears.

His horse stumbled slightly, jolting him out of his thoughts. "Are you sure there's a town ahead? I know Alonso said there was one in this direction but I got the impression it was farther away."

"Alonso's a fool, Harvard. Honest, but a fool. He should have known we could be at risk when he was carrying that money, but he's so dumb the thought didn't enter his head. I guess he knows about punching cattle but not much else."

He had to ask, needed to know. Swallowing hard, he asked, "Would you have shot him?" And then he tensed, hardly breathing, waiting for the answer.

Johnny looked at him through narrowed eyes. "Well, like I said, I was aching to shoot someone. What do you think?"

Johnny was watching him intently now, like everything depended on the answer to his question. Guy picked his words carefully. "I don't think you're so stupid as to shoot him in front of all the ranch hands."

Johnny raised an eyebrow and then glanced away before he looked back at Guy with a totally impassive expression. "Well, you won't ever know, will you?"

Guy smiled. "Not for sure, but I suppose I can't believe that you'd have shot him in cold blood."

Johnny shook his head slightly. "I done a lot of things I wouldn't want anyone to know about. A lot of things."

"Have you ever shot an unarmed man?"

Johnny looked at him. "A man not wearing a gun? It don't make no difference. Not if I want him dead." He smiled, more to himself, it seemed. "No, no difference."

The look in Johnny's eyes was unsettling. Perhaps it would be prudent to change the subject. He had a feeling that he really didn't want to know the worst of Johnny's life. He would content himself with the belief that there was a core of decency running through his brother. Just focus on that.

"So, how far to this town? Does your nose tell you that?"

Johnny looked amused, as though he guessed the reason for the sudden change of subject. The thought that Johnny could see through him so easily made him feel strangely uncomfort-

163

able. But presumably, it was that ability to read people so well that kept his brother alive. That, and the speed of his draw.

"It's a way off, but I can smell it and we won't go in 'til dusk."

"Why not until then?"

Johnny gave him a withering look. "Well, for starters that kid will recognize our horses. It's a hell of a lot easier to slip in once the town gets jumping. Until then, we'll bide our time. Hell, you can even tell me some more about your lady friends while we're waiting."

Guy grinned. "I suspect that yours are more interesting."

Johnny nodded. "And I expect I've had more, too, Harvard."

Why did everything have to be a competition with him? Like he always had to have the last word. Always prove he was right. He was so damn cocky and arrogant. God, it would be so good to put one over on him, just once. Still, having saddlebags packed with a change of clothes and books perhaps hadn't been the best way Guy could convince Johnny that he could cope with all eventualities. But Guy hadn't expected trouble on this sort of a trip. Hell, they were only meant to have been moving cattle. But it seemed Johnny was always prepared for trouble, and that was the difference between them. Guy was learning fast that Johnny had a very suspicious nature. He didn't appear to trust anyone. Had he ever trusted anyone? Somehow, Guy suspected not, or at least, not for a very long time.

"How old were you when . . . ?"

He didn't get a chance to finish the question. Johnny just looked at him, eyes narrowed, saying, "Ain't none of your damn business."

"You don't even know what I was going to ask you."

"Well, I guess you were going to be like all the rest, and want to know how old I was when I first killed someone. And it ain't none of your business."

"That's not what I was going to ask."

Johnny looked at him coolly. "Want to know how old I was when I had my first woman then?"

"Wrong again. I was going to ask how old you were when you got your first gun. I was wondering how long it takes to become as fast as you."

"Tell you one thing, Harvard, if you're hoping to become a fast gun you've left it far too late."

Guy rolled his eyes. The last thing he'd ever wanted was to be a fast gun. "No, I'm just curious, that's all."

Johnny shook his head slightly. "None of your business. Let's just say you were probably still playing with your fancy toys. Now shut up and let's just concentrate on the job in hand." He pushed his buckskin into a lope.

Guy pulled his bandana up over his mouth and nose—he was tired of breathing Johnny's dust. God, what an irritating man he was. And patronizing too. Keeping in Johnny's tracks, he followed him for another mile or so, only drawing level when Johnny suddenly reined in. It seemed that Johnny's senses had been right, for there, spread out beyond the ridge, was a small town. He glanced over at his brother, who was gazing down at it with a strange expression, as if he was almost excited by the thought of something. Guy felt an icy chill down his back. He shook himself; he was being fanciful. Johnny still had the same look though and there was something cold and hard about his eyes. Guy sighed. He had a bad feeling about this. Damn, what exactly was Johnny planning?

"We'll hole up here until dusk, Harvard. Make the horses comfortable and then I think I might have me a little siesta."

"A siesta?"

"Yeah, a siesta. A short sleep."

"I know what it is, Johnny," he snapped. "I just wondered if it was wise, this close to the town."

Johnny stepped out of the saddle looking bemused. "Why the hell not? Think those hombres are going to come looking for us? They'll be hell-bent on spending that money, and they're so dumb they think we can't track 'em. I've got a busy night ahead of me so I think I'll have a nap."

Guy felt even more uneasy. "A busy night? What do you have in mind?"

Johnny tethered his horse in the shade of some pine trees and hefted the saddle down, slinging it on the ground. He turned slowly back to face Guy, his eyes remote as if Guy were a total stranger. "Like I told you, Harvard, you're just along for the ride. If you don't think you can handle this, stay up here and I'll go into town alone." He paused. "I reckon it would be for the best, anyway."

"We just want to get the money back, nothing more. And we hand them over to the sheriff, agreed?"

Johnny smiled, but the smile didn't touch his eyes.

"We'll do this legally, OK?"

Johnny snorted. "They weren't worrying about being legal when they murdered our guards. Those were men with families. One of the vaqueros told me they'd got young kids. And I got to tell you, I don't think much of the law. Seems like it only looks after folk who can afford to pay for protection or it depends on the color of your skin. Not that you'd know about that. I guess in the world you come from, the law always looks after respectable folk like you . . ."

Guy cut across him, resenting Johnny's sneer as he emphasized the word respectable. "Whatever you might think of it, we rely on the law here. Let it do its job. It's what Father would want, and it's the right thing to do."

Johnny stared back with narrowed eyes. "I warned you. You ain't going to like what I got in mind. And I don't give a damn what Guthrie Sinclair thinks. Seems he didn't trust us enough to even tell us about this money, or more likely didn't trust me. But I ain't a thief and I don't take too kindly to folk thinking that of me. So, I sure as hell ain't going to worry about keeping him happy. And I'll damn well tell him so when I see him. Now, if you'll excuse me, I'm going to have my siesta." He settled himself on the ground and, tilting his hat over his eyes, leaned back against a tree.

Guy shook his head as he unsaddled his horse. Damn Johnny. He seemed set on fighting with their father. It was almost as though he'd go out of his way to find something to pick a fight over with the man. But now he came to think of it, Johnny had pushed their father in every single conversation over the past few days. But to what end? And then there had been his assertion that the range war wasn't over with the death of Chavez. Had he meant that, or had he said it for effect? There seemed to be no grounds for saying it. There was only one way to find out—always assuming that Johnny would even answer honestly. Sitting down close to his brother, he aimed a gentle kick at Johnny's boots. "What makes you think the range war isn't over? Surely now that Chavez is dead that should be an end of it?"

Johnny pushed his hat back and opened one eye with an irritated sigh. "I'm trying to sleep here, Harvard. Why don't you do the same?" Johnny tipped his hat forward again and wriggled away from a rough stump protruding from the tree trunk.

Guy aimed another kick at Johnny's feet. "I'd like an answer."

Johnny's eyes snapped open again. "You'll get a bullet in the head if you do that again. Why can't you just shut up and take a nap?"

"Just answer the question, Johnny. You've got me wondering about it, so I'll keep asking you until I get a response."

Johnny sighed loudly before making a big show of heaving himself back to sit straighter. He glared across at Guy. "You'll be the death of me, unless I shoot you first. Hell, if you were anyone else I would have shot you by now. I don't know why I put up with you." He shook his head, apparently puzzled by what he presumably saw as his tolerance.

Guy rolled his eyes. "I'm touched by your indulgence. Happy? Now, about Chavez—what bothers you exactly? It seems pretty cut and dried to me. The man's dead. The threat is gone."

Johnny ducked his head, seeming to study the ground for a few seconds before meeting Guy's eyes. "I don't know what bothers me . . ."

"You mean this is just a gut feeling? A hunch? I thought you had something definite to base your comments on." Guy couldn't keep the disbelief and irritation from his voice.

Johnny glared at him. "No, Harvard, it ain't just a hunch. It was something Chavez said that didn't sit right. But I can't remember what it was. It'll come to me."

Guy leaned forward curiously. He could see the concern etched in Johnny's face. "I can't say that I recall him saying anything odd."

Johnny chewed on his thumb, staring off into the distance. "He did, take it from me. I hoped if I didn't worry at it, it would come back to me."

"Well," Guy swatted a fly away from his neck, "let's try and recall the entire thing from when we saw Chavez and his men riding in. You and Father discussed the man, Mendoza, being a shootist. And then Chavez made his snide remarks about taking a last look at the land. And then he made his oily comments about how tragic it was that Father was shot." Guy furrowed his brow trying to recall exactly how events had played out. "You made your rather witty comment about cooking your frijoles in the oil that oozes out of him, and he started on about hired hands . . ."

"That's it, damn it!" Johnny slapped his hand down on his

thigh. "He said Sinclair hands wouldn't want to die over water rights and mineral deposits."

Guy shrugged. "I'm sorry. Am I missing something here? I don't see why that's . . ."

"Chavez wanted the water rights. Why did he mention mineral deposits? The man's a rancher. Wanting the water makes sense, but minerals?"

Guy shook his head. "You're grasping at straws. Maybe Chavez realizes the land could be worth a lot if it contains mineral deposits and wants to branch out."

"No, you're wrong."

Guy ground his teeth, aggravated that Johnny was so instantly dismissive of his opinion.

"Chavez ain't got the money to start up a mining operation. That takes serious money. More money than some Mex rancher has in his pocket. I thought it was strange when I heard the names of the guns he was hiring for this fight. They were top names and they don't come cheap. Even our old man would be pushed to hire those men—and I'll bet Chavez is the same. His money will be tied up in land and cattle, not sitting in the bank."

Guy frowned. "So would these top guns cost considerably more to hire than, for example, you?"

Johnny gave a cold, tight smile. "That's not what I said. I'm an awful expensive gun to hire and the likes of Chavez couldn't afford me."

Guy raised an eyebrow. He couldn't really believe that. Yes, Peggy had certainly reacted to the name Fierro, but then girls did tend to dramatize things. He eyed Johnny curiously. "How good are you?"

Johnny laughed softly but didn't answer, seemingly intent on studying the horizon. Eventually he sucked in a breath. "No, this whole thing stinks. It ain't over. And this attack on the herd? I'd lay money that's tied in with this somehow."

Guy bowed his head, pondering Johnny's words. "Surely Father would know if there was someone behind this as well as Chavez? No." Guy shook his head decisively. "The attack on the herd was just a coincidence."

"I don't believe in coincidences," Johnny said softly. "We ain't seen an end of this. There's more trouble coming. And I want to know who's pulling the strings." He smiled icily. "And then I'll cut off the head."

There was something in the tone of his voice that sent shivers down Guy's back. It put him in mind of a wild animal lying in wait to pounce on its prey. The thought was disturbing, and he wondered just how dangerous Johnny might be. It struck him that he'd been thinking of Johnny as his long-lost little brother. But this man next to him was a stranger—a very disturbing stranger who bore no resemblance to that happy, laughing child he remembered from his past. This was a man who seemed to have no compunction about killing.

"Worrying about what I'm really like, Harvard?" Johnny's sardonic voice jerked him back to the present. A sly smile pulled at Johnny's mouth. "I warned you not to underestimate me. That would be a big mistake. And so is keeping me from my siesta." And with that Johnny tilted his hat back down over his eyes.

Guy shifted his position, trying to get comfortable. He might as well sleep, too. He would need to be at his sharpest to keep Johnny in check. But hopefully he was just imagining the worst. Johnny wouldn't do anything stupid; he was far too smart.

When they woke, the heat of the sun had gone. Guy tentatively stretched his stiff legs. Hell, it wasn't just his legs and arms that ached; his back was sore, too. What he really wanted was a long soak in a tub and a proper bed. No wonder Guthrie had stayed at home. He glanced up at the snort of laughter from Johnny.

"You look real sore, Harvard. Missing your bed? You ain't cut out for this life, you know. You'd be better off in Boston."

Guy glared. "Do you have any idea how irritating you are? You think you're so superior, but you've got a shock coming. I'll get used to this life and give you a run for your money. Brother."

Johnny just cocked an eyebrow. "We'll see, we'll see. Now, get ready because we're riding into town."

They readied the horses, and then mounted up to start the descent down to the town.

A roughly carved sign announced the town as Bitterville. The place was a sprawling mass of wooden buildings and rutted alleys. It stank too. Music and raucous laughter reverberated from a couple of saloons on the main drag. Farther down the street, lights shone out a welcome from a hotel.

Johnny slid off his horse, leading it through a narrow alleyway between two large buildings. "We'll see to the horses and go get us a room."

They found the livery stables in the maze of alleys and handed the horses over to the care of a gnarled and wizened old man with bowed legs and a hacking cough. Then, keeping in the shadows, Johnny led them toward the hotel, pausing to glance cautiously over the batwing doors into one of the saloons. Guy's feeling of unease increased as a malevolent smile crept over Johnny's face as they saw a couple of the group from the holdup drinking at the bar.

"Let's go get us that room, and then I'm going to have me some fun," Johnny said softly.

They walked into the hotel, saddlebags over their shoulders, and after securing a one dollar room, headed up the stairs.

Guy stared around the room as Johnny pushed open the door. Well, the best that could be said was that he'd seen dirtier on his journey out West. But not much. Still, it would be a place to lay their heads. He was suddenly aware of a blur of movement in his peripheral vision and a searing pain as he fell forward and the world went black.

CHAPTER SIXTEEN

He felt a slight pang of guilt as he looked down at Harvard's unconscious form sprawled across the floor. He could already see the start of an ugly bruise where the butt of his gun had smashed into the back of his brother's neck.

"Sorry, Harvard," he said softly, as he checked his gun again. "But it's better this way. Ain't no place for you in this." Leaning down, he took his brother's gun from its holster and checked it for ammunition before sliding it into his own jacket. He looked down at Harvard again. Didn't seem right to take a man's gun. But an extra gun was going to come in real handy. Yeah, it was much better this way, because he sure didn't want his brother to see Fierro in action, not at his worst. He didn't want Harvard to know quite how bad Fierro could be. He paused briefly at the door, and then stepped back into the room. Grabbing a pillow from one of the beds, he stooped and gently eased it under his brother's head. He studied Harvard's face for a moment. The man was some greenhorn. Shaking his head, he left the room, locking the door behind him.

Once outside, he turned to the business at hand, his senses on edge as he moved swiftly down the stairs and out into the street. He tuned out the normal town sounds, listening past the two badly tuned pianos from the saloons either side of him vying for patrons. The blood was coursing through his veins, giving him that buzz he always got before a showdown. It never failed to excite him and he loved the feeling. It was the aftermath he hated, when he was ashamed and disgusted with himself. Shit. Why was he thinking of that already? Just enjoy the feeling now. After all, those men deserved what they had coming. There'd been no call to kill the lookouts. It wasn't like they'd been in the middle of a range war. Then, it was part of the game to kill lookouts—it went with the territory. But this had been different; they were just moving cattle. The lookouts had been ordinary ranch hands trying to do their job, simple men with wives and kids. No, there'd been no call to kill those men and now the bastards would pay for it.

They'd broken the rules so they deserved everything Fierro had in store for them. Yeah, revenge could be real sweet. He'd focus on that. He paused in the shadow of a doorway, shutting his eyes briefly as all the nerves in his body came to life and his blood pulsed faster. He'd felt like this at the Andersson spread before killing Mendoza and Chavez. And it wasn't like he hadn't given them a chance—he'd waited for Mendoza to make his move. He'd known then how much he'd missed this thrill since he'd been taken prisoner in Mexico. And now these men were going to see some killing—they shouldn't have tangled with Fierro.

He walked toward the saloon where he'd seen the men earlier, pausing just once more in a doorway. The hairs on his neck stood on end and he could swear someone was watching him. Squinting through the dusk, he scanned the buildings around him but there didn't seem to be anyone taking even a passing interest in him. Must be losing his grip, starting to imagine things. But a man couldn't be too careful. So he stood very still in the shadows for a few minutes, watching the street. And all the time, the prospect of what lay ahead excited him. He checked his gun again and moved on slowly, his spurs jingling as he walked.

He stopped at the doorway of the saloon. Through the haze

of smoke he saw a group of rough cowhands playing poker and joshing with each other while the piano player thumped out an off-key version of some song he vaguely recognized. The men he sought stood at the bar, downing drinks like there was no tomorrow. Good. Drink made men slow and stupid. More unpredictable, but definitely slower. He smiled to himself. Yeah. He was going to have himself some fun.

He pushed open the batwing doors and stepped inside. He stood motionless with his hand hovering near his gun, a faint smile pulling at his mouth as he surveyed the room, waiting for people to notice him. It didn't take the poker players long. They stared at him, frowning, as if sensing the menace. Flexing the fingers of his gun hand, he let his glance flicker briefly over them before returning to the group standing at the bar.

The poker players pushed their chairs back. "Yeah," he said softly, "best you leave." With a scraping of chairs, they stood and sidled out, relief written all over their faces.

As he spoke, the men at the bar turned and stared at him. Recognition dawned in their eyes. Johnny smiled, and spoke softly. "Evening."

The bearded man, who seemed to be their boss, laughed sourly. "You ain't got no sense, boy. You shouldn't have come looking for us. I hear you're Sinclair's son. He won't be happy to hear you got killed because you were too dumb to leave us alone."

Johnny raised an eyebrow. "I don't think he'd lose sleep over it. But I wanted a word with the kid there." He nodded toward the ranch hand they'd taken as their supposed hostage. The kid paled, his mouth working nervously, and suddenly he went for his gun.

It was the last thing he ever did. In death there was a look of stunned surprise on his face as blood oozed from the hole in his chest. Johnny glanced around at the other men, who seemed frozen in shock. He gave them a slow smile and drawled, "So, who else wants to try me? Ain't this fun?" Spinning his gun, he returned it to its holster. "Well, what you waiting for? Anyone would think you was scared or something." He shrugged. "Meanwhile, there's the matter of my money. You see, that kinda pisses me, that you took my money. An' you know, if I find that you been spending it, hell, I'm gonna be even more pissed. So, where is it?"

The men's leader spoke. "Think a lot of yourself, don't you, Sinclair? But I reckon you're forgetting that we outnumber you." He glanced at his companions, smirking.

"Sinclair?" Johnny sighed softly. "Well, yeah, that's my old man's name. But, you know something? I've never used that name. It never really sat right with me. Most folk know me by a different name."

The bearded man grunted. "Yeah? Well, I really ain't interested . . ."

"You should be." Johnny spoke real soft.

The men laughed. "And why's that, Sinclair?"

Johnny paused, savoring the moment. "Because it's Fierro. Johnny Fierro."

The reaction was all that he hoped for. The gray-haired barkeep scuttled to the far end of the bar. And the pianist slid off his stool, easing his way behind the piano, where he was out of any line of fire. The men looked at Johnny slack-jawed; their eyes wide open now despite the booze.

The bearded fellow moved his hand slowly toward his pocket. Johnny shook his head, speaking very softly. "You better not try anything, ain't nothing gonna give me greater pleasure than blowing your brains out."

The man paled, pulling his hand away. "Give him the money," he ordered one of the other men.

"Yeah, you do that, but make it real slow." Johnny watched as another man took a wad of notes and threw them down on the table. Johnny shook his head again. "Now, you really are starting to grate on me, because that don't look like as much money as you took. Where's the rest of it?"

The men shifted uneasily. The bartender moved carefully to the other side of the bar. Johnny stared at him. "You want to leave?"

The man nodded nervously. Johnny smiled slightly. "Might be a good idea, I wouldn't want you to get caught in any cross fire."

The bartender beat a hasty retreat while the men at the bar shifted uneasily, licking their lips. "Now, where's the rest of my money? I hope you're not going to tell me you spent a pile of it already? You see, if you have, someone's gonna have to pay—in blood." Johnny sighed and shook his head, as if in sorrow. "So, who's first?" Damn but he felt great, loved the buzz, he was so good at this. Sweat was running down their faces. And one of them moved slightly, his hand going for his gun.

The smell of cordite hung in the air. Johnny smiled as he spun the smoking gun. "Well, two down, only three of you to go."

"Look, Fierro, we can only give you what money we got. We didn't know it was you when we took it." The bearded man was shaking slightly.

"Well, trouble is, you knifed two of our ranch hands. An' their wives an' kids ain't gonna be too happy about that. So you see this ain't just about the money."

"For Christ's sake, Fierro. We're sorry. They were only ranch hands, how were we to know?" The man sucked in a breath, and licked his lips.

"You killed 'em, and you're going to pay."

"What ya gonna do? Gun us down? Turn us over to the sheriff." He was begging now, his mouth working frantically.

177

Johnny just smiled and raised his gun but as he did so there was a fumbling at the doors of the saloon. He turned fractionally and saw Guy stumble in. "Johnny, what the hell is going on?"

And that was all it took for the men to go for their guns. Johnny threw himself to one side as they fired, even as the thought flashed through his head that he should have bound and gagged his brother. His stomach lurched as he saw the bearded leader leveling his gun at Guy. Johnny flung himself across, trying to block the man's field of fire even as it registered that he would almost certainly wind up dead. And then seemingly out of nowhere, a rifle shot cracked, blasting into the chest of the man.

Johnny grabbed the chance and took down another man with a rapid shot, while the remaining man hurled down his gun in terror, screaming for them to stop. Guy was swaying at the door, stunned it seemed, and propped up by a man with a rifle who winked at Johnny. "Johnny. Saw you in the street earlier. I figured you was going to have yourself some fun. Guess it's lucky I was here."

Johnny grinned at the familiar face. "Eagle! You're a sight for sore eyes. Guess I owe you one now."

Johnny glared at Guy, who stood, looking confused, reeling slightly. "What the fuck did you think you were doing, Harvard? Trying to get us both killed? I told you to stay out of it. I was dealing with this."

"And if I'd stayed out of it, they'd all be dead," his brother slurred.

Johnny glanced at the one remaining outlaw, who stood with his hands high above his head. "Yeah, maybe they would, maybe they wouldn't. But as it is, you coming in like that nearly got us both killed. You're real dumb at times."

Guy shook his head, like he was trying to wake himself up. "I told you we'd let the law handle this. That's what we agreed."

"No!" Johnny stepped up close to Harvard, forcing his brother back against the wall. "We never agreed that. Letting the law deal with them is what you wanted, what you think the old man would have wanted. It ain't my way, but I guess you think the law should deal with him now?" Johnny gestured toward the surviving man. "Would that keep you happy, Harvard? Well, seeing as you got so much faith in your laws and doing everything legal, here's your gun back. Take this fellow to the sheriff." Johnny angrily pushed the gun into Guy's hand. "Well, go on. You wanted the law to handle it. Take him."

Guy stared at the gun, like he'd never seen one before. He looked dazed and a little green, his eyes dull. "Where are you going?"

Johnny swept the pile of money off the table. "Well, Eagle here is an old friend of mine. So I reckon Sinclair owes us some beers, and then, hell, old Eagle and I might go and get ourselves fucked, courtesy of Guthrie Sinclair." And pushing the money into his jacket, he put his arm around Eagle's shoulders and left the saloon.

CHAPTER SEVENTEEN

The hotel dining room was quiet, which was just as well because Guy's head throbbed and he couldn't remember ever being as angry as he was now. He added cream to his coffee, but pushed away a plate of food that had been put in front of him by a cheerful waitress. Her voice had jarred through him, making him flinch.

He'd been up half the night talking to the sheriff. Filing reports and sorting out the tedious paperwork, while all the time his head felt as though it was going to fall off his shoulders and roll across the floor. The sheriff had been reluctant to go and find Johnny and hear about the events from him—as soon as the name Fierro was mentioned, the sheriff had paled and demanded that Guy deal with everything. Luckily, the pianist had said that each time Johnny had drawn his gun the victim had gone for his gun first. Thank God the pianist had been there . . .

Or had that been part of Johnny's plan? Had he manipulated the whole situation to ensure he had a witness who could vouch for him? Had Johnny played the scene in such a way to force the men to draw first, knowing he could beat them? What was it Johnny had said to him during their journey? Something about the law not being able to touch him? And that look he'd seen in Johnny's eyes, it had been really chilling. Oh hell, he was sure that Johnny had manipulated the whole thing. The man was too damn clever. Machiavellian didn't come close.

And right now, Guy had a splitting headache and wanted nothing more than to knock Johnny senseless. Except, of course, Johnny hadn't come back last night. When Guy had awoken in the morning, Johnny's bed hadn't been slept in. Presumably he'd gone whoring with his friend Eagle, was that the name? Yes, Johnny had called the man Eagle. And who the hell was Eagle? Another gunfighter? Certainly neither of them had seemed at all concerned by the rifle blast that virtually splattered the bearded man across the room. Guy shuddered at the memory. So much blood. It had reminded him of the battlefield and scenes he would rather blot out.

He couldn't help but wonder now if he'd been a fool. He'd really thought that he and Johnny had made some progress on this trip, but maybe Johnny had been spinning him along. Maybe nothing that Johnny had divulged during their campfire chats could be believed. It hurt to think that might be the case. But then . . . He furrowed his brow as he tried to remember the way events had played out once he had staggered into the bar. He'd come to in the hotel room, sick and disoriented, but he knew he had to find Johnny. The door had been locked so he'd yelled and banged on it. It was just luck that the housekeeper had been passing and had been able to unlock it with her key. And he vaguely remembered stumbling up the road.

Hell, he was still feeling sick and disoriented now. He shouldn't have drunk the coffee—his stomach was rebelling and he felt very queasy. If only his head would stop throbbing long enough for him to think straight. Perhaps some fresh air would help. He pushed the table away and stumbled outside, blinking in the sunlight. A soft breeze ruffled his hair and it was tempting to shut his eyes and stand still while the nausea subsided.

"Morning, Harvard."

Did Johnny always sound so damn cocky and arrogant? Guy opened his heavy eyes and peered blearily at his brother, who looked particularly pleased with himself.

"Get your prisoner to the sheriff, did you? All nice and legal? Keep the old man happy, won't it?"

Guy glared at him. "Yes, I did. No thanks to you. I was up most of the night going through the paperwork with the man. Where were you?"

"Well, Eagle and I were having ourselves a little fun and then we got ourselves laid," Johnny drawled. "Should have let me finish the job, and then you could have come with us." Johnny paused, tilted his head to one side, and looked at Guy as if considering him. "Have to say, Harvard, you don't look too good this morning. Not pretty at all. You look like you had a rough night."

Guy stared at the self-satisfied smirk on his brother's face, and felt the rage building. He couldn't remember ever meeting anyone who'd made him quite this angry. And although he was feeling far from his best, the urge was too strong. Putting all his strength behind it, he threw a massive punch at his brother's smug face. Johnny was thrown backward onto the ground, totally poleaxed.

Guy stood waiting for Johnny to come back at him, fists flying. But he didn't; he just lay there and rubbed his jaw. "Guess I had that one coming."

"Well," snapped Guy, "Come on, because there's more than that coming." And growing impatient he grabbed hold of Johnny by his jacket and thumped him again. There was a satisfying crunch as his fist connected with the side of Johnny's face.

But still Johnny didn't come back at him. "Well, come on," snarled Guy, "fight me, damn you."

"I ain't fighting you. Like I said, I had it coming." Johnny grinned and then winced slightly as he gingerly tested a tooth. "Shit, Harvard, I'll say one thing for you, you do pack a mean punch."

Guy stared at him, still angry but now feeling more frustrated than anything else. Why wouldn't his brother fight him? He was certain he'd feel a lot better if he gave Johnny a real beating.

Still rubbing his jaw, Johnny got slowly to his knees. The temptation was too much. Guy hooked him again, sending him sprawling.

Johnny glared up at him. "Had your fill now? Because you're sure as hell going to piss me off if you do that again, Harvard."

"Just fight me, damn it. And stop calling me Harvard."

"I don't want to fight you." Johnny stared down at his own fists, which were tightly clenched. "I was trying to keep you out of it, last night."

"We had a deal. I was your backup."

"No!" Johnny exploded. "We didn't have a deal. I said you could come along for the ride. You could've got us both killed. Seems like I didn't hit you hard enough. You came round way too quick, and let's face it; you nearly did get us both killed." Johnny ran his hand through his hair as if in exasperation. Then, watching Guy warily, he stumbled to his feet.

"I wanted to keep this legal, Johnny. Instead we ended up with a bloodbath." Guy was still furious. His hand was just itching to punch Johnny again.

Johnny looked at him with narrowed eyes. "It was legal. It might not suit fancy folk back in Boston, but you're out West now and everything I did was legal. They had their chance. They could have taken me. Hell, it was five to one. What more do you fucking want?"

"Rubbish. You knew you could outsmart them and outdraw them. You manipulated the whole thing. It was tantamount to . . ." Guy stopped, could have bitten his tongue off. He'd gone too far.

"Are you accusing me of murder? I ain't no back shooter.

183

Those men had their chance." Johnny's eyes were very cold now.

Guy closed his eyes briefly and shook his head slowly. "No. No, I'm not accusing you of murder. But . . . hell, Johnny, you knew you'd come out of this OK."

"Oh for God's sake, Harvard!" Johnny threw up his arms in exasperation. "Of course I didn't know. You do talk horseshit at times. I gambled, OK? I figured I might outsmart 'em but I could just as easily have wound up dead. It's what I do. You just don't get it, do you? Every gunfight is a gamble. Yeah, I'm good. Hell, I'm real good. I'm fast and I keep my cool. That's what gives me my edge." Johnny sighed. "That, and not caring if I live or die."

Guy shook his head, bewildered. "How can you not care? You've got something to live for now. You've been offered a third of pretty much the biggest ranch in New Mexico."

Johnny rubbed his forehead, as if considering how to answer. He gave a slight laugh. "You really want me to answer that?"

"Yes, I do." But even as he said it, Guy felt his stomach contract. Did he really want to know?

Johnny raised his eyebrows slightly as he looked down and scuffed at the ground with his boot. Then he looked up again. His eyes were curiously bleak. "You know, I get a real buzz out of gunfights. I love that thrill of not knowing if I'll walk away. It excites me. Makes me feel really good for a while. But later . . ." He shook his head slowly. "Hell, later, it makes me sick inside. And every man I've ever killed comes visiting at night. Every damn night. I don't never get no peace. And I'm so damn tired I really don't care if I die. But anyone who wants my reputation can damn well earn it." He shrugged his shoulders. "I mean, I know I'm a cold-hearted bastard. I know I'll wind up in hell an' all because of the killings. But I figured those men should pay for what they done to those two cowhands. It wasn't right what they did, weren't no call for it. Someone had to make sure they paid."

A wave of compassion swept over Guy. It struck him that there was far more to Johnny than a cocky and manipulative gunfighter. There was a core of justice running through his brother. But it seemed that Johnny only saw himself at his blackest. "Johnny, you could have left it to the law to deal with those men," he said gently. "You didn't need to take it on yourself to mete out justice."

Johnny gave a short laugh. "Justice? There ain't any justice in the law. Not for poor folk. Who's going to care that a couple of Mex cowhands got killed? Oh, be different if it was some rich white fellow. It's always different for them. Maybe it's different out East, maybe the law there protects poor folk, but it sure as hell don't here, not that I've ever seen. Anyhow, how you going to prove which of those men took a knife and slit their throats? No, they'd have wriggled out of it. And while the lawyers fight over it, those cowhands' wives and kids will go hungry."

"The Sinclair Ranch will make sure that they're provided for."

Johnny stared at him in disbelief. "Provided for? How you going to replace a husband or a father? And whatever money the great Guthrie Sinclair decides to hand out, how long do you think that'll last? At least the kids won't go looking for revenge now. No point in them becoming killers too." Johnny was silent for a second. "Trouble is, people like you can't even begin to imagine what life's like for poor people. It ain't your fault, I'm not saying it is, but you can't ever understand, not unless you've grown up like that. Years and years of an empty belly, being walked over, treated like dirt because you live in some shack or ain't got any shoes. And all the while, folk who've got more look down on you."

Johnny kicked at a stone on the ground, sending it hurtling

down the street. "Anyway, a few pieces of shit wound up dead. What's a few more dead men to Johnny Fierro?"

"Sounds to me, Johnny, as if it's more ghosts to haunt your dreams."

Johnny gave a short, humorless laugh. "Hell, don't make no difference, I never get any damn sleep anyway. Like I said, it's stopped those kids ever looking for revenge, so . . ." He shrugged. "Still, Harvard, you do pack one hell of a punch, I got to hand it to you."

Guy had to smile at Johnny's effort to change the subject. "I'll tell you something, brother. Never has throwing a punch felt so good! I have a hell of a headache because of you." Guy paused, remembering the events of the previous evening. There was one question he had to ask. "Why did you put a pillow under my head?"

Johnny looked affronted. "A pillow? Think I'm soft or something? Didn't do nothing of the sort. Must have been on the floor and you just fell onto it, I guess."

Guy nodded, trying to keep a straight face. "Ah, that would explain it."

Johnny kicked at another stone and then flashed Guy a sudden smile. "For what it's worth, I really was trying to keep you out of all this. Couldn't think of any other way to do it. Figured I wasn't going to talk you out of tagging along. But this was a job for professionals." Johnny glanced quickly again at Guy. "And, well, sorry about your head."

Guy couldn't bite back the smile. Maybe they were making progress after all. He furrowed his brow suddenly, remembering something else from the previous evening. He'd known there was something, hovering on the edge of his memory, and now it came flooding back. Yes, Johnny had thrown himself in front of Guy, shielding him from the bearded man. Johnny could have been killed. Would have been killed if the rifle shot hadn't taken that fellow out. "I believe I also owe you thanks for saving my life. If it hadn't been for your friend, Eagle, and his fortuitous arrival, you'd have died saving me."

Johnny shook his head and laughed dismissively. "Think I'd risk my life for you? Reckon you must be confused, Harvard. Must be that bang on the head. Why don't we go get ourselves some coffee and I'll explain to you how life is out West? Oh, and I meant to tell you, Eagle said something about heading to Cimarron. I don't know why—I kind of had my hands full of a woman at the time." Johnny smiled, his eyes lighting up at some memory from the previous evening. "Anyway, I thought maybe we should offer him a job."

Guy tilted his head. "A job? As what, exactly? A guardian angel? Marksman? Slayer of would-be assassins?"

Johnny stared at him, bemused. "What? No, I just figured we'd be a couple of hands short now and if he's between jobs, it might help him out. He's done a bit of droving. Course, he ain't the hardest of workers." Johnny grinned. "Sort of man who'll sit back and take a breather and leave you to do his share if he can get away with it. But old Eagle, well, he won't stay long. He don't like to be fenced in, but I figure we owe him. Kinda hoped you'd clear it with the old man. He might take it from you." Johnny sighed, "Hell, we both know I just piss him off."

Guy rolled his eyes. "Hardly surprising when you apparently go out of your way to irritate him. You seem set on pissing him off. But it seems to me that he owes you a debt of gratitude for at least getting most of the money back."

Johnny grinned. "Well, Eagle and I kind of took our fee out of that last night. I was in the mood for a few girls and old Eagle had a girl and then there was the beer . . ."

Guy held his hand up. "Fine. I get the picture. But I assume that there is some money left?"

"Yeah, not even Eagle and I could get through that much

money in one evening. Well, not unless I let him play poker. He is one useless poker player, way too dumb. I reckon he's even too dumb for Faro."

Guy tilted his hat forward, shielding his eyes from the sun. "Is he a gunfighter?"

Johnny started laughing. "Eagle? Hell, no. He hires out as a gun in range wars, that sort of thing. He's real handy with a rifle, but a gunfighter? No. But he's a nice enough fellow, just ain't overly bright. You can trust him not to gun you or slit your throat. Leastways, not if you're on the same side. Yeah, I like old Eagle. And, we do owe him. So, if he wants a job, will you clear it with the old man?"

Guy grinned. "I think it's the least that Sinclair Ranch can do for the man who saved our lives."

"That's how I figured it. So, how about we go find Eagle, get a cup of coffee, and maybe find a cold compress for your head. Or do you want to hit me again?"

Guy choked off a laugh. "Well, I don't want to bruise my knuckles and it does seem that you have a particularly thick head, so coffee will do just fine. As long as you're buying."

Johnny gave a snort of laughter and threw his arm round Guy's shoulders to lead him to the hotel.

CHAPTER EIGHTEEN

They were drinking coffee when Eagle joined them. His eyes were bloodshot and his dark skin mottled after the previous night's drinking. Johnny bit back a grin. Eagle never had been too good with booze. The man blamed it on his part Comanche blood; Johnny blamed it on the fact that Eagle always drank more than any man should.

Eagle scraped out a chair to join them. "You going to introduce us, Johnny?" He nodded toward Guy, who looked as rough as Eagle. Johnny pushed away the twinge of guilt. He'd hit him for the right reasons . . . Harvard should be grateful.

Johnny shrugged. "His name's Guy Sinclair."

Eagle's eyes narrowed. "Sinclair?" He shot Johnny a sharp look. "I thought you mentioned Guthrie Sinclair last night." He glanced dismissively at Guy. "This his son?"

Johnny nodded; his senses suddenly on full alert. "You heard of Guthrie Sinclair?"

Eagle jerked his head at Johnny. "May be best if you and I have a word alone."

"Nope." Johnny shook his head. "You got something to say, you say it in front of him."

Eagle bit his lip, suddenly finding the table real interesting.

"What's on your mind, Eagle?" Johnny spoke softly but he knew the man wouldn't miss the edge in his voice.

Eagle huffed in a breath. "Damn it, Johnny, you signed on with Sinclair? That's why I'm heading to Cimarron—for the range war. But I signed on for the other side."

Guy's head jerked up even as Johnny leaned forward, his mind whirling. "Chavez hired you? If so, I got bad news for you. The man's dead. I killed him."

Eagle shuffled awkwardly, seemingly reluctant to talk.

Johnny glared at him. "I took care of Chavez and Mendoza. So I reckon you're out of a job, Eagle." Or was he? He'd got that feeling back—the one that said this thing wasn't over.

"It wasn't Chavez that hired me." Eagle sighed heavily. "Man called Wallace."

"The mine owner?" Guy banged his cup down, his eyes suddenly wide open. "He made Father an offer for that land. Father thought he might want the timber."

Johnny laughed sourly, remembering Chavez's comment about mineral deposits. It was all falling into place. "I always said Chavez didn't have enough money to finance those guns he was bringing in. But this? This makes sense. Mine owners ain't never short of money. And mineral deposits are a damn sight more valuable than water—or timber. I guess Wallace has been pulling the strings all along. How the hell could Sinclair not have figured that? Damn but the man is stupid."

"Thing is, Johnny," Eagle flushed. "I don't want to fight you if you've signed on with Sinclair. Hell, I'd like to live a little longer. And I reckon I got a better chance of that if we're on the same side."

Johnny eyed Eagle thoughtfully. "Thing is, I ain't hired on with Sinclair."

Eagle frowned. "But you're here with his son . . ."

"Sinclair's my old man." Johnny sat back in his chair, pleased to see Eagle lost for words. Stunned didn't come close to describing how surprised the man looked with his mouth opening and closing like a fish out of water.

"Your old man? Sinclair is your pa? You're his son? But your name's Fierro . . ."

Johnny sighed. Eagle always was slow. But he was real handy with a rifle. And it looked like the fight wasn't over so he'd be a good man to have on your side. "Yeah, he's my old man. That's what I said. So, will you join us?"

"Johnny." Harvard sounded worried. "Father is very against hiring guns . . ."

Johnny whipped around, his eyes icy. "I don't give a fuck what the old man wants. Firstly, we owe Eagle. Secondly, we're shorthanded thanks to those bastards who killed our vaqueros. Thirdly, we're going to need a good man with a rifle. I can give you a whole long list of reasons for hiring him." Johnny paused, thinking hard. "And I'd wager that those bastards were paid by Wallace to rob us. I don't believe in coincidences."

Guy nodded slowly. "Well, I'll back you. Your instincts have been right so far." He glanced at Eagle and raised an eyebrow. "So, Eagle, will you join us?"

Eagle grinned broadly. "Don't mind if I do! I sure as hell don't want to go up against Johnny. Like I said earlier, I'd like to live a few more years."

"And we'd best get to plotting," Johnny said softly. "Wallace is going to get one hell of a shock. He's just stepped way out of his league."

Johnny eyed his two companions as they all rode out of town the next day. Eagle had gone out drinking again the previous night and looked pretty rough. Johnny had left him to it. He'd stayed with Harvard instead, who still didn't look his normal self and had slept for hours while Johnny tried to figure out how to deal with Wallace.

Johnny sighed. He still felt guilty about hitting Harvard. But hell, he'd needed to keep him out of the way somehow. Maybe if Johnny had been to some fancy school he'd have had a better idea. But probably not. At least his brother seemed to have forgiven him. He knew it was more than he deserved. Hell, he'd gotten off light with just three punches. If someone had done that to him, he wouldn't have let 'em off with three punches. He'd have shot them. But then, Harvard was the better man, whereas Fierro wasn't worth shit. Why the hell Harvard wanted to get to know him was beyond him. 'Specially after seeing the end of the fracas in the saloon. He really hadn't wanted the man to witness any of that.

Eagle was prattling away about some prank he'd played. Johnny huffed out a breath, almost envying Eagle his easy approach to life. Eagle didn't spend all his time tearing himself apart, just said whatever came into his head and never gave a thought to the past or the future. Life would be so much simpler if he could be like Eagle. But oh no, Fierro had to go brooding over everything. Worrying away at everything like a coyote with a rotting corpse. Couldn't remember a time when he hadn't been like this. Even as a kid, when his mother would tell him to make himself scarce for a few days, he used to sit at his little hideout in the desert and worry over things. Shit, here he was, worrying about his worrying. Loco or what? Maybe that was it. Maybe he was just crazy. Look at his ammunition. Now that wasn't normal. Then there were the knives. How many knives did a man need? Most men would be content with one, but no, not him. Kept two in his boot, and often another in his jacket. But hell, you could only throw one.

He looked across at Harvard. The man still looked very pale. And he was riding with his face sort of creased up, like he had a real bad headache. He felt another stab of guilt. He'd really miscalculated on this one. Screwed up. He never had been any good at dealing with people. Like not knowing what to say to make things right. Well, leastways he could maybe shut old Eagle up. The man's voice grated after a while, and he'd bet it was grating on Harvard.

"Hey, Eagle, give it a rest will you. Just want to enjoy the peace and quiet. Be little enough of it when we get back to the ranch."

"Whoooeeeee, Johnny boy, still can't believe you got a pa who owns a big place like that." Eagle shook his head, laughing.

Johnny just smiled slightly and nodded. Luckily Eagle took the hint and settled back in his saddle. Out of the corner of his eye, Johnny noticed Harvard sigh with relief. Yeah, old Eagle could sure irritate a man.

They rode in silence for a few miles. And it was a whole lot more restful. In the distance he could see the outline of the mountains by the ranch. They'd be back tomorrow. Without the herd their progress was much faster, even allowing for not traveling too fast because of Harvard's headache. Trouble was he couldn't figure how to play it with the old man when they got back. He was furious that Sinclair hadn't told them about the money. He guessed it was because the old man didn't trust Fierro. And truth was, that hurt. Fierro was a lot of things, but he sure as hell wasn't no thief. Two innocent men had died, for no good reason, just because Guthrie Sinclair hadn't trusted Fierro. He and the old man would be butting heads over this.

"Shall we make camp here? It looks like a good place, what do you think?"

Harvard's words broke into his thoughts. Johnny glanced around him. "Yeah, this'll do just fine. How you feeling?"

Harvard smiled weakly. He really did look pale. "Better than I did. But to tell the truth I'm ready to call it a day. And I think I'll sit back and let you build the fire—I believe that you still owe me."

Johnny laughed. "Reckon you're right at that. Come on, Eagle, you see to the horses and I'll do the fire."

A little later they all sat around the fire eating the rabbit that

Johnny had caught and cooked. Or leastways, he and Harvard ate, seemed like Eagle never stopped yakking. Hell, the man could talk. Still, it was damn lucky that he'd turned up at the saloon when he did. They both owed him, so if the man wanted to talk, let him. The thought had no sooner flitted through his mind when Eagle stood up, stretching. "Well, boys, I'm going to go make myself a little camp somewhere."

Johnny stared at him, surprised. "Something wrong with this camp?"

Eagle grinned. "No offense, Johnny boy, but a man can't get a decent night's sleep with you yelling and hollering. You forget, I've shared camp with you in range wars and boy, I sure as hell didn't get too much sleep. So, I'll see you both in the morning. If you want, Mr. Sinclair, you're welcome to share my camp. You'll get a better night, I don't even snore."

Harvard smiled across at the man. "Thanks, Eagle, but I'll take my chances. Someone's got to keep him out of trouble and I'm not certain he should be left alone. Not too sure I can trust him to stay out of mischief."

Eagle laughed. "Rather you than me. Ain't no one I've ever known could keep Johnny Fierro outta trouble." And with a cheerful wave he ambled off into the trees.

Johnny shook his head. "I'd forgotten how that man talks. Made my head feel like it was going to drop off earlier."

His brother raised an eyebrow. "Now you know how I'm feeling."

"Ain't apologizing again. Just hope I knocked some sense into you." Johnny grinned as he spoke.

"Will you answer a question? There is something I'm very curious about. And I reckon you owe me at the moment, so I might as well play my advantage."

Johnny eyed him warily. "Depends on the question."

"I just can't help wondering when you got your first gun?"

Johnny stared at the fire. The charred remains of the rabbit lay in the embers. He threw some more sticks on and watched the flames catch on the dry wood and go licking skywards. The sun was dying in the west, going out in a blaze of colors. More colors than he could even put names to. Made him think of peaches and apricots, when they got so ripe that their skins split and they dripped their juice down his chin. He felt his brother's steady gaze on him, waiting for his answer. Brother . . . He still couldn't figure that. And he couldn't figure why he liked the man.

Johnny sighed. "Does it really matter?"

"No. But I'm curious. You're so fast. Hard to believe anyone can draw a gun that fast. And that puzzles me. So, really, how old were you?"

Johnny sighed. Ran his fingers through his hair. "About nine, I guess."

He heard Harvard's sharp intake of breath. Then a long silence.

"You got a problem with that?" Figured old Harvard was thinking that he'd been bad from the word go. And he probably wasn't far wrong. "Wonder where you got yourself such a shit brother?" He said the words lightly, but his gut clenched as he waited for the answer.

"Why do you think I would think that?" Harvard's voice sounded gentle. "I'm just amazed you were so young. At nine I was lining up toy soldiers in battle formations, and any guns were most definitely toys. How on earth did you get it?"

It was odd but he didn't sound disgusted, only curious. Shocked like, but curious and he didn't sound like he was judging him.

"When my mother had men in, some of them, well, she'd tell me to get lost for a few days. Sometimes it was better that I wasn't around." Johnny fell silent. Better not to be around. That was putting it mildly. Shit, don't go there. Don't even think about what those men did.

"Anyway, I had a hideout in the desert. Used to go there to be away from people. Most folk in those towns didn't like breeds, 'specially a whore's breed. So it was easier just to go off on my own for a few days."

"What did you do out there? It must have gotten kind of scary out there at night."

"Used to it." Johnny shrugged. It had been a hell of a lot more scary to stay around some of Mama's men. He shook himself slightly, trying to block out the memories. "Anyhow, this one time, I was in the desert and I found this fellow and his horse. Guess they'd been dead a while judging by the state of them. Looked like the horse had fallen and the man must have banged his head or something. Maybe he'd broken his neck. But they sure were dead and stinking.

"So I just sat nearby staring at them. Watching the flies on 'em and the vultures overhead. And I was staring at his saddlebags, wondering if maybe there was any food in them. But I couldn't stop thinking about his gun either."

He kicked the fire with his foot and threw some more sticks on, all the time feeling Harvard's eyes watching him, looking kinda serious.

"See, all I ever wanted was to be a pistolero, the greatest pistolero . . ." Johnny shook his head. God only knew what Harvard would say if he admitted how much he'd wanted to hunt down their old man and kill him. "And so, there I was looking at this man and his gun, thinking how was I ever going to become a great pistolero without a gun. Seemed the sooner I started practicing, the better. Anyway, I opened up the saddlebags to look for some food, and shit, couldn't believe what I found. Money. Lots of it. Piles of notes, all tied in bundles. I figured he must be really rich. He was a gringo and back then I thought all gringos were rich. Never occurred to me that he'd probably robbed a bank or a stage."

He grinned as he remembered his amazement. "So, I figured if he was so rich, people were bound to come looking for him. There was some jerky in the bags so I had some of that. And then I did up the bags real tight to make sure none of the money could blow away so it would all be there for them."

"You didn't think to take any?" His brother sounded amazed.

"No. Ain't a thief. Only thing I ever stole was a little food here and there. My mother used to send me out to steal food if she'd spent all our money on tequila, but I never stole anything else. But hell, I just sat there, munching on my jerky, looking at that damn gun belt around his hips. And then I got to thinking that by the time anyone found him, the gun would have seized up, gone rusty, and be no use to anyone. And I figured his family would be so glad to find him and all the money safe, they wouldn't care about his gun. So, I set about trying to get his holster off him. When I pulled it away he kind of broke up a bit, which made me puke." Johnny shook his head slowly. "God knows how long he'd been there. Anyway, I got the holster and the gun. And then I searched his saddlebags for extra ammunition and took it all back to my camp."

"What did you do then?" Harvard sounded real interested now.

"Tried to figure out how the gun worked. It was one of those old Colt Dragoon models and damn heavy. Not like this little beauty," he patted his modified Colt Army revolver. "Anyways, I was lucky I didn't blow my balls off. Damn gun went off and scared the shit out of me. Then I made a hole in the belt so I could make it small enough to fit me, because I wanted to practice drawing. And boy did I practice—for hours and hours. Only drawing the gun, not firing it. Then I set up some old cans and practiced shooting at them. But then I used the gun without drawing it, which is actually the right way to start. I didn't know that, all I worried about was not wasting ammunition, figured if I tried to draw and fire I might waste some. I was scared it'd run out and I didn't know how I'd replace it so I had to make it last.

"I practiced drawing for days until I was so damn hungry I had to go home. Before I went I wrapped up the gun real careful, and hid it away to keep it dry and where no one could find it. I used to go back and practice drawing whenever I needed to make myself scarce. And if I earned any money, I'd buy more powder and caps—always at the far end of town—say I was running an errand for someone so they wouldn't question why I needed them. Used to go without food to make sure I could buy ammunition for that gun, so as I could keep practicing. I was skinny anyway, but shit, I got even skinnier then, I reckon."

He kicked the fire with his boot, smiling as he remembered how the gun had ruled his life. "I used to sleep out there with that gun in my arms. Like I guess some kids will cuddle a blanket or something, I had that gun. I loved it. Made me feel safe too. As long as I knew I'd got that gun, I felt safe. When Mama decided we were moving on somewhere, I'd run off to get the gun and hide it somewhere in our stuff where she wouldn't find it. And first thing I'd do in a new town was work out where I could get ammunition and go find a hiding place for that gun."

"I can't even begin to imagine what your life was really like." Harvard shook his head. "I'm really sorry, Johnny."

Johnny stared at him, puzzled. "What are you sorry about?"

"What do you mean, what am I sorry about? I had such an easy life and you had it so tough."

"Ain't your fault. Hell, we all get dealt our cards; that's life." He shrugged, still puzzled as to why Harvard seemed so bothered. Didn't think he'd ever be able to figure the man.

Strange to think they were brothers. He kicked at the fire again. The flames had died away leaving just the glowing embers but there was little warmth in them. He shivered. The sun had long gone and the night air was chill. How many nights had he spent like this camped out by the remains of a fire wishing he was somewhere warm?

"Johnny, when we get back, let me handle things with Father." His brother's voice was quiet. "Trust me on this at least. I can handle this, and believe me, I'm not going to let him off lightly over why he didn't tell us about the money. And I certainly won't be letting go of the fact that two men died because of his omission. I'll clear things with him about Eagle joining us too. But let me do this, please."

Johnny was silent. Harvard did have a way with words. He could imagine the man could demolish the old man with some clever words, all strung together right. Whereas he knew he'd lose his temper with the old man, handle it wrong more than likely. And hell, he did owe Harvard.

He nodded slowly. "How you going to explain the fracas in the saloon?"

"Trust me, I'll handle it. Please, we do things my way over this." Harvard smiled suddenly. "Let's just say, brother, you're along for the ride."

CHAPTER NINETEEN

It was odd but he felt relieved. He really hadn't wanted a fight with the old man, though why he felt like that was a puzzle. Normally he relished a fight, and this would have been the perfect opportunity to push his father into drawing his gun. And then Fierro could kill him . . . And after all, that was why he'd first made the journey to Cimarron—to kill his father. The money hadn't really mattered. But now he figured he could sit back and let old Harvard deal with him. He suspected that Harvard needed to do something to prove he was as much a man as Fierro. But hell, everyone had different talents; it was simply that he was good with a gun. Well, old Harvard was good with words, so it seemed only fair to let him tackle the old man. Yeah. That explained why he'd agreed to Harvard's suggestion. It wasn't because maybe he didn't want to kill his father.

As long as Harvard was going to be tough. And somehow, Johnny had the feeling that he would be, and not just because he had a point to prove. Seemed Harvard really was mad at the old man. Hell, they could all have been killed. That would have pissed off Guthrie Sinclair. He'd have been left without his segundo. Johnny suspected that the man would have missed Alonso more than his two sons.

"Good morning."

Harvard's voice jerked him from his thoughts.

"You will doubtless be relieved to know that my head is feeling somewhat better this morning. It feels as though it is less inclined to sever itself from my neck and part company from the rest of me."

Sometimes, he wondered what language Harvard was talking. "What?"

"I mean my headache's better."

Johnny rolled his eyes. "Oh. Good. Well, yeah, I'm real pleased to hear that."

"I had rather assumed that you were still consumed with guilt about your unprovoked assault on my person. I thought you would like a progress report on my condition." His brother sounded very smug.

Johnny stared at him. Why couldn't the man just speak normal, like everyone else? Johnny clambered stiffly to his feet. "I guess we'd better find Eagle and push on."

Guy nodded. "I'm looking forward to my talk with our esteemed father." He grinned across at Johnny, as he bent to gather up his bedroll. "And don't worry. I won't let him off lightly."

Johnny stretched and gingerly tried to roll his shoulders. It would be good to sleep in a bed again. Shit. He really was getting soft. Or old. He was tying his bedroll onto the saddle when Eagle appeared in their clearing, and for once the man looked ready to ride. Johnny sometimes felt that Eagle was too lazy to even get himself on his horse. Still, he'd prove his worth in the fight that lay ahead. No way was Wallace going to win.

He was puzzled, though, as to why he cared so much about beating Wallace. OK, so his father had offered him a piece of the Sinclair spread, but he didn't believe the man would follow through on it. More likely as soon as the fight was done he'd want Fierro gone. People always wanted Fierro gone once he'd done their dirty work. Why should his father be any different? Hell, Fierro was trouble and the old man knew that. Seemed it was only Harvard who couldn't grasp how much trouble Fierro

201

could be. He smiled to himself as he swung himself up into the saddle. No one had ever believed in him before, but old Harvard, despite everything, well, seemed he had faith. It was kinda nice. He knew he didn't deserve it, but it was still good.

They kept up a brisk pace now that Harvard's head was better, stopping occasionally to rest the horses. But it seemed like even the horses knew that home was close and put on an extra spurt of energy. He loved this, riding free, smelling the sage, and no one ordering him around. This was the life he was used to. And yet, here he was considering a life of backbreaking hard work. And orders. Lots of orders if the old man made good on his promise. But he wouldn't make good, would he? Sinclair had thrown him and his mother out. Hadn't he? With a grunt of irritation he shook his head. Shit, there he went again, worrying at things. Damn it, enjoy the ride, Fierro.

He could see his mountain now, standing out in sharp relief against the purple backdrop. One mountain among a load of mountains but it pulled at him and he didn't know why. But each time he looked at it he felt good, like he belonged with it. Shit, he must be loco.

He was looking forward to seeing Harvard tackle the old man over the money; he had a feeling that might be quite a show. Even though he knew he probably wouldn't understand half the words the man used. Still, it'd be fun to see the old man's reaction. Bet he'd understand all those fancy words.

Approaching the ranch, Johnny could see the hands going about their chores, including the ones who'd been on the drive. Shit. They obviously hadn't gone on as instructed to check the farthest fence lines. Alonso had ignored Harvard's orders. Bet he just couldn't wait to get back to complain to the patron about Fierro. Son of a bitch.

He looked across at Guy, who was riding next to him. Yeah, he'd seen it too. The man's jaw had clenched, and his face looked harder now. Johnny grinned to himself. He was going to enjoy watching this showdown. He'd just make sure to steer clear of the cross fire. Hell, he was just along for the ride.

He pointed out the bunkhouse to Eagle and sent him over to introduce himself to the men. As he turned back to ride on with Guy, he spotted the old man standing outside the hacienda, watching them ride in. His face was like thunder. Yep. Harvard was welcome to this one.

Sinclair stood with his hands on his hips, his head thrust forward, looking like a grizzly. "Well? What the hell have you two got to say for yourselves?"

Guy glanced across at Johnny as they slid off their horses. "Don't forget, Johnny, this one's my fight."

Johnny grinned. "Believe me, Harvard, you're welcome. I'm going to sit back and enjoy the show."

"Sir." Harvard stepped toward the old man. "I believe we have something to discuss. Inside."

"Damn right, we have something to discuss." The man turned and strode into the house. He poured himself a large drink before turning to glare at them. "I told you two to follow Alonso's orders. But no, that would be too easy. Instead I hear that Alonso was insulted, threatened with a gun—and no guesses as to who threatened him. And then the two of you ride off and get involved in a bloodbath in a saloon. And you should know better, Guy, with your background, than to be led astray by your irresponsible brother."

He'd always known that the old man would turn this on him. He stared at the floor, bit at his lip, and kicked at the rug. He had to keep a lid on his temper. Just leave it to old Harvard.

Guy slammed his hat down on the desk. "My irresponsible brother? My irresponsible brother? If anyone is guilty here of irresponsible behavior, it's you. You neglected to tell us that we were carrying a large sum of money. You treated us as if we were nothing more than lackeys to do your bidding. You expected us to kowtow to your segundo. It is your behavior that culminated in two good men being killed as a direct result of your arrogance and high-handedness. Two men with wives and children.

"We thought this was a straightforward job of moving cattle. The only man smart enough to sense the danger was Johnny. He was convinced we were being followed. But because of your inability to trust us with the knowledge that we had that money with us, I, to my eternal regret, failed to take any account of Johnny's misgivings. And if Alonso's feelings were hurt, well, quite frankly, I really don't care."

"I wasn't to know . . ."

"Sir, I haven't finished yet." Harvard sounded cold as ice. "Johnny acted in the best interests of the men to find out as quickly as possible how much Alonso knew. I absolutely supported his actions. I believe you owe both Johnny and me an explanation as to why you didn't see fit to entrust us with the knowledge that we were carrying the money. We also expect, as we believe it is our money too, to be told for what purpose the money was there. And furthermore, we expect Sinclair to make provision for the wives and families of those two ranch hands."

The old man was turning a real interesting shade of purple. "I don't have to inform you of every decision I make. You were quick enough to accept a share of 150,000 acres—but until you gain some experience, I call the tune."

"By calling the tune, I take that to mean that in a dispute, you have the final say. It is not an unreasonable condition given your years of experience. However, a dispute would imply that all of the partners discuss possible issues. Here, you have blatantly neglected to consult either Johnny or myself. And whether you call the tune or not, it is still our money too. And quite frankly, the ranch was not the reason I chose to stay. I could make considerably more money from my family holdings in Boston."

"I bet it's the reason he's still hanging around." The old man gestured at Johnny, who stared back impassively. He was not going to rise to the bait.

"I feel that speculation about Johnny's motivation for being here is simply a diversionary tactic to deflect our attention from the main issue here, which is the matter of your irresponsible action."

Boy, Harvard could sound real smooth.

"So, why were we carrying the money, what was it for, and why did you neglect to tell us about it?"

The old man banged his fist down on the desk. "It was simply cash for a rancher I do business with, who doesn't like bank drafts. Alonso was to deliver the cash and arrange to collect a couple of bulls I wanted to purchase, together with a deed to a small parcel of land he and I had agreed on that has a good watering hole. Satisfied?"

"You neglected to discuss either the transaction or its conclusion. Why?"

Johnny stared impassively at the old man, watching the vein pulsing on the side of the man's head. Any minute now it would burst.

"I forgot, damn it. I forgot. It was that simple. With your brother and his damn gunfight before you left, it put the business side of the drive out of my head. There was the little matter of your brother gunning down Chavez and his shootist. Which leads us to the gun battle in Bitterville. I've heard all about it. The sheriff wired here to check up on the two of you. Why the hell didn't you leave it to the law to deal with? My God, four dead men. And I can guess who was to blame for that."

"I think it would be more appropriate to keep your concerns

205

for the two ranch hands we lost. Johnny and I were endeavoring to recover the stolen money. We acted as a team, and if those men chose to start a gunfight, that is hardly our fault. You surely don't believe that Johnny and I would be so foolish as to look for trouble with five men?"

Johnny looked quickly down at the floor, biting his lip and choking back a laugh. He had to hand it to Harvard, the man really had the upper hand here. And it even sounded believable too.

"Johnny and I are not fools. We were being totally responsible. We gave the men very specific orders about their next duties. Orders that Alonso apparently chose to ignore. It might be more to the point if you reminded him that Johnny and I are your sons and expect to be equal partners in this ranch, and therefore, inexperienced or not, entitled to have our instructions obeyed. Johnny and I jointly made a decision to pursue those men, bring them to justice, and retrieve our money, which is precisely what we did."

Johnny took the remainder of the money out of his jacket pocket and threw it down on the desk.

Harvard nodded to him in acknowledgment. "Unfortunately, the thieves spent some of the money before Johnny and I caught up with them, but at least we have something to bring back. No thanks to you."

"That's not the way I heard things went in that saloon . . ."

Harvard narrowed his eyes and took a step forward. "I really don't care what you heard. I was there and you weren't. Are you calling me a liar?"

The old man huffed at that, strode across the room, and poured himself another whiskey.

"Good," said Guy, sounding real smooth. "Now, there remains the fact that even if you forgot to tell Johnny and me that we were carrying the money, which I hope we really can attribute to lethargy or absentmindedness rather than strategy, you also neglected to tell us when you originally agreed to the deal. There is also the matter of the two men's families. What are you proposing to do for them?"

"They will be taken care of."

"How?" asked Guy. "How do you propose to replace husbands or fathers?"

Johnny permitted a ghost of a smile to himself as he heard the echo of his own words.

"I can't replace husbands or fathers as you damn well know. But I've already assured their widows that they can continue to live in their houses, and they will receive their husbands' pay each week. Sinclair Ranch will meet all the children's schooling fees as well."

Johnny smothered an exclamation of surprise. It was the right thing to do, but somehow he hadn't expected the old man to do it. He looked at his father curiously. He couldn't figure this man. Most of the time he seemed a cold-hearted bastard but just occasionally there was a glimmer of a more decent man inside. He didn't blame him for assuming that Johnny had been behind the latest gun battle. After all, he had been behind it and the old man knew it. But leastways he'd already done the right thing by the families of the two dead men. Said something about the man, seemed there was something buried under that cold exterior. He sure took some figuring.

"I think that I can speak for Johnny when I say that does seem an acceptable settlement, although I trust it can be arranged for someone to do any heavy work that needs doing at any time for the widows."

The old man glared. "That goes without saying."

"And would you like to explain why you neglected to even tell us about your business deal? Contrary to what you seem to think, I can assure you that in a proper legal partnership, which is what you have proposed for the three of us, you are not permitted to make major financial decisions without full consultation with your partners, Johnny and me."

The old man clenched his jaw. "I think, Guy, you have made your point." He swung round and gestured at Johnny. "Don't you have anything to say? Thought you'd be only to keen to join this discussion."

Johnny narrowed his eyes slightly. "Nope."

"Sir, you haven't answered my question."

Any second that vein would burst right outta the old man's head. Boy, it was really pulsing now.

"As I said, Guy, you have more than made your point. I am used to running things my way here, damn it. I've built this place up from nothing. I have sweated my guts out building it into what it is today, so, no, I didn't bother to consult you. Didn't even consider it. I've been running this ranch since before you were born. Old habits die hard. Ask your brother, he seems to have enough trouble with his old habits. He should understand."

Johnny bit his lip again, determined not to react. He wouldn't give the old man the satisfaction. But he wasn't surprised. Knew his father would have to take a potshot at Fierro. It was only a matter of time before the old man would throw him out—probably as soon as the fight with Wallace was over. And hell, Harvard hadn't even told him about that part yet.

"Well, it seems to me that you owe us some apologies rather than making cutting remarks at Johnny in a feeble effort to deflect our attention from the main issues. You proposed making us full partners in this ranch, and believe me, Johnny and I intend to exercise our legal rights to the full. We'll more than pull our weight but we expect to be treated as equals."

"I will consult you in the future, but I won't be treating you as equals until such time as you understand the full workings of this ranch. This isn't a Boston boardroom you're in now."

"And I'll remind you, sir, that neither is this your personal domain now."

The two men stood facing each other. The old man still looked like an angry bear and Harvard looked all calm and real superior, and like he'd stumbled over a rotting coyote. Boy, he was glad he'd left this one to his brother. Johnny knew if he'd handled it himself he probably would have ended up thumping the old man.

The old man snorted. Hell, he even sounded like a grizzly. Johnny grinned to himself, yeah, he was glad he'd let Harvard handle this one.

"So, I take it that we do have an understanding now?" Guy sounded as smooth as polished glass.

The old man gave him a grudging nod and stomped to the door. But he turned and looked hard at Johnny. "You and I will discuss your gunfights later. That subject isn't closed."

"I haven't finished yet." Harvard's cool voice stopped the old man in his tracks.

Sinclair turned slowly to face them, the nerve pulsing harder. "I think you've said enough, Guy."

Harvard shook his head. "Unfortunately, no. I haven't told you the rest of our news. And trust me, you're going to want to hear about this."

CHAPTER TWENTY

Guthrie stepped back into the room, throwing a sour glance at Johnny. "What? Don't tell me he's killed somebody else?"

Guy flinched, looking swiftly at Johnny, but his brother's face might have been a mask. Johnny showed no reaction to their father's insult. Guy took a deep breath, and counted to ten under his breath. It seemed he was going to need all the patience he could muster. "Wallace. That's who we need to discuss."

His father frowned. "Wallace? You mean the mine owner out near Elizabethtown?"

"The very same." Guy motioned toward a chair. "I suggest you sit down. I think you might find you need to." He strode to the liquor cabinet and poured two more glasses of malt, and handed one to Johnny before topping up their father's glass. He took a swift swallow before speaking. "Our troubles are far from over. Johnny and I have discovered that Chavez was not the driving force behind this range war. Wallace is."

His father jerked forward, spilling some of his drink. "Wallace? I don't believe it! Wallace is a respectable business-man. I've known him for years. The very idea of him being involved in planning a range war is ludicrous. He's not the sort of man to go hiring guns."

"He made you an offer for Andersson's land." Guy spoke calmly, but he suspected his father was not going to be easy to convince.

Guthrie grunted dismissively. "Yes, but that was purely a

business proposition because of the timber. I turned it down. And that was the end of it."

"Chavez mentioned mineral deposits." Johnny spoke very softly. "Water rights and mineral deposits. Why should he be interested in them?"

His father threw Johnny a contemptuous look. "And that's what you're basing this ridiculous assertion on? That Chavez mentioned mineral deposits? It doesn't mean a thing. And it certainly doesn't mean that Wallace had any involvement in this. It's over. When you killed Chavez it ended. But maybe you're disappointed! Maybe you'd like a full-blown range war . . ."

"You know fuck all about what I'd like." Johnny was on his feet, his fists clenched.

"Be quiet. Both of you," Guy snapped. "You might be interested to know, before you start flinging accusations around," he gave his father a steely eyed look. "That when Johnny and I were in Bitterville, we met an old acquaintance of Johnny's who had signed on with Wallace."

"An acquaintance of Johnny's?" There was a note of disbelief and a great deal of condescension in his father's voice. "Well, I can guess what line of work he's in. And you believe that sort of man? Oddly, Guy, shootists and such people are not the most reliable informants."

"The man in question saved our lives in the shootout in the saloon," Guy said icily. "When we talked later, he told us he was heading to Cimarron because he'd signed on for a range war. We assumed he meant with Chavez. He then told us it was with Wallace and I believe him. What reason would he have to invent that? Anyway, the result is he's now joined us—he seemed reluctant to side against Johnny. We were going to offer him a job droving, because we owed him, but when we found out that he was going to join the range war that Wallace is planning, it seemed sensible to get him on our side. And . . ." Guy held up his hand to stop his father, before he could jump in again. "And before you start on the topic of not hiring guns, the decision is already made. He's good with a rifle; he's not a shootist. And he seems like a good man to have around. Johnny, would you agree?"

Johnny nodded. "Yeah, Eagle's honest. Surprising, ain't it, for someone in my line of work?" Johnny's voice dripped with sarcasm. "He'll give his all to whoever's paying him. And that's us. And I trust him." Johnny flexed his fingers, staring at their father defiantly, obviously waiting for the man to jump down his throat. Guy sighed softly. It seemed that the two of them were determined to fight. He'd try to play peacekeeper—but he wouldn't bet on the chances of success.

"That you trust him does not engender confidence in me," Guthrie snapped. "I do not share your apparent faith in a man who accepts money to kill people."

"It's what soldiers do. That's all people like Eagle are— soldiers. Like old Harvard there was a soldier. What's the difference?" There was a challenge in the question.

"What's the difference?" Guthrie rose from his chair, shaking his head. "What's the difference? You cannot compare men who fight for an ideal or their country, with common mercenaries who fight for the highest bidder. And," Guthrie was turning a mottled shade of red. "Soldiers such as your brother had the benefit of the law on their side. I don't believe we can accord the same niceties to people like your friend Eagle."

"Or to people like me? It's people like him and me who sort out the dirty work for men like you. It was me who got your fucking money back." Johnny's voice was low, with an air of menace to it that made the hairs on Guy's neck stand on end. And the fingers of his brother's gun hand were tapping an incessant rhythm against his thigh as if they had a life of their own.

Johnny stepped forward, standing just inches from their

father. "So come on. Why don't you just say what you really think of me, Old Man? I know you've been itching to, ever since I arrived. Or haven't you got the guts to say it?"

Guthrie shook his head, looking at Johnny scathingly. "I know you're a killer. Whether there's more to you than that, God only knows."

Guy huffed out a sigh. He'd been right—they were determined to fight. They were as bad as each other. And any hopes of keeping the peace had gone up in flames.

The rhythm from Johnny's fingers was faster now, almost frenetic. But suddenly Johnny swung away. "Think what you damn well like. I've had enough of all this shit." Johnny strode to the door before turning and flinging his arm up to point at Guy. "But maybe you should listen to your blue-eyed boy there, because you got trouble coming, Old Man. You're going to end up with a bullet in the gut. And it'll serve you right."

"Johnny . . ." Guy wasn't quick enough. Everything in the room shook as Johnny slammed the door shut behind him. Guy glared at Guthrie. "Well, that went well! Why did you have to speak to him like that? Are you trying to make him leave?"

Guthrie snorted as he poured himself another slug of whiskey. "You're new to all of this and you've a lot to learn about the West, Guy. Men like your brother are holding it back. I want this to become a civilized place, a place where gunmen don't belong. But as long as nobody challenges their way, nothing will change. We need law here, not hired guns."

Guy perched on the edge of the desk. "I appreciate that things need to change, and I have no doubt that they will. But at the moment we're facing lawlessness and it seems to me that the only way to deal with it is to use whatever means are at our disposal. And in this instance it would be hiring gunmen—the same way that Wallace is."

Guthrie shook his head, sitting back down. "You're wrong

about Wallace. I've known him for years. I know he's not the sort of man to use those methods. Sure, he wanted to buy Steen's land, but when I said no, he didn't make an issue of it. He's a law-abiding citizen. He employs a lot of men up around Elizabethtown. The man is a friend of the governor. He gives money to numerous good causes. I've met him at various functions over the years. Take it from me; he would never be involved in anything underhand or dishonest."

Guy raised his eyebrows. He could think of more than one supposedly law-abiding citizen in Boston who'd proved to be less than honest. "Well, why would Eagle claim to have been hired by him then?"

Guthrie shrugged. "Guy, the man is, by his own admission, the sort of man who hires out his gun. That sort of man can never be trusted. They have no sense of honor. They're not the sort of men whose word you can lend any credence to. Believe me, I know what men like this man Eagle are like. I've seen enough of them over the years. And nothing they say can ever be believed. Doubtless he has his own reasons for wanting to stir up trouble."

Guy frowned. He couldn't think of a single reason why Eagle would lie to them. He'd seemed a straightforward sort of man. He'd obviously been pleased to see Johnny. He'd been quick enough to change side, but that was presumably out of loyalty to Johnny. Or fear of Johnny.

Guy paced to the window and stared out at the main corral. Johnny was intimidating and very dangerous, of that he had no doubt. He blanched, recalling the total lack of emotion shown by Johnny or Eagle over the men they killed in Bitterville. But then, Johnny had been determined to exact revenge for the deaths of the vaqueros. He'd risked his life taking on the men in the saloon. That showed he was a man with a sense of justice. He glanced around at his father. "And do you feel the same way about Johnny as you do about Eagle?"

His father didn't answer at first. Instead he stared into his glass as if hoping to find an answer there. "I don't know." Guthrie sighed. "I really don't know what to think of him. But he's done nothing to give me confidence in him."

Guy could understand that. Johnny had done nothing to endear himself to their father. He'd been confrontational since the moment he'd arrived, although Guy was still uncertain as to why Johnny had been so aggressive. "He risked his life getting your money back," Guy said softly. "He was incensed over the deaths of our two vaqueros. I think there's a good man under that rough exterior."

"That's what you want to believe. I can't say that I share the same opinion." Guthrie leaned back in his chair, stretching his legs out. "He's trouble, Guy, and the sooner you admit that the better. Even if he is, as you assert, a good man, trouble will follow him around. A gunfighter as notorious as him attracts trouble. It's why I chose not to contact him. He's grown into someone I have no use for."

Guy jerked his head around. "No use for? He's your son, for heaven's sake. And me? Do you have use for me?" The words were out before he could stop them. He'd suspected that his father had only been so insistent he should return home when the threat of a range war loomed, and Guthrie thought Guy's army experience would prove useful.

Guthrie waved his hand dismissively. "Don't be ridiculous, Guy. You and your brother are different as night and day. I've never had any time for shootists. Sadly, it is what your brother has become."

"But you offered him a share of this ranch, just as you offered it to me." Guy studied his father intently for a reaction, some sort of emotion. "Have you withdrawn that offer?"

His father flushed. "No. But I doubt your brother will stay.

You can see he's unsuited to this sort of life." He paused before adding sourly, "Ranching requires hard work. I suspect that is something your brother is totally unfamiliar with."

"I think you're wrong about him," said Guy softly. "But I hope to God you're not wrong about Wallace. Because if Johnny and Eagle are right, we have trouble coming. And we won't be ready for it." And even as he said the words he hoped that Johnny would stay. But on reflection, there had been something very final about the way Johnny had stormed out. What if Johnny wasn't coming back?

"I am not wrong about Wallace." Guthrie narrowed his eyes. "My judgment is sound, and far more reliable than this man, Eagle. Wallace is a good man, take it from me."

Guy sucked in a deep breath, hoping his father was right. The sound of hoofbeats caught his attention. He glanced through the window and his stomach lurched as he saw Johnny and Eagle taking off at a gallop. Both of their horses carried saddlebags and bedrolls.

CHAPTER TWENTY-ONE

"Where are we going?"

They'd reined in once they'd put some distance between themselves and the Sinclair spread. Johnny pushed his hat back and gazed back at the hacienda nestling in the valley. It sure was pretty. It was strange to think he might have been raised in that big house.

"Johnny, where are we going?" Eagle was persistent.

Johnny sighed. He should have shot Sinclair back at the house. But he couldn't do it. His hand had been itching to draw his gun and shoot him full of holes. But those voices from the past had been in his head, telling him to hear the man out, telling him there were "two sides to every story." And yet he hadn't been able to bring himself to ask the old man about the past. He should have just asked him straight out why he threw Johnny and his mother out. Why hadn't he asked? What the hell was wrong with him? Was it possible he was afraid of the answer? No. Fierro wasn't scared of nothing. But even so, it was odd, Harvard being so certain that the old man hadn't thrown them out.

"Johnny!"

He glanced at Eagle with a twinge of guilt. He owed the man an explanation. The fellow had only just gotten settled in the bunkhouse when Johnny had dragged him out, telling him they were leaving. He huffed out another sigh. "We're going to see Wallace."

Eagle leaned forward, wide-eyed, resting his hands on the saddle horn. "We're what?"

He couldn't blame the man for being surprised. "We're going to see Wallace. Just like you originally planned on doing."

Eagle opened his mouth. Then closed it. Then opened it again. Then he kind of sat with it open like he was planning on catching flies. "Wallace? But I thought I was working for Sinclair now."

Johnny bit back a grunt of irritation. It wasn't surprising that Eagle was confused. He never had been the sharpest of men. And to be fair, it wasn't like he'd explained anything to him. "Nope. You're going to sign on with Wallace—just like you figured to do when I met you in Bitterville. I'm going with you. And I'm going to sign on too."

Eagle frowned. "I know you only just met your old man, Johnny. But it don't seem right to go up against him. I wouldn't feel too good about that."

Johnny almost smiled. Eagle was a good man—even if Sinclair didn't believe it. Eagle knew right from wrong and his heart was in the right place.

"My old man don't believe Wallace is involved. He thinks you and I are talking a crock of shit. So, now you're working for me. But when we meet Wallace you don't mention being at the Sinclair place. You don't mention that I'm related to him. You don't mention Bitterville. All they need to know is we've worked together before and met up on the trail. And, I'll tell you something else," Johnny paused. "You ain't having a drink until this business is over. You talk too much when you've got a drink inside of you. You got all of that?"

Eagle chewed on his stampede string and nodded slowly. "I guess so, but I mean it, it don't sit right, you going against your family . . ."

Johnny shrugged. "Let's just say I got a plan. Trust me, OK?"

Eagle nodded slowly. "But no whiskey?" He sounded sad.

Johnny bit back a grin. "No. Not until this is over. But it won't be for long."

"What about women? If I can't have a drink, could I get me a woman? I got a real hankering for a woman." Eagle tilted his head hopefully.

Hell, the man had a point. A woman would be good. A woman was always good. And a man had needs and it always felt like he had more of those than other men. After all, if his plan went sour, this might be the last time. "Yeah, we'll stop in town before seeing Wallace."

Eagle brightened up instantly. "Well, I'll go along with that, as long as you got a plan." He shifted in the saddle, shooting a quick glance at Johnny, before examining his reins. "I got to tell you, Johnny, I wouldn't want to see your brother hurt. I kind of liked him—even though he's got a real odd way of talking."

His words were like arrows and they found their mark. Johnny bowed his head. "Yeah, he's a good fellow. Hard to believe we're brothers." He flashed a sudden grin at Eagle. "But you're right, he does talk real strange. And to tell you the truth I don't understand half of them words he uses."

Eagle laughed, and urged his horse forward. "Hell, I thought it was just that I was too dumb to figure them. Glad I ain't alone in that! Come on; let's go find us some women."

It was late by the time they arrived at the hotel in Elizabethtown where Eagle said Wallace would be hiring men. Glancing into the bar, Johnny saw five men with hard faces playing cards. It didn't take no genius to work out what they were. He thought a couple of them looked familiar, but they didn't spot him standing in the shadows at the doorway. He nodded to Eagle who sidled up to ask them where to find Wallace, and was directed to a room at the back of the hotel.

"Don't forget," Johnny said softly as they moved swiftly to the room where Wallace was reported to be, "you follow my lead. And don't talk too much. You leave this to me. And don't go getting friendly with any of the other men. I don't want you to let anything slip."

Eagle sighed loudly. "I got it, Johnny, OK. And let's face it. The men never want to get too friendly anyway, on account of me being part Indian."

That was true enough. Damn gringos always thought they were better than other folk. Johnny nodded and knocked sharply on the door. It was swung open by a burly man with a mop of yellow hair. He leveled a Colt Army revolver at them even as a look of recognition sparked in his eyes. "Fierro?"

Johnny smiled thinly. "Donner. I'm looking for Wallace."

Rip Donner's eyes narrowed a touch. "You mean, Mr. Wallace." He nodded at Eagle. "Been expecting you."

"Who is it, Donner?" A voice called from somewhere in the room, the voice of a man who was used to being the boss.

"Two guns here to see you, Mr. Wallace. One we were expecting, one we weren't." Donner motioned them into the room with his gun.

Wallace sat behind a desk, pen in hand, looking every inch the successful businessman in a fancy suit. He had the mottled face of a man who didn't get enough fresh air or exercise, and the broken veins in his nose told the story of a man who drank more than was good for him. He glanced up, surveying them with cold eyes. "Who are they, Donner?"

Donner pointed to Eagle. "This is Eagle, the rifleman we been expecting." He glared at Eagle. "Took your time, we were expecting you two days ago."

Eagle shrugged. "My horse lost a shoe. It slowed me down." Eagle pointed toward Johnny. "And I met him on the trail."

Wallace looked at Johnny. "And you are?"

"Fierro." Johnny spoke his name softly, and waited for the reaction, a hint of a smile pulling at his mouth.

"Fierro?" Wallace dropped his pen, glancing at Donner like he wanted an assurance. "Johnny Fierro?"

Johnny raised an eyebrow. "I see you've heard of me."

"We didn't send for you, Fierro." Donner had colored up, making his hair look even more yellow.

Johnny shrugged. "No, but you should have. Still, I guess anyone can make a mistake."

Wallace raised an eyebrow before glancing briefly at Eagle. "You can go and find yourself a bunk. The men have fitted out the barn behind the hotel as a temporary bunkhouse." He waited until Eagle closed the door behind him before fixing Johnny with an intent stare. "You think a lot of yourself, Fierro."

Johnny smiled, but didn't speak. He just waited for Wallace to speak again. Men always wanted to fill silences.

Wallace shifted in his seat. "You're an expensive gun to hire." It was a statement, not a question.

Johnny inclined his head. "Yeah, usually." That got the man's full attention, just like he knew it would. "But I heard you were going after Sinclair."

Wallace leaned back in his chair, swiveling around to get a better look at Fierro. "I've got a full quota. I haven't budgeted for another gun."

Johnny leaned against the door and laughed softly. "Now, I'd figure, Mr. Wallace, that you're the kind of man who likes quality. A man who wants the best. You're a man who leaves nothing to chance. And in this sort of dangerous game you're playing, if you want to guarantee success, you take the best you can get." Johnny paused. "And that's me."

Donner stepped forward, shoving his gun against Johnny's gut. "You always did think a lot of yourself, Fierro. But you

221

ain't wanted here . . ."

"Donner." Wallace's voice was like a whip crack.

Using just his fingertip, Johnny pushed Donner's gun barrel away. "Like I said, Mr. Wallace, you're a man who likes the best."

Donner's jaw was working furiously, and he turned aggressively toward Wallace. "You put me in charge, Mr. Wallace, and I don't want Fierro. We don't need him."

Wallace eyed Johnny thoughtfully, scratching his heavy jowls. "I had reckoned on Donner running this show. How would you feel about that?"

Johnny flicked his gaze over Donner. "I don't take orders from men who aren't as good as me. I'll hire on for short money, but I run things my way."

"Mr. Wallace . . ." Donner turned an even deeper shade of red.

"And why, Fierro, would a man like you be prepared to hire on for short money?" Wallace cut across Donner, silencing the man with a raised hand.

Johnny smiled coldly. "Because I want Sinclair too."

"What's your beef with Sinclair?" Wallace leaned forward, curious.

"It's personal." Johnny met Wallace's eyes, his mind working on a way to move the conversation away from Sinclair. "Maybe," Johnny nodded politely toward Donner, "we should have a little test to see who's the better man, if Donner ain't happy with taking orders from me."

The blood rushed from Donner's face and Wallace laughed sourly. "Yes, would you like to take Fierro on, Donner? Show me which of you should run this game?"

Donner swallowed hard. "You and me had a deal, Mr. Wallace, we agreed a price."

Wallace looked at Johnny and smiled thinly. "But if you run

things, Fierro, I only have to pay Donner the same rate as the others. I'll save some money."

Johnny shook his head, careful to keep the contempt from showing in his eyes. "If you agreed on a price with him, then that should stand. A deal's a deal." He noticed with a surge of satisfaction that Donner looked relieved at his answer—but the dumb devil would never get the chance to spend it if he kept pushing Fierro. And he'd lay money that Donner would keep pushing.

His meaning wasn't lost on Wallace, whose eyes hardened a touch. "But then he'd be paid more than I'd be paying you, Fierro. Now that's not exactly fair, is it?"

Johnny shrugged. "No matter. I ain't doing this for the money."

"But because it's personal?" Wallace steepled his fingers and rested his chin on them. "I promised Donner the girl when we take Sinclair's hacienda. But I suppose if you . . ."

"Girl? What girl?" Johnny glanced across at Donner. The man was sweating slightly and licking his lips.

"You promised her to me." Donner's chin jutted out.

Wallace leaned back in his chair, ignoring the interruption. "Sinclair's ward. It's her land that started this fight."

"Because it's full of gold?" Johnny kept his tone even.

Wallace narrowed his eyes. "That is no concern of yours, Fierro. Do you want the girl or not?"

Johnny shook his head slowly. "Nope."

Donner huffed out a sigh, and a laugh. "Maybe Fierro ain't the type of man who likes women."

Johnny turned his coldest look on Donner. "I like women, but if I want one, I pay."

"Very well, Donner, you can have the girl. She's of no importance." There was a note of distaste in Wallace's voice. "You will need to formulate a plan, Fierro. How much do you know about Sinclair and his spread?"

"I know he's supposed to be a friend of yours." Johnny watched Wallace for some sort of reaction, hoping to throw the man off balance. Although he suspected that Wallace would see nothing wrong in his actions. Doubtless he would justify it as business.

"I've known the man for many years." Wallace shrugged. "He's a fool. You know the type—scrupulously honest and naïve. There are lots of opportunities to make money out of this territory but he's only interested in his damn cows. I offered to buy the land and he refused. I don't give a man more than one chance. I want the land so I shall take it."

"I heard you were in partnership with a Mexican." Johnny kicked at the rug, wondering whether Wallace would admit to being involved with Chavez.

"You seem to hear a lot." Wallace shot him a suspicious look.

Johnny smiled. "I keep my ears open."

"All you need know, Fierro, is the Mexican is dead. He's out of the picture. This is my show now, and I want it finished as fast as possible. You get half of your fee now, and the rest when the job is completed." Wallace reached in his drawer and took out some notes, which he placed on the desk. "What do you have in mind?"

Johnny stepped forward and swept up the notes and stuck them inside his jacket. "Does Sinclair know you're hiring guns?" He paused as Wallace shook his head decisively. "Well, then, I reckon if this Mexican is dead, Sinclair will be relaxing. If he reckons the threat has gone, he'll send his men farther afield to catch up on the work. And that's when we'll hit him. I'll put on a good show for you. Come and watch—it'll be worth your while."

Wallace gave a snort of laughter. "I'd heard you were an arrogant bastard. But yes, I'd enjoy seeing that pompous oaf brought down. There's no place in my world for men like him. I'm in the business of making money. If you impress me I daresay there will be plenty more opportunities for you in my enterprise."

Johnny tipped his hat. "Obliged, Mr. Wallace. I can see it'll be a pleasure doing business. Now, I'll go and find myself a place in the bunkhouse."

CHAPTER TWENTY-TWO

The volume of snoring in the bunkhouse was enough to awaken the dead. And it was certainly loud enough to keep Johnny from sleeping. Instead, he lay in his bunk plotting. He'd told Wallace he had enough men. He sure as hell didn't want to cope with a whole crowd of guns. He had to move fast, before more arrived to sign on. Also, he couldn't risk anyone finding out that he was Sinclair's son. If truth be told, he didn't trust Eagle not to let that slip.

Hell, who was he kidding? If truth be told he never trusted anyone. It was how he survived. Never let anyone get close. Never give anyone any credit. The only thing a man could trust was his gun. And yet he'd talked to Harvard about stuff he'd never told anyone. Why? He shook his head, determined not to start thinking on that. He needed to concentrate on what to do next.

Whichever way he looked at this he knew that the longer he delayed, the more likely he was to fail. And he couldn't fail because of the girl and Harvard, especially the girl. The thought of what Donner would do to her made his skin crawl. And it wouldn't be just Donner; doubtless some of the other men would want a turn. He shook his head angrily. Wallace had a point: Sinclair was a damn fool. Had he really no idea of what men like Donner would do to a young girl? When this all kicked off with Chavez the old man should have sent the girl to safety. But Sinclair was either too fucking arrogant or too fucking

226

stupid. And if Johnny hadn't come along, God only knew what would have happened to her. Johnny gritted his teeth. He knew better than anyone what a bastard he was, but he'd never hurt a woman or stood by and seen one hurt. Never make war on women. That was one rule he'd always lived by. And he wasn't about to change.

How could Sinclair have failed to see through Wallace? How had Sinclair described him? A respectable businessman? He'd obviously known the man for a long time. How could he not notice that Wallace was a ruthless bastard? Johnny's jaw hardened, thinking of how dismissive Wallace had been about the girl, and how he'd leaped at the chance to wriggle out of the deal he'd reached with Donner. And how sneering he'd been about Sinclair's honesty.

Johnny sighed. He admired honesty. Sinclair might be a damn idiot but he obviously had some good qualities. Except when it came to his wife and child. He tried to push the thought away. But it never went far. It sat in the back of his mind taunting him, eating away at him. When this was over he'd have to have things out with Sinclair. He needed to know why the man had thrown Johnny and his mother out. Because, despite what Harvard had said, his mother wouldn't have lied. Harvard was just a little kid at the time and didn't know nothing.

With a grunt of irritation he swung himself from his bunk, pulled his jacket on, and headed outside for a smoke. He needed to concentrate on what lay ahead instead of dwelling on the past.

He squatted on the ground with his back against the bunkhouse and lit up a smoke, shielding the flare of the match from the breeze. He'd take a couple of men and head out early to spy on the ranch. Then, when he saw the ranch hands head out for their day's chores, he'd lead Wallace and his men over for a showdown. He'd have to take Eagle aside at some point.

Explain exactly what to do. And then he'd have to hope that Lady Luck was riding with him because his plan was crap. Couldn't even call it a plan—success depended on him being able to get Donner and Wallace so riled up that they went for their guns. It would likely work with Donner, but Wallace was an unknown. Still, it wouldn't be the first time he'd worked blind and trusted to the devil's own luck.

The most worrying bit was that he wouldn't have a chance to let Harvard know what he was planning. Although his brother probably figured he'd left for good, that could cause problems when he rode in with Donner's men. Harvard was going to think he'd sold out and joined the opposition. Shit. Hell, Harvard would probably take one look at Fierro and plug him.

He took a drag on his cigarette, exhaling slowly as he stared at the night sky. If he had any sense he'd walk away from this. Leave them all to it and not interfere. And if Sinclair got himself killed then that was a kind of justice.

He flicked the ash and it lay glowing on the ground before fading and dying.

But he didn't have any sense. And he wouldn't walk away. Soft. That was his problem. He was getting too damn soft.

Straightening up, he took one final drag on his cigarette before grinding out the stub with his heel. He might as well try and catch some sleep.

He didn't catch much. In the end he gave up trying. Just before dawn he woke Eagle and a couple of the men, telling them to ride with him to Sinclair's spread. He hated having to take the other two. If he just took Eagle, he could have sought out Harvard, explained what he was planning, but Wallace's men might get suspicious at being left behind. It was best to play things exactly as he would if he was working for Wallace.

He made a brief visit to the mining equipment storeroom to

collect what he needed, and then joined the three men. They rode in tight formation, at a ground-eating lope. The sun crept over the horizon, lighting the world with a golden glow that softened the harsh outlines of the mountains. The air was crisp and fresh, like it was brand-new. He smiled to himself. It was a beautiful day, and if everything went sour on him at least he'd picked a pretty day to die.

Eagle kept his mouth shut on the ride. And the other two men were professional. They didn't talk, or ask damn fool questions. They just accepted him as the boss and did what they were told. They slowed occasionally to give the horses a breather, but never for long. Johnny was determined that this business would be ended before nightfall—one way or another.

Eventually they reached a ridge where they had an uninterrupted view of the hacienda. His companions, Dexter and Red, together with Eagle, found a stand of trees, well out of sight of the house, and set about brewing up some welcome coffee. Johnny grabbed his saddlebags, found a sheltered spot, and threw himself on the ground, sending the loose scree pinging down the hillside. He took out a small spyglass. Propping himself up on his elbows, he trained the glass on the hacienda and studied the activity in the main corral. It looked like the hands were gathered together, getting their work assignments for the day. They were preparing a wagon, loading it with supplies. Obviously some big job was planned that involved most of the men. They'd be gone all day. It seemed life at the Sinclair spread was getting back to normal. All he could do was hope that there were a few hands left at the ranch to help out when the shooting started.

Dexter brought him a steaming mug and squatted next to him. "Anything happening down there?"

Johnny held his hand out for the mug, and swallowed a quick gulp, flinching as the hot liquid scalded his mouth. "They're loading a wagon. Looks like they're going to be heading out."

Dexter squinted in the sun, looking down at the corral. "So, what's the plan?"

"When they head out, we go get Wallace. He wants to be in on the showdown."

Dexter grunted. "That figures. Reckon the man's half crazy. He's a mean son of a bitch." He shot Johnny a shrewd look. "I warn you now, Fierro, I won't have nothing to do with hurting the girl. Donner can't wait to have a go at her—he's been bragging about it in the bunkhouse. But that don't sit right with me. Are you with him where the girl's concerned?"

Johnny flicked his gaze over Dexter before continuing to study the activity at the ranch. "Nope. I ain't with him."

Dexter huffed out a sigh. "So?"

Johnny peered through the spyglass again. "So, he won't be laying a finger on her. That's a promise." He shifted away from a stone that was digging into him. "But if you go spilling that to anyone before we get to that ranch, Dexter, I will kill you. That's a promise too."

Dexter laughed, but not like he thought anything was really funny. "I always heard you were a tough bastard. But fair enough. As long as we know where we stand."

"I don't make war on women." Johnny spoke softly as he slipped the spyglass back inside his jacket. "Yeah, I'm a tough bastard—you heard that right. And I'll kill anyone who crosses me. But I never seen no call to hurt women. That's a step too far. And any man who hurts a woman on my watch will end up wishing he wasn't never born."

Dexter nodded slowly. "Seems like you and me got something in common. Well, you're the boss on this show, so I'll follow your lead. I was thinking of quitting when Donner was put in charge. Can't stand the son of a bitch."

A smile tugged at Johnny's mouth. "Like you said, we got

something in common." He hauled himself to his feet. "Come on, I've got one last thing to do and then we'll head back to collect the men. I want this job finished today."

Dexter eyed him curiously, downing the last of his coffee. "You're in a hurry. Don't you want to wait till there's more of us? Some more fellows are supposed to get here tomorrow."

Johnny shrugged, as if he were relaxed and not wound as tight as a spring. "We don't need them. The hands are gone for the day, so let's use that to our advantage." But not all the hands had gone—he knew there were still some there. And Harvard was there. And Johnny had Eagle to watch his back.

Dexter nodded. "OK, you're the boss."

Johnny felt a twinge of guilt. Dexter seemed a decent kind and he had an honest face. He hated lying to him. But there was no way around it. Even so . . . "I'm making Eagle my second, Dexter. So, if he tells you men to do anything, I reckon it's good sense to follow his orders. And I guess you won't be following any orders that Donner tries to give you." It was the best he could do. Leastways Dexter had a chance of survival now. Maybe.

Dexter tilted his head to one side, giving him a sharp look. "Why do I get the feeling you're trying to tell me something, Fierro? Or that you're up to something? But like I said, you're the boss. I sure as hell don't think much of Donner. You can rely on me." He paused, squinting in the sunshine. "One last thing to do before we go back? What's that?"

Johnny grinned, and hefted up his saddlebags, beckoning Eagle over. "I got some sticks of dynamite from Wallace's mine supplies. I want to set up a fireworks show. I won't be long." With a brief nod at Dexter, he turned to Eagle. "You come with me."

Eagle followed him as he set off down a secluded and wooded track that ended in a small stand of aspens close to the ranch bunkhouse. There was nobody close by to catch sight of them; all of the activity was some distance away and he could work undisturbed while Eagle kept lookout. He just had to ensure that there was a direct line between the explosives and the main entrance of the house. When he'd finished packing the small sticks in a tight group, he explained his plan to Eagle. Eagle wasn't none too impressed—seemed to think they'd both wind up dead. Johnny couldn't blame him for thinking that because they probably would. It didn't really matter. He had to see Wallace and Donner defeated. He had to protect the girl and Harvard. Leastways, if he got gunned down in front of the old man, saving his precious ranch for him, there'd be a kind of justice in that. That would give the bastard something to think on.

He dragged his mind back to the job in hand, and looked searchingly at Eagle. "You clear about what you got to do?"

Eagle rolled his eyes. "It ain't too tricky, Johnny. Not exactly the best plan in the world, is it?"

Johnny grinned. "It'll have to do. Now, come on, let's get moving." And he turned and sped back to join Dexter and Red, who were waiting with the horses.

They made good time riding back and he was glad of it. He wanted to get this over. One way or another, it needed to be over.

He tethered Pistol outside Wallace's hotel, telling Dexter to get the men ready to ride. He hoped the speed of developments would throw the men off their usual game; it was the best he could hope for. He grunted in irritation. Eagle was right; this had to be the worst plan ever. Hell, it wasn't a plan—all he had going for him was his saint's medallion.

Wallace was in his office, with Donner on guard outside. Donner scowled as Johnny walked toward him. "The boss is busy. You'll have to wait."

Johnny ignored him, and tapped on the door. He didn't wait to be told to enter, just walked on in. Wallace was at his desk and he shot a look of annoyance at Johnny. "I didn't say to come in, Fierro. I'm busy."

"I came to tell you that we're ready for the show. I like to give a man his money's worth. And I did promise you some entertainment."

Wallace leaned forward with a thin smile. "Well, I'll say one thing for you—you certainly don't waste any time."

Johnny shrugged. "Sinclair is at the ranch, and his men are all out on the range. They won't be back until dark, or maybe not even until tomorrow. They took a lot of supplies."

Wallace nodded slowly. "What about Sinclair's son? Not that he's much of a rancher from what I hear. Is he there?"

"Yep. I reckon so. And no, he ain't a rancher. I hear he's from out East. Only just come home, a real greenhorn. You'll get both of them, Mr. Wallace. And that'll leave the way clear. But we need to move fast."

Wallace rose to his feet. "What exactly have you got in mind, Fierro? I'm not used to being kept in the dark by my employees."

"I promised you some entertainment and I never disappoint. It'll be quite a show." Johnny laughed softly. Wallace had a hell of a shock coming. But such was the price of greed. And Johnny had no doubt that Wallace was a greedy and ruthless man. Yeah, he deserved everything he'd got coming.

Wallace pulled his coat on. "I'm looking forward to it. I'll see you outside."

Johnny nodded briefly and turned back out of the office. "Come on, Donner," he ordered. "I want to get things moving."

The men kept in a tight group on the way to the ranch. He rode out front with Wallace and Donner, and Eagle close on his tail. When they were almost at the ranch, he signaled for the men to rein in. He leaned forward, hands resting on his saddle horn, to speak to Wallace. "We're just going to ride right on in, up to his front door, like you're paying a social visit, with a few of your employees."

Wallace frowned. "Why? What's your reasoning?"

Johnny grinned, like he was real easy about it. "Sinclair will see you ride in, and he'll come out of that big house of his to welcome you. You said yourself, he's a real innocent. He won't suspect a thing. And then you let me take him down. I promised you a show—you're going to get one."

Wallace smirked. "I'm looking forward to seeing Sinclair get what he deserves. I want to see him beg. And then he needs to be silenced—permanently. That leaves the field clear for me." He laughed. "And like I said, I need a good man for my empire, and I think you fit the bill."

His empire? Johnny bit back a laugh and tried to look suitably grateful. "Much obliged, Mr. Wallace."

Donner was unhappy. But then, Johnny knew he would be. He brought his horse in alongside Johnny. "What the hell are you up to, Fierro? This stinks. We should all gallop in together and shoot the place up. That's the way a job like this is handled."

Johnny shrugged. "You ain't subtle, Donner, that's your problem. You ain't got no . . . What's that word them Frenchies use? Finesse. That's it. You ain't got no finesse. Now I've promised Mr. Wallace a show and that's what he's going to get. But if you don't like my plan, why don't you try crowding me?" Johnny flexed the fingers of his gun hand, smiling coldly.

The man swallowed hard. "All I'm saying is it's a strange plan. That's all."

Johnny laughed softly. "Backing off, Donner? Anyone would think you were afraid to try me. Come on, why don't you make a play for that gun? Not much point in wearing it if you ain't prepared to use it."

A sheen of sweat glistened on Donner's face. "I ain't looking for a fight with you, Fierro."

Johnny leaned across and spoke real quiet, so that nobody else could hear. "Then get the fuck out of my face, Donner. We're doing things my way."

Wallace was watching them, licking his lips and breathing quicker than usual. Johnny turned swiftly away with a surge of revulsion but was not surprised that the sudden crackle of danger had excited the man. He was that type—a man who would like to watch others get hurt, just as long as there was no risk to his own precious skin.

At a leisurely walk, the men rode toward the main driveway of the hacienda. Donner reached for his gun, but Johnny shook his head at him. "No, we're going in like we've come for a visit. No guns. Yet. The only fellow with a gun out is Eagle. He can have his rifle out."

Donner muttered an oath but left his gun in its holster, while Johnny breathed a brief prayer of thanks. He sure as hell didn't want Donner with a gun ready in his hand. He could beat him on a straight draw, and that was what he was banking on.

He nodded to Wallace, signaling him to go in front, while the other riders fanned out behind. Wallace pushed his horse on to a brisker walk, sitting tall in the saddle, like he already owned the place. Probably thought it was all sewn up.

Eagle took his cue and moved in front of Johnny. The last thing they needed was Sinclair or Harvard seeing Johnny straight off and blurting something out. Dexter shot them a curious glance and edged his horse over, to ride alongside. He spoke quietly, so Johnny had to strain to hear him. "I wish you'd tell me what you're up to, Fierro. You sure got a crazy way to set up a range war. And that makes me wonder. Yes siree! Makes me wonder a lot." He jerked his head toward the other men. "Now they're too dumb or too scared to question you, but I got a sneaky feeling that you're planning something totally different for us. Just know I got your back."

Johnny ghosted a smile. Dexter was no fool. Whether he could be trusted was another matter. And he wasn't about to start trusting anyone. He inclined his head. "Let's just say I appreciate that."

The men reined in once they reached the front of the house. Johnny slid from his horse and moved to one side so that he wouldn't be too obvious to anyone standing at the door, then nodded to Wallace to step out of the saddle. Johnny figured his father would have spotted the men riding in and it would only be seconds before he came out to see what they wanted.

He was right.

The door was flung open and the old man stepped out, hesitating only briefly before nodding at Wallace. "Samuel! This is a surprise. What can I do for you?"

CHAPTER TWENTY-THREE

Johnny scanned the area between the house and the corral, noting all the places to take cover. When the shooting started he was going to need it. Johnny shook his head. He was going to be badly outnumbered, just him, Eagle, and maybe Dexter. There was really no telling which way Dexter would jump until the shooting started.

He watched his old man step toward Wallace to greet him. Damn it, did the rancher never wear a gun? And where the hell was Harvard? There was no sign of him anywhere. Johnny ducked his head as his father, with a slight frown, glanced over at the group of men behind Wallace.

"You've got a lot of men with you, Samuel. They don't look like miners." And now he could hear the first note of concern in his father's voice.

"Guthrie." Wallace paused as Harvard stepped out of the house. Damn it, he wasn't wearing a gun either. Wallace was talking again, sounding full of himself. "This is your son, is it? I heard he'd come home."

The old man nodded, turning to Harvard. "Guy, this is Samuel Wallace. We were discussing him only yesterday . . ." Harvard tensed and looked at Wallace with narrowed eyes.

"Mr. Wallace." Harvard nodded, but instead of stepping forward to shake hands, he thrust his hands into his pockets. Harvard was scanning the group of men, jerking upright, his mouth opening as he met Johnny's eyes. Johnny gave a sharp shake of his head, hoping his brother would keep quiet.

Harvard hesitated, a deep line showing between his eyes, so Johnny shook his head again, uncomfortably aware that Dexter was watching him. Eagle shifted his position, turning slightly to look at the small stand of aspens—searching for his target. He gave the tiniest of nods to Johnny. All was as they'd left it.

"Will you come inside, Samuel?" The old man sounded tense now.

"I don't think so, Guthrie." Wallace sounded very cool. "I'm afraid this is the end of the road for you. You really should have accepted my offer for that land. Since you didn't, I've taken matters into my own hands and now you've missed your chance. You wouldn't sell it, so I'm taking it."

Sinclair paled, his mouth opening and shutting before he finally found his voice. "Why? Why are you doing this, Wallace? You're a better man than this . . . Surely the timber?"

Wallace snorted. "Timber! You don't really think this is about timber, do you? The veins around Elizabethtown are running dry. I believe there's gold in Andersson's land and yours, and I intend to have it. As I said, you really should have sold it when you had the opportunity. I'd better introduce you to my new man. I've hired him to, um, how shall I put this . . . take care of unfinished business, such as yourself." Wallace turned to point Johnny out. "His name's Fierro."

Sinclair's head snapped around. "You!" He sprang forward. "What the hell are you doing here? I thought you'd cleared out. Gone for good."

Wallace cut across him. "Mr. Fierro's name is obviously familiar to you. Then I daresay you know the sort of business he's in." Wallace paused, as if Sinclair's words had just registered. "You've met Fierro already?"

"Met him?" Sinclair almost spat the words out. "Yes, I've met him. Can't believe you'd stoop to this, Wallace. Hiring Fierro?

And believe me, I know all about him—I'm ashamed to say he's my son."

Johnny flinched at the words even as Wallace swung around to look at Fierro with fury. "You're Sinclair's son? What the hell game are you playing, Fierro?"

"Now!" Johnny yelled, and Eagle swung his rifle and fired into the aspens.

"Kill him, Donner! Kill Fierro!" screamed Wallace.

Johnny went for his gun but an immense blast sent him hurtling through the air and crashing to the ground. The aspens were alight, showering fragments of burning wood, and casting a pall of smoke over everything. And even with his ears ringing and his head reeling, the thought flashed in Johnny's mind that maybe he hadn't needed quite as much explosive.

Above the crackle of flames, Eagle yelled out, "Do you think you used enough dynamite there, Johnny?"

He scrambled to his feet amid the chaos. The terrified horses had scattered in all directions, men lay stunned on the ground, and through the thick, swirling smoke, Johnny could just make out his father crouching in the doorway of the hacienda, clinging to the pillar. Harvard was struggling to his feet near the door, dazed.

He'd have thrown Harvard his spare gun, but he had to find Donner. And Wallace. Before they found him. One of Wallace's men poked his head out from behind the water trough. Johnny fired off a round, and felt a surge of satisfaction as the man fell backwards and lay still.

Shielding his face with his arm, he stalked through the dust and smoke, looking for Wallace and Donner. He squinted through the haze to see Donner scramble to his feet and fumble for his gun. Johnny swung his gun up and fired, but scalding ash landed on his hand and threw his aim off. He cursed as

Donner jumped to one side and dove for cover behind the water trough.

Glancing around, Johnny saw the buggy just a few yards from where he stood. He threw himself behind it, taking down another of Wallace's men who was headed for the same spot. While he had the chance, he fed a few bullets into his gun to fill up the cylinder. Cocking it, he peered out. Through the smoke, he could see Donner crouched down with Wallace, right beside him, gesturing wildly. Now that was a perfect setup. He could end this right now. He lifted his gun to fire but jerked back as a bullet whistled past his ear, close enough to feel the heat.

Sparks from the aspens had landed on the bunkhouse roof, which must have been tinder dry, because it was now well alight and sending a fresh cloud of black smoke across the yard. Squinting through the flying ash, he glimpsed Donner and Wallace peering from behind the trough again. Johnny lifted his gun again, but another explosion rocked the ground around him, throwing him off balance. He hissed in a breath. The ammunition stored in the bunkhouse shed had blown.

One of Wallace's men stuck his head around from the side of the burning bunkhouse, yelling to Wallace and pointing to the buggy. "Fierro's there!"

Johnny swung his gun up and took the fellow down with a direct shot to the head, even as gunfire started from the hacienda porch. Johnny grinned. Harvard had found himself a gun. Now all Johnny needed was to get Donner and Wallace. His brother and Eagle could take care of the rest of the men.

Donner's shoulder was just visible at the side of the trough— Johnny recognized his shirt. He fired a shot and caught Donner in the arm. He heard the man give a roar of fury and clutch at his arm, pulling himself back out of sight.

A heartbeat later, Donner fired a volley of shots in Johnny's direction. The bullets screamed through the spokes of the buggy wheels.

Sucking in a breath, Johnny peered through the smoke toward the barn. He could make out Eagle and Dexter crouched together, busy in a firefight with a group of Wallace's men. He'd been right about Dexter being a good man.

But with Eagle and Dexter busy, and Harvard pinned down on the porch, staying behind the buggy wasn't an option. He needed to flush out Donner and Wallace. And that meant slipping behind them to get the jump on them.

He quickly filled the Colt again, figuring the best route. The explosions from the guns echoed around him and the smell of cordite filled the air. The horses in the corral, their nostrils flared, were galloping around wildly, terrified of the noise and smells. Peering through the herd, he could see one of Donner's men creeping along the far side of the corral toward him. Taking aim, he waited for a momentary break when the crazed horses were headed toward the other end of the corral, and fired. The man flew back, and lay still.

The corral offered the solution. If he used the horses as cover he could get himself in position to take out Wallace and Donner and finish this. Taking his spare gun from his jacket, so he had one in each hand, he ran firing and scrambled under the corral rails even as bullets kicked up the dust at his feet. His heart pounding, he tore toward the far end of the corral, through the horses, and paused breathlessly. Wallace was screaming out orders, still crouching by the trough, taking potshots at anyone he could spot, regardless of whether they were on his side or not. Johnny lifted his gun and fired, hitting Wallace in the chest. The mine owner dropped like a rock.

But where the hell had Donner gone? Johnny licked dry lips. He knew he'd grazed him, but the man sure wasn't dead—yet. Sucking in a gulp of air, Johnny peered through the swirling smoke. Donner was there somewhere. All he had to do was find the bastard.

The old man and Harvard were still pinned down on either side of the porch. Johnny scanned the yard. A couple of ranch hands were flattened against the side of the barn. There was a lot of shooting—but not many bullets were hitting home. Amateurs!

Where was Donner, damn it? Maybe behind the barn? Checking his gun, Johnny got ready to slip into the barn. But the breath caught in his throat as a movement caught his eye and he saw Red stalking the old man. He didn't have a shot at Red from here. "No!" Johnny tore into the open, firing repeatedly at Red, who staggered and fell to his knees before going facedown in the dust.

His heart racing, he let out a sigh of relief, and then he was slammed forward into the ground. Heat seared through his back.

The world around him slowed down, the gunfire and crackling flames suddenly far away as he lay with one side of his face in the dirt. His shirt was wet; he could feel the damp spreading across his back. A pool of red spread out next to him. And that was strange because he couldn't figure where it was coming from. It looked like blood. But it couldn't be his blood. Blood was warm, and he was so cold. A voice somewhere in his head was telling him he shouldn't stay here. He should move. But it was peaceful here. Moving would be an effort . . .

His gun was still in his hand. He could feel it, but couldn't really see it. Everything was very misty. Someone was running toward him. But the figure was blurred. Who was it? He tried to lift his gun, but his hand didn't seem to be working.

Was that Harvard running? But that was Donner's voice. And he still couldn't lift his gun. It was heavy.

And everything was growing faint.

A crack.

A rifle crack.

Someone was falling. He hoped it wasn't Harvard.

If only he could move.

He was trying but it hurt so bad to move.

And he was so damn cold.

The world closed in, fading into black.

CHAPTER TWENTY-FOUR

Guy's stomach lurched as he saw Johnny fall. He started to run forward but hesitated at a warning shout from someone—Eagle. Then the breeze made a momentary clearing in the smoke that swirled around the hacienda, and he saw someone walk toward Johnny with a gun pointing at his brother's head. Donner. Blood soaked Donner's shirt but he seemed oblivious to that and to the chaos around him. A couple of his comrades were in a gun battle with a small group of Sinclair hands, but Donner just walked on, his left hand clasped over his wound, and his gun steady in his right hand. Guy's eyes watered in the smoke. He swiped his arm across them and leveled his gun at Donner even as the man raised his hand to make his shot, but before he could squeeze the trigger, the crack of a rifle echoed around the valley. Donner staggered and then crumpled forward, landing just feet from where Johnny lay.

Firing blindly now, hoping to give himself some cover from the battle still raging between the remaining few men, Guy rushed to Johnny's side, crouching over him, searching desperately for some sign of life. "What the hell were you thinking, Johnny?" His voice was a croak, but there was no sign that Johnny had heard him. He lay immobile in a growing pool of blood.

Somewhere a voice shouted that Donner was dead, and the last of Wallace's men made a run for it. Apart from the crackle of flames and the thuds of falling timbers, the scene was eerily quiet for a moment.

He looked up at the sound of running feet. Eagle and another man pounded across to him, their faces blackened. "How is he?" Eagle dropped down next to him.

"Not good. His pulse is very weak," Guy said softly. "What the hell was he trying to do? The way you both left, my father and I assumed that you'd gone for good."

Eagle shrugged. "Johnny figured this was the best way to bring Wallace out in the open. Come on, let's get him in the house." He gestured toward his companion. "This is Dexter."

As they stooped to lift Johnny, with Guy taking his shoulders and the other two his legs, Guthrie arrived, breathless and limping badly. "Is he dead?" There was a note of fear in his voice.

Guy shook his head. "We're moving him to the house. We'll know more once we get his jacket off and get a proper look at him. But . . ." He hesitated. "It doesn't look good."

Guthrie sucked in a breath, and gave a sharp nod. "As you say, get him inside."

Peggy stood waiting inside the hall, her face white with shock. Her eyes widened at the sight of Johnny and she smothered a gasp. But drawing her shoulders back, and standing a little taller, she snapped, "Take him upstairs. I'll get some water boiling, and bandages. When we've taken the bullet out, we can put him straight to bed."

Once they got Johnny to the room, Eagle nodded to Guy. "We'll go and help the men put out the fire in the barn. Has someone sent for a doctor? Or do you want us to . . ."

"I've already dealt with that," Peggy's voice was brisk as she ran into the room, her arms full of bandages. "I know he was expected to visit the vaqueros' families today, and I sent one of the hands to fetch him if he's there. I'll bring hot water as soon as it boils, and the medicine chest."

Eagle, Dexter, and Peggy hurried out as Guthrie limped in.

His face was gray and he seemed to have aged ten years. "Well? Still alive?"

Guy nodded, his mouth suddenly dry as Johnny's blood soaked through the material that Peggy had brought. "Yes, but he's losing too much blood. We need to stop the bleeding. I need pads so I can keep the pressure on the wound. Torn-up sheets, anything will do." Guy shifted Johnny slightly, trying to peer under him. "I don't think the bullet went through. It's still in him."

Guthrie muttered a curse as he hurried off while Guy kept pushing on the wound. He needed to cut Johnny's jacket off so he could see what he was dealing with but he didn't want to risk easing the pressure yet. Guy gritted his teeth, wishing he'd told Guthrie to bring a knife too.

"Damn it, Johnny," he muttered as he pushed his brother's jacket up so that he had more room to apply pressure. "That was a stupid stunt to pull. But just hold on now. You've got to hold on. For God's sake don't die on me."

Guthrie arrived with a stack of sheets. "I'll tear these up. Here's a knife. We need to get his jacket off him. And if Ben isn't nearby, we'll just have to deal with the bullet ourselves. It won't be the first time I've had to do it." He crouched down. "You keep the pressure on, and I'll cut his jacket away."

Guy nodded, trying to keep his arms clear so that his father could work unimpeded, watching as the blade cut through the soft leather. His father tossed the jacket to one side, lifted the blood-soaked shirt a few inches from Johnny's back, and cut that away too, leaving his bare back exposed. Guy bit back an oath, even as his father exclaimed. Faded wheals and puckered scars covered Johnny's back.

"My God," whispered Guthrie. "My boy. What in heaven's name happened to him?"

Guy shook his head, trying not to be distracted from keeping the pressure on the new wound. Even so, he couldn't take his eyes off the whip marks and other scars. Gunshots? Knives?

"Should we start? Or give the doctor more time?" Guy looked at his father's ashen face, hoping to divert his attention.

"The doctor's here!" Ben strode into the room, clutching his black bag. "I heard the firefight in the distance. Now, let me see my patient. I understand there's just one casualty. Are you both OK?" He shot them a sharp look as he leaned down to examine Johnny.

"We're fine, Ben, but those scars on his back, how recent are they?" Guthrie pointed to the marks.

Ben pushed Guthrie's hand away. "Damn it, Guthrie, never mind old injuries, let me look at this gunshot wound."

"Ben! How old are they?" Guthrie shook Ben's shoulder.

"For God's sake, Guthrie, let me do my job," Ben snapped, but he touched the scars briefly. "Some are very old, dating from when he was a young child—you can tell by the way the skin has stretched as he's grown. He's had more than a few beatings in his time. Who is he anyway? A new hand?"

"No." Guthrie's voice shook. "Not a new hand. It's John. He came home."

Ben jerked around to look at them. "John? This is Fierro?"

Guy nodded. "Yes. Can you help him, Ben? He's lost a lot of blood."

Ben sucked in a deep breath. "Move the dressing table near to the window. We'll stretch him out there so I can see what I'm doing. I need to get that bullet out fast. He's already lost too much blood, and he's in shock, judging from how cold he is." He clambered stiffly to his feet. "I'll do my best. But, I'm sorry, Guthrie." He shook his head. "It doesn't look good. He's in a bad way. Now, come and move this table."

Guy moved to help Guthrie and Ben push it closer to the window. A sheen of sweat showed on Guthrie's forehead and he was breathing heavily. Ben looked at him sharply. "Guthrie, go and ask Peggy to make coffee—everyone's going to need it. You shouldn't be exerting yourself this much. It's not long since you yourself were shot." Ben gave a grunt of irritation. "Go on! Guy can help me. Tell Peggy to bring some hot water."

Guthrie limped from the room, leaving Guy and Ben bending to their work.

As he watched Ben work, Guy recalled how impressed he'd been with the doctor when Guthrie had been shot. He was a man who always focused on the job at hand. And right now that was the best chance Johnny had.

Ben worked steadily, his head bent as he probed gently searching for the bullet. After what seemed an age, he suddenly grunted in triumph. "Found it!"

He extracted the bullet with infinite care, dropping it onto a saucer, and huffed out a sigh of relief. Ben glanced at Guy. "So, tell me, what's he like? Fierro?"

The question, coming out of the blue, threw him. He frowned. "You mean Johnny?" Guy sucked in a breath. "I don't know."

"Hmmm." Ben didn't sound impressed. "He has quite a reputation."

"Reputations don't always match the man they purport to describe," Guy said.

Ben didn't respond for a few minutes, intent now on cleaning the wound. He paused to move his head from side to side, as if easing a crick in his neck. He glanced at Guy. "There's usually an element of truth in them, though. And being from out East, perhaps you don't realize the sort of reputation Fierro has."

"Father was at great pains to point it out to me," Guy huffed. "Great pains!"

Ben gave the briefest of smiles. "Yes, I imagine he would have done that. But whether you like it or not, Guy, Fierro has a fearsome reputation. A man doesn't end up with that kind of reputation by accident. Still, I am curious, which is why I wondered what your impressions of him are."

And there was the rub. Exactly what were his impressions of Johnny? He'd been so relieved initially to discover that his brother was alive. But it had been such a shock to discover that he made his living by hiring out his gun. Hiring out his gun! What a very discreet way of saying his brother killed people for a living—was a paid killer. There was no getting away from that unpalatable truth.

And yet . . .

Guy winced as Ben started the delicate procedure of stitching the wound. "I can understand your reservations. But there is much more to him. I'm sure of it. The day he arrived, he was incredibly rude to Father, but it was almost as though he was trying to provoke him. And he doesn't appear to have had any education at all but he's very intelligent. There's something about him and I don't know what it is. Something I can't put my finger on but I think there's more to him than meets the eye. For one thing, I think he has a strong sense of justice and compassion."

"Compassion?" The tone of Ben's voice suggested it would be a cold day in hell before he believed that.

"Yes," Guy said firmly. "Compassion. Unexpected, I'll grant you, but it's there. We were moving cattle when two of our hands were killed for no reason other than they were in the wrong place at the wrong time. Johnny was incensed. He risked his life, hopelessly outnumbered, to get justice for those men. Nobody was paying him to do that. He had no personal interest, but he put his life on the line just the same. And today, he took an incredible risk to engineer a showdown so that we could end the threat of this range war, and prove that Wallace was indeed behind it."

"I find it hard to believe that a man like Samuel Wallace could have stooped to something like this." Ben shook his head in disbelief. "It's incredible."

"Well, he did, as Johnny proved. Wallace manipulated Chavez and funded the hiring of guns. Chavez hoped to get the water rights, but it was mainly about Wallace's greed. Johnny's been vindicated but he's paid a high price for it." Guy reached out and gently touched his brother's head. It was too hot. Far too hot. "What he did today was crazy. I can't believe he didn't realize he was setting himself up as a target. It was almost as if he was sacrificing himself, it was so reckless. Although he makes it difficult for anyone to get to know him, I think it would be worth the effort to learn more about him. And," Guy paused, "I want that opportunity."

Ben raised his eyebrows. "I confess to being surprised, and curious too. But I have to warn you, Guy. He's very sick. He's lost a great deal of blood, he's in severe shock, and there's a grave risk of infection."

Guy swallowed hard. "You don't think he'll make it, do you?"

Ben put in a final stitch before looking back at Guy. "I'm sorry, but if I'm honest, I don't. I've cleaned the wound as well as I possibly can. But, now, it's in God's hands."

Guy nodded slowly. "I know you're right. And it doesn't look good. But judging from the state of him, he's survived an awful lot in his life. Look at those old scars . . ."

Ben patted Guy on the shoulder. "Yes, he's survived a lot. But there's only so much the human body can take, and this could be the wound that breaks him."

CHAPTER TWENTY-FIVE

Ben left Guy watching over Johnny and trudged down the stairs to the kitchen, where Peggy was busy making soup. His old friend was nursing a large whiskey and staring out the doorway to the mountains beyond. Guthrie turned to face him, still shaken. "How is he, Ben?"

"Not good. He's lost a lot of blood. All we can do now is pray. Peggy, could you go and help Guy make him comfortable please?" Ben smiled as she rushed from the room, obviously keen to help. He was very fond of Steen's daughter; she was a credit to his old friend.

Guthrie ran his fingers through his hair, seemingly oblivious to the fact that it was still full of ash and dust. "Those scars, Ben. I've never seen anything like it. How could anyone do that to a child? I keep telling myself it's not him; that the Pinkerton Agency got it wrong. But then, I look at his eyes, and I know it's him." Guthrie sighed heavily. "Do you remember John's smile? There's no trace of that smile in that young man upstairs."

Ben folded his arms. "So tell me, what is he like?"

Guthrie snorted. "Rude, foul-mouthed, truculent, cold, insolent. Shall I go on?"

"But?" prompted Ben, gently.

"I just don't know, Ben. Yesterday, he and I locked horns. Hell, that's all we've done! He said Wallace was involved in this business. I didn't believe it. I mean, we've known Samuel for years. And, on top of that, Johnny had been in a shootout over in Bitterville. He rode in and killed several men who'd robbed the cattle drive."

Ben nodded. "I'd heard that there'd been trouble. News travels fast. But I didn't realize it was Fierro."

"We argued over the way he handled it. He challenged me to say what I really thought of him. I said some things. Um. I was angry, maybe a little rash."

Ben shut his eyes briefly. Another intemperate Guthrie Sinclair outburst! The frustrating part was that he was a good and honorable man—but he sometimes said the first thing that came into his head rather than weighing his words. And considering what Guthrie's views were on gunfighters, he could imagine, only too well, the sort of things he might have said to his son.

Guthrie took another swig of his drink. "It was the strangest thing, Ben. There was a look in his eyes, almost of pain. I could swear that I'd hurt him. But then the look was gone and I thought maybe I'd imagined it." Guthrie shook his head, frowning. "And then he rode out. He took his things, what little he has. And heavens, he doesn't seem to have much of anything. But he got on his horse and went without a word. I thought he'd left. God, I hoped he had left, if I'm honest. But then he arrived today with Wallace and a bunch of hired gunmen. I don't know what the hell he thought he was doing. It was crazy to come here with all those men—he was setting himself up to be taken down. He was hopelessly outnumbered." Guthrie turned again to look out at the mountains. "Even so, he seemed to be everywhere. He took down a lot of men. And he got Wallace. But then, he suddenly ran out, with no cover at all. He shot a man who was coming up close to where I was on the porch. I hadn't seen the fellow, not until Johnny shot him. Why did Johnny run out without any cover?" He turned and looked at Ben searchingly. "It was the most reckless thing of all." Guthrie paused, running his hand through his hair again, sending a small cloud of ash showering down. "He couldn't have taken that risk to save me. Could he?"

Ben shrugged. "I don't know, Guthrie. What do you think?"

Guthrie hesitated. "He hates me. He wouldn't have risked his life for me. That first night he was here, he scared the hell out of me. It was obvious how much he hates me." He paused again. "But if he hates me that much, why didn't he just help Wallace instead of double-crossing him?"

Ben perched on the edge of the table. "Guy seems to have some faith in him. I confess I was surprised. They certainly can't have anything in common, but Guy seems to think there's some good in him. He didn't describe John in the same way as you."

Guthrie interrupted, on the defensive now. "Guy wants to believe that his younger brother is everything he wants him to be."

Ben snorted. "Guy's not a child, Guthrie. He's a well-educated and intelligent man."

Guthrie poured more whiskey and offered a glass to the doctor. "The fact remains that Guy is very accepting of him and supported his actions in Bitterville. I don't understand it. Believe me, Fierro is no angel."

"Fierro?" Ben raised an eyebrow. "I do realize, Guthrie, how humiliating you find it having Fierro for a son, but perhaps you should ponder on why Guy is supportive of him. As I said, Guy's no innocent—he's nobody's fool."

Guthrie bowed his head before looking back at Ben bleakly. "You're right—I do find it humiliating. I don't think I can handle it and, to be honest I'm not sure I want to. He's so hard. Like I said, he scares the hell out of me. But I still don't understand why he did what he did. If he hadn't . . ."

Ben felt a pang of sympathy for his friend. He looked so defeated and Ben couldn't think of anything to say that would make the man feel any better. He had no answers for him.

He took a sip of his malt as Peggy burst in, breathless. "I think you'd better come quickly, Uncle Ben. Johnny's already started a fever. He's burning up."

He slammed his glass down, and he and Guthrie took off up the stairs to Johnny's room. Ben hurried to the bed, where Guy was struggling to restrain the young man who was thrashing around, calling out in Spanish. Peggy set about laying damp cloths on him to cool his fever. She turned frightened eyes to the men. "How could he get a fever so quickly? We got him settled and then he started calling to his mother, begging her not to die. It was awful."

Ben stared down at his patient. The boy was drenched in sweat and muttering incoherently, with just odd words recognizable. "Looks like I'll be staying a while, Guthrie. Guy, do me a favor and take your father downstairs please. Leave this to Peggy and me."

Ben found the ensuing hours some of the most harrowing of his life. Afraid that Peggy would understand some of the things that John was saying, he sent her to cook a meal. His own Spanish was good enough to understand the delirious ramblings and he hated what he was hearing. Although some of it seemed to be about gunfights, the worst was when John was reliving his childhood. He was just glad that Guthrie wasn't there to hear it, for it turned his own stomach. God only knew how his friend would cope.

What on earth had Gabriela done after leaving with the child? Where had they lived? And why hadn't she sent the boy back to the ranch for his own safety? It wasn't as though she'd been the most attentive of mothers. She'd never bothered much with her baby. He'd always had the impression that she saw John as an inconvenience. Shaking his head, he wondered how old John had been when Gabriela died because it was obvious from the garbled ramblings that she was dead. And at this rate, judging from the boy's labored breathing, the son would soon be joining his mother.

But John was stronger than he looked. Despite the high fever, he clung stubbornly to life.

Guy arrived with a mug of steaming coffee. "How's he doing?"

Ben seized the coffee gratefully. "Hanging on, but only just. If this fever breaks, we have a chance." He watched Guy put a hand on John's forehead.

"Not much of a homecoming for either of us," Guy said softly.

"Is it home?"

Guy shrugged. "I don't know. I was curious to meet my father again. It's been too many years. The war and everything." Guy's voice trailed off, and for a few seconds he seemed lost in memories. "But it was time to come back, even though I knew it would all seem so very alien. And of course I never expected Johnny. I believed him to be dead. So it was quite a shock, especially to find him so different from anyone I've ever known before.

"It's strange though, before I came back, I told myself this was just going to be a visit, that I'd stay a few weeks and then return to Boston before the fall. But now I've told Father I'll stay." He smiled apologetically. "He wants me here, and to be honest, I said yes because this life, this ranch, seems like a challenge. I've been bored stiff in Boston since the war." He hesitated. "It's certainly different here. I think I need that. I needed to get away from Boston."

Ben nodded. He liked Guy. And the young man's presence would be good for Guthrie. He'd been without his sons for too many years. But he wondered what Guy would think if he heard some of the stories about his brother. Still, it wasn't his place to tell him. Guy would doubtless hear them at some stage and have to make up his own mind about John Sinclair. Or Johnny Fierro.

The sound of Guthrie's heavy footsteps echoed along the landing, and Ben felt a twinge of concern as the man limped into the room, his face haggard. "How is he, Ben?"

"He's holding on. Everything depends on how resilient he is and I've no way of knowing that. But if it's any comfort, he's obviously survived a lot in his life so maybe he's stronger than he looks. If the fever breaks he has a fighting chance. I'll do everything I can."

Guthrie walked stiffly across the room, his leg obviously troubling him. He stood at the edge of the bed and tentatively put his hand out to push the sweat-soaked hair from his son's eyes. He stood with his head bowed, leaving his hand on John's head. Then he looked across at Ben and said, "I don't want to lose him. Not after what he did. He put his life on the line today for us and I don't know why. But I do know I'll never forget seeing him fall when that bastard shot him in the back. It'll haunt me. God help me. That image will haunt me."

Guy pulled up a chair to the bed for his father. "Sir, why don't you sit with him for a while? I'll take the doctor downstairs for a bite to eat and some rest."

Guthrie nodded, and Ben followed Guy down the stairs to the living room.

Guy disappeared in search of food, and Ben sank thankfully into a deep comfortable chair. It felt good just to relax for a few moments. Not for too long though.

When he awoke he could see the first streaks of dawn in the sky. He'd slept for far too long. Guthrie was snoring in the chair opposite him, still frowning even in sleep. Struggling to his feet, Ben hurried upstairs to John's room where he found Peggy sitting by the bed. Guy was slumped asleep in the corner, traces of exhaustion etched across his face. Peggy smiled as he came in. "I think the fever's broken. He's cooler and he's been quiet for some time. He's breathing a little better too."

Ben felt his patient's forehead. He certainly felt cooler. Checking Johnny's pulse, he was relieved to find it stronger.

"Will he be all right?"

He smiled gently at Peggy's hopeful face, "Well, it looks more promising now than a few hours ago. But the fever could return and there's a risk of infection, so it's still too early to say. But yes, it is looking better." He rubbed his chin. He needed to check on his other patients in the district. He had two expectant mothers he should see, and it did seem that John was more stable now. Perhaps he could be left for a few hours. Peggy was competent; she'd cope for a while.

He hurried through his other visits before returning to the ranch later in the day. He sighed with relief when he looked at his patient. There was no sign of the fever. John moaned in his sleep from pain when he moved but his breathing was better and his pulse was stronger. Maybe he'd awaken soon.

He returned the next day and went to join Peggy in John's room. "How is he? Has he taken some fluids?"

She frowned, and shook her head as if confused, "Well, he hasn't woken up yet."

Ben felt a stab of concern. Damn it, the boy should have been awake, albeit briefly, long before now. What the hell was wrong? His pulse was strong, his forehead was cool. It made no sense. "What happens when you try and give him fluids?"

"He swallows them. But he hasn't opened his eyes at all."

Why the hell not, he wondered. He gave John another examination but there was little response. Had he hit his head when he fell? He opened John's eyes and looked thoughtfully at the pupils before letting go. A suspicion was starting to form in his mind.

"Peggy, what say you and I go and get a cup of coffee? It's been a long day and I could really use one now. And I'm sure you could too."

"But what about Johnny? I can't leave him. What if he wakes up and there's no one here?"

"He's sound asleep, my dear; he'll be fine for a while."

With a worried glance at her patient, she walked with Ben to the door. But then he put his finger to his lips and shook his head, signaling her not to speak. "Come on, leave him be, Peggy." And with that he pushed the girl out of the room and shut the door firmly after her.

He stood motionless at the door and watched the dark figure in the bed. He felt a stab of satisfaction as he saw his patient's eyes open, and he looked into the coldest and most unfriendly eyes he'd ever seen.

CHAPTER TWENTY-SIX

"I thought you were faking. Nice of you to join us." Ben glared back at his patient.

John's eyes raked over him. "Oh, you're real clever, Doc, ain't you?"

"What I don't understand is why?" Ben stared at him, puzzled.

John grunted. "I ain't much for talking. Just want to be left alone."

Ben poured some water into a glass and put it to John's lips for him to drink. But he swiped it away, splashing water over the blankets. "I don't need no help."

Ben held the glass out, watching impassively as he struggled to take it. Lines of pain were etched across John's face as he tried to grasp the glass before his arm fell back to his side. "I'm not thirsty." There was defiance in his voice and in the look he threw at Ben.

A thought flashed through the doctor's mind. The young man was as difficult as his father. Ben bit back a smile. He suspected his patient wouldn't care for the comparison. Instead, he said firmly, "If you want to recover, you'll have to drink lots of fluids and if that means accepting a little help initially, tough! Do as you're told."

John's eyes narrowed and when he spoke his voice was very soft. "I've killed men for less than that, Doc."

Ben gritted his teeth. He was damned if he'd be intimidated.

"Just drink the damn water." He pressed the glass to John's lips again—and this time his patient drank some before jerking his head back and glancing around the room.

John struggled to raise himself up onto his elbow, even as Ben tried to push him back down. "You need to stay down, young man."

John's eyes flashed. "My gun. Where the hell is my gun? I need it."

Ben frowned, wondering if John was still feverish. "You don't need it. You're safe here. The fighting's finished."

"I said," John hissed, "where's my gun?"

Ben swallowed hard. "Why?"

John rolled his eyes. "Well, I ain't planning on shooting you, if that's what you're worried about. Leastways not yet."

Was that an attempt at humor, or a threat? Ben shook his head and went to fetch the gun from the chest by the window. He paused to draw the drapes open, permitting himself a small smile at Fierro's grunt of irritation. "Thought we needed some more light in here." He smiled benignly at his patient as he handed over the Colt.

John grimaced in pain as he took his gun and checked it. He glared at Ben. "It ain't no good without any damn bullets."

Ben huffed out a sigh, but passed him a handful of bullets from the gun belt. It was painful to watch as John tried to load the gun, but he finally succeeded. Pushing it under his pillow, he fell back, looking flushed and worn out by the effort.

Ben looked at him, bemused. "Do you always sleep with a gun under your pillow?"

Pain dulled those blue eyes. "What of it?"

Ben quirked an eyebrow. "I'm curious. It seems an unnecessary precaution when you're safe here."

"Safe!" John snorted. "Someone like me ain't ever safe. Always someone who'd like to take me down."

"John, I'm sure you don't need . . ."

"It ain't John." His voice was flat. "John Sinclair's long gone."

"Gone?" Ben frowned as he tried to figure what John meant. "You mean you're Johnny Fierro now? That, as far as you're concerned, John Sinclair no longer exists?"

John rolled his eyes. "Look, Doc, let's cut the crap. I'll be out of here in a day or two."

Ben snorted. "You won't be going anywhere ever unless you start letting people help you. You need to drink plenty of fluids; otherwise that fever will come back." He paused. "And it will probably kill you. So will you let us all help you, or would you rather be dead?" He knew his words were harsh, but hoped they might have some effect. Oddly, his patient just smiled. A smile that didn't warm those eyes.

"We all got to go sometime, don't we?"

The words, spoken so casually, chilled Ben. "John . . . Johnny, you're a young man with your whole life ahead of you."

Johnny laughed humorlessly. "Young? I ain't young. I ain't been young for a long time. And I've already lived way longer than I expected."

Ben furrowed his brow. "Is that why you were so reckless? Your family says your plan was crazy and it was almost certain to end up with you being shot. Did that not bother you?"

Johnny didn't speak for a few seconds. He flinched as another wave of pain seemed to wash over him. He sucked in a breath and shrugged. "Figured it was the best way to bring it to a head. It worked. And not that it's any of your business, but no, I ain't scared of dying. Scares the shit out of the man you're facing when he realizes you don't care. But anyone who wants my reputation can fuckin' well earn it. Like I did."

Unbidden, the picture came to mind of a young gunfighter standing over a man, watching him die in agony, and smiling all the while. Ben tried to push the picture from his mind, but it hovered there, taunting him, daring him to ask Fierro about that gunfight.

"So, like I said, I'll be outta here soon."

His patient's voice jerked him back to the present. Ben shook his head. "You won't be going anywhere soon. But if you do as I tell you, start eating and drinking, we might get you downstairs in a few days' time."

John's eyes sparked with fury. "Downstairs! I'm talkin' about riding out. I been shot up worse than this."

Ben bit his lip. Having seen the scars on the young man's body, he could well believe that. "While you're my patient, you'll do as you're told, young man. If you try to ride too soon, that wound will open up and could easily become infected. Anyway, I thought you'd come home. Why the hurry to ride?"

"Because I ain't planning on staying in these parts. Just need you to get me fit enough to get the hell out of here." Johnny paused with a chilling smile. "You get it right, Doc, and I might let you live to see another birthday."

Ben raised an eyebrow. "Very generous of you."

Johnny laughed softly. "See. We understand each other perfectly."

Ben sat down on the edge of the bed. Johnny obviously didn't like that. He was trying to draw back from the close contact, even though the pain showed clearly in his face. Ben knew it was petty but he liked having this young man at a disadvantage. No patient was going to threaten him. "So why aren't you staying for your share of the ranch? I understand you've been offered a third. That's a lot of land. It would tempt most men."

Still trying to draw away, Johnny grimaced. "I ain't like most men. Anyway, he ain't never going to give me a piece of his precious ranch. He sure as hell don't want me here." Johnny hissed in a breath, shutting his eyes briefly. "Just can't figure out why he sent for me. Could understand him wanting my gun in a range war." He paused, fighting another wave of pain. "But it was like he didn't want my gun. So why the hell am I here?"

Ben reached out to check his forehead for fever, even as Johnny jerked away. "Do you want something to ease the pain? Laudanum would help."

"No! Like I said, I've had worse."

Johnny's skin had lost all its color. Ben reached over to check his pulse. "I think you'll find Guthrie's offer stands. He's a man of his word."

Johnny gave a grunt of derision and glanced at Ben. "So is that it? Are we done here?"

Ben chewed his lip. The picture of that gunfight was still playing on his mind. He knew it was crazy, but he had to ask. He swallowed hard. "I wanted to ask you about a gunfight."

There was a brief flicker of surprise in Johnny's eyes, but it went so quickly, Ben wondered if he'd imagined it.

"Any particular one or just gunfights in general?"

Ben sat a little straighter and looked his patient in the eye. "One in particular. Down in Santa Fe."

Johnny raised an eyebrow. "Been in a lot of gunfights down there."

"You were facing down two men." Ben spoke firmly.

Johnny laughed softly. "I need a bit more than that. Facing two men ain't unusual for me."

"You shot one of them dead with a clean shot. But the other man . . ." Ben hesitated. "You shot him in the gut, and then in the hand when he tried to reach for his gun."

Johnny held his gaze without speaking for a few seconds before shrugging. "Like I said, I'd need more details. One gunfight is pretty much like another. Someone winds up dead, and so far it ain't been me. So, are we done? I'm tired." As if to signal the conversation was over, he shut his eyes.

Ben berated himself silently. He'd known what to expect: a

cold-blooded killer. Nothing more. But he knew, deep down, he wanted to be wrong. He hoped to see some trace of the child he knew, the one with the engaging smile. But then, given what he'd heard of Johnny's delirious ramblings, how could there be any trace of that child left?

He suddenly felt very old and tired. He walked from the room, shutting the door quietly behind him. Obviously there'd been nothing memorable about that gunfight. Apparently, to kill somebody in such a cruel way was nothing out of the ordinary for the gunfighter. To Johnny Fierro, it was just another dead man.

But as he trudged downstairs, an insistent voice in his ear said, *if that's the case, why does Guy think he's worth getting to know?*

He ran into Peggy in the downstairs hall and gave her new instructions for Johnny's care. "He woke and drank some water, but he's sleeping again now. Wake him every two or three hours to get him to take fluids. Don't try to talk to him, Peggy. He's in a lot of pain and needs to be left quiet." He hoped that would keep her from bothering Johnny. Otherwise he had a suspicion that his patient would lose consciousness again.

He was climbing into his buggy when Guthrie hurried over. "How is he?"

Ben shrugged. "In a lot of pain, but wanting to know how soon he can leave."

"He's talking about leaving?"

Guthrie sounded hopeful at the prospect. Ben frowned. "Yes. He seems to think you won't honor your offer of a share of the ranch. He's also puzzled about why you asked him here. Are you going to tell him Peggy and Guy sent for him?"

Guthrie scowled. "I don't think there's any need for him to know that. Anyway, if John leaves, it's probably for the best."

Ben's mouth dropped open. He shook his head in disbelief.

"Best! Best for whom? You? Peggy? Guy? It certainly can't be best for Johnny. He's on a fast road to nowhere and is going to wind up dead before much longer. The real tragedy is that he doesn't care. And neither, it appears, do you."

Guthrie bristled. "Damn it, of course I care. I told you when he was so ill that I don't want to lose him. But you didn't see him when he arrived. I don't see how he could ever fit in here. He doesn't seem to care about anything or anyone."

Ben felt a flash of irritation. Guthrie was determined not to find any redeeming qualities in his son. "Well, maybe you'll get lucky and the wound will get infected. He's very weak, and it might kill him!"

"I don't enjoy this, Ben. But anyone can see the boy is just like his mother, totally wild."

Ben gathered up the reins. "That's odd, Guthrie, because I was thinking earlier how much like you he is." And with that parting shot, Ben clicked to his horse and drove away.

He returned the next day, hoping to avoid Guthrie. He suspected he'd get enough of a battle from his patient.

He bustled into Johnny's room to find him apparently asleep, but he could just as easily have been feigning. Ben opened his bag, and said loudly, "So, how are you feeling today?"

Johnny opened his eyes and shot him an icy look. "I was asleep."

Ben snorted with laughter. "Sorry, son, but I don't buy that. You don't look bleary enough. So, how are you?"

"Fine."

He looked anything but fine. His face was flushed and beads of sweat sat in furrows on his brow. Ben set his bag down. "I want to look at that wound." Removing the bandages, he saw the stitches had pulled and the wound was red and angry. He shot Johnny a sharp look. "Have you been trying to get out of bed?"

"No." The answer was sullen and unconvincing.

Ben snorted. Like hell he hadn't been trying to get out of bed. "Are you trying to kill yourself? I'm trying to help you but you're going to make my job impossible if you pull stupid stunts like this. Look at the state of you." He threw his hands in the air. "Your fever is back, you've pulled your stitches, and there's a risk of infection."

Johnny rolled his eyes. "You're starting to piss me off. I don't need no lectures."

"And you watch your language. You should treat me with a little courtesy, young man."

"Why should I?" Johnny's eyes flashed.

"Well, for starters, you've known me longer than anyone else so that entitles me to a little courtesy."

Johnny frowned. "What the hell d'you mean? I only just met you."

Ben smiled smugly. "Actually, my face was the very first you ever saw in this world."

Johnny looked at Ben sharply. "What d'you mean?"

Ben was ridiculously pleased to see interest now in Johnny's eyes. "I delivered you. I brought you into this world."

A smile spread across Johnny's face, transforming it. Despite his obvious pain, he suddenly looked years younger. Ben felt a surge of pleasure for it was the smile he remembered, one that could lighten the darkest day.

"You knew my mother?"

Ben laughed; he had to at the sudden enthusiasm. "Of course I knew her. I was here when she first arrived at Sinclair." He rummaged in his bag for his stethoscope before turning back to his patient. He felt a clutch of fear as he found himself staring down the barrel of the Colt. The smile was gone and Johnny's eyes were remote. Ben opened his mouth but no sound came out.

"So what I want to know, Doc, is why the old man threw us out." His voice was emotionless.

Ben sank onto a chair, startled by the change in Johnny and by the question. He shook his head. "What in the world are you talking about? Guthrie didn't throw you out."

"You got just one chance to tell me the truth. And if I find out you've lied, I'll kill you. That's a promise."

Looking into Fierro's eyes, Ben felt a jolt of fear. The words were no idle threat. It hit him that the young man was every bit as dangerous as his reputation suggested. Ben swallowed hard. "I'm sorry, but I don't know what you're talking about."

There was a loud click as Johnny cocked the gun. "All you got to do is tell me why the old man threw us out. It ain't that difficult. Was it because I'm a breed? Or some other reason?"

Ben's mouth dropped open, too shocked to speak for a second. "Where the hell did you get that crazy idea from? Guthrie didn't throw you out. Surely Gabriela didn't tell you that. It makes no sense."

"Just tell me why he threw us out," hissed Johnny.

Ben stood and paced around the room. "I can't tell you about something that never happened. You've got it all wrong. Your mother ran off and took you with her. Nobody threw you out. Damn it, I had to deal with Guthrie after she took off. He was in a hell of a state. Half the town knew she'd been seeing someone while he was away on a cattle drive. I thought once he was back, the affair would die a natural death. I was wrong. She took off with the fellow and took you with her.

"Guthrie spent years trying to find you. Steen and I were convinced that you were both dead, but Guthrie never gave up. He used to go and trawl the border towns searching for you. He hired the Pinkerton Agency too, whenever he had enough money.

"And why do you think he'd care that you're part Apache?

He didn't care that Gabriela was half Apache. Hell, he was so proud of you, he used to ride around with you sitting in front of him. I'm sorry, but you've got it all wrong."

Johnny shook his head slowly, his face ashen. When he spoke his voice was barely a whisper. "You're lying, Doc. I said I'd kill you if you lied."

Ben shook his head. "You can kill me if you like, but it won't alter the fact that I've told you the truth."

"The old man, did . . . did the old man knock her around?"

The question was so soft Ben had to strain to hear it. He frowned, confused. "You mean did Guthrie hit Gabriela?"

Johnny nodded.

"No, Johnny. Guthrie didn't hit her. I'd have known. I was her doctor. Did she tell you these things?" He looked searchingly at Johnny, appalled by the sudden despair in the boy's face.

Johnny turned his face away, staring out of the window. "I want to go to sleep now."

Ben shook his head. "Firstly, young man, you're going to drink some water, and no arguments. Then I'm going to dress that wound. And I'm not leaving until you're more comfortable. I don't want you dying on me. It wouldn't do my reputation any good at all."

He was rewarded by the ghost of a smile. "And neither do I want to hear that you don't care if you die," Ben added. "I care so you can just put up with it."

He set about cleaning the wound, and put in some extra stitches. Johnny didn't flinch. It was as though he'd gone someplace where he could no longer be reached. He didn't react when Ben replaced the bandages.

Ben eyed him, feeling only compassion now. "I'm really sorry, Johnny, but I've told you the truth. Guy was so young that he may not remember much, but if you don't believe me or your father, a lot of people in town remember what happened. They'll confirm what I've said."

Johnny nodded slowly, his eyes dulled by pain. "It's OK, Doc. I know the truth when I hear it." He shrugged. "Trouble is, it means I've based my whole life on a lie. The things I've done . . ." He lifted his gun briefly before dropping it back on the bed by his side. "The things I've done . . . Get me fit enough to travel. I got no place here. They'll be better off without me. Either that, or let me die, I really don't care, even though I know that's hard for you to understand. I've had enough."

Ben had no answer. The boy looked worn out. Hardened gunfighter or not, he suddenly looked very much a boy. Ben took Johnny's wrist to check his pulse. It was too fast. God, the boy looked sick.

Ben spoke gruffly. "I told you, I'll be damned if you're going to die on me, boy. I don't like losing patients, particularly the ones I brought into the world. You'll stay in bed and do as you're told. Understand? Now, get some rest. I'll be back later."

He was halfway through the door when Johnny spoke again, so softly that Ben had to step back into the room to hear him. "About that gunfight. I do remember it. Just so as you know, it's not the way I usually do things."

Ben opened his mouth to speak, but Johnny shook his head. "Too tired. Just didn't want you to think . . ." He left his sentence unfinished and looked away.

Ben smiled, and spoke gently. "Thank you, Johnny."

CHAPTER TWENTY-SEVEN

Guthrie stood at Johnny's window, glass in hand, looking out over the ranch. It had been a dreadful few days and now he felt exhausted. Not knowing if Johnny would live or die. Not knowing if he even cared. He didn't know what he really felt about the boy. Boy or gunfighter? But all he could see in his mind's eye was Johnny tearing toward the hacienda through the smoke and dust and being gunned down. He didn't think he would ever be able to forget that. That image haunted him. It had been crazy. Had Johnny been trying to save him? No. That really was crazy. Maybe Johnny had simply miscalculated. And yet, the one thing he'd felt certain of, as soon as he met Fierro, was that he wasn't a fool. Johnny Fierro was a man who weighed everything, of that he was certain.

And he still couldn't get any answers. He knew the boy had been awake at times. Ben had spoken with him. And so had Peggy. But whenever he'd visited Johnny's room, the boy had always been sleeping. And so he'd stood at the window, staring out at the mountains in the distance, lost in his own thoughts. There'd been moments when he'd felt he was being watched. But whenever he had turned from the window to look at Johnny, thinking he was awake, those eyes had been shut. Johnny still slept.

He looked at the boy now. God, he looked ill. He was certainly still very sick. Ben had expressed concern, worried about infection. Guthrie walked to the boy's bedside and looked down at him. He tentatively put out his hand to brush the unruly hair off the boy's face. Johnny seemed to flinch at the touch, although he slept. His face was flushed with fever, and he looked very young. Guthrie could almost forget this was a killer.

His mind went back to that afternoon, so long ago, when he'd sat with Steen and Ben in the saloon in town, the day they heard a story about Fierro. Of how he had gutshot a man and then stood smiling while the man died slowly. Guthrie shuddered. He knew he could well believe such a thing of the man who had arrived a few days ago. But to believe it of this sick boy, who had risked his life for the ranch . . . well, that was a different thing altogether.

He wondered, for what felt like the millionth time, what had happened to Johnny in those years before he came home. What had driven that laughing toddler to turn into a hardened and feared gunfighter? And what the hell had Gabriela been doing while someone had whipped their son? He couldn't believe she would have done it. She'd never seemed to care much about the boy, which had made it all the more shocking that she had taken him with her. But whipping? No, she wouldn't, couldn't have done that.

God, it still hurt to think of her leaving. She'd left him for another man, the implication being that he couldn't satisfy her. God, that had hurt. He knew that men had sniggered and whispered behind his back.

He shook himself back to the present. There was no point in dwelling on the past. He needed to look to the future now. And the one positive thing in all of this was that Guy had announced he intended to stay, rather than return to Boston. He was already proving himself a good worker. He'd been working flat out with the hands to try and restore some semblance of order to the ranch.

Guthrie was surprised that Guy seemed so concerned about Johnny. Hell, he'd risked his life, running out under fire to drag Johnny to cover.

While they'd been waiting for Johnny to regain consciousness, Guy's words had surprised him. "I want the chance to get to know him. I suspect it won't be easy, but I think it'll be worth the effort—if he lives."

He'd tried to allay Guy's fears. "Ben's a good doctor. He's in good hands." His gentle words had surprised himself. He realized he meant it, and was praying it would be true. He hated everything Fierro represented, but Johnny was his son. It had been easy not to care before. Fierro had just been a name, someone to be dreaded or despised. But now, he was flesh and blood. Guthrie's flesh and blood.

He gazed out over his land, reflecting on their hard won victory. For they had won; Wallace was dead. Chavez was dead. Life could get back to normal. Normal! That was a joke. What was going to be normal now?

There was the damn partnership deal. He shouldn't have been in such a hurry to offer that, although he'd hoped the idea of real work would scare Fierro off. But why had he taken that huge risk for the ranch? Was it just greed? Had Fierro thought he'd be rich if he owned part of this ranch? Fierro or Johnny? He glanced once more at the figure lying on the bed. Was it really his Johnny? Could the Pinkerton Agency have got it wrong? So many questions, so many doubts. There was no trace of that wonderful smile he remembered in his young son. He'd hoped to see something that would make him believe there was still a remnant of John Sinclair. But there had been nothing. And now he'd have to live with the memory of his son running through the smoke, running toward the guns, and falling.

He looked again at Johnny, willing him to wake up. Would he be all right? Oh God, he had to be all right. He was still so very young. And there it was. He did care; he had to admit to himself that he cared. He hadn't wanted to care. Didn't think he could, wasn't sure he should. But when he'd stood with Ben after the operation, seeing his boy burning up, perhaps dying, it had finally hit him.

The door opened and Guy peered in. "Has he woken up?"

Guthrie shook his head. "No, he's always sleeping when I'm here. I'll come back later, but it worries me, him sleeping so much. He should be awake for longer periods by now, but there seems to be no change at all. I'll send Peggy up to sit with him. At least then, someone will be here if he wakes."

It was much later when he had another chance to go to see Johnny. He knew Ben had seen Johnny and gone again. And Peggy said the boy had been awake and taken some broth. He opened the door quietly and saw Johnny lying, staring out of the window at the far peaks where the sun was already low in the sky.

"It's good to see you awake at last. How do you feel?" His voice sounded forced to his own ears. Why couldn't he just relax?

"Fine, I feel fine." Johnny's voice was flat, disinterested.

"That was a pretty damn stupid thing to do out there." Guthrie inclined his head toward the window. "You could have been killed." He felt the cold gaze turn to him now, and forced himself to look at his son.

Johnny seemed to shrug. "Well, I'm still here, ain't I? I had to bring Wallace into the open somehow. Seeing as how you didn't believe me."

Guthrie ignored the jibe. "It was crazy, that's what it was. Totally reckless. As I said, you could have been killed."

Johnny looked away, out of the window, apparently disinterested in the conversation.

Guthrie ground his teeth. He felt helpless. Frustrated, angry, and helpless. How could he have a discussion with the boy? Johnny wasn't going to give him an inch. Well, perhaps this wasn't the time. Perhaps it would be easier when Johnny was a little stronger. He still looked very ill.

"Was there anything else, Old Man?" Johnny had turned his head once more and was looking at him now. "Because I'm real tired."

Guthrie knew he was being dismissed. Damn it, this was his house and if he wanted to stand here, he would. Hell, he was entitled to feel concerned. His son had almost died. He couldn't understand the boy's attitude. Maybe, there was no Johnny, maybe all that was left was just Fierro. But if that was the case, why had he risked his life?

"Well?" Johnny's voice was cold.

"Why did you do it? If you hate us so much, why did you risk your life?"

"Well, I sure as hell didn't do it for you, Old Man. Now, will you go?"

His son's words cut him. It was as he'd suspected. Johnny hadn't been running to save him. He kept his voice even. "Don't you think you owe me an answer? And Guy risked his life running out to help you when you were shot. Maybe you didn't know?"

"I don't owe you nothin'. An' if Harvard chose to risk his life, that's his affair. I sure as hell wouldn't do it for him."

Guthrie threw his hands in the air. "So why did you help us? You must have had some reason."

Johnny looked very tired now. His face was gray and drawn. "Please, go. Leave me be."

Guthrie felt a twinge of guilt. And concern. "Shall I draw your curtains?"

"No, just leave 'em. I like being able to see out."

"You always did." The smile came unbidden. "I used to find

you kneeling at that window, always looking out at your mountain."

That got a reaction. Johnny turned sharply now, the sudden movement causing him to wince with pain. "What d'you mean, my mountain?"

"That's what you always called it, that one with the funny shaped peak. You always said it was your mountain. I used to tell you, when I was rich enough, I'd buy it for you."

He looked at Johnny again. Now the boy looked stricken, pain etched in his face.

"Please, go now." Johnny's voice was so faint that he had to strain to catch the words. The boy looked as though his heart was breaking. But that couldn't be so, not this hardened gunfighter. There was nothing he'd said that could upset Johnny Fierro. Hell, he'd only mentioned the mountain.

"You're sure there's nothing I can get you?" But the boy didn't even look at him. He merely shook his head and stared into the distance, at that damn mountain. Guthrie turned stiffly, to leave the room.

He was almost out of the door when he heard Johnny speak again. Very softly. "You don't have to worry. I'll be out of here as soon as I can ride."

Guthrie turned sharply. "You're leaving? What about the partnership, your share? Why'd you risk your life for it if you didn't want it?"

"I don't want nothing. Don't belong here, that's all."

Guthrie's gut tightened. Hell, the boy had only just come back. He couldn't leave again. He thought of how disappointed Guy would be. Funny, though, only days ago, he'd have been delighted if Johnny had said he was leaving. But now . . .

If Johnny left, what in hell would become of him? He'd bet that the boy would wind up dead in some dusty street in a meaningless gunfight. And they'd learn about it from the newspapers. And he suddenly knew he had to convince Johnny to reconsider. He had to keep his boy safe.

"Look, Johnny. You're really not in any state at the moment to make decisions. Let yourself get better. Heal up a bit. And then we'll talk about it. Guy's hoping you'll stay. We . . . we all are." There, he'd said it aloud. Admitted he wanted him to stay.

But Johnny only looked at him with the ghost of a smile playing at his lips. "I'm trouble. And we both know it. Harvard don't realize what me staying could mean. But you do. And I reckon if he understood what it really means, he'd be glad to see me gone."

"I'm sure that Guy would feel exactly the same as he does now." His words sounded stiff and formal even to himself. And unconvincing.

"Well, why don't you go find out? Like I said, I'm real tired now." And with that, his son rolled over and shut his eyes.

Guthrie stood at the door. He knew he'd been dismissed, knew he'd usually be furious at such behavior. But instead he found himself looking at an angry but very ill young man, one who seemed determined to mask his weakness at all costs— even if that cost was his future. He felt an urge to break through the boy's walls and hold him—like he used to before Gabriela snatched him away.

CHAPTER TWENTY-EIGHT

He felt sick. Not that he'd admit it. Ever. His back was on fire and yet he felt cold. That didn't make sense. He tried to focus on the window but even his mountain was blurry. Funny that it really was "his" mountain. The old man had shocked him with that. And yet, that very first morning when he looked out at it, it had seemed familiar, like an old friend. Now, he knew why.

Trouble was, since talking to the doc, finding out that the old man hadn't kicked him and his mother out, he'd lost his only reason for living. It was the hatred that had kept him going all these years, he knew that. But now . . . Hell, he had nothing left to hate. No reason for anything, anymore. Well, he'd be on his way soon. One way or the other. One thing was certain, he couldn't stay here. Even if the old man did mean it about the share of the ranch, it wouldn't be fair to them to stay. He was probably only offering it because he felt guilty about all those missing years. Hell, he wouldn't really want someone like Fierro around. Not now with the trouble over and Wallace gone. No one ever wanted Fierro around once he'd finished a job.

He'd probably have left already if he hadn't been so damn stupid as to get himself shot up. If he hadn't broken cover, running out when he did, he wouldn't be lying here burning up. Wouldn't have got a bullet in the back. And he still couldn't figure why he'd done it. When he saw Red stalking the old man . . . Shit. He had to stop thinking of it. Felt too damn sick to be worrying about that. He'd screwed up. That was all. Made a mistake. And he wasn't going to think on it no more.

He struggled against the feeling of nausea that swept over him. He didn't want to puke all over the bed and make more work for the girl. Surely he hadn't felt this bad earlier? The old man had worn him out, that's what it was. But hell, he felt sick. Talking to the doc had been tiring, but not like this. And shit, of all the gunfights for the doc to hear about, it had to be that one. The one he'd rather forget. He'd done a lot of things to be ashamed of, but that gunfight had to be near the top of the list. But the man had deserved what he got, least that's what he told himself.

Johnny hissed in a breath as another wave of pain rushed through him. Women. They were always his weak spot. Even so, he should have stuck to his rule in that gunfight. Quick and clean. But he hadn't. And, worse still, he'd enjoyed seeing that piece of shit suffer. Well, it was yet another thing to pay for when he went to hell. There'd be a lot of things to pay for one day.

He hoped the girl would leave him alone for a while. She'd been in and fussed around. She'd laid a soft, cool hand on his forehead and seemed concerned that he didn't want any water. He couldn't tell her he'd puke it back up. Anyway, she'd gone now, rushing off and muttering about the doctor.

So he could relax, for a moment. At least he had his gun. He could feel it under his pillow. Had the doc told her to leave it alone? She'd seen the gun but hadn't moved it. He felt safer with the gun. Yeah. Good to have it there, in case he needed it. Though, at the moment he wasn't sure he even had the strength to lift it. Shit, his back hurt. If only he could get warm—should've asked the girl for a blanket.

The door opened. Why couldn't they leave him in peace? He prayed it wouldn't be the old man again. It wasn't. It was Harvard.

"I thought I'd come and see how you're feeling."

"Fine. I'm doing fine." No way was he going to give up how weak he was, not even to this so-called brother. Why wouldn't they leave him alone? Still, least it wasn't the old man. What the hell was Harvard doing now? Shit. Pulling up a chair, sitting down.

He closed his eyes, hoping Harvard would get the message and leave. Instead, Harvard spoke. "Peggy said you didn't look too good. I'm not sure that 'fine' is a true assessment of how you're feeling."

Johnny opened his eyes but shut them again. Harvard looked very blurry. Shit, if only he didn't feel so ill. "I'm fine. Leave me alone."

"Were you trying to get yourself killed? I ran out to help you, but it was Eagle who took Donner down in the end."

"So? I ain't thanking you, if that's what you want. Just fuck off and leave me alone, Harvard."

"Do you always curse this much?"

Johnny opened his eyes again. But Harvard looked even more blurry now. "What?"

"Your vocabulary, you seem to swear a lot."

What the hell was Harvard talking about? "Just . . . leave me . . . be." His mouth was dry and it was hard to talk. If only Harvard would go. Didn't want people seeing him like this. Never let anyone see your weak spot. Never let your guard down. And he felt so cold. Maybe Harvard would get him a blanket. But he couldn't ask.

"Would you like a drink?"

Harvard seemed to be offering him a glass of something. Johnny tried to focus on it and pushed it away. "Not . . . thirsty." He swiped at the glass again, and felt the water spill over his arm. It made him even colder.

Harvard started wiping his arm with a cloth, drying him

off—like he was some little kid. No, please, not that. Johnny struck out, trying to push him away. Why wouldn't he go? But now Harvard was lifting him and putting the glass to his lips. Johnny swallowed some of the water but it made him feel like puking. He lay trying to fight the new wave of nausea before losing the battle and puking the water and foul bile all over himself. He could feel himself choking on it, unable to breathe, before Harvard pulled him up and propped him in place with a pillow. He couldn't focus on Harvard's face but felt his brother wiping the bile away. And being real gentle. Johnny felt like howling and he hadn't cried since he was a little kid. Instead he said, "Leave . . . the fuck . . . alone."

Harvard just pushed another pillow under him.

Johnny swallowed hard, trying to speak. "Don't touch . . . my gun."

"It's OK." His brother spoke softly. "I won't touch your gun. Are you cold?"

He nodded. He was too tired to talk. Felt worse now; the puking had worn him out.

"I'll get you another blanket."

He was vaguely aware of Harvard going out of the room and then the next thing he felt was his brother wrapping another blanket around him. It didn't help—he was still cold. He just wanted to shut his eyes. And not wake up. But Harvard was talking again.

"I think you need to stay awake, Johnny. The doctor is coming to see you soon. I'm sure he'd want you to stay awake."

"What's he comin' for? 'Fraid I'm gonna die on you?"

"He likes to check up on his patients. That's all."

Johnny tried to think of something to say, but his head felt odder now. Kinda muddled. Hell, was that his mother standing by the door? No, couldn't be. She was long dead. Shit. Don't think of that. Not her dying.

280

Sure looked like her though. And now it seemed like she'd lied to him. That everything she'd told him had been lies. Or had he dreamed that? Yeah. Maybe he'd dreamed that. If only Harvard would let him sleep. He needed to sleep.

"Johnny, don't go to sleep. Try and listen to me."

Who was that? Oh, Harvard. Brother. Didn't know about a brother. She never said nothing about a brother. Everyone lied. She'd lied. Why was she standing at the door? Thought she was dead. But she was here now, at the door.

"Johnny, can you hear me?"

He tried to open his eyes to look at Harvard. So tired, though. Felt like someone was wiping his face. Who'd do that? There'd been a girl, but she'd gone.

"Johnny, come on. You've got to try and stay awake."

Harvard sounded odd. Worried. What about? There was more noise now. Voices. If only they'd shut up, let him sleep.

Now there was a new voice. "Johnny. It's Doc. Can you hear me?"

Course he could hear. He tried to nod.

"Can you look at me, Johnny? I'm going to have to have another look at your back. Do you understand? It's infected. But we'll sort it out, OK?"

He tried to speak. " 'Bout that gunfight."

"Johnny, I can't hear you, what's that?" The doc sounded a long way away.

"That gunfight, had . . . had . . . my reasons."

"Don't worry about the gunfight. We just need to get you better."

"Let me . . . go . . . Doc."

"Johnny, I don't like losing patients, I told you that before. But what I'm going to do is going to hurt, I'm afraid."

He tried to focus on Doc but everything was slipping away. He could feel hands on him. But he was so tired and cold.

There was a glow by the door. Looked warm there. If only he could get there. So cold.

CHAPTER TWENTY-NINE

Guy grunted as he tried to ease the crick in his neck. Everything ached, his back, his shoulders, his head. Despite wearing gloves, his hands were raw, too. He'd never realized what hard work ranching was. He thought back wryly to his early thoughts that other people on the ranch would do the physical work, that as owner he would delegate the hard labor. He couldn't have been more wrong. But at least the hard work was taking his mind off Johnny.

He was surprised at how concerned he felt about his brother. Particularly in view of what he had learned about Johnny Fierro. Once the ranch hands had learned who Guthrie's long-lost son was, they'd been only too keen to fill him in on all the stories surrounding his gunfighter brother. They weren't pretty stories.

He'd been unsuccessful in getting any more information out of Guthrie. The man seemed shocked by Johnny's relapse and sat for hours by Johnny's bed, staring at his extremely sick son. Ben seemed to think they would lose Johnny. When Guy asked what his brother's chances were, Ben had shaken his head sadly and said: "Virtually nil. He was weak from the operation and this infection is very severe. Add to that the fact that he doesn't appear to want to live, well . . ."

Wearily, Guy climbed the stairs. Tired as he was, he wanted to see how Johnny was doing. He'd been appalled that Ben thought Johnny didn't want to live. How could anyone not want to survive? His brother was the strangest man he'd ever met and he didn't know what to make of him.

He walked into Johnny's room. Guthrie was sitting by the bed, studying Johnny's face intently. Guy quirked an eyebrow. "How is he? Is there any change?"

His father didn't seem to hear. He continued to stare at Johnny, lost in thought.

"Sir, are you all right? Staring at him like that, it's as if you're looking for something, what do you hope to see?"

Guthrie looked at him. "Some trace of the child I once knew, I suppose. He had a smile that could light up a room, but I haven't seen that smile since he came home."

Guy paused, before saying gently, "That was a long time ago. He's a man now. He's bound to be different. People change, sir."

His father shook his head sadly. "I still hoped for the smile. If only I knew what had happened to him in the missing years. Those scars . . . I tried so hard to find him. Spent years, on and off, searching. Every time I had money, I started another search. But those border towns, it's easy to disappear in those towns. I tried so hard . . ." he trailed off. Guthrie shook his head again. "As to how he is, I really don't know. He looks dreadful. His breathing is very shallow but I don't think he's worse than he was. Holding his own is the best I can say. Ben seems to think that he doesn't want to live." He sighed, heavily. "How can someone so young be so tired of life?"

Guy looked down at Johnny. He'd heard Johnny ask Ben to let him go, and the meaning had been clear. "I don't think he's as tough as he tries to make out. When I came up to sit with him, before Ben arrived, he was sick all over himself and I sponged him off and washed his face. But the strangest thing was, it looked like his eyes were . . . Well, he almost looked like he was going to cry." Guy wondered how to explain it. "It was almost as though he couldn't believe someone was caring for him. The way he looked, it was really sad. Of course, he told me to leave him alone, but not so politely."

Guthrie snorted. "I can certainly believe that. His language is appalling."

"I told him that too."

Guy stretched to ease his aching back. Then he rolled his head from side to side. He flushed as he realized that Guthrie was watching him, looking faintly amused.

"Ranching's hard work. Any regrets about deciding to stay?"

Guy shook his head. "No. I was bored in Boston and I can honestly say that there seems to be no chance of that here. In fact, a little boredom would be very welcome right now." He glanced again at Johnny's pallid face before adding, "I wasn't sure what to think when you told me about Johnny being a gunfighter. The idea of someone making a living by being fast with a gun is so alien to me. Abhorrent, if I'm honest. But then I tell myself that Boston rules don't apply out here."

"Guy, even out here, gunfighting is abhorrent. We're not that uncivilized."

"I meant no offense . . ."

"I know, but make no mistake, if Johnny lives and if he decides to stay, he will not be considered a welcome addition to the neighborhood. I suspect that a lot of my oldest friends will want nothing to do with him, or me, if I encourage him to stay. They won't want him near their wives or their daughters, that's for sure. They will simply view him as a killer—a hired gun, not Johnny Sinclair."

Guy huffed, and nodded slowly. "I'm sorry. I guess I never considered how difficult this is for you."

His father shrugged. "It's not just what the neighbors will think. His staying could bring other types of trouble—other gunfighters who want his reputation. When they find out where he is, they might come looking. They'll come to challenge him because killing him boosts their own reputations. It's all about reputation. And believe me, Johnny's is fearsome. His being here brings danger to us all. I want to save him from that life, if it's not too late already. But the way he was when he arrived . . . He was cold, hard, brutal. The things he said, his language, the way he looked at Peggy that first evening. I'll be honest, he frightens me. But I am even more frightened of reading about his death in some seedy border town, gunned down in a senseless gunfight. I dream now of that, when I'm not dreaming of him being gunned down here during the battle."

It was probably the first really frank speech he'd heard from his father. He felt compassion for the man; he looked so defeated. Although the ranch was saved, the battle was far from over, assuming Johnny lived. But that looked far from certain, and if Johnny died, he suspected that his father would still feel defeated. After all those years of searching, it would be a very cruel blow for Guthrie to lose him now.

"For what it's worth, sir, I really do feel that there's more to him than what we saw that first evening. Did you know he believes you threw him and his mother out? Thinks you never wanted him?"

The color drained from Guthrie's face. "He told you that? What did he say? When was this?"

"It was the evening he and I were moving the cattle. He said you threw him and his mother out because you didn't want a mixed-breed son."

His father looked white and shaken. "Who would have told him that nonsense? Surely Gabriela wouldn't have told him that? Oh, my God." He held his head in his hands before looking up, a dawning realization on his face. "My God," he said softly. "No wonder he hates me, if he believes that. Is that why he was trying to make me angry, so I would draw on him, so he could kill me? It would explain his attitude toward me. But if so, if he really does hate me, why did he risk his life to save the ranch? To save me?"

Guy flushed, uncertain of what to say. What could he say? He didn't know what the hell Johnny had been thinking when he came up with his plan to draw Wallace out into the open. Was it possible that Johnny had figured on getting killed?

And when he was honest with himself, it was that part of his brother he found most disturbing. It was why he felt there had to be more to Johnny. He was a man who was tired of life, and who'd chosen to risk making the ultimate sacrifice to save the ranch, but for what? Surely not for Guthrie, so why?

He stared again at the enigma lying in the bed, struggling to breathe, but holding on. He wondered if Johnny would live to answer some of these questions. God, he hoped so. Heavy footsteps on the stairs dragged his mind back. Hopefully it was Ben. At least he would be able to tell them how Johnny was doing.

As the doctor appeared in the doorway, Guy sighed with relief and Guthrie lifted his head from his hands. He still seemed sunk in despair.

"How's he doing?" asked Ben.

"We were rather hoping that you would tell us that," Guy responded dryly.

"Well, at least he's still with us, so let me take a look at him. Help me turn him, Guy, so that I can take a proper look at that wound."

Guy hurried to help and then stood back while Ben inspected the bullet wound and checked Johnny's pulse.

After a few moments the doctor stood back, viewing Johnny thoughtfully. "Well, he's holding his own. His pulse is still weak but the wound looks a lot better, no sign of new infection. I really didn't think he had a chance." Ben paused, his lips twitching. "I have to tell you, Guthrie, gunfighter or not, I rather like him. I admit, at first, I was like you, just seeing the reputation, but there's more to this young man than meets the eye. I hope we all have the chance to see what else is there, besides Johnny Fierro, gun for hire."

Guthrie rubbed his chin. "Aye, well, I hope you're right. But what's worrying me right now is that Guy's just told me Johnny believes I threw him and Gabriela out! The only explanation is that she lied to him."

The doctor nodded his head slowly and said, "I know, Johnny and I discussed it briefly. He has some very strange ideas."

"And it didn't occur to you to tell me about this?" Guthrie demanded angrily.

Ben shot him a look. "Guthrie, he's my patient, anything Johnny says to me is confidential. I was going to speak to him about discussing it with you when he was stronger, but in case you hadn't noticed, he had a relapse. However, I did tell him that he was mistaken, and I told him you'd been searching for him for years. But I am not telling you what he said. That is for him to tell you, when he's ready."

Guthrie's shoulders sagged. "And if he dies, I'll never know."

CHAPTER THIRTY

He managed to pull himself round and get his feet to the floor. Now, if only he could walk. Gritting his teeth, he managed to force himself to his feet and stood swaying for a second, clinging to the bedpost. The room spun and for a moment he thought the floor was coming up to meet him. He closed his eyes briefly until the feeling of nausea passed. The next challenge was to reach the window. Find out how strong he was. How soon could he get out of here? He had to get out, get away from these people. He didn't belong here and they sure as hell didn't need someone like him around.

And they never left him alone. There was always someone hovering. Why? They couldn't care about him so why wouldn't they just leave him alone? The easiest thing was to pretend to be tired. They'd nod, and look like they felt sorry for him, and leave. Trouble was it didn't work with the doc. The doc just snorted and told him to stop faking. He seemed surprised that Johnny had survived. Hell, Johnny was surprised that he'd survived. It hadn't been part of his plan. He'd almost been looking forward to meeting his old friend, Death. It was time. And now that he knew Mama had lied to him all those years, well, there really wasn't much point in anything, anymore.

Of course, if he wasn't so dumb, he'd have seen through her lies. When he was a little kid he used to ask her why they never stayed long in one place. And she always told him the same thing: because of the men searching for them. And he'd asked why, if his father didn't want them, was he trying to find them? But she never answered that question. More often than not he got slapped, or pushed out the door. He'd soon learned not to ask. He'd learned to do a lot of things real fast. Like walking real quiet, so if Mama had a man with her, they wouldn't hear if he walked in by mistake. That always led to a beating, or worse, depending on the man.

Still, no sense brooding on the past. It couldn't be changed, no more than the future could. A future? That was the one thing he'd never had. Not like other people. He was too far down the road he was traveling to hope for anything. If only he could get the hell out of here. He needed to get away from the old man, Harvard, and the girl. He couldn't think of them by their names. That would be too personal and he didn't want anything personal.

He let go of the bedpost, relieved the room had stopped swaying. Slowly, with a hiss of pain, he made his way to the window. Enjoying the feel of the soft breeze blowing his hair, he looked across the yard, where the men were busy rebuilding the bunkhouse, to the hazy outline of his mountain. Fuck! There he went again, thinking of the damn mountain. Why did he keep looking at it? What did it matter if he'd liked it when he was a little kid? He should be thinking about the gun instead. The gun the doc had passed to him was his spare gun and that was still under his pillow. But he needed to check his other one, the modified gun that he used for gunfights—the killing gun. Where the hell was it? Maybe it was in the chest of drawers. He pulled the top drawer open and felt a surge of relief to see his gun. Lifting it out, he smiled at the weight of it in his hand. The butt molded perfectly into his palm. It belonged there like the gun almost grew from him. It was who he was. The only thing he was sure of.

He stroked it tenderly. God, it felt good to have it in his

hand. To know it was safe. Was the Derringer in the drawer too? Yes, that was there so it was one less thing to worry about. But his knives? He frowned, were his knives still in his boot? His boots stood against the wall by the chest. It looked a long way down to reach them. He tried to bend to pick them up, grunting at the sharp stab of pain and then the room starting spinning. He leaned against the oak chest, trying to catch his breath and praying he wouldn't collapse. He knew he'd never get back up without help, and he sure as hell couldn't risk anyone seeing him like that. The gun was the main thing; he needed to check that it was loaded. Suddenly his senses were on full alert. Cocking his head, and listening hard, he could hear footsteps outside in the passage. Shit! He stood, swaying, hoping that whoever it was would walk past his room.

He muttered an oath as the door opened and his father came in, frowning when he saw Johnny standing. "What are you doing out of bed?"

Johnny glared. "Gettin' my gun. Not that it's your business. I got to get up sometime. I need to be out of here soon."

"Where you need to be is back in bed." His father hurried across the room, crowding him and trying to get hold of him.

Johnny struck the proffered hand away, hissing, "Leave me alone. I'm fine." He wished he felt fine. And if the old man was going to stand watching him as he tried to struggle back to bed, he'd soon figure out that Fierro was anything but fine. Johnny sucked in a breath, building himself up for those agonizing steps. Still, he'd got the gun, which was what he'd wanted. Maybe if he kept quiet and stood at the window for a few moments longer, the old man would give up and leave. Johnny shut his eyes briefly, his head was throbbing now—that was all he needed. Everything was such an effort and the old man still hadn't moved. He was just standing there, watching him. Waiting. Fuck.

"Do you want a hand?" The old man sounded kind of smug, like he knew Fierro needed help.

"No!" And with shuffling steps, Johnny started his slow trek back to his bed. It felt like a mile, and the old man hovered alongside of him, looking like he was ready to grab him at any second. Johnny ground his teeth. What was it with the old man? Why couldn't he just go away and leave Fierro alone?

Johnny smothered a sigh of relief as he finally reached the bed. Grabbing the bedpost and holding on tight, he eased himself down to sit on the edge of the bed. He was worn out. He was breathing hard and each breath made him flinch with pain. What he really wanted was to lie down, but there was no way he could manage to lift his legs up. All he could do was sit there like it was exactly where he wanted to be.

"Shall I help lift your legs up? Ease you round?"

Shit! It was like the old man knew how much he wanted to lie down. But Fierro would never admit to needing that. He glared at his father, hoping that if he was rude enough, the old man would leave him alone. "I'm right where I want to be, so fuck off." Johnny fiddled with the gun in his hand, anything rather than look at the old man. But he could feel those blue eyes boring into him. Blue—just like his own eyes.

But if he'd hoped his father would leave, it was a vain hope. The man was pulling up a chair. Why couldn't he just go? Why wouldn't they all leave him in peace? Were they afraid he was going to steal the silver?

Johnny narrowed his eyes. "I'm not in the mood to talk. I'm tired."

"Well, then you'd better let me help you into bed as you quite obviously can't manage it alone." The old man sounded pleased about that, knowing he'd got the upper hand. And the old man knew that Johnny knew who'd got the upper hand.

Johnny gritted his teeth. "I'm fine, right here."

"Well, in that case you won't mind me sitting and having a talk."

Damn. There was no getting out of this, leastways not if he wanted to keep his dignity. He sighed. "About what?" He'd bet the old man wanted to talk about Wallace.

The old man hesitated, like he wasn't sure how to go on, almost like he was embarrassed about something. Hell, he'd bet the man was probably desperate to see the back of Fierro. And he couldn't blame him for that.

"I heard that you think I threw you and your mother out."

Johnny tried to keep his face expressionless, but shit, he hadn't seen that one coming. He felt a pang of disappointment—he'd thought the doc would keep things to himself. He should have known better. "So the doc told you that, huh?"

He was surprised when the old man shook his head. "No, Ben didn't tell me anything. You're his patient; he would never divulge anything a patient told him. He takes that oath of his very seriously. No, it was Guy who told me."

Of course! Funny, he'd forgotten all about that evening when they were on the trail. He still didn't know why he'd talked as much as he did to old Harvard.

He shrugged. "Seems I might have heard things wrong."

"I didn't throw you out. I woke one morning and found you both gone and I did everything I could to find you. That's the truth. Did your mother tell you I'd thrown you out?" His father's eyes bore into him.

He sure as hell didn't want to discuss his mother with the old man. He shrugged again. "Don't remember."

It didn't sound convincing and he knew the old man didn't believe him. The bastard sat silently watching him, waiting for more. Well, he'd have to wait a long time, because Fierro sure as hell wasn't saying any more.

Eventually the old man broke the silence. "It seems she'd

been seeing someone. I . . . I knew nothing about it. Other people did, but not me. I was the last one to know."

That was a tough admission to make. And knowing his mother as he did, it was no surprise that she'd had a man on the side. Johnny looked at him from under half-closed eyes before glancing away and saying softly, "Husband's always the last to know."

"I tried hard to find you. I even hired Pinkerton men whenever I could afford it. But there was never any trace."

Johnny shrugged again. "We moved 'round a lot." He wasn't going to tell the old man that they were always trying to keep one step ahead of the Pinkerton men or an unpaid landlord.

"Where did you live? Did your mother stay with him?"

"Don't remember where. Like I said we moved around a lot. And I don't remember no man either." Just hundreds of men. Dios, his mama had liked men. Not surprising she'd left the old man.

His father leaned forward, frowning. "Well, if she didn't stay with him, how did the two of you live? Did your mother work?"

He'd been expecting the question, so the lie came easily. "Yeah. In a cantina." That was a joke. She'd never work for an honest buck, not when she could make it on her back. And any money she made went to tequila. But the way the old man was nodding, looked like he'd bought it. What was the point in telling him his wife was a whore? She was dead and it seemed she was the one who'd lied, so why upset the man?

"Your back . . . Who whipped you? Surely not your mother?"

"No! Wasn't her."

His father tilted his head, his brow furrowed. "Well then, who?"

"I don't remember." And that was the truth. There'd been too many of them. But the whippings were the least of it . . . Shit! He couldn't think about that. Johnny gritted his teeth, trying to push the memories away.

He fiddled with the gun again, weighing it in his hand, loving the smoothness of the handle against his hand. He must oil it. He must oil all the guns. Maybe the girl would bring him up a cloth to cover the bed so he could oil them. He'd ask her when his father and brother were out working. She'd be easy to get around.

"So, are you going to stay?" His father's voice dragged him back to the present.

Johnny ducked his head. Perhaps it was time for a little honesty. Just a little. He met his father's eyes and sighed softly. "We both know I don't belong here and I'd only bring trouble. It's best that I leave."

The old man shook his head like Fierro was talking garbage. "But you do belong here. You were born here. I built this place assuming that one day my sons would have it."

Johnny raised an eyebrow. "Well, I'm sure old Harvard will be real pleased about that. But he sure as hell won't want me around."

"He's hoping you'll stay, he said so."

Johnny shrugged. "Yeah, well, let's face it. Being from back East, he don't know what it really means. You an' me do, though. How would you introduce me to all your fancy friends? And you really think your neighbors want someone like me around?"

"That's their problem. The fact remains that you're my son."

"Ain't that easy, though. What about when people come looking for me? A gunfighter maybe, who wants my reputation. How you going to deal with that, Old Man?"

The old man looked really pissed now. "I don't know how I'll deal with it. I suppose we'll just have to deal with it as a family, if and when it happens."

Johnny threw his hands up with a grunt of irritation. "You don't get it, do you? I'm trouble. And I bring trouble. And hell, if we're being honest, why do you want me to stay anyway? You sure didn't want me here when I arrived. You were shittin' yourself you were so scared of me. What changed?"

His father moved to the window, staring out at the mountains. He spoke so softly Johnny had to strain to hear him. "I don't want to read of your death in the papers. Dead in some dusty street, killed in some pointless gunfight."

Johnny furrowed his brow, puzzled. "It's what I do. I don't care; why should you?"

"Damn it!" His father banged his fist down on the desk by the window. "I'm your father, of course I care. You have your whole life ahead of you and you're just throwing it away. You've everything to lose."

Johnny laughed humorlessly. "Hell, I got nothing to lose. And I gave up caring whether I live or die a long time ago. I don't see why you should give a shit. You couldn't wait to get me out of here a few days ago. People don't change that fast. And I still can't figure why you sent for me in the first place, because it sure seemed like you didn't want my gun." Johnny paused, shooting him a sharp look. "When did you find out who I was?"

His father flushed but didn't answer. Instead he turned back to stare through the window.

Johnny hesitated as a wave of pain surged through his body, grateful that the man was looking the other way. He sucked in a breath. "I asked you a question. When did you find out?"

His father turned to look at him. "Almost two years ago. I . . . I didn't know what to do."

"Until you needed my gun." Johnny laughed coldly.

His father shook his head. "No, that's not how it was."

"Well, why don't you tell me how it was?"

The old man looked real uncomfortable now. Good. Fierro was getting his edge back—he had the old man on the run.

"I didn't send for you." His father snapped the words out.

"Guy sent for you when I was sick. Peggy told him you were still alive."

Johnny bit back a laugh. Oh boy, he'd love to have been a fly on the wall when the old man found they'd sent for the infamous gunfighter. Still, to give the old man credit, he'd had the guts to admit it, even though he looked like he expected Johnny to shoot him. Yeah, Fierro definitely had his edge back.

"Well, Old Man," he drawled, "sure explains why you were real unfriendly when I showed up. No wonder you had my money ready an' waiting. But, you needn't worry, like I said, I'll be leaving as soon as I can ride."

The pulse started going in his father's temple. "I'm offering you a third of this ranch and you're going to walk away from it? You must see that this is a better life. You'll end up dead in no time if you go back to your old one."

Johnny shrugged. "We all gotta go sometime, don't we?"

"What are you scared of?"

Johnny jerked his head up. "I ain't scared of nothing, Old Man."

"I'm offering you a chance of a different life, Johnny. A fresh start, a family, land, a home. Isn't that worth having?"

A fresh start? Yeah, as if someone like Fierro could ever have that. It was way too late for that. "Like I said, you'll be a lot better off without me around. I'll only bring trouble. And we both know that's the truth."

The pulse in his father's temple was off again, and his face red. Johnny sighed. It seemed he had a talent for pissing off his father. But he wished the man would go. This talk was wearing him out. All he wanted was to lie down, and sleep.

The old man stood up and walked slowly to the door. He'd finally got the message.

His father paused in the doorway. "I'm offering you a chance here, Johnny. The best you've ever had. But it seems to me, you're scared to take it." And the man walked out of the room.

CHAPTER THIRTY-ONE

He felt like throwing something at his father's departing back—preferably a sharp knife. The sooner he got out of here the better. He didn't need these people, or their fancy words. If he had the strength, he'd walk out right now. But he didn't think he could even lift his legs into the bed. Shit. Just keep sitting right here. If someone else came in, and it seemed like that was all they did do, they'd think he wanted to be sitting here. But hell, his head hurt.

Still, leastways the old man had been honest. Admitting he hadn't sent for him. And why would he have sent for him? It wasn't like he was the sort of a son a man like Sinclair could be proud of. Not like Harvard. Now he was everything Fierro wasn't. He was the sort of man Sinclair could introduce to his friends and neighbors. Johnny grinned, imagining the reaction in town to the arrival of Johnny Fierro as a permanent fixture. Hell, they'd all be cowering in their houses and locking up their daughters. Not that he'd be interested in their dull daughters. He liked fire in his women. And that was a good sign—he must be on the mend if he was thinking about women. If only he didn't feel like shit. He couldn't imagine being much use to any woman at the moment.

Gritting his teeth, he strained to lift his legs into the bed but still couldn't manage. Shit, he'd be sitting here forever at this rate. Shit! Footsteps were coming along the corridor. Surely not someone else coming to bother him? He grunted in irritation as the door opened. It was Harvard with a tray.

"I brought you some soup. I thought you might be starting to feel hungry."

"Well, I ain't. Just sitting here, that's all. Fed up with lying down."

Harvard raised an eyebrow, like he didn't believe that. Johnny fought the urge to glare at him. Instead he tried to look relaxed, and gazed toward the window like he was perfectly happy. But instead of leaving, Harvard put the tray down on the dresser, frowning.

"Would you like a hand into bed? You look absolutely exhausted."

Johnny gave him the benefit of his best scowl. "No, I don't need a fucking hand . . ." But Harvard ignored him, lifting his legs up and gently supporting him into the bed. Then, he leaned Johnny forward and propped him up with some pillows. Johnny ground his teeth, feeling the heat flushing his face. Hell, if he could reach his gun, he'd blow Harvard's head off for this. But he felt too damn tired even for that. Trouble was he felt too tired for anything. And if he was honest he had been for a long time now.

"Would you like the soup?"

"No!" Truth was, even the smell was making him feel queasy. And why the hell did Harvard have to stand there, just looking at him? And for the millionth time he wondered why wouldn't they all just leave him alone?

Harvard leaned against the chest of drawers. "So, have you decided to stay?"

"Nope. Soon as I can ride, I'm outta here."

His brother raised an eyebrow. "Why?"

"What the hell do you mean, why?"

"Just that, why leave?"

What sort of question was that? He tried to think of some

smart answer, but his head was throbbing. "No reason to stay."

"Don't you think this land, this ranch, is a good reason?"

Johnny snorted. "Is that why you're staying then, for the land? Wouldn't have thought it would mean much to you. I'd have figured you'd want to hightail it back to Boston." That's it. Try and get the edge back.

Harvard grinned and pulled up a chair. "Actually, it's not the land I'm staying for."

He had to admit, he was curious now. "Then for what?"

The older man hesitated, looking thoughtful. "For the challenge, I think. And curiosity. I'm interested in getting to know our father better. It's been too many years since I spent any time with him. I mean there were occasional visits to Boston, and letters, but to be honest I can't say that I know him. Aren't you curious to know him better?"

Johnny shrugged. "No. He's nothin' to me."

"Aren't you curious to get to know me better? I'd like the chance to know you."

Johnny glared. "Ain't none of you anything to me."

"So why risk your life helping us?"

Johnny narrowed his eyes. "None of your fucking business."

"Your language is atrocious, you know. We're going to have to do something about your appalling lack of more suitable adjectives."

Was the man talking a foreign language now? Johnny felt off balance, he'd lost his edge. Try a different ploy. He yawned. "I'm tired, Harvard, so if you don't mind . . ."

Harvard smiled. "Oh, don't mind me. I'll just sit and chat until you nod off."

Damn, the man was stubborn. Why wouldn't he just leave?

Harvard leaned back, crossing his legs. "So, as I was saying, why did you risk your life? I really am very curious, given your apparent disregard for our well-being."

Johnny wondered how many fancy words old Harvard actually knew. He had a feeling that his brother wasn't going to let up on this line of questioning. Hell, maybe if he answered the question he'd go away and leave Fierro in peace. "You an' the old man really don't have any idea do you about what Donner would have done to the women here?"

His brother frowned. "You mean he'd have killed them?"

"Eventually, yeah. But he'd have wanted his fun first. Wouldn't make no difference who the women were, Donner and some of those men would have taken turns at raping them and then killed them, including the old man's precious darling. It's what Donner always does."

"But he was a gunfighter, like you."

Johnny jerked forward. "No! Not like me, Harvard. I might be a hell of a lot of things but I don't make war on women and I ain't nothing like Donner. Nothing! An' I tell you, if you ever say that again, I really will kill you." He felt the blood pumping in his head. If he'd had enough energy he'd have knocked Harvard out for daring to suggest he was anything like that piece of shit, Donner.

"So you did it because of the women? Johnny Fierro, gun for hire, has a weak spot?" His brother looked at him curiously. "I thought you were supposed to be a really hardened gunfighter, it's what everyone says. The ranch hands are terrified of you. They say you're as cold and hard as they come. And yet you risked your life for some women you didn't know." Harvard shook his head slowly. "You're not stupid. You must have calculated the risk to yourself. So the only conclusion I can reach is that you have an Achilles heel, brother. Under that cold exterior you hide behind, you have a soft spot when it comes to seeing the weak suffer."

What the fuck was an acklees heel? "Don't call me brother. You ain't nothing to me."

"Yes, you said that already." Harvard smiled suddenly. "I was delighted when Peggy told me that you were alive. I was looking forward to being reunited, but I have to be honest and say I never envisaged you to be the way you are now!"

Envisaged, what the hell sort of word was that? Did Harvard use these words deliberately, to try to appear smart? No, somehow that didn't fit. It was simply that he knew these words and they came real natural to him. Oddly, he didn't think Harvard was trying to talk down to him. Was just talking to him like he'd talk to anyone he knew, assuming Johnny would understand, because he didn't think Fierro was stupid. It was kind of good not to be thought stupid. Most folk seemed to think breeds were dumb.

"When you were a child did you ever think it would be nice to have a brother?" The question broke into his thoughts.

"What the hell would I have wanted a brother for?" He laughed. No way would he tell old Harvard how he'd longed for one when he was a kid. An older brother who'd have stuck up for him, fought for him, maybe stopped Mama's men . . . no! Don't think about that. Anything but that. "Sorry, Harvard, but, no. An' if I had, he wouldn't have been nothing like you." He was amused to see his brother looked kind of disappointed.

"So, why don't you want to stay?"

"Told you, nothing for me here."

"You'd rather go back to being a gunfighter? You might get killed."

Johnny laughed. "Yeah, well, that comes to us all, sooner or later."

His brother leaned forward, frowning. "Yes, but most people envisage a long life first."

Shit, envisage, he'd said it again. "Well, Harvard, I ain't most people." What sort of word was envisage anyway?

"No, you're certainly not." His brother paused. "I'm not

ignoring the business in Bitterville, but I understand why that happened. You had good reason for that. But putting that to one side, I have to say, that despite your tough gunfighter image, you don't seem very dangerous."

Johnny looked at him and said very softly, "I am." He paused, let the words sink in. "Don't make that mistake, Harvard. Don't go thinking it's all talk. I done things you can't even begin to imagine, an' believe me, they ain't nice."

The curtain billowed in the breeze at the open window. His brother bowed his head as if lost in thought. "I killed, as a soldier in the war."

Johnny shrugged. "That's different. Hell, people think you're a hero in a war. No one thinks I'm a hero. Just a paid killer."

Harvard looked up, the breeze ruffling his hair. "How many men have you killed?"

Why did people always ask that? They were so predictable. Hell, the old man had been dying to know the same thing. Kind of funny, really. He'd seen the curiosity in the old man's eyes and had expected the question. But in the end his father hadn't had the guts to ask.

But he sure as hell wasn't going to get into it with Harvard. It wasn't nobody's business. "I haven't been counting."

"I thought gunfighters had notches on their guns."

Johnny smiled thinly. "My gun wouldn't be big enough."

His brother flinched, like he'd been struck. Johnny chalked one up to himself. It had shut Harvard up. But not for long, the man was opening his mouth again. Did he never tire of talking?

"You must know how many gunfights you've been in."

"No, I don't." Except, he did. "Anyway, in a range war you never know if the people you shoot live or die. Tend not to hang around to find out."

"How old were you? When you first . . . ?" Harvard couldn't even say it.

Johnny stared at him icily. "None of your damn business." Hell, if his brother knew just how young Johnny had been, he'd never believe it.

His brother sighed. "OK, but this life of yours, is it so wonderful that you'd rather go back to it than stay here?"

Johnny ran his hand through his hair, and huffed out a sigh. "It's what I know. It's who I am. You don't get it, do you?"

"I know you'll end up dead before long. When you could stay here and have a life, a future."

A future. That was rich. It was the one thing he'd always known he didn't have. Futures were for other people, not him. "It's too late to change. Even if I wanted to."

That seemed to rile Harvard; he colored up and the nerve started pulsing in his temple, just like the old man's did. "Rubbish! Of course it's not too late. You're young. You can have a whole different life, if you want it."

Johnny shuffled down under the covers, shutting his eyes, hoping Harvard would leave.

"And don't think that if you shut your eyes, I'll just tiptoe away. I want an answer. Why won't you stay?"

Johnny opened his eyes. "Like I said, I'm dangerous, Harvard. I'm also dangerous to be around. And believe me; people will come looking for me, at some stage. And that puts everyone near me at risk—including you. So maybe you should start thinking about that. Worry about your own skin instead of mine. And you should realize how lucky you are that I'm going to ride outta here. Hell, you'll get half a ranch instead of a third."

"I'd rather have a brother."

Johnny rolled his eyes. "Funny, you don't seem stupid. Except when you wear them damn stupid Eastern clothes. But believe me; you don't want me anywhere near."

"If people come looking for you, we'll deal with it when it happens."

It was odd, but the old man had used almost the same sort of words. What was it he'd said? Something about what families did. But neither the old man, nor Harvard, seemed to realize that they weren't family—they were strangers. "Just get the fuck out of here. I'm leaving, as soon as I can ride. An' that's an end of it."

"You still haven't said why. If you dislike us so much, you can't be worried about our safety. I'm just wondering what it is you're so scared of, surely not us?"

The dry heat of anger came rushing over him and he reached under the pillow for his gun. "Get out of here, now!" He cocked the gun, and hissed, "Now, Harvard."

His brother stood, and picking up the dish, walked slowly to the door. He turned again and smiled almost sadly. "Calm down, I'm going. But you're wrong, you know. You've got to learn to trust someone and you might as well start with family." He closed the door behind him and Johnny fell back onto his pillows, feeling like someone had torn his guts out.

CHAPTER THIRTY-TWO

Ben drove his buggy up the long approach to the hacienda. It was an imposing entrance and never failed to impress him. The grand gates and the sweeping driveway announced the presence of a successful man. It always puzzled him. Guthrie wasn't a boastful man. He was a good employer and loyal to his friends. Ben suspected that it had been Guthrie's way of dealing with Gabriela's departure. It had been a desperate attempt to shore up his pride when he'd failed to find her or Johnny. It was too out of character for him to have built it for any other reason.

What a family! Guthrie was all stubborn pride, with a hell of a temper. And Guy was reserved in the extreme. A man could never guess what he was thinking. Those dispassionate eyes and carefully chosen words didn't give a thing away. And as for Johnny, it seemed he'd inherited his father's temper. And stubborn didn't begin to describe him. God only knew what would become of him if no one could convince him to stay. Ben shuddered, remembering Johnny's ramblings during his fever. He'd been sickened and filled with a murderous rage when he'd made sense of some of it. No wonder Johnny had turned out wild. But there was also a core of decency running through the young man, a miracle given the circumstances of his youth. He wished Johnny would tell him more about the gunfight; he had a feeling the story would reveal a lot.

What he couldn't understand was what Gabriela had been doing when Johnny was being abused. Why hadn't she sent him home for his own safety? Had she really hated Guthrie that much? Ben shook his head, wondering sadly if Johnny realized the implications of learning that he and his mother hadn't been thrown out—that there had been a place of safety for him all along. Johnny's life could have been very different. But it was obvious that Johnny thought it too late to change course now, or that he no longer had the energy. Ben couldn't blame him for that hard shell or the cynicism but it tore at his heart to see the hard young man, knowing life could have been so very different.

Guthrie and Guy were standing outside the hacienda and he wondered briefly if Guthrie had the faintest idea of what sort of abuse Johnny had suffered. Probably not. He could see the scarred back, but not beyond.

He reined in the horse and smiled at the two men. "It's a lovely day, isn't it? And how's my patient doing?"

Guthrie shook his head. "That's what Guy and I were talking about. His recovery seems very slow, Ben, but he's still hell-bent on leaving as soon as he can ride."

Ben looked at them. "It may seem an obvious question, but have you tried talking to him?"

Guthrie glared at him. "Of course I've tried talking to him. It . . . It didn't go very well. I . . ." He paused. "I don't understand the boy."

"He's not a boy," Ben snapped. "He hasn't been for a very long time, I would say. And I suppose you lost your temper. Why doesn't that surprise me?" Ben was gratified to see that his sarcasm had the expected response. Guthrie looked even crosser.

"I tried talking to him last night, Ben." Guy smiled disarmingly. "I didn't have any success either. He actually pulled a gun on me." Guy said it as if he still couldn't quite believe it.

Ben tried to hide a smile. "But it seems you're still in one piece, Guy," he said gently.

"Yes. I don't think he had the strength to pull the trigger! But what I find strange is that he doesn't seem to care about his future, or what happens to him. He's being offered a wonderful opportunity for a new life but isn't interested."

Ben was silent as he reflected on what Guy said. How could these two men ever understand someone like Johnny Fierro? Guy had enjoyed a privileged upbringing, living in luxury. Guthrie, while he'd worked hard to build his ranch, had never known real hardship.

Ben sighed. "He's tired."

"Tired!" snorted Guthrie. "He's young, why should he be tired?"

"I mean, Guthrie, he's tired of life. He's seen more in his few years than all of us put together, I suspect. You've seen his back; doesn't that make you wonder what else has happened to him?"

Guthrie shrugged. "I know it's not easy growing up in the border towns, especially for a boy of mixed ancestry. But no one forced him to pick up a gun."

Ben stared at Guthrie. The man really had no idea what he meant—no idea at all. And it wasn't his place to tell Guthrie what he suspected. It would be unprofessional. And, besides, Johnny would probably shoot him for it. "Do you want him to stay, Guthrie?"

His friend sighed heavily and then nodded slowly. "Yes, I do. And I told him so. But I don't know how to deal with him. It's like he's built a stone wall around himself and I haven't a clue how to get through it or over it."

Ben smiled; it summed up his patient rather well. "Perhaps then, Guthrie, we'll have to sneak under his defenses instead! I know one thing; I haven't gone to all this trouble of saving his life to have him walk out of here and get killed in a gunfight. I don't give in without a fight." And with that Ben walked into the house and up the stairs.

He walked straight into Johnny's room without knocking. Johnny was staring out of the window, apparently at the distant mountains.

"So, how are you today, Johnny?"

"Fine." The reply was sullen. "I'm fine. Just tell me when I can expect to get outta here."

"Well, I'm glad to hear you're fine. In that case, get yourself up out of bed and walk to the window." Ben was amused at the faint flicker of panic in Johnny's eyes. It was gone in a flash and he felt he could almost have imagined it. But he knew this exercise was going to prove interesting. "Come on then, show me how well you're doing."

He watched as Johnny, keeping his face averted from Ben, swung his legs out of bed and grasped the headboard, pushing himself onto his feet. He stood, white knuckles clutching the bedpost, swaying. "Just need to get my balance a minute, been lying down too long."

Ben watched as Johnny let go of the headboard and moved quickly to catch him as he fell forward.

"Feeling fine, are you? Well, you go right on downstairs and ride out of here then."

"Just dizzy. Got up too quickly. I'm fine." Sweat trickled down Johnny's face.

Ben snorted, shaking his head. "God, you're a hard one, aren't you? And of course, you have no pain whatsoever."

He was treated to a full Fierro scowl. "I said, I'm fine. Just got up too quick."

"Johnny, you can lie to Guthrie and Guy, but you don't need to lie to me. You're still in considerable pain and nowhere near ready to get on a horse to ride anywhere. Are you eating properly yet?" He helped Johnny sit back down on the edge of the bed.

"Yeah."

"I will check with Peggy."

"OK!" Johnny snapped. "Sometimes I feel like I'm going to puke."

"How often?"

"Sometimes." Johnny sighed, looking defeated. "Most of the time. Just the thought of food makes me feel sick."

Ben nodded. "I'll give you something that might help with that. But the best thing for you would be to relax a little."

Johnny's mouth dropped open. "What the hell do you mean? Relax! That's all I can do lying here."

Ben counted to ten and prayed for patience. "I mean stop being so tense and angry and let these people look after you."

Johnny rolled his eyes. "I'd be just fine if they'd all leave me alone. But there's always someone coming in—either the old man, Harvard, or the girl. They never leave me in peace."

"They're concerned about you, it's natural they should come in."

"Why should they care? I ain't nothing to them." Johnny sounded genuinely bewildered.

"Johnny, you're a member of their family, of course they care."

Johnny snorted. "Family don't mean nothing."

Ben eyed him curiously. "Why don't you use their names, Johnny? I've never heard you call them by their names."

Johnny shrugged but avoided Ben's eyes.

Ben pulled a chair over and sat down. "Why don't you call them by their names? Are you afraid they'll start to mean something to you?"

Johnny glared at him. "I ain't afraid of nothing, Doc."

"You don't even use my name. It's Ben."

"I know!" Johnny snapped the words out.

"Where was Gabriela when you were being beaten?"

The abrupt change of tack seemed to throw Johnny. "What?"

Ben kept his voice calm. "I take it that it wasn't her who beat you?"

Johnny narrowed his eyes. "No!"

"So who?"

Johnny huffed in a breath and stared out of the window again, but his body was tense.

Ben persevered. "Who were they? It obviously happened over years."

Johnny shot him a sharp look. "An' how do you figure that, Doc?"

Ben shrugged. "I can tell by the scarring."

Johnny just glared again. God, he was good at glaring.

Ben pushed on. "Were they friends of your mother?"

At least the question got a reaction, because a ghost of a smile passed over Johnny's face, but it didn't touch his eyes. "Yeah, friends."

Ben looked him in the eyes. "What else did they do to you, Johnny?"

There was a momentary flicker in Johnny's eyes and he seemed to shrink back into his pillows. Ben felt a surge of guilt but it confirmed his suspicions.

"Dunno what you mean. They didn't do nothing."

Ben watched as Johnny ducked his head before looking up again, his face impassive now. It was as if he'd put on a mask.

"So, when can I get outta here, Doc?"

"Changing the subject, are we? You won't be going anywhere soon. You're not out of the woods yet, young man. And although I know you don't care, I do, and I've told you that I don't like losing patients. So, was Gabriela a good mother?"

He was pleased to see that the sudden change of subject again threw his patient.

"What the fuck d'you mean? Yeah, she was my mother, like any mother I suppose." But Johnny's eyes were evasive now. He looked out of the window again, avoiding Ben's gaze.

Ben frowned and tried his luck with another question. "So what happened in that gunfight?" Johnny looked almost relieved at the new topic.

Relieved or not, he still bucked. "Why the fuck d'you keep on about that damn gunfight?"

Ben decided to stay silent.

Johnny shook his head. "Look, it was only a job. Some men wanted him dead—that's all."

Ben raised an eyebrow and sat back, folding his arms. "Why?"

Johnny shut his eyes briefly. "I'm real tired, Doc."

Ben shook his head. "Not that tired, Johnny. Why?"

Johnny set his jaw. "I don't know why I don't shoot you. It would make life a lot easier."

Ben smiled benignly. "Ah, but then who would help you get better? Stop trying to change the subject and tell me why."

Johnny fiddled with the blanket, pulling at a thread, and then shrugged. "They came to me because the law wouldn't touch him. He was white and rich. But he'd raped their daughters. He'd cut them too. He was real vicious. The one girl, well, she went crazy. Her pa said she had to be put away somewhere, she went so crazy." He picked at the blanket again, unraveling more of the thread. "He was a piece of shit. I gave the other guy his chance. He could have walked away. But he went for his gun, so I killed him. The other, well, I figured those girls were going to suffer for the rest of their lives, so he suffered for two or three minutes. He had it easy."

He unraveled a little more of the blanket and looked up. "I broke my rule, OK? I always try to do it quick and clean. Just figured that was too good for him. Satisfied?"

Ben stared at him, thoughtful now. The boy really was a puzzle. But Ben was also strangely relieved. He'd known there had to be something, that the boy wasn't just "bad." He wondered how best to proceed. Somehow he had to make Johnny understand that he had a place here, people to care about him. Care more than Gabriela ever had, he thought sourly.

"Thank you, Johnny, yes. So, why do you want to leave here?"

"You don't quit, do you, Doc?" He ran his hand through his hair. "Let's face it, I'm trouble and they sure as hell don't need the trouble I'll bring."

Ben scratched his chin, leaning back in the chair. "Don't you think that's up to them to decide?"

Johnny laughed humorlessly. "They don't realize what it could mean, me being here."

"You're underestimating them. They're not stupid, Guthrie knows the risks, but he still wants you to stay."

Johnny snorted derisively. "Don't believe that. Anyway, if I'm here I put them in danger, so best I leave."

"I think you're afraid to admit that anyone wants you." Ben bit back a smile as he was treated to the full Fierro glare. "Have you ever loved anyone, Johnny?"

The question seemed to puzzle him. "Love? What d'you mean? Like women? I've sure as hell fucked a lot of 'em, Doc."

Ben bit back another smile. "That wasn't quite what I meant. I'm talking about love, caring about someone and trusting them totally. It's what families do, Johnny. It's why Guthrie spent years trying to find you; it's why he wants you to stay. It's why he'll take the risk, and deal with the consequences of your past if and when they happen."

"Love!" Johnny threw his head back with a bitter laugh. "Love! No one would love me—especially if they knew the things I've done. Now, just get the fuck outta here, Doc, I'm tired."

Ben turned and headed for the door but paused and turned again to look at Johnny. "You're heading nowhere fast, Johnny.

314

But I think you deserve more than a bloody death in some nameless town. Much more."

CHAPTER THIRTY-THREE

His fingers tapped restlessly on the table. Inactivity was driving him crazy. And so was sitting here while Harvard and the old man droned on about their day. Surely there was only so much to say about cattle. They were pretty dumb animals, 'nough said. And he longed for some food that tasted of something, not plain roast meat with tasteless gravy. He wanted chilies and tortillas and tamales. Real food. Soon as he could ride he was goin' looking for real food and a woman. His fingers beat a louder rhythm and he was suddenly aware they were all looking at him.

"Do you want to sit in a more comfortable chair, Johnny?" The old man sounded a touch sour.

"Yeah, think I will." He braced his hands on the table as he stood, trying to make it look casual and not let any pain show on his face. The next test was to walk like it was easy—when his back was killing him. Every single thing he did hurt. He was even forced to admit to himself that there was no way he was riding out of here for another day or two. He'd never make it onto his horse. And it didn't take no genius to work out that no one was going to help him. All they did was go on about him resting up, taking it easy. Madre de Dios! Maybe he should butter up the cook. Get her to make him some real meals. Trouble was the doc had said plain food. Well, they sure understood plain food in this house.

He deliberately chose a high-backed chair with arms. It would make it easier to stand later. Now they all seemed to be coming in. The girl settled down with her sewing. The old man was going to the liquor cabinet and Harvard was ferreting around in some cupboard.

The old man was holding out a bottle. "Whiskey, Johnny?"

He shook his head. He sure didn't trust these men enough to drink with them.

The old man tilted his head. "I bought you some tequila, if you would prefer that?"

That surprised him. Didn't think the old man would even think about tequila. He almost felt guilty refusing. Hell, he did feel guilty. "I ain't fancying liquor yet. But, thanks anyway." He felt awkward and the old man looked kind of surprised. Hell, he was probably surprised that Fierro knew to say thank you.

Harvard took a carved wooden box out of the cupboard and looked across at him. "I wondered if you'd like a game of checkers?"

Checkers? Did his brother think he was some little kid? Johnny fixed him with his coolest stare. Didn't say nothing, just waited to see what Harvard would come up with next.

His brother frowned. "Perhaps you're not familiar with the game? I could teach you."

Johnny narrowed his eyes. "Kind of a kid's game, ain't it? I prefer chess. Maybe I could teach you?"

That put Harvard in his place—he turned bright red and shuffled from one foot to the other.

"I . . . I didn't think you played chess. Sorry."

Johnny kept his gaze on him, unblinking for a second, enjoying the sight of his brother looking even more uncomfortable. Johnny raised an eyebrow. "You mean you thought I was too dumb to play chess? That only people who go to fancy schools know how? But then, maybe you do need me to teach you."

Harvard ground his teeth. "I'll happily give you a game of

chess. I'll get the board."

"Yeah, you do that, Harvard." He sat back in his chair and watched the man go and get the set. He was looking forward to this.

Harvard's game was good, solid and very predictable. But he took ages to make his move. Johnny knew his style of reading the board in a flash would throw the other man. As would his restless fingers tapping while he waited for Harvard to make his move. If he could get out of the damn chair he'd have walked around the room out of sheer boredom. But he had to save his energy for getting up the stairs to bed—that was a challenge in itself.

The old man was watching their game from behind the book he was pretending to read. Seemed amused too.

Harvard looked irritated by the restless fingers, but finally advanced his piece. "This is a game of strategy, Johnny. You should take more time to consider your options. One is meant to consider all possible moves."

Johnny bit back a grin and immediately moved his knight. "Is one? Check."

He heard the old man snort with laughter from behind his book. Harvard was looking real irritated now, and shit, he was going to take ages to consider his "options."

He heard his old man snicker again. It was kind of strange. It was almost like he wanted Johnny to win. Like they were on the same side. Johnny looked across and caught him looking at him. The old man smiled and gave him a wink. Shit! Johnny permitted a ghost of a smile to cross his face. He was almost tempted to ask for a tequila.

His father must have read his mind. He got up to pour himself another drink and held up the tequila bottle. "Sure you won't change your mind, Johnny?"

Johnny hesitated, and then nodded. "Why not? Just a small

one, please." He took the glass. It was good tequila too. Not like some of the rotgut you could get.

His brother finally made his move and sat back looking smug. It was a bad move. Johnny swallowed the rest of the tequila. Then, without taking his eyes off old Harvard's face, he made his own move. "Mate."

The old man snorted with laughter, even as Harvard looked frantically to see if it really was checkmate.

He threw his hands in the air, and looked at Johnny with a grin. "You have to give me a return game."

"Nope." Johnny pushed himself to his feet. Damn, that hurt. "I'm turning in."

"Where did you learn to play, Johnny? You play a very good game." His father cocked his eyebrow, leaning forward.

Johnny walked to the door before turning. He knew his answer would startle them and he wanted to see their reactions. "Prison."

His father frowned. "Prison? You mean jail? You've been in jail?"

"Nope. Prison. Real prison."

"When were you in prison?" There was just the slightest shake in the man's voice, and the girl and Harvard were staring at Johnny like he'd got two heads.

"Didn't your Pinkerton men find that out? I thought they'd have told you all about it." He wondered briefly what the hell the Pinkerton people had told the old man.

"No, they didn't. When were you in prison?"

Boy, they did want to know everything. But this was his fault—he only had himself to blame. He shouldn't have said anything. Even so, he'd enjoyed shocking them, so what the hell. "I dunno. I was maybe about twelve, thirteen. Can't remember."

"So not proper prison then." The old man sounded relieved.

"They don't put boys of that age in prison."

Johnny smiled at that. "Breeds they do."

His father swallowed hard. "What had you done? Why did they put you in prison?"

Johnny shrugged. "Stealing."

The old man stared at him, like he was disappointed. "I didn't take you for a thief. What did you steal?"

Johnny wondered briefly whether to invent something that would really shock them. But he might as well stick to the truth. "A loaf of bread, 'cause I was starving. Hadn't eaten in days. See you in the morning."

No need to tell the old man that the loaf of bread had just been the start of it. That he'd been thrown in jail and knocked out the sheriff trying to escape.

He was halfway through the door when his father spoke again. "Johnny, I'm sorry."

Johnny stared at him, puzzled. What the hell was he sorry for? Looked kinda pale too. Unsure of how to react, Johnny nodded and left the room. He wanted his bed. If only he could make it up the stairs without falling over.

He trudged up the stairs, hissing with pain at each jarring step. It was with a big sigh of relief that he finally made it to his room. He shut the door behind him, leaning against it for a few minutes as another wave of pain washed over him. The curtains blew gently in the breeze at the open window. Moving slowly, he limped across to stare out into the night. The sky was almost purple and full of brilliant stars. And the scent of the flowers in the girl's garden wafted on the warm air up into his room. The sound of the cattle lowing in the distance and the horses snorting in the corral were carried on the breeze. His mouth quirked into a smile as a shooting star shot across the sky. He remembered someone telling him that people were meant to make a wish when they saw a shooting star. He wondered what he'd wish for if he believed in such things. He figured that to belong somewhere like this, to be able to call it home, was probably as good as it got.

He stripped his clothes off and slid between the sheets, thankful that now he was no longer confined to bed, he didn't have to wear that damn nightshirt anymore. The moon was almost full and cast a brilliant light. It was strange how comfortable he felt here. Could he have a future here? It was tempting. But somehow, he didn't feel it was fair to these people.

No, as soon as he could get on his horse, he'd leave. He'd got five hundred dollars out of the trip. A small fortune. Maybe he should ride north, some place where people wouldn't know him. Get a place of his own. But it would only be a matter of time before someone showed up who'd recognize him. Then it would all start over again. No good blaming anyone. He'd chosen this life and now he had to live and die with it. But it was sure tempting to just stay. Trouble was, when the old man realized what he was really like and kicked him out, it would be even harder to leave. Better not to have it in the first place. It would be easier that way. Just take the money. Forget about trying to get a place of his own—that couldn't work out. No, he'd end up spending the money on women, same as always.

Women. He smiled to himself. Yeah, it would be good to be able to ride free and go get a woman. Hell, who needed a home anyway?

He sat in the girl's garden enjoying the sun on his face while he dismantled his guns. They needed cleaning and he'd been fretting over it. Pathetic, really, he thought as he dealt with the Derringer. Worrying about the fact he hadn't cleaned his guns for a few days. The routine made him feel better. He'd intended to clean them in private, in his room. But the warmth of the sun and the fresh air were too strong a pull.

He wanted to get the job done before some friends of the old man arrived—he thought it would be better if he wasn't around for that. The girl was hanging washing out, humming to herself. She turned and smiled at him. "Can I get you anything, Johnny?"

He shook his head and busied himself with cleaning his spare gun. She walked over and looked at the other gun, his fighting gun, in its holster next to him on the bench. She looked at it curiously.

"That's a strange holster. I've never seen one like it before. Why's it cut away like that?"

He shrugged, not wanting to answer that question. But like all women she was determined to press the point.

"Wouldn't the gun fall out? It's cut right away. Why?"

He sighed. "Gun clears the holster quicker that way." He couldn't look at her. But he could feel her eyes on him while she figured out what he meant.

"Oh! Oh, I see."

And he knew she did see. God, he felt small. What a dirty way to earn a living. Suddenly he saw her start to take the gun from the holster. "Don't! Don't touch it!"

She jumped, looking at him fearfully as he grabbed the gun. "It's a hair trigger and could go off real easy." He felt clumsy trying to explain. Hair trigger didn't begin to describe how easily that gun would fire. But the feel of the gun in his hand calmed him. It was a perfect fit. He loved the feel of it in his hand. It was part of him. Sometimes, when he lifted his arm he expected to see the gun growing from him. He caressed the gun, unaware for a second of her presence. Then he felt her eyes on him, watching him with a mixture of fear and curiosity.

"Sorry," he muttered. He couldn't look at her now. He carried on cleaning his guns, resisting the urge to hold the one gun close to him. To caress it. It would make him feel safe. It always made him feel safe.

"Did you alter that gun? I've never heard of one that fires so easily. And the handle looks odd, like it's been carved."

"Yeah. It's . . . modified." He knew that was the right word.

"Modified for what?"

The abruptness of the question surprised him and he looked up, meeting her gaze. "It's what keeps me alive."

To his surprise she smiled then. "Well, I'm glad then."

Her reaction puzzled him. Why would she care? He was nothing to her. He was a passing stranger—a very dangerous stranger. But even so, it made him feel good.

She sat on the seat opposite him, swinging her legs and seemingly lost in thought. She tilted her head to one side. "Why do you want to leave here, Johnny?"

He wondered what to say. He shrugged, to buy himself more time. "Don't belong here."

"You were born here, of course you belong here. It's your home."

He smiled at that. "Just because I was born here don't make it home."

"Is there some place you'd rather be?"

He didn't know how to answer that. Because right now he couldn't think of any place he'd rather be. But it didn't make staying the right thing to do.

He looked at her. "I got lots of places to go."

"That's not what I asked." He heard the reproach in her voice.

"Look, fact is, I'm trouble and I'll bring trouble. None of you needs that."

"Families face trouble together, Johnny. It's what they do."

"You ain't family."

"I am, sort of. Uncle Guthrie's my guardian, so that makes you my foster brother."

He sighed. "Some brother I'd be. Like I said, I'd bring trouble."

"What do we have to do to persuade you to stay? We all want you to. And Uncle Guthrie, well, right through my childhood all I can remember is him searching for you. He never gave up. He used to talk to my father about how he hoped he'd find you and bring you safely home. And although it's difficult for you to see, because you don't know him, he is happy you're here. At least give this life a try. Don't give up on us; we don't want to give up on you."

She smiled and suddenly leaned over and gave him a kiss on his cheek before hurrying back into the house.

He stared down at his gun, and tried to swallow the lump in his throat. Hell! The sooner he got away from here the better.

CHAPTER THIRTY-FOUR

He stood up slowly, wondering how soon he could ride. He'd stayed too long. He fastened his gun belt around his hips, relishing the feel of it. He'd missed it while he was sick, and now the feel of the belt soothed him. It was strange, though, he'd put on his fighting gun without even thinking about it. It must be the girl's fault. She'd unsettled him. All that talk about staying. This gun made him feel safe. Protected. Nothing could touch him now. Sooner he was outta here, the better.

He watched the bees hovering at the girl's flowers, buzzing drowsily in the heat. The scent of roses was heavy in the air and he shut his eyes briefly, soaking up the sounds and the perfume. A man could get way too comfortable here. Never want to leave.

The sound of approaching hoofbeats dragged him back to the present. Two men were riding in. Older men. Shit. Talking to the girl, he'd forgotten about the old man's friends coming. He'd meant to be out of the way before they arrived. They reined their horses in and looked over the wall at him.

"Boy. See to our horses."

He stiffened. Narrowed his eyes and looked at them.

The other man, with a swollen red nose that said he drank too much and a gut that said he ate too much, ordered, "Perhaps you didn't hear what my friend here said. Come and take our horses, damn you. I'll have your boss fire your half-breed ass otherwise."

"I heard." Johnny spoke softly and walked out from behind

the wall. So they could see the gun that sat low on his thigh. He stood, relaxed, but with his right hand very close to his gun, watching them. Enjoying the looks on their faces as they realized who he was.

The first one looked at him with open disgust. "It's all over town that you showed up, but I thought you'd have gone by now, Fierro. The range war's over and your kind has no place mixing with decent folk. Guthrie's a good friend of ours and he sure as hell doesn't need your kind here, or anywhere near here."

"And just what is my kind?"

"Scum, Fierro. Murdering scum. You're not wanted in this valley and I warn you, if you go near anyone's daughter, you'll end up with a bullet in the back."

The other man nodded in agreement. "They'll be standing in line to do that, Fierro. So take some advice, and get out while you still can. Guthrie's a decent man and he doesn't want the likes of you around his ranch, or anywhere near that ward of his."

Johnny didn't react. No expression crossed his face. He just stretched his fingers, almost imperceptibly, and let his hand go a fraction closer to his gun. He was enjoying this. They looked nervous now. The fat one was starting to sweat.

"We aren't wearing guns, Fierro."

He narrowed his eyes. "That don't make no difference." He allowed his words to sink in. " 'Specially to murdering scum like me." He continued to stand motionless, with his right hand just a hair's breadth from his gun. They were both sweating now. Licking their lips nervously. Any minute now they'd be pissing themselves.

"I really should put a bullet right between your eyes." He spoke very softly. "It wouldn't make no mess, because it seems to me you ain't got nothing between your ears."

Before they could respond, he heard the old man calling out. "Matt, Henry, I didn't hear you arrive." And the old man walked over smiling, pleased to see 'em.

"I'd like to introduce you both to my son, Johnny. He's been laid up a while, but he's on the mend now. Johnny, these are two old friends of mine. Matt Dixon and Henry Carter."

"We met already." And Johnny turned abruptly on his heel and walked off, sensing rather than seeing the old man staring after him in annoyance.

He went to the barn where the buckskin was stabled. The horse nickered at him. He laid his head against the horse's neck. "I think it's time for us to leave, amigo."

The barn door creaked and he turned to see his brother. Harvard was fidgeting a little, like he didn't know what to say.

"What's the matter, Harvard? Still not gotten over being beaten at chess?"

The other man smiled slightly at that. "It is a rare occurrence." He paused, chewing on his lip. "I heard what those men said to you, Johnny. I'm sorry. They were rude and ignorant and totally out of line."

"What the hell are you sorry for? You think they said anything I haven't heard a thousand times before? It sure as hell don't bother me none."

His brother frowned. "I thought from your reaction that they must have upset you."

Johnny had to grin at that. "Nope. They didn't upset me. I just couldn't resist scaring the shit outta them."

The man stood looking at him. Still bothered, it seemed. "Other people aren't like them, Johnny. The things they said . . . That's not what people think."

Johnny kicked at a bit of straw caught on his boot. Seemed it was time for some truth. "Harvard, it's exactly what people think. That's how it is. Don't bother me none. Hell, I chose this life. No one forced a gun into my hand. When I was kid, I used to see gunfighters, and people used to step out of their way. I thought it was respect and I wanted it. I guess I was just too young to know the difference between respect and fear." He ducked his head, remembering how in awe he'd been of those men. "See, the thing is, folks round here won't want to know me. You seem to think I can stay and fit in. Life ain't like that. Leastways, not for me it ain't."

His brother shook his head. "Everyone won't be like that. Let people get to know you. Those men today, well, who needs them?"

"Who needs 'em? The old man needs 'em, Harvard. They're his friends."

"I don't think he'd be happy if he knew how they behaved."

"Yeah, well, I sure ain't gonna tell him. And neither are you. Like I said, it's what people round here will think. I'm a killer, an' that scares the shit out of them."

His brother shook his head again. "You're wrong, Johnny. If you let people get to know the real you . . ."

Johnny stepped forward, the blood pulsing. "You don't know what the real me is, so don't give me that shit," he snapped. "You don't know me at all, Harvard. So what if I told you a couple of stories on the trail. You got no way of knowing if they were even true. Maybe I was spinning you a tale. You know nothin' about me, an' you sure as hell don't know what I'm really like. Hell, I don't know what you're really like, so why the fuck d'you think you know all about me? Just because you went to some fancy school don't mean you know it all."

"I didn't say I knew it all. I don't think you're as bad as you seem to want us all to think you are. You risked your life for the women on this ranch. I happen to think that says a lot about you. Why do you want us to think the worst? It really does seem at times that you want us to hate you or be scared of you. It makes me wonder what you're scared of. Getting too close, maybe?"

Dios! Why did everyone here think he was scared of something? "I ain't scared of nothing. But it seems to me it wouldn't be right if you all get your heads blown off because I decide to hang around."

"Sorry, Johnny, but I don't believe that's the only reason. I think you're scared of admitting that you'd like another life, a family, a home. All the things you've never had."

"Fuck you, Harvard." Johnny turned on his heel and walked out of the barn. Hell, fuck all of 'em. They didn't seem to realize what a favor he'd be doing them if he left.

He walked into the house, but paused at the sound of raised voices coming from the great room. He walked softly as a cat and stood at the door listening.

"Guthrie, why won't you listen to sense? He's a killer and he'll bring trouble to this valley. There'll be other killers looking for him and no one will be safe. And as for the women folk . . ."

"Matt's right, Guthrie. I know you've spent years looking for him, but that was before you found out who he is, what he is."

"He's my son, Henry, that's who he is. As for what he is, well, I'm prepared to give him a chance. He took a bullet helping save this ranch. He damn near died and I think he's earned his right to a chance here."

"All he's ever earned, Guthrie, is a hangman's noose, and you know it. God, you've said yourself often enough what scum gunfighters are."

He'd heard enough. He trudged up the stairs to his room. He closed the door and took his money from under the mattress and shoved it inside his jacket. He slung his saddlebags over his shoulder and checked that he hadn't left anything behind. Although that wasn't likely—he always traveled light. He sighed. Yeah, he traveled light because he owned next to nothing. Glancing a last time around the room, he found himself once more at the open window, drawn by the vaqueros calling to each other and the sound of hammering. The scent of wood smoke hung in the air. It all seemed familiar and almost dream-like. His eyes settled again on the distant mountain range. The mountains were purple against the blue sky. God, it was beauti-ful here. And it could have been where he belonged, if things hadn't turned out the way they did.

He walked quietly down the stairs and out of the side door. He made it to the barn without meeting anyone, and saddled Pistol before leading him around to the back of the barn, out of sight of the main house. If only he could manage to mount, it would be fine. Hissing in pain, he struggled to lift his foot into the stirrup. Fighting a wave of nausea he made it into the saddle. He clung to the saddle horn trying to catch his breath before urging the horse into a lope, gritting his teeth against the stab-bing pains in his back.

He didn't look back until he got to the ridge above the hacienda. He stared back across the sun-dappled green valley and the sparkling river. It really was beautiful. As good as it got, probably. He swallowed the lump in his throat. He couldn't stay, but he'd sure been tempted. But who needed to be fenced in, anyhow? There was freedom out here. Hell, he could start living again.

CHAPTER THIRTY-FIVE

He breathed a sigh of relief as he rounded the ridge. He was out of sight of the ranch. And better yet, it was out of his sight too. He could put the whole thing behind him. Tell himself it was just a job, like any other. He'd been well paid. What more could he ask for? He rode on along a well-worn track until he came to a fork. Question was, which way to go? He could toss a coin; heads, south to the border, or tails, onwards to Cimarron.

If anyone from the ranch followed, they'd be bound to think he'd head for the border. It was the obvious thing to do. But hell, he needed a woman and that was a better reason than any for heading on to the town. One thing Johnny did recall was that the doc had, after much pressing, told him there was a bordello in Cimarron. That made heading for the town an even better idea—there'd be a far better choice of girls in a bordello than in the saloon. Well-run, and clean, the doc had said. Johnny had enjoyed ribbing him about that. But the old doc had sniffed and said the woman who ran it was a friend. And Johnny had ribbed him even more. Then the doc said when he used the word friend, he meant just that. Johnny grinned at the memory. Leastways if he ran into the doc in town, he could pay for his treatment—he didn't like the thought of his old man paying for him. The doc would be mad as hell if he saw Johnny on a horse, but he probably wouldn't see the doc anyway. He was a busy man and would be out treating patients somewhere.

Johnny kept the horse at a gentle pace. His back hurt way too much to go any faster. And he was sure no one had seen him leave so there was no need to hurry. Yeah, Cimarron was the right choice. He could enjoy a woman, or maybe two, and take his time. The border could wait.

The town stood shuttered and quiet. Some tumbleweed blew along the sidewalk past a small trading store. Last time he'd been here it had been busier. Maybe that had been payday for the miners. A small group of men stood talking outside the largest of the saloons, but otherwise there were few people on the streets. It seemed an odd place to find a bordello. If it had been Santa Fe that would make sense, but surely there couldn't be enough business here? Still, maybe it was one of those towns that didn't get to jumping until nightfall.

Glancing up and down the main street, and with an unerring instinct that had never yet let him down, he spotted the bordello straight away. It looked respectable from the outside, the sort of place people could walk into without realizing what it was. Johnny grinned at the thought. The owner must have a sense of humor.

He reined in and swung his leg over the saddle to dismount but pain shot through him, making him gasp and fall forward onto the saddle horn. Fuck! That hurt. Whatever he'd done had pulled the stitches too. He paused for a few moments, fighting for breath and waiting for the pain to ease. Then, still moving gingerly, he tied the buckskin to the hitching rail.

He paused for a moment at the heavy door as another wave of pain washed over him. Taking a deep breath he pushed open the door and walked in. It obviously didn't do much afternoon business because some girls looked up, surprised, from where they were sitting chatting. But they sure were pretty in their flouncy dresses. There was a bar with all fancy mirrors, and a piano, and huge glass things with candles hanging from the ceiling, which sparkled when they caught the light. Yep, Doc was right when he said it was a classy place. One of the girls called to someone sitting out back in an office. He grinned broadly at the girls and touched his hat. "Ladies." It always tickled working girls to be called that and it seemed this lot was no different from all the others because they started giggling and coloring up. He was just toying with which one to pick when a woman came out of the back office.

She was tall, as tall as he was, and had dark hair scraped back from her face into one of the ugliest hairdos he'd ever seen. Her hard face was overly made up, with painted brows and a scarlet gash for a mouth. He swept his hat off, turning his most winning smile on her, knowing that it always charmed the ladies. Except she didn't look charmed. She just stared at him and said, "Yes?"

Like she didn't know what he was there for. Dios! "Ma'am. I was kinda wondering, you open for business?"

She looked him up and down slowly, her eyes lingering briefly on his low-slung gun, like he was something real unpleasant. "We're open for business, but not yours. I'm sure you'll find something to your liking at the other end of town."

She made as if to go back into her office. What the hell was wrong with his business? "Ma'am, I was thinking of staying right here, seems just fine to me."

She turned back to face him, eyeing him coldly. "And I just said we don't want your business."

"What's wrong with my business? Or is it the color of my skin?" His voice was hard now. And the girls started fidgeting like they were nervous. But the woman looked unmoved. And she didn't look bothered at his change of tone.

"The color of your skin has nothing to do with it. The way you wear your gun does. I don't know who you are, but I know what you are and I don't have gunfighters on my premises. So, out, now."

He stared at her in amazement. Shit, why couldn't he think of something smart to say? Damn woman, just standing there, staring at him from the greenest eyes he'd ever seen, unflinching. She'd got guts, he had to admit. Most people wouldn't dare refuse a gunfighter anything.

Maybe a little charm would work. He turned on a wider smile. "Ma'am . . ."

"I said out and I mean it. Now, you can either turn around and walk out, or I'll call some help and have you thrown out. It's your decision entirely; I have no preference, one way or the other." She sounded bored now. Used fancy words too, like she was educated. Hell, she even sounded educated, bit like old Harvard.

He swallowed hard, realizing she meant what she said. And oddly, he felt a pang of shame that this stranger held him in such contempt. "Ma'am, I ain't never been thrown out of a bordello in my life."

There was a momentary flicker of something in her eyes, but he couldn't read it. But he'd swear that her mouth twitched slightly. Then again, maybe not. She raised a painted brow, and tilted her head to one side. "Well, honey, there's a first time for everything. Now, out."

Her gaze didn't falter, and he couldn't think of a damn thing to say to her. He couldn't remember ever meeting a woman he hadn't been able to charm his way round. Charming the women and killing—it was what he did best. But damn, she was sure of herself; kind of confident and untouchable—and bored.

He opened his mouth, but the steely look in her eyes defeated him. He knew it was pointless. No one could beat him with a gun, but this woman . . . Still, with a face like that, no wonder she was sour.

He gave her a mock bow and left with as much dignity as he could muster. He stood outside wondering whether to go to the place at the other end of town. But he was no longer in the mood. His back was hurting like hell now; it had since he'd got off his horse. He moved his hand behind him to rub the area around the wound—it was very wet. Shit, he really had opened it up. It was bleeding.

As his eyes scanned the street, he saw the doctor's nameplate above one of the doors. He sighed. It would be the sensible thing to do. Get the damn thing stitched again before he rode on. He wasn't usually very sensible, but hell, the doc's place was right there.

Moving slowly, he made his way over and reluctantly knocked on the door, already regretting the decision. Maybe the doc wouldn't be there, and then the decision would be made for him. He felt like running away as he heard the footsteps approaching, like some little kid. Doc Greenlaw opened the door, his eyes widening with surprise. Johnny swallowed hard as the doc's expression hardened. Shit, he looked pretty pissed off too.

"Johnny, what are you doing here? You're supposed to be taking it easy on the ranch." He leaned forward to look outside, like he was expecting to see the old man's wagon. "How did you get to town? I didn't give you permission to ride yet."

"Was on my way through, Doc. Thought I'd call in and settle my bill." Somehow, he didn't think the doc was going to be too impressed if he saw Johnny's back right now.

The doctor narrowed his eyes. "On your way through? Going somewhere?"

"Yeah, well, thought it was time to move on, you know?"

The doctor stood back and motioned Johnny inside. Johnny could feel the way the doc was watching him move, looking for signs that all wasn't as it should be. "Well, if you're so hell-bent on leaving, I'll have one last look at your back before you go."

Johnny looked at the man, but the doc stared at him unflinchingly. Hell, could the doc see right through his jacket? He didn't think the doc was fooled. He sighed and went to remove his jacket. He could feel blood soaking his shirt. The doc stood expressionless, with his arms folded, as Johnny tried to pull the blood-soaked shirt away from the wound.

"I think it's kind of a mess," he muttered.

"Kind of a mess?" Doc narrowed his eyes. "Kind of a mess? That's one way of describing it, I suppose." He sucked in a big breath, like he was going to start yelling. "There are times, Johnny, when I wonder if you have any brains at all! What the hell do you think you're doing?" He threw his hands in the air. "No way are you fit to ride yet. We talked about this. You agreed to let it heal, so why the sudden change of plan?" The doc's eyes bored into him, demanding a straight answer, even as he beckoned Johnny into some kind of treatment room.

Johnny sighed, and said softly, "I couldn't stay any longer, Doc. Had my reasons." He watched the doc collect stuff together to clean the wound.

"And would you care to share those reasons with me? Something must have happened for you to do something so damn foolish. Did you have a fight with Guthrie?"

Johnny shook his head. He didn't know what to say or how to explain.

"Well, something happened. What?"

The old doc just never gave in, did he? He was going to push and push until he got an answer. It would be easier, and a lot quicker, to answer his damn questions. "Couple of the old man's friends turned up." He tried to sound casual.

The doc looked at him sharply. "Rancher friends?"

Johnny nodded. But avoided meeting the doctor's eyes.

"You had words with them?"

"They didn't bother to introduce themselves, if that's what you mean. But they weren't too friendly." His face hardened as he thought of the insults, boy and half-breed and then once they knew who he was . . .

He felt the old doc watching him. He shrugged and said, "Then later, I heard 'em talking to the old man. All about how much he hates gunfighters, thinks they're scum . . ." He paused, uncertain how to continue. "So, I figured it's best I leave. Save everyone a lot of bother. Then saw the track to town, thought I'd stop at the bordello and pay your bill."

"In that order?"

Johnny grinned. "Well, that was the plan. But shit! I went to that damn bordello you told me about, and the owner threw me out." He shook his head again in disbelief. "She didn't like gunfighters either!"

Ben threw back his head, laughing like it was a great joke. "That sounds like Delice. She's something, isn't she? But I daresay, if I put in a word for you, she might permit you to use the amenities."

Shit, another one intent on using fancy words. But Johnny got the message, and grinned again. "Hell, they'd have taken one look at my back and thrown me out anyway, Doc!"

The man laughed. "Somehow I don't think Delice would have appreciated you bleeding all over the place, that's for sure. Now, for God's sake, stay still while I stitch you back together."

He stayed still, gritting his teeth, determined not to show how much it hurt. Still, he only had himself to blame. He regretted his impulse now. Should have stayed another day or two and then lit out. But it felt that the longer he stayed, the more difficult it was to leave.

"You're not fit to ride, Johnny. Will you at least agree to stay here for a day or two?"

"I don't want the old man to know where I am." He might as well admit it.

The doc looked at him sharply. "You did tell them you were leaving?"

He found himself unable to look the doc in the face. He shrugged, then wished he hadn't because it hurt like hell.

"You didn't, did you?" Doc looked him up and down in a way that made Johnny feel like he could see through anything he might say. He shook his head and started in on Johnny like he was some dumb kid. "You are the most stubborn and difficult man I've ever met. And do tell me what did Guthrie say, when these men were talking about how much he hated gunfighters?"

Johnny shrugged again. Even with the pain it seemed easier than trying to come up with an answer.

"You didn't stay to listen to his answer, did you?" Hell, where did the old doc get so smart?

Doc looked kind of like he couldn't believe quite how dumb Fierro was. "There are times, Johnny, when I despair of you. And that father of yours too! Guy seems a little more sensible, but I'm not holding my breath. What a family!"

Johnny stared down at his boots. They sure looked scuffed. Hell, that bit of straw was still stuck in the sole. He rubbed it with the other boot.

"Will you at least agree to stay here, for a day or two?"

"You won't tell the old man I'm here?"

The doc sighed. "No, I won't tell Guthrie. I'll put your horse in my stable, no one will know."

Johnny bowed his head. His back was throbbing and so was his head. Wouldn't do no harm to stay for a few hours, till he felt better. He looked up. "Yeah, OK. Thanks, Doc."

The doc nodded. "I'll put your horse away. It's the flashy buckskin, yes? Seems very appropriate for you." Johnny looked at him sharply, but saw the twinkle in the man's eyes.

When Johnny awoke it was dusk. The scent of frying bacon wafted into his room, and he realized how hungry he was. He made his way to the kitchen, where the doc stood over a sizzling pan of bacon and eggs. He looked at Johnny. "How do you feel now? And please don't say fine, because that one never works on me."

Johnny grinned. "Well, better than I did, honest."

"Well, you do look better now, I'll grant you that. Come and sit down and have some supper. And you can tell me what your plans are."

"Plans?"

"Yes, Johnny. Plans. As you're prepared to toss away the prospect of a third ownership of one of the largest ranches in New Mexico you must have some other, more pressing plan for your future."

Johnny pushed the bacon around his plate, his appetite suddenly gone.

"Eat your dinner first. Then we'll discuss your plans."

"Never give up, do you, Doc? And you say I'm stubborn."

The doc just laughed. "Eat your supper. I'm willing to bet you went without lunch. How you think you're ever going to get fit, I can't imagine."

Johnny picked at his food; he was starting to regret coming here. Doc Greenlaw was no fool, and he seemed to have a way of seeing right through a man. It was kinda disturbing, knowing that whatever he said the doc probably wouldn't buy into it. What could he say? That he hadn't got any plans. The only plan he'd ever had was to be the fastest and best pistolero. He'd never thought beyond that. It was all he'd ever wanted.

Well, people sure knew the name of Johnny Fierro and all it brought was trouble. Time was he'd enjoyed that. Loved the rush he got when he faced a man, knowing one of them wouldn't be walking away. Hell, he'd loved seeing the fear in people's faces, the sharp intake of breath when they heard his name. It had all made him feel good. The women found it exciting too. They loved that Fierro had chosen them. Hell, women had begged him to take them. And that had made him feel good, too. Hadn't impressed that damn woman today though. She'd looked down on him. She knew a gunfighter wasn't worth shit.

And the trouble was she was right. It was only a matter of time before some younger wolf came along and took him down. His luck was bound to run out sooner or later. He supposed his plan would be to just keep doing the same as he'd always done. Take a job and then take a woman to forget the killing. Didn't sound too good when he put it like that. But he'd never apologize for Johnny Fierro. Fierro had kept him alive. Course, at some stage Fierro would get him killed.

Doc wiped his mouth with a napkin, and leaned back in his chair. "So, Johnny, what's your big plan?"

He found himself shrugging, again. "Gunfightin', I guess. It's who I am."

"It doesn't have to be, you know. You finally have a choice. You can choose a different life. A more rewarding one."

"You don't know shit about my life."

"You think killing is rewarding?"

Johnny pushed his plate around the table. "It's what I am."

Doc rolled his eyes. "You said that already. As I said, for the first time you have a real choice. You have the chance of a new life, a family. Are you going to throw that chance away?"

"It ain't that easy."

Doc raised an eyebrow. "I never said it was easy. What it boils down to is whether you have the guts to make the change. Even if it doesn't work out, at least you'll know you tried."

"An' what if someone winds up dead because of me?"

"Life is full of risks, but that doesn't mean we shouldn't take chances. You're not responsible for making other people's choices. Guthrie's not a fool. He knows the risks but he's prepared to take a chance on you. Don't you owe him the same?"

"I don't owe him nothing. And I don't need nobody."

"Are you trying to convince me or yourself? And as for family, well, I suppose until you have one, you won't know what the rewards are. People need companionship and love; those are things that a family provides. I do wonder why you find the prospect of getting to know your family so frightening."

Johnny glared. Why the hell was he sitting here listening to this shit? But before he could say anything there was a loud knock on the door. The doc got to his feet. "Take the plates and go into the kitchen. Whoever it is needn't know you're here. It'll be a patient needing something. Go on."

Johnny picked up the plates and moved into the kitchen. There was a comfy rocking chair near the big stove. He settled himself down as he heard the doc opening the door. His heart lurched as he heard the doc's words. "Guthrie! What brings you here this evening?"

CHAPTER THIRTY-SIX

He shrank back into the rocking chair, praying that the damn thing wouldn't squeak. He knew the doc wouldn't let on that he was there, but he didn't want to give himself away. Surely the old man couldn't know he was here? There had been nobody around when he came in. Damn town was so dead there'd been no one anywhere.

His father's voice rang through the house. "Ben, can I come in? I need to talk. Johnny's gone, taken off without a word to anyone."

"Of course you can come in. Let me get you a drink and then you can tell me what's happened."

He could hear the clink of glass as the doc poured a couple of drinks. "So, tell me, did you two have a quarrel?"

"No!" His father sounded snappy. "I mean, I know he and I don't exactly see eye to eye, but no, we didn't fight, I hadn't even seen him today. Peggy said he was cleaning his guns this morning. Then Matt Dixon and Henry Carter arrived for lunch."

Doc snorted at the names. "Don't know why you put up with those old devils, Guthrie. Talk about intolerant . . ."

"I know, I know. But I've always done business with them, Ben. I wanted them to meet the boys. I thought it would show that I see them both as part of the ranch. But it seems they met Johnny before I arrived. And when I tried to introduce them, Johnny stalked off. I thought he was being his usual rude self.

342

Then Henry and Matt started on about how I shouldn't have Johnny anywhere near here. God, Ben, you should have heard them."

"I can imagine." Old Doc didn't sound too impressed.

"They went on and on, Ben. How no women would be safe and he'd bring crowds of gunfighters to the valley. I mean, it was ridiculous. And of course, they threw my views on gunfighters in my face. Because of all the things I used to say. But damn it, he's my son. And those two didn't know when to stop."

"They wouldn't."

"I threw them out, Ben."

"You did what?" Doc sounded stunned.

Johnny almost rose out of the chair in surprise.

"I threw them out. Told them they could keep their narrow-minded bigotry to themselves. They said Johnny threatened to kill them, that he threatened to blow their brains out. But after they left, Guy told me he'd overheard them with Johnny. He said they treated him appallingly. So I went to look for Johnny and couldn't find him anywhere. I assumed he'd gone to cool off. It was only later we found his horse gone, and his room as empty as when he came.

"He didn't have much, but it was all gone. It was as though he'd never been there, Ben. And now I haven't a clue where he's gone. And of course Guy and Peggy both blame me. Said I hadn't made him welcome."

There was a pause and Johnny heard the glasses being moved again.

The old man spoke again, but softly now. "Trouble is they're right. As you know, I was horrified when I discovered that Guy had sent for him. I sure as hell didn't want him here, not once I knew he was a gunfighter. But damn it, now I want him to stay. I admit, he scared me at first, but he risked his life for the ranch. And Peggy and Guy both seem to think he's worth getting to know.

And the other night when he played chess with Guy . . ."

"Chess?" The doc sounded surprised. Why did everyone find it surprising that he could play chess? Did they really think that all gunfighters were dumb? Hell, two of the smartest men he'd ever known had been gunfighters, and the most trustworthy.

His father laughed. "Oh, it was great. You'd have enjoyed it. Guy asked Johnny if he wanted to play checkers. Johnny sneered, saying it was a kid's game and what about chess. And I could see Guy thought he'd wipe the floor with Johnny."

"And do I take it that Johnny was a match for him?" The doc sounded amused.

"Wiped the floor with Guy." His father chuckled at the memory. "And I thought perhaps that evening, he and I had made some progress. He even had a drink with me. Believe me, that's progress. But now . . ."

"Now he's left, just like that." Doc sounded very gentle. It struck Johnny what a kind man he was. Yeah, a real good man. He hadn't known many of those.

"Yes. Now he's left. It hurts, to think he didn't even care enough to say goodbye, to offer some sort of explanation."

"Maybe he didn't know how. Maybe he couldn't explain. It doesn't mean he didn't care." Ben spoke gently.

"Doesn't it?" His father grunted. "I wouldn't be too sure of that. He never seemed to care about any of us. He was always remote. You never knew what he was thinking. He'd just look at you with those damn cold eyes. Hell, Ben, I wanted to see him smile. He came close, the night of the chess game, but that was it."

"He didn't want you to know what he was thinking, Guthrie. He's a very proud young man. And a stubborn one. And so like his father."

"Like me! Don't be ridiculous. He's like Gabriela."

"To look at, yes. But he's all Sinclair. He's had a rough life and he's built a wall around himself."

"What'll become of him? It scares me. Someone as infamous as him, well, we both know . . . I dread it. The thought of picking up a newspaper and reading an account of his death, like it's entertainment. It's all such a waste. He should have grown up here, not in those border towns."

Johnny sat motionless in the chair, listening to the passion in the old man's voice. He found it hard to swallow. Shit. He shouldn't let this get to him; the old man was probably saying it for effect. But it sounded real.

"So, what would you say to him, Guthrie, if he was here now?"

Damn, the doc was a cunning old devil.

"Ben, we both know, if he was here now I probably wouldn't say a thing to him. I'd growl at him or say the wrong thing. We'd end up arguing or with him stalking off. I'd be bound to put my foot in it."

"You do seem to have a talent for that, particularly where Johnny's concerned."

"Don't I know it! But I get so mad about what he's done with his life. I mean, why the hell did he become a gunfighter in the first place?"

Yeah, that sounded more like the old man.

He heard the doc sigh. "Maybe he saw it as an escape from the life he faced in Mexico, a case of get tough or die, perhaps. As I said, I think he's had a very rough life."

"Well, I wouldn't know about that, as he doesn't see fit to tell me anything about his early life." The old man's voice was bitter.

"Maybe it's too painful. Maybe he's worried that you'll think badly of him."

"Why should I think badly of him over his childhood? I know he's been whipped badly at some stage but whatever he did, no child deserves that."

"I think we're talking about more than whippings, Guthrie."

Shit. Johnny gritted his teeth, praying that the doc would shut up. Otherwise he might have to put a bullet in the man.

"I don't know about his childhood, Ben, or why he made the choices he did, but I do know that I didn't want him to leave. I know it would be tough if he stayed. I'm not a fool. But I already have too many regrets in my life. I didn't want to look back and think that we didn't even give it a try. More than likely he wouldn't have stayed, but I wanted us all to give it a go. See if we could make it work. I hoped he might see the opportunity and seize it—seems I was wrong."

Johnny felt a surge of relief that the conversation seemed to have moved away from dangerous territory. He heard Ben walking to the liquor cabinet. "Another whiskey, Guthrie?"

"Why not? I certainly need it."

He could hear the splash of liquid pouring into a glass. "I assume you want my opinion, Guthrie, for what it's worth. You think he left because he doesn't care. I think he left because he's so damned scared of caring. He's afraid of causing everyone trouble and he's afraid of caring for you all and he's afraid that, ultimately, you'll be disappointed in him."

Johnny hissed in a breath. Why did everyone think he was scared? Well, fuck 'em all, he didn't need nobody. Did he? He'd ride out in the morning and they could all go to hell. He wasn't going to sit here and listen to this shit any longer. Heaving himself out of the chair, he strode into the parlor where the two men were sitting. The look on the old man's face was priceless.

"Johnny!" His father looked from the doc to Johnny and back again.

"I'm sorry, Guthrie." Doc sounded relaxed, like he wasn't surprised by Johnny's sudden appearance. "Johnny stopped by earlier. He's spending the night here."

Johnny stared at his father defiantly, waiting for him to lose his temper. He'd show him he did exactly what he wanted. Oddly though, the old man didn't look mad, just kinda sad.

"You left. You didn't even say goodbye. Not even to Peggy or Guy. That hurt them. You hurt us all." There was a slight tremor in his father's voice.

Hurt! That was rich. He doubted they were heartbroken. An' old Harvard, well, he'd get half the ranch now, instead of just a third. He felt the doc's eyes on him, waiting for Johnny to say something. Except he couldn't think of anything to say. It was easier to shrug. He dropped his gaze, couldn't look at his father now. Instead, he muttered, "Got places to go."

His father tilted his head. "More important than family, Johnny? We're offering you a new life, a chance to be part of something you can be proud of."

"I'm proud of being a gunfighter, one of the best, but I don't suppose you can understand that." The words came like bullets from a gun.

"Proud of killing?" He heard the contempt in his father's voice.

"It ain't about the killing."

"Then what is it about? Tell me, because I'm trying to understand what it is that's so important out there that you'll throw away your whole future."

"It's about being fast, good at my trade, respect." But even as he said the words, an image of the woman in the bordello flashed through his mind. She hadn't respected him. And he remembered how earlier, when he'd cleaned his guns, he'd felt ashamed and thought what a dirty way to earn a living.

His father sighed. "The lawyer is coming to the ranch at ten tomorrow morning. I had him draw up a partnership agreement. I'd like it if you were there. I can't offer you any guarantees that things will work out, but it's worth trying, worth fighting for. I do think if you turn this down you're making a big mistake. The tragedy is you probably won't live long enough to even realize how big a mistake."

He tried to think of some real smart comment to make. And he felt he'd used up all his shrugs. "I ain't afraid of dying."

"No, you're not. But I think you're afraid of living." His father stood up. "Ben, thanks for the drink. I'll head on back." He looked across again to Johnny. "I hope I see you tomorrow. Like I said, at ten."

The door closed behind him and Johnny could feel Doc Greenlaw's eyes boring into him. "What?"

The doc shook his head at him. "God, you're a hard one, Johnny. Not an inch of give. At least Guthrie was trying; couldn't you meet him halfway? You heard what he said, he wants you to stay. What the hell have you got to lose? If it doesn't work out, well, you can leave later, but at least try it."

Johnny shook his head. "I'm too tired for all this now, Doc. I'll see you in the morning." And turning on his heel he walked upstairs to the small room he'd slept in earlier. He looked through the window over the small town. There was music coming from the saloon and a welcoming glow from the bordello at the end of the street—welcoming everyone except him. Shutting his eyes, he recalled the view of his mountain from his bedroom at the ranch. He'd never had his own room before, and it had been kinda nice. The girl had put fresh flowers in it. He'd thought that was stupid, but they had smelled good.

Hell, stop thinking about it and get some sleep. He slipped out of his things, wincing as he tried to get his shirt off, and huddled beneath the blankets.

He should have known he wouldn't get much sleep. He dozed fitfully, as images of gunfights flashed through his mind. And then all his ghosts came visiting, mocking him with their lifeless eyes as blood oozed from their mouths.

Shit! He woke with sweat pouring off him and tried to sleep again. But then he dreamed of his mother and her men and . . .

He jerked awake, trembling, his heart thumping like it was going to explode in his chest.

He huffed out a sigh and padded to the window. The first wispy fingers of dawn were spreading across the sky, reminding him of all the nights he'd spent on the trail, sleeping under the stars and then watching the dawn.

And he thought of how the dawn had set his mountain on fire when he watched it from his bedroom window. Fuck! He had to stop thinking about the damn mountain. Instead, he pulled his clothes on, wishing his back didn't feel like it was on fire. He'd check his kit in the stable and get his horse ready. Moving silently through the quiet house, he closed the door softly behind him as he crossed to the stable.

He'd just finished feeding the horse when a voice made him jump. "Taking off again, Johnny, like a thief in the night?"

"Hell, Doc, you scared the shit out of me!"

"And you not scared of anything!"

Johnny glared at him. "You know what I mean. And no, I wasn't going without saying goodbye."

The doctor raised a disbelieving eyebrow at that. "Do you want some breakfast, before you go to wherever you're going?"

Johnny felt distinctly uncomfortable. "No, but thanks. I ain't really hungry."

"That's a shame. I have a big piece of humble pie in the larder and I thought you might like to eat that."

What the hell was the doc talking about? Narrowing his eyes and looking at Doc Greenlaw, he had a pretty good idea the man was getting at him. "I'm just fine, thanks."

"Actually, you look terrible. Bad night?" The doc didn't sound real sympathetic.

"I slept fine, thanks."

"Hmm. I seem to remember telling you that your 'fines' don't work on me. Still, if you want to kill yourself that's your affair. Just ride on out. Turn your back on the first people to care about you in a long time. After all, in your parlance, you don't need nobody."

Johnny tried to meet the doc's gaze. The man had a way of seeming to look right through him. "I'll be on my way, Doc, but thanks for everything. You haven't told me what I owe you."

"I'll settle the bill with Guthrie. What you owe me is some peace of mind."

"I pay my debts. Don't need the old man settling my bills. What do I owe you?"

"OK, Johnny. How about one honest answer? What is it about staying that frightens you so much?"

He scuffed the ground with his boot. He looked at the doc's kind face and sighed. "Trouble is, I guess, nothing lasts. Every time you trust someone they let you down. I don't think I believe in anything anymore, or anyone."

"Just because people you've cared about in the past let you down, it doesn't mean they all will, Johnny. I guess Gabriela let you down the most."

"She did the best she could." He didn't want to talk about his mother. He suspected he must have talked a lot when he was sick, since old Doc seemed to know way too much about him. "Anyway, I ain't taking no chances. Got places to go. There's freedom out there, Doc."

"Freedom means nothing when you're all alone. A man has need for companionship, friendship, family. We all need affection, love. Life is about taking chances. Even when things go wrong at least you can look back and know you lived."

Johnny swung himself with some difficulty onto his horse and held his hand out to shake hands with the doc. But instead of taking it, the man shook his head sadly. "No. I wish you well,

Johnny, but I won't shake. It seems you're not the man I thought
you were. Good luck, you're going to need it." And the doctor
turned and walked back to his house.

Johnny sat, stunned for a second. Couldn't believe the doctor
wouldn't shake hands. Well, fuck him, fuck the lot of them. And
spurring the horse, he rode out of town.

Mierda, he felt angry. Angry with all of them. And his back
was throbbing. Damn them all. What gave them all the right to
think they knew what was best for him? They should all mind
their own business. What was it to them, what he did? He
paused. What was it to them? Why should they care? The girl
saying he shouldn't give up on them because they didn't want
to give up on him. Old Harvard all upset because those two
jerks had called him a few names. The old man searching for
him all those years. Was this what families did?

The horse stopped suddenly and he realized he hadn't been
looking at which way they were heading. The damn animal had
stopped on the ridge overlooking Sinclair. It turned its head
and nickered at him and then lowered its head to graze.

"You telling me what to do too?" He slid down and propped
himself against a tree, looking out across the valley to the
mountains beyond. The sun was almost full up, flushing the
tops of them the color of ripe apricots and throwing a golden
halo around the bald tip of his mountain. It seemed like the
most beautiful place on earth. And he could be a part of it.

He must have sat for an hour there while the horse dozed
next to him. Even though his eyes seemed misty he could see
activity down on the ranch. Hammering echoed across the valley where a man was working on building a new barn, and
another group of hands were branding calves.

A buggy made its way up the long winding drive. The lawyer
maybe, and a passenger.

He scrambled to his feet, cursing his sore back. He needed to get moving. He needed to get on with his life and head for the border. He stood on a stone to make it easier to mount. Dios, he was as bad as a girl. Turning his horse he rode out of sight of the ranch. He came to the fork where he tried to turn the horse south, but it dug its heels in. He gritted his teeth. It seemed like he was in for a battle of wills with the damn animal.

They stood at the desk, with a dapper, gray-haired man. "Shall we start, Mr. Sinclair? I have the papers ready. All they need are your signatures. Dr. Greenlaw can witness the agreement." The man gestured to the doctor, who stood a little apart from the others, chewing on his thumb as if lost in thought.

"Just one more minute, please. I'd like to wait a little longer."

"I do have other appointments, Mr. Sinclair. I'm sorry but I really need to get on."

Johnny slipped in through the door and spoke softly. "Yeah, we're all ready. We're all here now."

He bit back a smile as they all jumped, every eye in the room focused on him. He nodded at his old man, who smiled, like he really was pleased to see him. A huge smile split the girl's face, and Harvard raised an eyebrow, saying, "You cut that a bit fine, didn't you?" The doc looked smug.

They each stepped forward to sign the thick parchment document. Johnny hesitated for just a second, and then dipped the pen in the ink to sign his name beneath the others. John Sinclair. It looked odd. A little voice inside his head asked who the hell was John Sinclair—but he figured maybe it was time to find out.

As soon as the document was sealed, Harvard opened a bottle of champagne with a flourish, pouring the fizzing golden liquid into glasses he passed around to everyone.

Harvard raised his own glass. "To new beginnings!"

And as they all echoed his words, Johnny leaned across to

whisper in Ben's ear. "I'm only doing this because you promised to put in a word for me with that damn woman at the bordello." He stifled a hiss as the wound in his back pulled, and then grinned. "A man has needs, you know."

ABOUT THE AUTHOR

Adventurer and journalist **JD March** has tracked leopards in the Masai Mara, skied competitively, ridden to hounds, paddled dugout canoes on the Indian Ocean, and is an accomplished sailor. JD has lived in a series of unusual homes, including a haunted twelfth-century house in Cornwall in Britain and a chalet in the French Alps. But a lifelong passion for the old West means JD is happiest in the saddle, rounding up cattle on the Bighorn Mountains in Wyoming.

www.jdmarch.com